PRAISE FOR DEREK KÜNSKEN

"An audacious con job, scintillating future technology, and meditations on the nature of fractured humanity."

Yoon Ha Lee

"Technology changes us—even our bodies—in fundamental ways, and Künsken handles this wonderfully."

Cixin Liu

"Künsken has a wonderfully ingenious imagination."

Adam Roberts, *Locus*

"I have no problems raving about this book. A truly wild backdrop of space-opera with wormholes, big space-fleet conflict and empires.... What could go wrong?"

Brad K. Horner

"A boldly ambitious debut."

SFX Magazine

"*The House of Styx* is a stunning new sci-fi family drama that admirably shoulders the burden of two heavy genres and distills them into an exhilarating and heart-breaking journey of discovery."

***SciFiNow*, 5 star review**

FLIGHT FROM THE AGES

& other stories

FLIGHT FROM THE AGES

& other stories

DEREK KÜNSKEN

SOLARIS

First published 2022 by Solaris
an imprint of Rebellion Publishing Ltd,
Riverside House, Osney Mead,
Oxford, OX2 0ES, UK

www.solarisbooks.com

ISBN: 978-1-78618-728-4

Designed & typeset by Rebellion Publishing

Printed and bound by CPI Group (UK) Ltd, Croydon CR0 4YY

For editors Sheila Williams at *Asimov's*,
Trevor Quachri at *Analog*,
and Alex Li and Vera Sun at *Non-Exist*.
Their encouragement touched me profoundly.

CONTENTS

PREFACE

I'M A SENSE of wonder junkie. I always have been.

The world I grew up in, while picturesque, vaguely rural, and slow-paced with wonderfully long summer days, felt like the start of a journey rather than a destination. I remember Saturday morning cartoons, the occasional scifi show in prime time, and eventually comic books and novels transporting me to strange places, but always leaving me wanting more.

I knew early that I wanted to write—for no reason at all I'd started writing a story in Grade Two and finished a modest book in Grade Four, which Mr. McCurdy kindly published for my class. But between Grade Four and *Beneath Sunlit Shallows*, I had to learn to really write. While I took long years to learn, my sense of wonder continued to transport before I could quite transport myself.

Science fiction TV like *Star Trek*, books like *Star Wars* tie-ins, and novels like *Mythago Wood*, *Dune* and *The Lord of the Rings* brought me to different places and hinted at ideas not yet revealed, leaving me hunting for more. My mind was really blown when I learned the weirdness of quantum mechanics, the non-intuitiveness of general relativity, the vast space and time that failed to contain cosmology, and the tirelessly iterative, dumb imagination of evolution. I wanted that feeling of big ideas in what I read and I wanted it in what I wrote.

And at some point, I'd finally learned enough that magazines started buying my stories.

Beneath Sunlit Shallows was the first story I sold to *Asimov's* magazine. It was inspired by reading about extreme life on the ocean floor. It got me thinking that "it must suck to live in the benthic parts of the ocean." And readers liked it.

Persephone Descending was the first story I ever sold to *Analog* magazine, and it was the culmination of my lifelong fascination with Venus. A lot of stories are set on Mars, but I felt that scifi writers had been short-changing the goddess of love for some time. I wanted to see what kind of life would evolve in Venus' clouds and what kind of people would choose to colonize those clouds. Even as I wrote it, I knew one story wouldn't be enough, and a few years later, *The House of Styx* became my third novel sale.

Around 2011 or 2012, I listened to an anthology of time travel stories and was vaguely disappointed. I realized that I'd wanted that anthology to push the boundaries of time travel harder. The stories felt sterile in that they ignored biology; none of them considered the implications of evolution and time travel. So I resolved to write three time travel stories: one about evolution and forward time travel, one about evolution and travel back in time, and a third about how many forms of life might adapt differently to many kinds of time travel devices.

Schools of Clay was my story about how evolution might interact with forward jumps through time. *Pollen From a Future Harvest* was my attempt to knit evolution with movement back in time. Sheila Williams at *Asimov's* magazine bought and edited both. It took until this year to finish the third and I really should have sent it to Sheila by now...

I read Alastair Reynolds' collection *Galactic North* and if you haven't, then run, don't walk, to your local book store. You can thank me later. The title story blew my mind with a relativistic chase across the millennia. But, as with everything else I read, I asked "what if *Galactic North*, but bigger and with a cosmological-level catastrophe?" The answer to that question was *Flight From the Ages,* in which my mind got to travel across all the space and time I could imagine. The story found a home in *Asimov's*.

But I really journeyed and the jetlag really hit me in *Tool Use By the Humans of Danzhai County*. My stories had been doing well in translation in China and in 2018, I was invited to Danzhai County in Guizhou, one of China's poorest provinces. One of my Mandarin-language publishers was commissioning science fiction inspired by real situations in China—in this case, a massive anti-poverty initiative in Danzhai county. Poverty is a complex problem and I wanted to approach it honestly. So I asked a lot of awkward and personal questions to understand how poverty manifested itself in China. My hosts answered my questions frankly. We talked about gender pay gaps, what sexual harassment looks like in China, the way society treats people with disabilities and members of LGBTQ communities, what family mores and sexual freedoms look like in different parts of

China, all of which I needed to try to write meaningful near-future science fiction. *Tool Use by the Humans of Danzhai County* is still one of my personal favourite stories and it found a home in *Asimov's* magazine.

As you read, you may notice that most of these stories have elements that appear in my novel series. That wasn't on purpose when I wrote the stories at first, but it was on purpose when I wrote the novels. One of the things *Galactic North* inspired me to do was to set my stories and novels in the same universe, so that the weirdness of each might interact with the weirdness of the others. So in the end, the stories themselves went on a journey together.

I hope you're transported the way I was when I wrote these stories.

Derek Künsken
19 July, 2022
Gatineau, Québec

BENEATH SUNLIT SHALLOWS

VINCENT DREAMED AGAIN that he swam behind a child-like Merced, out of the cold dark, rising towards an unknown sun. He didn't see the sun, which could only penetrate two hundred meters of water. He wanted, the way one does in dreams, to see it, ignoring the fact that if he saw even its depth-attenuated blue light, he would already be dead. The dream ended inconclusively and he dreamed inconsequential things. When he woke, he remembered the first dream as if his waking had cut the ending. It had been a long time since he'd thought of Merced. She'd been his best friend, but memories of her only reminded him of how he'd never been brave enough to follow her.

His room was black and cool. He felt the heating coils, not by their warmth, but by the electric current and the way they bent the local magnetic field. The electrical sense, for all that he'd been born with it, felt strange, off angle, while his sight always seemed to be the first thing he turned to when waking.

Don't trust instinct, he'd been told all his life.

His eyes yawned, seeing nothing. Beneath layers of blubber and muscle and rib lay two columns of muscular disks called electroplaques. Plagiarized from electrical eels, they stored electrical charge. Vincent sent a weak current along his left electroplaque. A sensor in the wall detected the change and lit the clear water of his room, showing flakes of white silt.

His tired gills churned. Months might pass before his blood adapted to the oxygen starvation of the ocean floor. They'd told him not to rush, to adapt to his new home slowly, but that's not why he nearly returned to sleep. Loneliness gnawed at him. Indecision exhausted him.

He felt something odd in his right side and shrugged at it. It was more than a twinge. He pushed a charge through the electroplaque under his ribs and found an unexpected resistance under his skin.

To protect him from the intense cold of the alien ocean floor, Vincent's designers had left room in the blubber layer to retract his arms into its warmth. That was how he slept, and he now pushed his arms out and felt around his torso. The thick skin, engineered from walrus and shark DNA, slid under his fingers. At first, he found nothing more than a film of algae, a hygienic faux pas, but over his ribs, he found a lump that hadn't been there a month ago.

He'd spent the last month descending through layers of ocean. The magnetic field shifted direction and strength slightly at each depth. He hadn't become used to any single pattern long enough to notice changes within himself. Until today. No more moving. It was day thirty of the move, day one on the floor, but only a fraction of the interminable night of his life. The feeling that he was a coward rose again.

Beneath the mottled grey skin of his forehead, instinct tried to frown, but the massive engineered scalp immobilized inadequate muscles. He twisted his inexpressive face to look at the blubbery rib cage. He couldn't see anything. He'd check himself with the CAT scan later.

Although they'd been designed to thrive in the benthic zones of the ocean, there was a chance that one organ or another had herniated because of some pressure imbalance. He stretched, chubby grey arms wide, blunt head back, flukes twisting and extended, gills open enough to eat a fish. He knew he was a monster, but he didn't have the courage he needed.

VINCENT SPENT A lot of time thinking about the people whose decisions had, generation after generation, put him at the bottom of the ocean of the world they'd named Indi's Tear. He could not sum the series of seemingly well-intentioned choices with a result he clearly considered immoral. Where was the breakdown? He thought he knew where to lay the blame, but was blame even meaningful?

Vincent regarded the colonists who left Earth as crazy, but didn't think that they had crossed any ethical line. Earth had successfully launched many colony ships. The one to Epsilon Indi was certainly among the most ambitious, but they were trusting proven technology and skills. The risk was acceptable. Vincent was even prepared to accept as ethical the decision to permanently cut off their future descendants from Earth. No matter which way you looked at it, any trip that took more than a thousand years was a one way trip. Most of the original colonists had died of old age before they'd even left the solar system.

But their children and grandchildren, who now ran the colony ship, were still human, even if they'd never see Earth again, or any humans other than the ones they'd brought with them. He felt that there was a lot of weight in that choice, but accepted it as reasonable, even responsible. He understood the argument that the farther humans colonized, the more likely that they as a species, a culture and a civilization would persist.

THE DOOR SLID into the wall and Vincent left his room. He was shocked by water so cold that only pressure kept it from freezing. A snap of his body propelled him into the middle of the dark camp. No lights were on, which meant that Renald and Amanda hadn't yet risen, but that wasn't surprising. It was early yet.

He didn't need light anyway. He navigated like an electric eel or fish would, orienting himself by the way the camp equipment distorted the planet's magnetic field. He glided over the powdered sediment floor of the ocean, grabbing a hand lamp from a pile of boxes. Without lighting it, he surged ahead, leaving the cluster of cylinder shelters and containers.

Chill water squeezed through his gills, offering little oxygen, but his hyperactive hemoglobins seized even the trace amounts. The water held other scents. He smelled the stale odor of sand mixed with carbon dioxide, the stink of decaying amides and the taint of sulfur as he approached the smoker.

He switched the light as he felt the water get warmer. It lit the white ocean floor and a lumpy reddish-black tube of rocky mineral deposits that thrust five meters out of the sand. It was called a smoker and they'd surrounded and penetrated it with wires. One hundred and fifteen degree water burned out the top, rippling against the dark, benthic world. An algae-coated turbine spun in the smoker provided the limited power for their settlement. It would be months and years before they could build a full geothermal plant.

Robots crept in and around the superheated water, culling worms, clams and little lobsters. The harvest required prodigious processing to remove toxic minerals and heavy metals, but the eventual slush was to be a staple of their ocean-floor diet. Once more electricity was available, they would grow modified plankton in deep sea green houses. It was difficult to imagine food more revolting than what they'd eaten growing up, yet here he didn't need to imagine. Vincent flexed away, gliding farther afield.

He left the light on, following the depressing endlessness of sand. Ahead of him, he saw a dim glow and felt an electrical disturbance. Bait. A dozen fine-meshed cages stood on mounds of sand. Inside each one hung a rolled metal screen covered in bioluminescent bacteria. Their light was fuzzy, as if out of focus, mostly blue, but some patches hazing to lime. The color didn't really matter. Any light would draw deep ocean fish.

Two of the traps had sprung. In the first trap, expressionless, black eyes similar to his own regarded him from over serrated, bony lips. The scaled body was spiny and thin, mottled by some filamentous, fungal infection. It beat against the cage, reacting to Vincent's lamp. The second trap had caught a transparent ball covered with fine threads.

Both animals were native to Indi's Tear and were unfortunately edible, meaning that they weren't toxic, but weren't wholly digestible either. Some of the amino acids in the animals and plants of Indi's Tear were identical to those in Vincent's body. Others were different, but digestible. But there were enough amino acids that couldn't be metabolized that each meal fulfilled a sickening, cramping promise.

He returned the catch to camp, but arrived short of breath. His large gills churned, sucking chill water, scavenging oxygen. There would never be more oxygen at the bottom of the ocean than there was now and he knew his body wouldn't adapt until it was forced. But the suffocation worsened. His heart beat faster and he felt himself dizzying.

He waited, but finally, he swam to the wall of the main building and fit his face into a mask-shaped hollow. A stream of oxygenated water poured out of the emergency station, and the pressure on his chest slowly abated. He thought that maybe today he would have the courage he needed.

VINCENT SUPPOSED THAT those who had arrived at the star Epsilon Indi, after a voyage of eleven hundred years, were still human. A millennium was too short a period of isolation to produce a new species, but he found it telling that he had to ask the question. Humanity had to be more that biological compatibility. What referents could a town of colonists share with humans on Earth if they'd spent thirty-seven generations in a steel cylinder, never seeing sun or moon, never feeling wind?

But he pitied those colonists in their metal case. He couldn't imagine the communal and cultural horror of looking through their telescopes and seeing Indi's Eye, their destination planet, devastated by a hit from a rogue moon. They couldn't turn around. They couldn't change course. They'd accelerated in Earth's solar systems on disposable boosters and carried enough fuel to brake at their destination, eleven hundred years later.

Did they understand that they were a population whose death was only a formality? He guessed that they didn't. Otherwise their choices would have been not only unethical, but deliberately cruel.

TOO EXHAUSTED TO wash, he moved to the side doorway of the shelter and swam through. The dim lights lit for his entry, seeming overbright. His huge eyes had been designed a generation earlier, a preliminary step to humanity's expansion to the deeper ocean of Indi's Tear. The water inside was three or four degrees warmer, and oxygenated to simulate the rich upper ocean where he'd grown up.

Vincent couldn't stomach the thought of breakfast and went to his workstation. A network of sonar stations that transmitted in frequencies Vincent couldn't hear connected the fifteen aquatic communities on Indi's Tear and this camp. The nearest was Charlotte's Web, the town of four hundred souls where Vincent, Amanda and Renald had grown up. It floated five hundred meters below the surface of the ocean and exactly two kilometers above where Vincent was now. Two messages waited on his desktop.

He opened the first. An electrical echo formed, invisible to ears, eyes and smell, but leaving a faint tangy taste in the water and a clean image in his electrical receptors. It was a likeness of his lawyer perceived through his electric organs. Tiny crackles of static discharged from the display: language, borrowed conceptually from dolphins, but electrical instead of acoustic. It was a recording of his lawyer's electrical voice.

"Vincent, I've spoken with the prosecutor and convinced him not to press charges. Given your current service to the community and the impossibility of re-offending, we've agreed that it would be a waste of time. Congratulations."

The electrical image faded. Vincent felt nothing. He hadn't been worried.

The next message was in text. The faint blue letters were from his psychiatrist. He'd listed some times when Vincent could call for his mandatory therapy. One of them was now. Vincent's inexpressive face sucked water. He chattered electrically to the sensor and the call was made. He might as well get it done. It would only take half an hour and with the proper external events, twenty minutes.

The psychiatrist answered and an electrical image formed. The face was less fishlike, more human, more flexible and evocative. Vincent had seen the psychiatrist many times and knew that the image forming, although mostly correct, wasn't accurate. It was a psychiatrist trick, using hints of what humans used to look like to trigger positive emotional responses in patients.

"Vincent," the doctor said, "congratulations on reaching the bottom."

The image formed something like a smile. Vincent felt himself react to the artifice, but beat down the feeling. The doctor was as incapable of smiling as Vincent, but his communication system was programmed to alter the image, evoking reactions locked into thousands of generations of human evolution, recalling shadows of joy.

"I didn't do anything special," Vincent said. "We just sank for a month."

"You underestimate your accomplishment. The whole town is ecstatic."

The doctor waited, but Vincent was determined not to cooperate today.

"How are the others?" the doctor asked finally.

"Still asleep."

"And on the trip?"

"Same old irritating."

"They aren't like you," the doctor said. "They aren't as talented, or as independent as you are. Everything that comes hard to everyone else comes easy to you. They look up to you, even Renald, who wishes he were more like you." The psychiatrist paused, trying to pry a response from Vincent with silence. Vincent was quiet. "I don't think they understand why you won't speak to them," the psychiatrist finished.

"They know why. Whether they choose to understand is their problem."

"You hurt a lot of people with your principles, Vincent, including yourself. Part of life is about understanding how to balance a moral stand with other things that are important. None of us chose to come to Epsilon Indi. We're living the consequences of decisions made by our ancestors. We're just trying to survive."

"I'm not bringing children into the world who have to live like this."

"You won't be separated from your children, Vincent."

"I won't have any."

"You don't have the right to decide that. We're trying to survive as a species."

"What species? *Homo sapiens*? They're on Earth and colonizing other planets. *Homo indis*? We're not even one species. We're *costalis, pelagius* and now *benthus*. How many limping, pathetic things have to suffer through short lives so we can say we succeeded?"

"Have you dreamed of Merced again?"

Vincent felt himself gulping for oxygen, gills churning. Anger was a hormonal state that didn't mesh with the hemoglobins modified for deep sea survival. Genetic engineers would modify either the hemoglobins or the hormones in the next generation of *Homo sapiens benthus* to avoid this problem, but Vincent, Amanda and Renald were stuck with it. Vincent also guessed that the change would cause other problems that were just as likely to wipe out dozens of embryos or babies. Vincent calmed himself, but it was an artificial solution.

"No," he said.

The psychiatrist paused, waiting for more. "It appears your wishes in the end will be respected and they won't even press charges," the doctor said finally.

"I knew they couldn't press charges. They need me. They would have tolerated far worse."

"Destroying your stored germ lines deprived society other safe successes."

"I'm not a success! You're not a success. We're successful relative to miserable, painful failures. We're awful."

"Do you still have a plan?"

"What?"

"Do you still have a plan to kill yourself?"

Vincent filled the room with silence for a meaningful, revealing time.

"Of course I do," he said. Then he cut the connection.

He huffed at his anger, his gills flexing. This was only the most recent of a lifetime unpleasant conversations. He'd chosen at some point not to take them personally. These conversations were very much about him and very much not about him.

THE COLONISTS ARRIVING at Epsilon Indi had weighed their options and picked the only one that made any sense. There was too much debris orbiting Indi's Eye to set up orbital habitats, but the same amount of fuel could stop them at Indi's Tear, a heavier, colder world, farther from the dim star. They set up an orbital colony there and set out to weigh their next steps. The asteroid that struck next was not thought to be more than sixty centimeters in diameter, but had been travelling at better than twenty-six kilometers per second. It killed half the orbiting community instantly. It was also not alone. There was far more debris in the system than they'd guessed. The only thing that could protect them from most of the impacts was a thick atmosphere, like the one on the world beneath them. So they'd abandoned their habitat and descended to the chill surface of Indi's Tear, despite its three crushing gravities.

VINCENT LEFT THE habitat, gliding into the cold, anoxic darkness. The currents had shifted and unfortunately, he smelled their kitchen. He glided towards a cylindrical habitat set away from their compound and the smell intensified. The door of the habitat slid away as he approached and he passed into the concentrated stink of fishy nitrogen compounds and sulfur. In sealed boxes incapable of containing the smell were the slurries and pastes of the catches made yesterday by robots. Although they were ground to mush and leeched of not only heavy metals, but most of the cramping minerals and sulfur, they were still repellent.

The first box had his name on it and he pulled it from the shelf with his hands. It was slick with a bacterial growth on the outside, but he set it on the table and opened it. He could not close his eyes, nor escape the smell. His jaws opened with designed efficiency, and he shoveled the slurry in, gulping clumps around a gag reflex his designers hoped to remove in the next generation. The cartilaginous grounds lodged under his tongue and at the edges of his throat. The handfuls of sulfurous flesh were like bite after bite of rotting eggs. He emptied the box without vomiting, but the bloated queasiness that accompanied every feeding lurched in him.

His stomach gurgled and twisted. The bacteria in his gut had been modified to metabolize and neutralize the sulfur, and he swore, as he always did, that he could feel them work. These bacteria were nearly as critical to his survival as his other adaptations, because they carried enzymes that would digest some of the strange amino acids of Indi's Tear, increasing the caloric value of food by almost forty percent. Newborns had to be fed special cultures which sometimes didn't take to their intestinal tracts. When they didn't, the newborns were euthanized. It was so difficult to survive that the towns had no flexibility to even try to keep the weak alive.

Thoughts of newborns saddened yet satisfied him. In Charlotte's Web, he'd entered the storehouse that held his germ cell stocks and had set them adrift in the ocean.

They'd charged him with a crime, but had not dared convict him. He was irreplaceable and as an adult, he would not let them take any more sperm. They could not use him or his genes for any further failed generations of sacrificial litters. The line of descent and inserted genes that connected Vincent through all his ancestors, back through all of evolution to the dawn of life on Earth would stop with him. Someone had to say stop. All he had to do was follow Merced and it frightened him that today he might have the courage.

IT WAS NOT long before the new inhabitants of Indi's Tear had started dying. Fewer meteors reached the surface, but those that did devastated. And three gravities, every hour of every day, was too much. Every task made them dizzy. Every fall broke a bone. Exhausted hearts failed in young and old. Only immersion in water made the fierce gravity bearable. They took to the coastal shallows at first, layered with survival equipment. But this was a temporary solution. Human skin was not built for constant soaking. They diseased.

Even though no one knew how to genetically modify adults, they could tinker with fertilized eggs. They could try to spare them the ravages of gravity and of the rotting diseases of the skin. Mostly they failed.

At first, the changes were small. They had carried the complete DNA sequences of hundreds of thousands of species from Earth with which to terraform and colonize Indi's Eye. They used these on their offspring, toughening and thickening the skin with artificial chromosomes made from walrus and seal DNA and layering fat beneath that skin to keep them warmer. Even so, engineering a new kind of human was a complex thing. Many new genes interfered with one another. For years they had nothing but spontaneous abortions until they figured out how to modify all the genes being interfered with.

Then infants started to survive.

But they'd crossed a line. The children of this new generation were still air-breathing mammals, but they were a new species. With an extra pair of chromosomes and hundreds of modified genes, there was no chance of a successful mating with *Homo sapiens*. *Homo indis* was born.

And the line was more than biological. They'd planted a permanent barrier, cultural and emotional, between the two generations. Family and parenting as practiced by *Homo sapiens* was meaningless in this new context. The gene swapping involved in success meant that those new children belonged both to no one and to everyone. Direct lineage, the unbroken line of descent from parent to offspring that ran from the origin of life to the shores of the oceans of Indi's Tear, ended.

Lack of belonging and descent coloured other perceptions. Although the new babies were grown in artificial litters of fifty, only a fraction survived. No one would, or could, invest their emotions in things that were not theirs and were likely to die.

Beauty and sexuality also separated the generations. These new creatures, *Homo indis*, were hideous, to their many parents, and to themselves. The broad standards of beauty, the mate recognition hardware in mammals, were evolved through thousands of generations of gradual change. The genetic engineers had no idea of how it worked or how to change it and the longing for physical beauty became a torment. In a practical sense, it didn't matter. The *Homo indis* could not reproduce without technological assistance.

No one foresaw the consequences beyond the goal of this genetic tinkering. Their choices seemed eminently reasonable, if coloured by desperation.

BEFORE AMANDA OPENED the door, Vincent felt her electrical signature, the unique pattern of moving charge associated with her. This level of discernment, being able to distinguish one person from another by electrical sense only, was unique to Vincent among the *Homo indis*.

Amanda slid in and he felt his contempt rise, like the breakfast he'd eaten an hour ago. Since childhood, he'd watched her flounder in every subject in school. She was vacuous and missed the implications of almost every conversation he'd ever had with her. But she was here, for the same reason that he was: she'd survived to maturity. What little pride he took in his abilities and his role in the community bled in her presence.

"Good morning, Vincent," she said in lumpy electrical echoes. Her speech was atonal. She had nothing of the musical inflections he used to nuance even his most careless statements. "How long have you been up?"

"Less than an hour."

"It feels strange being this deep, finally being away from home."

Nothing she said was wrong, but her presence grated.

"Do you feel the same, Vincent?"

Contempt welled. She knew he barely stomached her, but she still needed his approval, the approval of others. She was a shell of a person, waiting to be defined, rated, and assigned a role. He fantasized about leaving her alone for months or years. However long the solitude took to give her an identity. He wanted desperately for her to be someone he respected. He didn't speak, but swam away from her, towards the lab. She followed him as he knew she would.

THEY BECAME BETTER at reproducing. By the time the last of the *Homo sapiens* had died, the *Homo indis* had established themselves in murky river zones and along coastlines. They mastered the engineering skills of their dead ancestors. Every generation modified the next, racing against time to spread themselves wherever they could survive. It was now part of their culture. The costs were acceptable, normal.

Meteors rained onto Indi's Tear. *Homo indis* spread to different continents to minimize their chances of extinction, but even at that, coastal shallows were a grim place to weather the tsunamis following an asteroid impact. The *Homo indis* were almost wiped out. They fled again, modifying themselves into true water-breathers to colonize the upper layers of the open sea, becoming *Homo indis pelagius*. But even here, they were not safe. They worried and watched the sky, for the impact that would be inescapable.

He cursed his collective ancestors, those who were neither mothers, nor fathers, and felt close to ready. Today felt like the day he could be as brave as Merced, even if he was twelve years late.

IT WAS NEARLY twelve hours later that Renald and Amanda entered the lab for the third time to see how Vincent was doing. Vincent had taken scans and biopsies of all three of them in the morning and now floated in front of screens data. He turned as they stopped behind him.

Renald was slightly bigger than Vincent, with pale, mottled skin stretched over fatty flesh. He tended to defer to Vincent, but not for lack of competence. Renald had never tried very hard, leaving most problems for Vincent, because everyone knew Vincent was the best. Renald's large, expressionless face, framed by slowly pulsing gills and centered under bulbous black eyes, perused the medical scans.

"It's not an infection," Vincent said to him. "It looks like cancer, pre-metastatic, many different kinds, all forming now."

"What does it mean?" Amanda asked. She hadn't Vincent's or Renald's training in molecular biology. She was a technician and mechanic, and not even a good one at that. "Is this something else that they didn't see in our generation?"

Her meaning was clear. They three were the only survivors of a litter of fifty of the new subspecies *Homo indis benthus*, engineered to live on the floor of the ocean. None of the four preceding litters had survived.

It was a tricky thing, redesigning the development of a whole being. Growth factors, gravity, nutrient concentration, temperature and pressure interacted with some sixty thousand human genes to produce a person. The complexities of neurology still escaped the genetic engineers, which was why they still ached for human food, human smells, human sights and human beauty. These were hard-wired by hundreds of thousands of years of evolution.

"I don't think so," Vincent said to Renald. "If it was

something designed wrong, we would have found it before now and we'd probably all have the same cancer."

Vincent knew Renald had also guessed the cause as well.

"The change in pressure we've gone through over the last month has been enormous," Vincent said. "Thousands of proteins in our bodies have been modified so as not to change shape because of the pressure, but it was suspected that there might be some gene products we wouldn't know about, like alternate splices or undiscovered post-translation modifications. You only need a couple dozen of these unknowns to explain all our cancers."

"What does it mean?" Amanda asked.

"It means our gene engineers have screwed up and that our lives have been thrown away for nothing," Vincent said. "It means we head back up to town. The pressure change may solve the problem and we can live the rest of our lives with our friends. The next generation can live on the bottom of the ocean, if they decide to keep pushing this stupid plan."

Vincent observed Renald, not with his eyes, because they could discern no more emotion from Renald's face than he could from a carp's. He listened to the electrical pulses, shielding his own. Renald obviously disagreed with him, but they'd trod those arguments many times. Vincent doubted Renald was interested in repeating them today. But Amanda had no notion of social politics and the concept of unwinnable battles.

"None of us should be here, Vincent," she said. "The colonists couldn't have known."

"I don't blame the colonists for arriving," Vincent said. "I blame them for sacrificing the humanity of their children. They didn't have to live with the consequences.

We did and we do. This is not life. It's purgatory, for us and all our children."

"You have the choice they had, Vincent," Renald said. "You have the choice of letting this cancer kill you."

"You know what my choice is," Vincent snapped. "No more speciation. No more separation of family and friends. We take what we have and build on that. No more of this," he said, waving his fatty, gray arm wide. "Is this your dream? Spending the rest of your life on the bottom of the ocean with me and Amanda?"

"We're better off than those who didn't make it," Renald said.

"Are we?"

Renald did not reply and left, his swishing tail fin driving him through the door. Disconcertingly, Amanda did not leave. He ignored her and sputtered an electrical signal to the communications system on his desktop. A minute later, a fuzzy image formed, part faint blue light, part diffuse standing electrical waves. The two parts complemented each other poorly to build a picture of Kent, the head of operations and Vincent's nominal superior.

"Kent," Vincent said, "we're having some problems and I'm going to ascend. We need medical treatment. We've each developed multiple, pressure-related tumors."

The Kent image stilled. "Are they immediately life threatening?" he asked.

Vincent didn't shrug. He had no shoulders, but he used an electrical equivalent that transmitted well. "We have tumors, Kent. How immediate do you want it?"

"Between fifty-six and seventy hours, Vincent," Kent replied. "That's when a big rock is going to hit this hemisphere. We can't get more information because another watch satellite was struck by debris. Our best guess is that it's between a kilometer and a kilometer and a half wide."

Vincent didn't respond. Whether it struck land or sea, an asteroid of that size would leave a big hole, blocking the sun for weeks or months with atmospheric debris. The shear forces of the shock wave would ravage the towns and maybe even kill the population outright. He had close friends in Charlotte's Web.

"What can we do?" Vincent asked.

"Batten down everything. Secure the computer systems as best you can. You may want to get a little distance between yourself and the ocean floor. Shock waves will be bad."

"What about you?"

"The towns may survive, depending on what happens to sunlight and how many toxic minerals rain down on the ocean's surface. We're scattering everyone as far and as deep as we can, but it may be no use. In a week any town that survives will start sending out radio signals. Any survivors will rendezvous on those."

"I wish I was there," Vincent said.

Kent was silent again. There was history and respect between these two, polarized sides of a debate, generation past and generation present. "This is why we've done everything we've done, Vincent. This is to survive."

"Plankton survives, Kent. Humanity has to live. We have no dignity and we have no hope. I'm here because someone was so afraid that he didn't know that sometimes being true to what you are means admitting you lost."

"We all make sacrifices, Vincent," Kent said. "The costs are high, but we live and we dream. Thousands of generations before us stuck through misery because they hoped tomorrow would be better. It won't always be like this."

"Good luck, Kent," Vincent said finally. "I'll talk to you when we start picking up the pieces."

WHILE RENALD AND Amanda were securing the camp, Vincent stayed in the lab, supposedly working on the problem of the tumours. He wasn't. He'd figured out what was wrong before even speaking to Kent.

He'd never been short of ways to kill himself. In the middle layers of a deep ocean, only a dozen generations from terrestrial life, the trick was more keeping yourself alive. When people like Kent had found no traction for their arguments with the sanctity of life, they'd inevitably turned to community interest. It had never been difficult to show that Vincent was not only a biological, but an intellectual luminary. His death would be a serious loss to the community, making everyone's life that much harder. But the community, whether Charlotte's Web or the larger network of towns, was a fuzzy target and Vincent had never accepted that the needs of the others should stop him from ending a life of misery. Now, today, he felt he had the strength to overcome the survival instinct, the same dumb instinct that had kept mindless creatures alive through eons of suffering. But today, his decision suddenly implicated Renald and Amanda, not a fuzzy concept.

The biochemical problem was simple in comparison. The genetic engineers had modified every one of Vincent's sixty thousand genes to produce proteins that would survive the pressure at the bottom of the ocean. An extra two kilometers of water above them pressing down with three gravities was enough to squash and change the shape of every protein, which changed the way it functioned. So the engineers had tested and made changes in each individual gene, one by one. And they hadn't missed a single gene.

They'd missed the entire specific immune system. They'd missed the immune proteins on all B-cells and all T-cells. It wasn't their fault. The proteins on immune cells and in antibodies were not produced by regular genes. The immune elements of T-cells and anti-bodies developed in the fetus. Each B-cell and T-cell shuffled sets of DNA fragments like cards in a deck, keeping any combination that didn't attack the host.

The problem was that in coming to the ocean floor, the pressure had squashed the immune elements of every antibody and T-cell. Vincent, Renald and Amanda had entirely different immune systems down here, none of which were tailored to the bodies that contained them. There were undoubtedly some autoimmune diseases forming right now. And a handful of benign tumors in each of them had now escaped immune surveillance.

If they stayed down here, they would die, unless Vincent could find some medical solution before the tumours or autoimmune diseases killed them. Renald was a good physician and geneticist, but he didn't have Vincent's leaps of intuition and creativity.

His first idea had been the one with the most promise: return to Charlotte's Web and hope that the pressure changes would be reversible, or at least treatable. The immune cells should be fine, and they would regain the immunities they had before. The ruined antibodies that were now probably in the early stages of attacking their bodies would do a great deal of damage, but might eventually wear out before Vincent, Renald and Amanda died. But now, there was every chance that there would be no town to return to. There was a chance that the three of them would be the last survivors of all the dreams and aspirations of the thousands who'd lived and died to come to colonize this system. And he was likely the only person who had a chance of saving Renald and Amanda. Vincent left the lab, gagging down a slimy lump in the kitchen while his stomach prepared to send it back.

IN MANY DREAMS, Vincent had legs and saw the sun. It was a spotlight in a black sea with sediment drifting in front of it. He didn't know what legs felt like, but faithless instinct suggested. It was an erotic feeling. He'd lived so long among alien things that elicited no sexual recognition in his brain that arms and legs were deeply sexual. They felt natural, frustratingly, hauntingly compelling.

As in most dreams, some part of him was detached, critical, realistic. This part repeated the childhood litany: *Don't trust your instincts. They aren't for here.* But instinct seduced and in dream he drifted over a field of floating, waving grass, fat-leaved and tickling his dreamed legs. A woman appeared beneath him, with pale grey skin, plump with spaghetti hair floating about her large, bulbous eyes. Her arms and legs spread straight out and he throbbed at her beauty and didn't know what to do. He ached and woke frustrated.

He remembered the dream with painful precision. Very deeply and very powerfully, he hated who he was. Sexuality was not safe for them. Pregnancy was too complicated to design. So Vincent, Amanda, and everyone in the towns squirted eggs and sperm into containers, for the genetic engineers. There was no pleasure. A pharmaceutical injection triggered the release. The neural circuitry for reproduction existed in their brains, but led nowhere. The genetic engineers didn't know how to rewrite the neural patterns that were hardwired by evolution into instinct. Every one of them was haunted by a desire that ran nowhere.

RENALD AND AMANDA found Vincent much later before an inactive work station in a still lab. They were winded. They gulped the oxygenated water, listening to the electrical movement in the room.

"We've gotten everything ready outside," Amanda said. "We can detach the main building from the sea floor whenever you want."

Vincent had no authority over them, but it was indicative of their relationship that they cleared most plans with him before acting. He considered not responding, but didn't want to be artificial, affected.

"I've figured out what our problem is," he said.

"How bad is it?" Renald asked.

"Bad enough. Our immune systems were initialized, so to speak, under one pressure. They're not set for this new depth. Benign tumors that were being controlled under the weight of the middle ocean have now escaped immune surveillance on the bottom. And I think our immune systems are probably attacking our bodies too, although it's too early to see symptoms."

"Can we fix it?" Renald asked.

"Maybe," Vincent said.

His companions shot forward.

"If you think it's possible, that's great!" Renald said.

"Is it?" Vincent swung his expressionless face towards them. "Look at you. What are you? What are we here? We're freaks on the bottom of the ocean."

"It's better than being dead," Amanda said.

"Is it? Where we grew up was barely better than being dead. And it certainly wasn't for our friends. Was it for Colin, or Darla, or Sergei?"

He didn't calculate the comment to bite, but the names carried emotional weight. They summoned memories of childhood friends with painful, wasting autoimmune diseases. Torturous, experimental therapies were ineffective and the playmates expired, faded to nothing by genetic errors.

"We aren't free," he said, more quietly. In his mind, he saw Merced, his best friend at ten years old, a horrifying barracuda-faced girl who'd wanted to see the sun and who had risen into the photosynthesizing zone in the top two hundred meters of the ocean. Designed for the ocean floor and barely surviving the limited pressure in the upper dark zone of the sea, all her proteins had denatured in the reduced pressure, the opposite of what had happened to their immune systems on the bottom. She'd floated dead while the townspeople, those who weren't cursed at conception to exile on the bottom of the ocean, collected her. There was no starker reminder that none of the survivors of Vincent's generation would ever see the sun.

"We aren't really alive," he said. "The people who made us sacrificed everything human just so we could exist. We're human brains living in alien bodies that don't connect right. There's no beauty, no attraction, no love. We don't have parents. We don't have children. We don't have family. Humans on Earth and on other colonies, even the most worthless exile or prisoner can taste food, see and feel sunlight, look in the mirror and not frighten himself."

"We're your family, Vincent," Amanda said.

"What are you saying?" Renald asked Vincent.

"We've surrendered too much, suffered too much. We don't live in dignity because those who came before us were not brave enough to accept that their runs were over."

"You're not going make the cure?" Renald said.

"I'm saying we have a chance to right a mistake."

"I'm not ready to die, Vincent," Amanda said.

Renald stared silently at Vincent. "The three of us dying won't accomplish anything," he said finally. "Towns across the world have the plans to make more of us, literally more of you and me."

Vincent swished his arm like an ax chopping.

"Stop thinking about accomplishment! It's not about the dream or the goal or extinction. Too much has been done for the sake of fear masquerading as vision. This is about us, as people, and only about us. Think about this as people. Not the vilest criminal on Earth has to live like this."

"I think it's immoral to throw away lives for no reason," Renald said.

"You've bought the company line without thinking, Renald. Think!"

"I haven't bought anything, Vincent. I'm just willing to stick it out."

"Kent's words."

"Mine. And I'm not going to absolve you."

Vincent and Renald stared at each other.

"What does that mean, Renald?" Amanda asked.

Neither answered.

"What does that mean, Vincent? What about absolving? Is this about the germ cells you destroyed in Charlotte's Web?"

"Vincent's looking for a moral out," Renald said. "He knows that I can't figure out the treatment to this immune problem, not like he could. I think he's getting ready to tell us he's ready to kill himself after talking about it for so long. The problem is that if he kills himself now, he takes us with him. He's trying to find a way out of being a murderer by inaction. So much for the brave and ethical Vincent."

Vincent said nothing and Amanda stared at him with her huge, vacuous eyes. He thought of Merced. The path she'd taken, intentionally or not, had always been open to him. And now it seemed to be closing again. He'd never ended things when he should have, made his statement, made his choice the way he'd always argued that the first human colonists should have taken.

He cracked inside, the sadness, the frustration trapped, as much as laughter was, aching for release from a bulky, fleshy prison. He was and was not the person he'd thought he was, wanted to be. He was neither the courageous forerunner like Merced, not the protector like Kent. He was weak and strong, just like everyone else, but in the wrong places. His tearless, lidless eyes stared uselessly at Renald and Amanda. He cried without physical release, for lost friends, lost dreams and lost self.

Others thought that Merced had gone crazy, had cracked like so many others. But he and Merced had known that the sun's light contained the trappings of humanity that had been stripped from them: beauty, pleasure, passion, love.

45

"Amanda and I will finish unhooking the base from the sea floor," Renald said. "The asteroid is due sometime in the next ninety minutes. You decide what you're going to do. Come on, Amanda."

"I've already decided what I'm going to do."

Their faces, like dead fish in the dark, carried no nuance, nor had Vincent inflected the statement with any hint of his choice. They waited and even he waited.

"I'm following Merced."

SCHOOLS OF CLAY

Present

THE WORKERS' REVOLUTION began on the hive's nine hundred and third day, when the Hero pulsar was above the horizon to the north. A pod of predatory shaghāl emerged from behind a small asteroid to the west. The exhaust of their thrust was shielded by their bodies, but the point shines of their souls were visible to those in the colony who had souls. The shine was just slightly blue-shifting.

The skates were not ready. Only half the princesses were fueled in the launch tubes of the hive. Indecision washed over the colony. Skates and souls yelled over each other. Then, a thousand tiny reactions bloomed. The colony panicked. The flat, triangular skates hopped along the regolith in different directions on steely fingers.

Diviya stood above the rising dust, on a mound of mine tailings. He had been meeting with a half-dozen revolutionaries in the slums past the worker shanties.

None of his revolutionaries possessed souls, so they could not see the shaghāl, but the panicked radio bursts from the hive alarmed them. Some thought that a squad of hive drones had found them.

"Oh no," Diviya said.

"Flee!" Diviya's soul crackled to him in the radio static. "Save the princesses!"

"Diviya, the revolution isn't ready!" Tejas said. Tejas was a soulless worker, made of carbon-reinforced ceramic. He was triangular and flat, with a single, lightly abraded lens on the vertex of the leading edges of his wide fins. "The workers are not assembled."

Hours away yet, the shaghāl split into two pods. The first pod of predators continued toward the hive. The second angled to intercept the migration, before it had even launched.

"The whole colony is already late," Diviya said. "The revolution must happen now."

Nearby, three skates hopped between the dusty mounds of mine tailings toward the hive. Their radioactive souls shone hot behind their eyes: tax farmers, coming from the farms to join the migration.

"We have only minutes," Diviya said in a radio discharge. He felt sick with doubt. He led his followers forward.

The revolutionaries leapt upon the three tax farmers. Diviya screamed out his own fears. The violence against kin was surreal, matching the strange panic that exploded all over the colony as its last hours played out.

The tax farmers struggled, stirring graphite fines in the vanishing gravity of the asteroid. The revolutionaries pinned the tax farmers upside down. Their steel fingers waved uselessly and their mouths were exposed. Diviya's conspirators held tight to the frozen subsurface.

The tax collectors cried out with crackling radio noise that carried far on the great asteroid. But while the colony was launching the migration, no one would notice. Too many hurried to save the princesses, the princes, and themselves.

In this chaos, the workers' revolution could become real.

One of the three tax farmers appeared to be a landlord by the brightness of his soul. He was the most dangerous. Beneath the hardened carapace of boron carbide, his soul spattered the hard, energetic radiation from uranium and thorium, and the soft, diffuse glow from tritium and potassium. The landlord's soul spoke frantically. Diviya's soul was strangely quiet; it feared Diviya.

The landlord's rows of short legs waved helplessly and he was hot. His soul heated the landlord's whole triangular body. Although it was a sin to waste reaction mass, Diviya did not put it past the landlord to pour the stored volatiles over his soul, launching himself, and everyone on him, into orbit. They could not hold him if that happened.

Diviya reached into the landlord's mouth with the pry and pliers that doctors carried. Deep in the landlord's mouth, Diviya pried back supporting metal bands made to hold the soul. The landlord understood what Diviya was doing and in his horror released a cool spray of thrust from the trailing edge of his fins.

But then Diviya had the soul free and he held the rectangular cake of radioactive isotopes in the shine of the pulsar. They all stared and listened in awe. Only Diviya had ever seen a naked soul. These revolutionaries were farm workers, ore processors, and haulers of regolith.

Diviya turned to Tejas. The skate turned onto his back, exposing fingers blunted from months of scratching frozen nitrogen and graphite from around hard chondrules. Charged regolith dust grimed his open mouth. Diviya set the still-screaming soul within Tejas' mouth.

Any skate could have a soul. Souls gestated in the large ore plants within the queen, near the kilns where the skates themselves were fired. Diviya had been chosen to be a doctor and received a soul only by chance. The soulless could farm volatiles, but could never find radioactive isotopes in the regolith, or fly from the asteroid. Diviya fastened the bands, locking the soul into place. They turned over the newly ensouled skate.

The panic of the hive heightened. The throbbing radio signals from the queen signaled that she was preparing to launch the first wave of princesses. Diviya hurried to remove the souls from the other two tax farmers and place them into Barini and Ugra.

The souls beamed their fear and outrage in radio static. Once, hive drones would have come and arrested them all, but this was the end of the world the souls had preached.

Far off, above the great bulk of the queen, the leaders of the migration launched. Bursts of hot volatiles, briefly visible through the thickening dust, launched princesses at tremendous velocities. Six. Seven. Eight. Waves of princes and their courtiers threw themselves into space after the potential hive queens. Then, a wave of slower-moving, uncoordinated tax farmers and landlords. Diviya's soul began speaking, at first in quiet, fearful tones, but then more strongly.

"Come," Diviya said. "There is no more time!"

Dozens of revolutionaries had crowded them. The soulless. They had put their faith in Diviya. They retreated at his words, stunned. And Diviya's heart cracked. Of everything that they had hoped for all of the workers, they only had time to save three.

Not even save. There was every chance that Diviya and his three ensouled revolutionaries would be killed by either the shaghāl or the migration itself. They were not princes, fed volatiles and radioactive dust by scores of workers. They had been given every nugget of frozen volatiles that could be smuggled out of the work camps, but it was probably not enough.

Diviya opened a valve. A trickle of the volatiles he had stored in his body passed over his soul, super-heating. A searing mix of water, methane, ammonia, and nitrogen shot from the spouts on Diviya's trailing edge, launching him over the hive. The great, sintered ceramic bulk of the queen, dwarfing all the piles of mine tailings, and studded with the launch tubes of the princesses, lay beneath him, shrinking as he rose. The ordered lines of skates carrying ore and volatiles to her had dissolved. They fled into her now for protection she could not offer.

Beneath him, a new volley of princesses burst from the tubes, shooting past Diviya. Their steel fingers were tucked tightly beneath them and the spray of their thrust sent shivers of aching attraction through him. A squadron of princes and their servants followed. Their wide, dust-free fins turned gracefully, briefly reflecting starlight from smooth carapaces of boron carbide, beneath fine, tight nets of steel mesh. They turned the webs of steel to face the Hero pulsar, absorbing its microwaves as they thrust.

Breath-taking. Intimidating. Kin.

Diviya and his revolutionaries thrust hard after them. The horizon of the great asteroid fell away on all sides, revealing the clean dark of space. The colony, with the hive and its halo of slums became a dark, irregular shape, lit only by the bright points of the few souls still there. Then the third and last wave of princesses launched, with every soul that could, even those who could only thrust briefly.

Invisible were the workers left behind, colorless as the dirt. He'd fought for them, tended their hurts, and had wanted to bring them on migration. Those brother skates tugged at his heart, but eerily, less than he expected. Diviya was enlightened, rational, but the strength of instinct surprised him. Diviya felt the urge to protect the princes, clouded with his attraction for the princesses. He needed to control both feelings.

His soul whispered the navigational liturgy to him and he wanted to follow its lead. His soul had migrated before, in a successful prince of a generation past. His soul carried the wisdom of flight angles through the vastness of space and time, how to block the shaghāl from reaching the princesses and the princes. Each soul knew the same way to the same spawning ground waiting for them in the future. But to his soul, those workers left behind were no more important than the giant shell of the abandoned queen after the princesses had launched.

The smaller pod of shaghāl proceeded to the hive. They were radio-reflective, not thrusting, but riding the Hero's Voice with mesh sails catching the powerful microwaves shouting out each second. The dying queen served by soulless skates would feed the predators. The larger pod's course would intercept the migration.

* * *

Past

DIVIYA HOPPED OVER the regolith, arriving at Work Farm Number Seven. Several days of bribing low-level officials with frozen nitrogen had gotten him a permit. A big skate with a sleek carapace patrolled the edge of the farm. Under a thin layer of dust, the grand prince's insignia was visible, scored in the ceramic on both leading edges of his wide horizontal fins. The lens at the front of his head showed the hot radioactive light of his soul behind it.

"What do you want?" the tax farmer said.

"Someone called for a doctor," Diviya said. He tilted his leading edges lower, showing less of his own soul. The landlord's thugs were not worth antagonizing. From his gullet, Diviya pulled a thin sheet of beaten aluminum inscribed with his permit.

"Go back to the hive," the tax farmer said. "We got the lazy skate back to work."

"I've come all this way. I may as well check on the other workers," Diviya said.

The tax farmer threw the permit. "Waste your time if you want."

"Thank you," Diviya said, retrieving the permit. Rows of steel fingers undulated beneath him and he hopped onto the work farm.

The farm was so large that the curvature of the asteroid nearly hid the great mounds of debris at the far end. The flat, triangular bodies of the skates moved over the regolith, digging and sifting with sharp fingers. Their radio sails were pulled tight across the tops of their wide horizontal fins, to feed on the radio and microwaves of the Hero's Voice.

The workers were almost all soulless. Some few were given weak souls to find radioactive grains during their sifting. Diviya had received a respectable soul. Doctors needed keen, penetrating sight. The tiniest injuries and earliest-stage material stresses could only be detected with radiation reflected back from ceramic carapaces.

Diviya passed a mound of regolith scraped from the surface of the asteroid, sifted for icy clays, hard nuggets of nitrogen and carbon dioxide, and iron-nickel granules for the foundries and kilns within the queen. The tailing mounds were chondrules of silicates and magnetites. Atop the hill was one of the grand prince's landlords.

The landlord preached a droning liturgy from the apex of the mound, but the words were not his. The soul behind his eye recited the sagas for him to repeat. The metronomic rhythms of electrical buzzing and snapping carried some distance before they were drowned by the inscrutable mystery of the Hero's Voice. Tax farmers and other landlords heard the liturgy, and retransmitted it, complete with its numbing, repetitive rhythms.

Diviya had become adept at ignoring his soul. Otherwise he would spend his days in sagas and parables that froze the class struggle into hardened clay. He moved among the workers. He knew many of them by name, from protests and rallies.

"Good morning, Esha," Diviya said to a dusty skate. Esha's fingers moved in a blur beneath him, scrabbling at the hard regolith, creating a cloud of dust in the microgravity. Esha was a good worker. Several nuggets of nitrogen and carbon dioxide shone in dusty pride beside him. A respectable meal for a prince or even one of the princesses.

"Good morning, Diviya. What brings you out here?"

"I heard a doctor was needed."

"That was days ago. Dwani was beaten."

"Where is he?"

"They're supervising him close to the west mound."

A tax farmer approached.

"Get back to work!" he said. "Hey! Who are you?"

Diviya turned to show the mark of a doctor that had been scored onto both leading edges of his fins. The tax farmer grunted derisively. Diviya was a doctor to workers. If he'd had a patron, he would have been the doctor to princes and perhaps even the princesses. Tax farmers did not consider country doctors like Diviya anything more than workers reaching above their station, although they themselves happily came to him with their aches.

"Hoy!" the tax farmer said. "You didn't call me to pick this up," he said, pushing both Diviya and Esha aside to grab the nuggets of frozen gasses.

"I just found them," Esha said.

"That's what they all say! Get back to work. And you, doctor, get done whatever you were doing before I revoke your permit." The tax farmer hopped towards the next worker.

"Go see the skates after you see Dwani," Esha said. "They'll want news of him. The workers look up to you. You received a soul, but you haven't forgotten them."

The droning of the liturgy resumed. Like the Hero's Voice, the meaning of the words had decayed.

* * *

Present

THE HIVE VANISHED behind him. The minuteness of their former home was spiritually humbling. Stippled stars on black night, close companions since birth, now wrapped him in their vastness. His struggle for the workers, all his words to free his brothers, seemed hollow here. And the migration might still die stillborn, like a drone without a soul. No future. Not even a present.

His soul was silent, perhaps hoping that Diviya had resolved himself to his duty. He fell behind the thrusting princes, still so far that they were just tiny points of hot breath. Perspective placed them near the unknowable voice of the pulsar. The thought of approaching the Hero terrified him.

Diviya's soul began, in staccato radio crackles, the liturgy of migration: vectors and star sightings, landmarks, and flight speeds drawn from the sagas. The souls had done this before. They adjusted the liturgy each migration, to account for the drift of the asteroids, but the mythic arc of the Hero and the Maw was unchanging.

Diviya knew the migration route. He'd studied it, perhaps in a way unseemly for a country doctor. He eased his thrust, contrary to the liturgy. His soul repeated the timings of the thrusts, and their strengths. Diviya ignored his soul. He needed to be trailing the princes and princesses for what he wanted to try. And he needed his thrust later.

THE PULSAR BECAME a fat dot. Its gravity drew him onward and its voice had become a deafening, constant shout. Diviya unfurled his radio sail. It bloomed outward, bound to him by many fine steel wires. He angled his sail so that the microwaves pushed him off a collision with the collapsed star. The force would grow as he approached, compensating for the rising gravity.

THE PULSAR HAD bloated into a fat disk. The Hero's Voice was too pure and loud to be audible. Microwaves seared tiny arcs of electricity across Diviya twice each second, filling him with life for what must come. He was sick with overcharging. His soul recited the prayer of brushing against divinity. When that finished, his soul told the parable of the prince fleeing before waves of the shaghāl. The Hero made Diviya large and small. Diviya could not turn to look how close the shaghāl might be, nor even if his fellow revolutionaries had kept pace with him. One approached divinity alone.

Past

DIVIYA HOPPED TO find Dwani. The strip-mined regolith fields were uneven; layers of frozen dust revealed blocks of immovable iron-nickel. Such large masses of exposed iron-nickel did strange things to the Hero's Voice. Where they could, workers dumped mine tailings upon them. But sometimes all the fingers in the colony could not cover them and the odd protrusions sparked and crackled, interpreting the Hero's Voice in their own way, like the mad.

Diviya reached the west mound, an immense pile of mine tailings looking over the entirety of the plain. It had been here long before the queen and her grand prince had arrived.

"Poor workers," Diviya said. "How long had they toiled to make that mound?"

"Long enough to launch generations of princesses and princes onto the migration," his soul said, "fully fueled, with discerning souls to guide the foundation of new colonies."

"At remarkable cost," Diviya said.

"Remarkable that we survive at all," the soul said.

The tax farmers inspected his permit. His soul shone as brightly as theirs, although these skates had likely been extorting bribes of volatiles from the workers for months. They might have enough breath to migrate with the princes and courtiers. The work of tax farmer and landlord was difficult, but could be lucrative.

Difficult skates worked the fields around the west mound. Fewer breaks, harsher discipline. Not that workers had many privileges. The workers here were slower, and the digging was hard. A tax farmer indicated a lone worker close by the base of the mound.

"Dwani?" Diviya asked when he had neared.

The skate turned and Diviya recoiled. The worker's carapace had been smashed where the clean lines of the leading edge came to a point. Near the vertex was a jagged hole, dusted with regolith attracted by the electricity within Dwani. The lens of the eye was so scratched that no part of its surface was smooth.

"Who is it?" Dwani said.

"Diviya."

"The doctor?"

"What happened, Dwani?"

"The tax farmers went after a few organizers. Reinforced ceramic doesn't stand up well to iron rods."

A horrified sadness crept over Diviya as he neared

Dwani. The radioactive shine of Diviya's soul scattered back from Dwani's carapace, revealing many microscopic fractures. Some of the cracks were so large that Diviya would not have even needed a soul to see them. They reached far along Dwani's fins, one nearly to the trailing edge. Dust, especially the static-charged graphite fines of the regolith, infected the cracks. To say nothing of the dust entering through the hole near Dwani's damaged eye. The dust would soon interfere with the neural wiring.

"Whoever did this didn't mean for you to live long," Diviya said.

"I can't move some of my fingers, but I can still work." As if to make light of it, Dwani moved his fingers. Only a half-dozen of the steel limbs moved. The rest dangled.

"I hope you didn't come all this way just for me. Unless you have some cure."

"One of the committee members got word out. I came as soon as I could."

"It won't do any good," Dwani said. "The tax farmers know their job."

"I'm sorry."

"Don't be sorry. Do something. More than just writing little manifestos and three-point plans on committee broadsheets."

"Violence isn't getting us anywhere, Dwani."

"Coward."

"There's no end in what you're doing. You and a school of other committee leaders make it sound as if a total upset of the hive will somehow make us free."

"We'll be free when we are not oppressed."

"Half of us will be dead, win or lose," Diviya said. "And the chaos will do nothing except cripple the hive. We'll be easy pickings for the shaghāl."

"We already are."

"The princesses too?" Diviya said. "What is the point of all our work if even the princesses do not get away? Extinction is not social change."

"You never resist," Dwani said. "That's why they gave you a soul."

Present

DIVIYA'S CRY OF suffering mixed with the tireless booming of the Hero's Voice. His soul had begun crying long ago. Weight crushed them. Diviya felt as heavy as an asteroid or a star, important to the world, possessing meaning. And yet, he was tiny. The Hero was now an angry blue and purple sphere. A beam of burning microwaves ripped across its face twice a second, throwing Diviya back by his radio sail. Strange radiations he'd never seen swirled in sickly oranges and reds on the pulsar's surface.

Diviya reached perigee, the closest approach to the Hero, and he thrust. It ached. His thrust burned. The Hero's Voice stung. The pull of his radio sail creaked his whole carapace. He was going to snap.

And then the Hero was behind him, His Voice throwing Diviya forward. His soul, between bouts of terror, repeated the correct speeds and distances of the migration. The temptation to relent to the soul was strong, but Diviya followed the migration at a distance with his co-revolutionaries in clumsy formation around him.

The lighthouse beams of the Hero's Voice propelled them faster and faster. On this course, the radio waves would accelerate and charge them continuously as they flew straight and true towards the black hole called the Maw.

It was a long way between the Hero and the Maw. Sometimes half or more of a migration could fall to the shaghāl before the Maw had a chance to destroy them. And that was when the courtiers distracted the shaghāl and led them away.

And the shaghāl certainly followed. Diviya held his terror in check. The shaghāl were big, strong and fast, riding under enormous radio sails, leading with maws large enough to crush a skate.

The Hero's Voice already dimmed as they moved away. But Diviya listened for any drop in the Voice beyond that, which would be the first sign that the shaghāl had found him, had picked him as food. In all the sagas and the teachings of the souls, the pursuing shaghāl placed themselves between their prey and the Hero so that the creatures of appetite slowly crept up with their great mouths while the skates drifted helplessly in their silent shadow.

Yet sometimes the ways of the devil were instructive. Diviya settled behind a distant prince, cutting off the radio and microwaves with his sail. The prince tilted his sail, this way and that, trying to escape the shadow, but without the Voice, his sail was just wire mesh.

The prince retracted his sail, a prelude in the sagas to thrusting. He extended the sail indecisively. Breath was a hard object, sifted or picked from the regolith, but it possessed a holiness. It was the Hero's gift for the migration. The taboo of its use was both spiritual and pragmatic. Any use of breath except in the approaches to the Hero and the Maw, in strict, soul-guided accelerations, could mean not having enough later.

"No!" Diviya's soul said, suddenly realizing what he was doing. "Stop it, you monster!"

The shadowed prince chittered electrical static, passing alarm across the migration, but it did him no good. The formation spread out. Over long hours, it passed the prince and Diviya finally moved aside, choosing another target to shadow. He drifted past the prince, who, suddenly hearing the Hero's Voice, began accelerating again. But it would not be enough.

The shaghāl had been accelerating all this time too. They were closing faster than the prince could accelerate. They would consume him, volatiles, radioisotopes, rare metals and all.

Diviya's three revolutionaries shadowed other princes. They were not as nimble as Diviya. More often than not, the princes escaped, catching radio waves that the revolutionaries had not quite blocked with their sails. But the princes still lost precious moments or minutes of acceleration.

It was working. The satisfaction tasted bitter to Diviya. He hadn't wanted this and was the first to regret it. He'd wanted some end to the suffering of the workers. The princes had forced this revolution on themselves.

One of the courtiers, trailing so far back that he perhaps sensed he would soon be shadowed, retracted his sail and gently spun in flight. Instead of an approaching shaghāl, he saw Diviya, Tejas, Barini, and Ugra. He transmitted a radio shout in anger, and unfurled his sail. He rode the microwaves expertly, sweeping close to Tejas.

Diviya cried a warning, but it was too late. The courtier crashed into Tejas and dug with sharp fingers at Tejas' eye, at his mouth, and at the wires holding his radio sail. The fingers snapped two of Tejas' four wires. Tejas pitched as his sail tilted. The courtier leapt away.

"Tejas!" Diviya yelled.

Tejas began to tumble slowly. He could not retract his sail, nor right it.

"Diviya!" Tejas called. Diviya slowly pulled ahead as all of Tejas' acceleration spun into his wild careening. "Fix my sail! Help!"

Diviya's heart cracked. There was nothing to be done. On the migration, Diviya hadn't the materials to replace snapped wires. And the shaghāl approached.

"Leave!" his soul said. "Fly on! Protect the princes and the princesses now."

"I'm sorry, Tejas!" Diviya said.

"Please!" Tejas called.

Diviya slipped behind Tejas' attacker before he could spread news of their betrayal. The courtier, suddenly without the Hero's Voice, tilted his sail, to no effect. The migration crept away from him. He shrieked warnings, but he was too far for anyone to hear, except Diviya. The migration had dispersed widely, a scripturally pure defense against shadowing by shaghāl.

"No, do not do this!" his soul said. Perhaps it had overcome its fear of Diviya.

"Please."

"Do you know how many workers have suffered because of the princes?" Diviya asked. "Do you know how many have been beaten and killed?"

"You are angry," his soul said. "You do not completely understand the way the Hero has organized the hives so that the finest and strongest of skates are sent upon migration."

"They are not the best," Diviya said disgustedly. "They are the skates who have been given a soul, and then use that soul to enslave workers."

"You are wrong. You are special."

"I am not. A doctor wore out. Another was needed. I was the easiest to train. That is all. We are all the same. Souls create divisions for their own benefit."

"The hereditary information you carry in clays are all the same. Circumstances and accidents of feeding and luck have their roles, but you are all kin. We are one colony. The success of a prince is your success. We make sure our kin succeed."

"We are more than schools of clay," Diviya said. "And if we truly are all the same kin, you won't mind if it is I instead of the princes who make the final journey with the princess."

The Hero's thinning Voice pushed Diviya toward the courtier he shadowed. When they were almost touching, Diviya tilted his sail, veered aside, and passed him. The courtier's radio sail caught the pulsar's beam and started accelerating, but the shaghāl would finish what Diviya had started.

Past

THE FOUNDING QUEEN and her grand prince had located the hive on an asteroid with a lazy rotation around an axis that pointed almost directly at the pulsar. At the pole, the queen heard the Hero's Voice tirelessly, but in the piled rubble fields near the worker slums, the low ensouled lived with short nights of quiet starvation and lethargy. The pulsar had set an hour ago and Diviya should have been resting, but he'd been invited to a workers' rally. He entered the slums.

"These are not elements of society you should be associating with," his soul said. "You and I may have a future. There may yet be time to show your talents and come into a more lucrative position, like a tax farmer, a minor landlord, or even the personal physician to a courtier. Imagine the resources you would have then for the migration."

"My future will hardly be determined by a meeting," Diviya said. A group of skates congregated ahead of them. "Look, other souls are here."

"Ensouled workers!" his soul said dismissively. "Workers are where they put souls that are incapable of memorizing the migratory routes. No one here can help you."

"Diviya!" Abhisri said. "You made it." His friend Abhisri edged from the crowd, the flat ceramic triangle of his carapace worn by months of hard building. A soul winked behind the lens of his eye. Like Diviya, he had received his soul late in life, and had become an engineer. He often spoke at rallies.

"I heard you went to the work farms? You saw Dwani?" Abhisri asked.

"The drones were thorough," Diviya said. "They cracked him."

Abhisri made a sound.

"Change is slow," Diviya said.

"Not just slow," Abhisri said, not for Diviya, but for the others. "There is no change!"

Around them, workers sparked loudly in their heads, casting radio waves. Yelling. Cheering. They knew Diviya here, but he felt trapped in the center of attention as Abhisri spoke. Diviya was not a leader. Although they read his manifestos, Diviya didn't agree with their methods.

"We cannot have slow change," Abhisri said, warming to his oration. "We cannot hop or crawl toward freedom!"

More cheers. Diviya felt like cheering, too. The gaping hole in Dwani's face would not leave his thoughts.

"We must go!" his soul said. "Now!"

"All of us are wiped out at every migration," Abhisri said. "We never migrate. Only nobles. Their hangers-on. Their enforcers."

"Revolution now!" someone yelled in the darkness.

"Overthrow the hive!"

Diviya's soul shrieked in panic. So loud that surely others around them heard it. Diviya was also alarmed. He cared about these workers. Many were his friends. He was one of them. Revolution would get them killed. A terrible nervousness crept over him as he realized that he was going to speak.

"We cannot overthrow the hive," Diviya said. "Violence will not free us."

They hissed at him in electrical static.

"The princes and their courtiers are big, well-fed, and ensouled," Diviya said. "They can fly while most of us cannot. The hive is built to repel us."

"Excellent," Diviya's soul said.

"Defeatist!" someone yelled.

"Collaborator!" someone yelled.

"Leave!" Diviya's soul said.

"This is Diviya!" Abhisri said. "Let him say his piece."

"How much time is left, do you suppose?" Diviya asked. He was nervous with all eyes upon him. "A few months? The nobles fear that they haven't enough volatiles to migrate. Courtiers fear they will not have the fuel to follow. Princes know that without the courtiers, the shaghāl will pursue them."

No one spoke. No one moved. "And we fear being left behind."

Diviya felt dizzy. He never threw himself into the middle. "What if we ask for souls for some workers?" Diviya said. "Would they give them?"

"No!" someone yelled from the darkness. "They'd beat us 'til we crack."

"Yes, they would," Abhisri said.

"So what do we do?" someone demanded.

"Offer them something," Diviya said.

A chorus of protests rose all about him.

"Offer them more than what you are producing, in exchange for souls."

"We can't do that!" someone said.

"We ask for souls? For some of us? To go on the migration?"

"Yes," Abhisri said, sounding intrigued.

"That won't work for everyone!" someone said.

"But if a dozen workers survive the migration, they become the princes of the next generation," Diviya said. "They can change the colonies that follow. Fewer tax farmers. Fewer nobles. More souls for the workers."

"It isn't enough!" someone yelled. A chorus supported him.

"Of course it isn't enough," Diviya said. "But it is the best we can get right now. As long as all the workers are wiped out every generation, the workers of the next must restart the struggle as if it were the first time. We must be in solidarity with the brothers of tomorrow whose clay has not yet been fired."

The crowd silenced. A shade of the immensity of their task, of a sense of history and time slipped over them.

"Abhisri!" they cried. And some yelled "Diviya."

"No!" his soul said. "This is against the will of the Hero."

"Some will say this is against the will of the Hero," Diviya said to the workers.

"The Hero made the princesses and their suitors and the migration, but where in the sagas did the Hero make tax farmers?"

Laughter greeted his joke, but sparking anger, too. "Nowhere!"

"And we have a leader," Diviya said. "Abhisri can take our ideas to the princes."

"Diviya!" some said, including Abhisri.

"Abhisri!" Diviya said, and was relieved when that cry was taken up.

Then other skates spoke. They hadn't the rhetoric to speak at a prince's reception, but their strength as orators lay in the visceral reality of their wanting. These workers scratched and scrubbed the regolith each day for nuggets of gasses to launch princesses and their suitors into the future. They had more right to their words than Diviya had to his. They deserved to migrate. As the speeches went on, workers gave Diviya gentle double-knocks of approval with the tips of their fins.

"Leave!" his soul said. "You endanger yourself and me!"

"Hive drones won't come here," Diviya whispered to his soul. "Drones are lazy and greedy and spend their time on the hills."

"They employ informants."

"Among the workers?"

"The soulless will die when the shaghāl come, but many seek to ease their time with easier work."

A worker neared, leaning the whole leading edge of his fin against Diviya's, until their faces were close.

"Will you migrate, Diviya?" the worker asked.

"I have no patron. I have not been given any breath either."

"You will not be given any," the worker said. "This is a bad year and a bad site for the hive. Many of the landlords will be here with us in the end."

"Famine," Diviya said.

"Take this." Beneath them, the worker's fingers passed Diviya a half-dozen large nuggets of frozen gases. Nitrogen. Carbon dioxide. Methane. "Eat it!" the worker whispered, so close that only the two of them could hear.

"I can't," Diviya said.

"You must! You are one of us, Diviya."

Diviya stared at the gift. The worker might have done any number of things with this much raw reaction mass. He could have bribed tax counters, or even a low-status prince if he could get close enough.

"Hide them, quick!" the worker said.

Diviya put them in his mouth and deep into his gullet, past his soul, so as to not melt them. Over time, he could melt and refreeze the gases to purify them.

The worker melted into the crowd, as if suddenly shy. Diviya retreated, too. This was enormous. When he'd been apprenticed to a doctor, he'd expected to die in terror when the shaghāl came. Even when the hive had given him a soul, elevating him into the lowest of the privileged, he'd not changed his thinking. Without volatiles, there was no point in dreaming wishes. But now, this stranger, from nowhere, had given him a gift, one that separated him from the workers as irrevocably as a soul could.

"We will migrate!" said Diviya's soul. "Although this is not nearly enough breath for such a journey, it is a start. Let us leave."

"The meeting is not finished," Diviya said.

"Everyone here is a revolutionary!" the soul said. "Someone will denounce them all to the hive drones and the princes."

Present

THE MIGRATION HAD broken into three streams, each with at least one princess and a dozen or so attendant princes and courtiers. Diviya followed the fastest princess, the one farthest ahead. She was the least likely to be targeted by the shaghāl.

Barini and Ugra followed. He did not know either one well. Barini was a hauler of regolith who participated in rallies. Ugra had tilled the soil and his musical talent produced electrical melodies, into which others fit political rhymes and slogans. Neither seemed a likely revolutionary, but perhaps he wasn't either. Dwani, Abhisri, and all the real leaders were dead, with all the workers of their generation except for three.

The three of them became methodical and pitiless. Their targets tried to evade the sudden silencing of the Hero's Voice, with only some success. Hours passed. Then days. Then weeks. The Hero's Voice attenuated. The best acceleration from the pulsar was in the past. Now, speed grew in slow increments. The princess was a point far ahead, but the courtiers and the princes had fallen behind.

Diviya retracted his sail, and exhaled a puff of volatiles. He slowly pivoted, until he faced the pulsar. The Hero was a sad, cool point in the blackness, flashing thin radio and microwaves twice a second, lower in tone and quieter. Diviya felt dislocated. His class struggle felt minuscule. This cold vastness offered neither light, nor asteroids upon which to shelter. Far behind, the shaghāl appeared tiny, but their radioactive souls shone hard and point-like. Seven of them followed. Diviya exhaled another puff to stop his rotation, and unfurled his radio sail.

THEY WERE CLOSE to the princes and courtiers. Weeks of slow work had made each of them adept at stealing the microwaves destined for the sails of the princes. The pulsar's beam was so distant now that its push was faint. Diviya and his companions were tiring.

A lone princess sailed ahead of the princes and the revolutionaries. The sounds of the souls far in front of them were frantic. The princess ought to be protected at all times.

Diviya felt the Voice of the Hero abruptly thin. A moment of panic stole over him. His soul shrieked. Diviya had been preparing for this for weeks, imagining the angles, the time he would have. He was not completely shadowed, not yet. Some of the distant Voice reached him still. He tilted his sail hard, catching the few microwaves reaching him, accelerating sideways. At first, nothing seemed to be happening. His soul recited the litany of the sacrifice, for both of them. But it was working. Slowly. After long minutes, the Hero's Voice became louder, and he emerged from the shadow.

Diviya sailed wide to stay away from the shaghāl who had found him, and then snapped his sail back to accelerate again. He felt weak. The sagas called the starvation from the Hero's Voice the small death. His soul quieted for a long time.

"It is not what we wanted," his soul whispered. "We dream of being at the front of the school, with the princess. But we are not. We too must serve. We will not escape again, but we may atone for our crimes by leading the shaghāl away. I was weak. I should have opposed you more. Morality is the responsibility of the soul. I have failed, but we now may seek redemption."

"I never wanted to be a prince," Diviya whispered back.

"Come!" Diviya cried to Barini and Ugra. "Let us create a new hive where workers are free!" Diviya slowly slipped into place to shadow another prince.

In the fourth month of the migration, a shadow fell over Barini. It was sudden and complete. The shaghāl was close and Barini had no hope of sailing free.

"Barini!" Diviya cried in radio static. "Thrust! Exhale!"

"No!" Diviya's soul said. "On the migration, only a princess may exhale. All breath must be saved for the Maw."

"Barini!" Diviya said. "Thrust!"

"Everyone has a place. He too who is caught serves the hive," Diviya's soul said.

The soul was not wrong. Every courtier and prince lost kept a shaghāl occupied long enough for time dilation to mean they would never be seen again.

But the soul was also wrong. The calculation was grimly mathematical and religious, weighted to favor the nobility. The princess was indispensable, but the princes and courtiers were more than interchangeable. Barini had tilled the soil, given the princesses breath, given flesh and life to new souls. He had as much right as any to be among the fathers of a new generation.

Diviya's words did nothing for Barini. Diviya's soul recited a litany of complacency and sacrifice, as Barini's soul probably whispered to him. The soul seduced, by pulling on instinct.

Barini retracted his radio sail against his back. He began to silently rotate, his mouth and eye shut, hiding the hard radiation of his soul. Instinct was stronger.

Past

DIVIYA MOVED IN the low circles of the hive itself, with ensouled skates whose skills were too valuable to be spent on farming. Accountants and building engineers worked around the queen and hive, erecting the nets of fine wire on high scaffolds, capturing the constantly beamed Voice for the queen, weighing workers bearing regolith and frozen volatiles into the hive, scheduling work.

The low ensouled had some leisure with which to imitate the princes and courtiers. They did not have the opera house in which to put on the sagas, but they performed for each other in the hollows between mounds. They did not have libraries, but they retold legends and parables, refining their manners, so that someday, if the chance came, they might mingle successfully with the princes and their courtiers.

Although he mostly tended workers, Diviya was also physician to clerks and petty functionaries who could not get higher-status physicians. It was always difficult for a cold skate, living at the temperature of the surrounding regolith, to carry a hot soul. Even the ceramics of boron carbide sintered and fired in the kilns of the queen creaked with distortions of temperature. In the worst cases, carapaces could even crack.

Diviya's hive patients possessed souls, and jockeyed for patronage. They guarded their own opportunities and blocked skates like Diviya from the princes. This, from what Diviya understood, suited the princes, who received gifts constantly from these petty clerks.

They were all taught to sacrifice, and for a while the idea of sacrifice could be romantic and ennobling. Freshly kilned skates were reared on the parables of the good worker, and especially the sacrifices of Narah the courtier. Narah had led away some of the shaghāl and the saga spoke lovingly of his last moments. It felt heroic, its romance layered by generations of retelling.

Yet it ran deeper than sacrifice. The males of the hive carried the same hereditary clays from the queen. The contributions of the few grand princes who had survived the migration accounted for limited variation in the hive. Diviya was brother to the princes, the tax farmers, the landlords, and the workers.

But privilege and status did not creep into a hive. Inequity stormed in, like hive drones breaking up a protest. The queen produced new souls with the radioisotopes sifted out of the regolith. Those who received souls no longer depended on capacitors to work and move through the night. The spiritual wealth became the power to see the radioisotopes of other souls or find more in the regolith. Most importantly, radioactive souls turned frozen gases into hot thrust.

Diviya met with Abhisri in the camps of the low ensouled outside the hive. Abhisri had bribed a courtier for a meeting with Prince Lasiya. Diviya was nervous. He had never met a prince. He doubted his ability to persuade. He had channeled debate among like-minded skates, but this was his own idea now and a high audience. It had been easy to speak in the dark to workers, deep in the slums. This was the hive, vast and monumental.

"This is bad," whispered his soul. "Once you speak with this prince, we are marked, you and I. The accountants will look in their records to see what soul you have and they will put marks there against both of us."

Diviya and Abhisri approached a side entrance guarded by two big drones. Prince Lasiya's secretary emerged from behind the drones. The brightness of his soul was stabbing. The lines of his ceramic shell were sleek and clean. The leading edges bore the emblems of his patron. Abhisri pulled a lump of distilled and refrozen breath from his gullet. Possessing it was a crime. So much breath ought to have been destined for the princes and princesses. The secretary took the bribe without otherwise moving. It vanished into his gullet. The hive drones studiously ignored the transaction.

"I am listening," the secretary said.

"We were told we would be speaking with Prince Lasiya," Diviya said.

"The prince is not available."

"My words are for him alone," Diviya said.

The hot circle of radiation from the secretary's soul shone full on Diviya. A submissive reverence stole over Diviya's soul. A fearful thought crept into Diviya's mind. Might the souls have some secret language, mediated perhaps by particle decay? It was an eerie, paranoid thought, and yet, something of substance passed between these souls and Diviya imagined his whole life being reported.

"I will bring any message to Prince Lasiya."

Diviya and Abhisri backed away and spoke in low tones, in the rough dialect of the workers.

"He won't bring the message anywhere," Abhisri said.

"We have no other choice."

"Do what he says!" Diviya's soul whispered. "There is danger here."

"A prince would have listened on his own authority," Abhisri said. "This courtier will report what we say in the worst light if you tell him your offer."

"The workers held back a riot so we could make this offer. We must try." Diviya turned to the courtier. "Tell Prince Lasiya that there may be a way for the workers and the princes to come to an understanding to increase farm yields."

"Go on."

"This is a message for Prince Lasiya."

"Something as important as farm yields should not be toyed with. Where are your loyalties, doctor?"

"My loyalties are with the hive."

"Would your soul say the same?" the secretary asked. The shine of his soul was a beam, like the Voice of the Hero itself, focused through the smooth lens of his eye, in through Diviya's eye. Diviya felt hot.

"Of course," Diviya said.

"If your loyalties are correct, then speak of increasing farm yields, doctor."

Diviya hesitated. "The workers dig hard, but the regolith is poor. Additional incentives could make them eager to work even harder."

"Any worker who is not working as hard as he can is guilty of a crime," the secretary said.

"The treatment of the workers makes them less effective," Diviya said. "Beatings make them resentful. I have seen skates broken and killed by tax farmers. Broken skates produce nothing."

"Slack workers must be forced to do their duty. Examples inspire others."

Diviya's quick words were difficult to contain. He had urged restraint on workers on so many occasions, so that they could bring forward something of substance. Only the thought that he was representing many workers held his anger back.

"There is a better way to inspire workers," Diviya said.

"Odd that centuries of experience did not find it, yet a country doctor has," the secretary said.

Diviya controlled his fear. Abhisri edged backward.

"Workers move regolith, find the volatiles and radioisotopes, yet know they will never migrate. If a few workers could receive souls, the additional radioisotopes found would soon repay the gift."

"Souls for the workers?" the secretary scoffed. "The apportionment of souls is a sober process. There are not enough volatiles now for the court. If breath were further thinned, instead of a quarter of the migration outrunning the shaghāl and the Maw, no one would."

"More skates on migration will draw away more shaghāl from the princesses," Diviya said, "especially if they are slower."

"You consign them to die? Do they know this?"

"They are already dead. We all are. When the migration flees, every worker will sit waiting with the empty hive for the shaghāl to come."

"You are naïve, doctor," the secretary said. "Every additional migrating skate takes breath from the princesses and princes. The sagas are filled with cautionary tales of migrants falling into the Maw, or even the Hero, when they lack breath. Your reckless ideas would jeopardize the whole migration."

"Not if we could find more volatiles," Diviya said.

"Ah," the secretary said, and Diviya felt as if he'd stepped into a trap. "Let us explore your thoughts on farming. How much more could workers do?"

"That would be based on how much incentive was offered."

"Treason," the secretary said, with the tone of someone commenting on the procession of the stars. "Do you know the punishment for treason? For withholding breath or radioisotopes?"

"I know it," Diviya said. He was cold beneath that hot stare.

"Then let us pick a strategy to get those additional volatiles."

"Incentives?" Diviya asked.

"I do not trust incentives. Even among the princes, not every skate can be trusted. Fear and disincentives are the most consistently effective methods."

Present

THE FLASHES OF radiation from near the black hole resolved into searing weaves of curtained light. Oranges. Reds. Whites. Sharp rays leapt from infalling gas, heating Diviya's soul, even though they were still days away. And the Maw was loud. It endlessly consumed the breath of the world. The infalling volatiles crackled with electrical panic. Loud, frightening snaps.

The enormity of what they approached dwarfed even Diviya's imagination. The rain of hot particles traced a line around the Maw, outlining a monster large enough to swallow even the Hero.

Weeks of careful work by Diviya and Ugra had pulled four more princes from the school. Soon, the princess would be unguided. Her soul carried other liturgies, secrets of growing a hive and waves and waves of little skates, but not navigational liturgies. Diviya had caught up to the trailing edge of the school. Ugra was close.

The Maw's own kin, the shaghāl, followed and Diviya imagined their enthusiasm as they neared the hive of their master. They shadowed the princes and courtiers, creeping closer and closer hour by hour. Diviya retracted his sail and exhaled the faintest of breaths to rotate slowly. His insides went cold.

He'd never seen a shaghāl. Three of them followed, one closely. He'd pieced his imaginings from the liturgies and sagas. Reality outstripped his nightmares. The shaghāl were big, reflecting light from hard ceramic and metal. Their bodies, triangular and flattened like a skate's, had long steel fingers for sharp grasping. It was as if a school of grand princes had been transformed by the Maw itself into engines of appetite.

The leading shaghāl thrust powerfully, leaping forward to hug Ugra in great fingers. It stuck a tube into Ugra's mouth and sucked away his breath. Ugra's fingers waved wildly, scratching at the carapace of his captor, until the shaghāl cracked Ugra open around the mouth, exposing the soul. Diviya did not see the rest. The shaghāl held Ugra and thrust outward, onto an orbit to carry it far around the black hole and back to the archipelago of asteroids where new hives would be founded.

And then Diviya was alone. There was no more revolution. There was only he, a princess, a prince, and a pair of pursuing shaghāl. Between Diviya and the prince, Diviya would always be second. The prince's soul was larger, hotter, making his thrust more powerful than anything Diviya could make. The shaghāl would reach Diviya first.

Then Diviya too fell into shadow.

"He too who is caught serves the hive," his soul whispered. That was the role the princes had for him. And the priesthood of souls. The poor brother must die for the rich brother to live.

He too who is caught serves the hive.

Diviya thrust.

"No!" his soul said. Diviya blasted precious volatiles behind him, emerging from the shadow of the shaghāl and even accelerating closer to the lead prince, the one closest to the princess.

"Monster!" the prince said. "I saw you waste your breath on yourself!"

Diviya rode his exhalation, coming close to the prince. Both souls protested, shrieking, warning the prince with panicked static, but the prince did not understand. Diviya clamped onto him, undersurface to undersurface where his fingers could reach the prince's mouth. Belatedly, the prince scored Diviya's carapace with sharp fingers.

The prince's violence almost shook Diviya away. Diviya dug into the prince's mouth, for the hot radioactive soul. Recriminations were loud in Diviya's head, difficult to block out.

The prince's soul was enormous. He had taken the

best radioisotopes. And many ices to be sure, enough to become the next Grand Prince, if Diviya had not caught up to him.

Diviya had learned from Dwani. He would rather end the next generation than let this prince recreate the colony they had left.

Diviya's fingers scrabbled at the fine bands holding the prince's soul. The souls screamed. Diviya's with memory. The prince's with terror. Princely fingers broke off some of Diviya's. Diviya snapped one of the bands, then another, then another.

The prince's soul drifted free.

The four of them shared a moment of disembodied terror. They screamed. And the prince went perfectly still.

Diviya held the screaming soul, its radioactive shine lighting the tireless night, as he pushed away the stunned prince. Diviya slipped the soul into his gullet, unfurled his radio sail and drifted clear.

The prince wobbled and drifted. What were his thoughts now as justice was given to him? Did he blame Diviya, blind to his own role? Perhaps this was not even justice. They approached the Maw, where death became victorious over life, darkness over light. They raced so quickly that the red stars stippling the darkness had brightened to blue. Only Diviya, the princess, and the shaghāl following them remained and they lived a quiescent fugue. Time became meaningless and long. The great sail of the shaghāl was furled. The Hero was so far, his Voice so quiet, that sails were decorations of brighter lives while they entered the mythic land of the dead.

Before them, the Maw cloaked itself in vast fields of hot clouds, but the breath of a thousand migrations was a poor shroud for the monstrosity of the Maw's hunger.

Light burned from beneath the clouds as warning. Speeding blues, falling greens, and throbbing reds each marked some particle falling into the Maw.

Diviya's spiritual terror, for all that he had set aside the sermons and sagas, was visceral. He trembled. The souls within him, his own and the stolen one, quaked. His soul's whispers had become hypnotic and he wanted to surrender. To believe.

He was falling, accelerating. The Maw had noticed him and it summoned him. It was dangerous to be seen by the Maw, yet only here could the migration be completed. Here, any differences in speed would be multiplied. The princess was still ahead of him. No one had been showing her the way. Diviya's soul, between bouts of confession and recriminations, recited coordinates he would not follow. Diviya thrust forward, using up more of his precious volatiles, until he was beside her.

She was a sleek, flat skate, larger than he, but built more toughly. Her soul was incoherent with fear, but she was brave. Within her she carried flat matrices of clay, stacked one upon the other, containing the hereditary secrets for the next generation encoded in the atomic gaps in the lattice of the clay crystals themselves. These leaves, paired with the ones he carried, would create the next generation.

"Are you ready, my prince?" she asked. Diviya shivered with excitement. *My Prince*. To be beside a princess, near the eerie strangeness of the Maw, was like being in a saga.

"I will lead you past the Maw," Diviya said.

"We are only two."

He found her suddenly young, although they were pressed and kilned in the same queen. She'd surely never questioned the powers who had cosseted her. She'd never had friends starved or beaten to death. Of course she was young.

"We must go," Diviya said, taking a star fix and comparing it to what he'd been taught by the souls. He was not taking their path.

Diviya understood the role of time dilation in the migration. Skates launched themselves into the future, leaping over generations of shaghāl whose population collapsed when bereft of prey. And when the skates established a new colony, few shaghāl were left to hunt them.

To the skates migrating around the Maw and back to the archipelago of asteroids, the trip lasted a single year. To the unmoving world, they were gone for seventeen. The skates coordinated their leap. Those who survived reunited not only in space, but also in time. Every acceleration and angle was perfectly calculated. The smallest error might leave a skate weeks, months, or even years from the rest of the migration.

But Diviya was not leading the princess seventeen years into the future. Their culture was bankrupt, built upon the broken carapaces of workers. No matter what happened, neither Diviya nor the princess would ever see anyone from their hive again. Shorter migrations were more dangerous, taking paths closer to the Maw and harder accelerations at perigee. Diviya had worked out the trajectories, without the help of his soul. He was leaping thirteen years into the future.

"Follow!" Diviya cried, over the protest of his soul. Diviya aimed into the hot clouds around the Maw and thrust.

* * *

Past

DIVIYA AND ABHISRI had left the secretary, shaken in themselves. The secretary had issued remarkably detailed instructions to them on who he wanted watched among the workers. There was little doubt that should Diviya or Abhisri fail to report to him, their souls would be removed, and the two of them killed.

"Disincentive," the secretary had said, "is more reliable."

Diviya and Abhisri had no intention of reporting on the workers, but they had a little time before they had to give something to the secretary. They passed messages to Esha and other work farm unionists. They struck secret committees, to plan a true strike, to grind the industry of the hive to a halt. They met in the worst of the shanties, where hive drones seldom passed.

The Hero precessed auspiciously from the Constellation of the Good Courtier to the Constellation of the Farmer, signaling the arrival of the longest night of the year. Workers could not move regolith without the shine of the Hero. Even the tax collectors were reluctant to push workers on the longest night, which became a time for singing and performing the snippets of the sagas in the regolith fields and the slums.

Diviya was with the workers' committee when the hive drones thrust in, carrying metal weights. They threw the weights just before landing, cracking workers. Diviya barely leapt out of the way. Workers scattered in terror as drones landed on them, striking ceramic with steel, tearing out wires that absorbed microwaves. Rows of hive drones ringed them.

Abhisri pushed Diviya into an alley filled with panicking workers. "Fly!" Abhisri said.

"I can't!"

"You're the only one who can! This is big! They don't know you carry breath."

A hive drone fell upon Abhisri, striking with a pick in its hard fingers. Diviya leapt on the drone, scratching and hitting. Diviya had never fought anything, and the drone was trained for this. The drone jerked, sending Diviya tumbling high in the microgravity. Below, the workers were awash in hive drones. They were lost.

Diviya exhaled a breath to correct his tumble as his trajectory carried him out of the slums. He thrust gently, turning, and settled to the regolith. A few skates, too weak or worn to work, saw him land, but did not move. They surely took him for some wayward tax farmer.

Even this far away, Diviya heard the panicked electrical sputtering of terrified skates. Friends and brothers. But the commands of the hive drones were louder, more calm, angry, and organized. Crackles of electrical static shot orders, some encoded. Abhisri was right. This was big.

"Flee!" his soul said stridently. "Flee!"

Diviya rocked back and forth on his fingers. He itched to run. To help. To run. His thoughts were jumbled. He feared he would only think of the right thing to do when it was too late. And he feared the sure beating. The work farms. The amputation of his soul. The true darkness of being a worker again, detached from a whole world he could only perceive through his soul.

Present

They thrust hard. The princess flew close. Hot violet radiation bathed them as the hunger of the Maw's gravity sped them faster. They fell from heaven, like the Hero himself. The whole world shifted into the blue. The sounds of static came tight and high-pitched. Tense. Near the Maw, space itself feared, releasing ghostly sounds and strange discharges.

The searing cloud abraded Diviya. The keening of his soul heightened in pitch. Radiation and particle strikes corroded the little soul. It was not made to fly this close to the Maw. It was composed of so many different radioisotopes that no matter what struck it, some part of it changed to something inert or something inappropriately active. The soul was going mad.

They neared perigee. Their speed was terrifying. Stars multiplied, filling the sky. Their haunting chorus blended with the relentless screams of the souls.

"Pray!" Diviya yelled to the souls. "Pray!" They did. In warbling tones of panic, the souls recited the metronomic cadences of the liturgy. Diviya listened to the prayers as he never had before.

Diviya's carapace creaked. He was so close to the edge of the Maw that the difference in gravity from his ventral side to his dorsal threatened to crack him. And still the Maw accelerated him.

No sounds of the living world remained, except for the chanting of his soul, a simple prayer to a hero who had no authority here. A new, eerie ocean of slow echoes filled his senses. His stars, radiant microwave stars, were all gone. New stars appeared. They were dead, their glows constant and unblinking as the sleet of passing clouds flayed and scorched him. He counted time by the cadences of the souls' prayers.

The intensity of the radioactive hail burned his soul, making Diviya's exhaust so hot that it felt like riding a star. And the clay wafers that he carried, his gametic contribution to the future, hardened in the heat and pressure, forming the crystalline structures that could be laid over the wafers carried by the princess. The possibility of new life quickened in this crushing furnace. Diviya counted the prayers and then, at a precise moment, he redoubled his thrust.

Diviya could not hear the princess. He stayed fixed on the strange stars. If he looked back for her, they would both be lost. Among these ghost stars, he could only trust. If she had not been able to follow, everything they had suffered at home was for naught.

The Maw grasped at him, to crush, stretch, and snap him. The heat of Diviya's thrust burned his own carapace. The clouds of hot gas brightened. He became so fast that even the ghost stars became too blue to see. The acidic particles shooting at the Maw crowded out the darkness, filling Diviya's world.

Then the Maw flung Diviya away.

The clouds thinned, but did not cool. Each grain floating in his path zipped into his carapace at nearly the speed of light. The world was eerie. He had left the Maw, but not the land of the dead. Strange purple colors and warped, fluid sounds drifted past him. He was a ghost and the living world had closed itself to him.

Yet amidst this dislocation, far away, faint, a point pulsed, frenetically like a young pulsar. Its microwaves were blue-shifted to a pitch that was visible instead of audible. The world was covered in a cloak of strangeness, yet he had to have faith that this was the Hero, summoning him back from death.

He was far from home, and had only whispers of breath left. He had used everything in the slingshot passage around the Maw and he did not even know if he had succeeded in leading the princess.

He exhaled the tiniest gasp of breath. Achingly slow, he pivoted. And his heart grew, in a primal way. A few body lengths from him was the princess. He had led her into the land of death and past the Maw. They could see the world of life, even if they were still fast-moving ghosts. It would take weeks to slow down. Her sleek carapace was striped and pitted with fine burns. Her soul was bright, but quiet and reverent.

Beyond her, the great bulk of the Maw had begun to shroud itself again under layers of bright, doomed clouds. The gases in palliative spirals spit hard radiation, but now that they had passed the Maw, their spite was thin and reddened and sepulchral.

The king of the underworld receded majestically. In the last moments of that hypnotic view, Diviya saw a tiny, distant silhouette, carrying a point of hard, hot radioisotopes.

No.

No. No. No.

The Maw had scarred them as they passed, and had not let them truly escape. The Maw let through one of its own, an engine of death, a famished monster that had nothing to eat but Diviya and the princess.

Past

DIVIYA HAD CEASED to sympathize with his soul. In the beginning, he understood it as a gift from the Hero and the queen, as a guide for the migration. The soul was, in some ways, an alien presence, but partly comprehensible within its role as the voice of eternity. But it was pitiless. Petty. Commitment became inflexibility. Resolve turned to stubbornness. Morality deafened reason. Diviya's soul argued, becoming more shrill. It was difficult to ignore the voice in his head.

In part to draw the soul away from its recriminations, Diviya spoke to his soul about the migration. Skates were taught nothing of the migration. This was safer ground to till. His soul calmed while considering the migration. Perhaps it thought that Diviya was opening himself to redemption.

At first petulantly, then with increasing enthusiasm, the soul spoke to Diviya of what was to come. Even when Diviya probed at the mystery of time dilation itself, the speeds and accelerations needed to achieve the magical dilation of seventeen, his soul answered him. Some of the pieces were symbols, or worse yet, allegories Diviya had to suffer through to keep his soul talking. More useful were the liturgies containing mathematical proportions, and angles and curves. Diviya read meaning into the liturgies that perhaps his soul did not mean for him to understand.

On the third day, Diviya descended from the mound. He left the slums and hopped into the worker districts where tailing hills were evenly rowed and the workers were healthier, younger. The neighborhood seemed lonely. This was a rest period, so most workers should have been back. In the distance, he saw the shine of another soul and turned away, so as not to give himself away. Between dusty piles he recognized a worker.

"Tejas!" he said.

Tejas approached. He had new scratches on the tops of his fins. Chips were missing along his leading edges. "Diviya," he whispered. "I thought you'd been arrested."

"Abhisri got me out a back alley. What happened?"

Tejas had difficulty speaking. The sparks he made were mistimed and sometimes sputtering. "We were all beaten. Most were arrested. I thought they were going to crack me."

Diviya's strength left him. "What charges?"

"I don't know," Tejas whispered. "They're all being sent to work farm number seven."

Dwani's broken face stared out of memory. Tejas sputtered and shorted over his words. "Abhisri got it bad, Diviya. They took out his soul right there. They weren't careful. I don't think he made it."

Diviya sank into the packed regolith. Adding or removing a soul was dangerous. Diviya had done it many times, but had not always been successful. The radioactive souls heated the ceramics and metals of the carapace and the neural wiring, while the skates cooled the souls. Sometimes the stresses on the skate and on the soul were too much. Tejas neared.

"They told me he didn't say nothing to the interrogators, but his soul did. They're looking for you, Diviya. You've got to hide."

"I told you!" Diviya's soul said. "Turn yourself in! Name names!"

But Diviya's soul had no hold on him anymore. The crushing pressure of the hive and his soul had crystallized a sense of mission in him. They had hardened his wavering resolve into the seed of something much more permanent. He was deathly frightened of being cracked open like Dwani, of having his soul torn away, but he heard the sagas through Dwani's eyes now.

"I'll hide in the slums, Tejas," Diviya said, "where the broken workers lie. Send me the leaders, yourself included."

"I'm no leader. I wasn't even a committee member."

"We're all committee members now," Diviya said. "The revolution must begin. Not the one Dwani and Abhisri wanted, but a larger one."

Present

DIVIYA AND THE princess had little with which to escape the shaghāl. Diviya had intended to unfurl his sail to brake beyond the black hole, but that would do nothing more than bring the fast-moving shaghāl to them faster. They flew so quickly that the gulf between the Maw and the Hero, that had taken the migration many months to cross before, now took only days. Yet if they did not slow soon, they would overshoot their home.

They unfurled their sails together. Blue-shifted radio waves punched their sails and the shock of slowing dizzied. As the tremendous deceleration intensified and the Hero fed them, they became less ghostly. The world abandoned its frenetic blue-shift. Strange stars faded, their haunted voices quieting. Stars he knew began to shine as if just reborn and the Hero's Voice aged centuries every minute, slowing finally to two flashes per second. Diviya and the princess were reborn.

"We will find a way to survive," the princess said.

No. Not princess. She was the queen now. But no. Not that either. No queens after the revolution. No princes. No grand princes. Just skates, sharing what they had.

"Yes, we will."

His words felt false. If they overshot their home, deep, deep space was a different kind of death than being crushed by the Maw.

"I will try to shadow the shaghāl," Diviya said.

"That will bring it to us faster!"

"Yes," Diviya said. Diviya adjusted his path, spotting the shaghāl's soul, as it shone in faintly blue-shifted hunger, far distant. "It will be ravenous now, and desperate."

Far behind, but still close enough to chill Diviya's marrow, a great radio sail unfurled. Diviya would make a poor shadow. The shaghāl was close and closing, decelerating at a furious rate.

Diviya slipped into the path of the pulsar's beam, cutting a shadow in the center of the shaghāl's sail. The shadow grew as the shaghāl neared. The shaghāl seemed to realize what was happening and angled its sail to escape the shadowing. Diviya followed.

The shaghāl jerked its sail the other way. It had no experience in avoiding a shadow. It hurtled closer, unable to do more than edge slowly sideways. The shaghāl tilted its sail wildly, trying to get around Diviya.

Diviya jerked his sail opposite to the shaghāl's tilt. The Hero's Voice veered Diviya aside, but not fast enough. The shaghāl's wing tip struck Diviya. The knock was tremendous, accompanied by a snap.

Diviya spun. Pain. Sharp pain. And fear and screaming. The second soul nearly flew from Diviya's mouth. Diviya righted his sail, catching the Hero's Voice, slowing his spin. Finally, he controlled his spin.

The shaghāl plunged far ahead, toward the asteroid field. It was slowing, but Diviya had robbed it of time. Now it would need every bit of effort to avoid overshooting the asteroid field.

The ragged princess neared. Diviya felt strange. His sail still pulled oddly, producing an ache under him.

"Your soul is glowing through a long crack beneath you," she said. The rhythms of her sparking speech were quick, fearful. He feared, too.

Cracked. He was cracked. Dwani's broken face haunted his thoughts. Dust would get into his carapace and would scour his wiring and joints. Soon, he would only be good for resting on mounds.

"You will survive," she said. "We will survive. You will make a magnificent grand prince."

His soul, and the stolen one, made sounds of relief. The princess had accepted him as her mate. Despite his crimes and the hardships of the migration, the souls sounded guardedly elated. A new hive. His hive. Grand prince. Diviya would be the father of a new generation, one that, due to the separation of time dilation, would never see any skates from another colony. And his colony would have no landlords, no tax collectors, and no beatings.

Past

FURTIVELY, WORKERS CAME to Diviya in the slums, atop his mound. Most had never been unionists. Diviya recognized his old fear in them. They came to speak to Diviya about the massacre. Few had been there, but they knew the workers who had been killed, and the workers who had been exiled to the work farms. They came as cowards might, shamefully, weighed by the guilt that they were happy not to have been there.

The idea of sacrifice in them was strong, as it was in Diviya. The Hero had built them to sacrifice for each other, for kin. They were pressed of the same clay. The success of a brother worker or a prince felt like a success for all of them. Demanding something for themselves was difficult. The newly ensouled like Diviya had to be taught selfishness, acquisitiveness by the souls. Yet these skates, who had not been brave enough to attend a union rally to help all of them, now slinked to the last committee leader, a skate who shared their guilt. They formed new committees.

"Tell them what to do," his soul said. "You are better than this rabble. Leverage your influence here for patronage. Deliver the malcontents to the hive. Give bribes."

Diviya had bribes. The workers smuggled innumerable tiny nuggets of frozen volatiles to him. This struggle with his soul could not go on.

And then, he saw it again.

In the distance, the brief, hot shine of a soul, looking this way. The sleet of radioactive particles stilled his soul. Diviya shut his eye, shuttering the emissions of his own soul.

"Open your eye!" his soul said.

"You can guess as well as I what that was," Diviya whispered.

Diviya's soul laughed. "More unionists have been picked up by hive drones," the soul guessed. "The rascals must have spoken of an ensouled committee member dispensing fratricidal treason from a mound in the slums."

"It is rich that you would call me fratricidal, when I have never hurt another skate, while the hive beats, imprisons, and kills my brothers," Diviya said.

"Your disloyalty endangers every skate and princess in the hive. Open your eye."

Diviya descended the mound with his eye closed. Tejas

was with him, as were Barini and Ugra. They did not have souls and were accustomed to Diviya's silences while he communed with his own. With his eye closed, the world was dark, but loud, filled with the Hero's Voice and the scraping vibration of his own movement. But in this way, he was invisible to the other ensouled skate in the slums.

"What are you doing, Diviya?" Tejas asked.

"An ensouled skate has been moving at the edge of the slums," Diviya said to Tejas.

"I have seen him several times today. He is looking for something."

"Or someone," Tejas said.

"I saw only one skate. Perhaps an ambitious tax farmer seeks favor by catching a union leader."

"Hide!" Tejas said. "We must get you away."

"Me?" Diviya said.

"You're the key to the revolution," Tejas said. His voice was charged, tense. He believed what he was saying. And Diviya felt as he had when he'd first spoken at the rally. Exposed. Undeserving.

"Tejas, Barini, and Ugra," Diviya said, "lead me closer, so that we can see, but not be seen. You will need to be my eye."

"What are you doing?" his soul demanded.

Tejas walked Diviya on a winding, blind way around the tailing mounds.

The Hero was high in the sky, so none of the mounds cast shadows. Diviya heard the Hero's Voice change tone when they turned. Catching the subtleties in the polarization of the radio waves was a different way of experiencing the Hero, one perhaps more primal, and it calmed Diviya, as much as his new resolve.

Diviya was built for peace, but the princes, and those

who spoke in their name, had taken matters too far for Diviya to stay still.

They were kin, pressed from the same clays, made to launch princesses and some males into the migration. Their success was his success, in the flat equations of biology, but skates had grown. They were no longer the primitives of the sagas. They reasoned. They were more than their instincts. They had grown past the need for souls to tell them how to treat each other. Souls created and perpetuated divisions in the hive. Princes. Landlords. Workers. But the skates carried their own blame for taking what was given to them, as blindly as Diviya was being led through the slums. The souls had their own interests. Not least Diviya's soul.

Brother and enemy. Family and opponent.

Diviya's steel fingers sunk into the thick regolith. Pebbles and larger fragments of iron-nickel and hard, volatile-dry silicates were so numerous and uneven as to be stumbled over, especially blind. The four of them walked and hopped. From a distance, they would just be four soulless workers.

"He is to our left now," Tejas whispered.

"Take me onto a mound," Diviya said.

Tejas led Diviya scrabbling to the top of the hillock.

"What are you doing? Open your eye!" his soul said.

"Is he facing us?" Diviya asked.

"No," Tejas said. "We are facing north. He is facing west."

The revolution needed to happen. Working with the souls as they had was no longer possible. Diviya lifted a large chunk of iron-nickel in his fingers. He snapped his eye open and thrust, hurling himself toward the ensouled skate.

"You are wasting breath!" his soul shrieked. "Stop! Stop!"

Diviya released the iron-nickel chunk as he flew past, as a hive drone would have. It crashed into the other skate with such force that ceramic chips rattled against Diviya's underside.

"Murderer," his soul whispered.

Diviya puffed breath sideways to spin, and then thrust to a stop and landed. He hopped to the ensouled skate. His three fellows were already there.

Diviya's attack had struck the skate's left leading edge, near the eye. A gaping hole exposed the hot soul beneath.

"You are beyond redemption," his soul said. "I will not rest until justice is done."

"I know," Diviya said.

Diviya removed medical pliers and a small pry from his gullet. Dust caked them. He had been ensouled to help skates, to mend their minor wounds, to make them well enough to get back to the mines and farms. The hive had taught him anatomy and science for a skill he hadn't practiced in weeks.

"Do not touch that soul!" his soul said. Both Diviya and his soul could plainly hear the electrical panic of the soul in the fallen skate. "Report this to the hive! No one may touch a soul without the authorization of the princes."

Diviya reached into the corpse, prying away the bands around the soul. He lifted it gently, leaving the inside of the carcass warm and hollow.

"No!" his soul said.

"You must be destroyed, Diviya!" the soul said. "You are the most vile criminal ever fired in the hive."

Diviya reached into his own gullet with his pliers.

Diviya's own soul screamed as he pried it loose and pulled it from his mouth.

And then, Diviya was a worker again, for the first time in a long time. He had no sensitivity to most of the wavelengths of radiation and energetic particles. The world was quiet and cold. The stars were colorless. The souls before him were gray lumps, hotter than the regolith, but otherwise unremarkable.

Diviya set his soul in the cold, dry dirt. The temperature stresses crackled in the radio bands. He put the other soul carefully in his mouth and onto the mounting. As Diviya lowered the bands to hold it into place and clipped it tight, the beauty of the spiritual world washed back in. And he was himself.

The new soul spoke immediately, more timidly than Diviya's soul. "What are you doing?" it whispered.

"Do not leave me here!" his old soul cried from the cold regolith. "Summon the hive!"

Diviya took his own soul in his fingers and inserted it into his gullet where its shine would not show.

"Bury the body," Diviya said to his co-conspirators. "When it is completely frozen, we will take whatever volatiles it may have."

Diviya launched himself from the surface of the asteroid. It did not take much breath. The microgravity of the asteroid barely pulled the dust back to the surface. As the hive receded, he exhaled again and sailed away from his home and from the Hero.

His former soul was apoplectic.

"I might have migrated with you," Diviya said to his soul. "I had even thought of putting you into another worker, for the revolution, for more workers to migrate." Diviya removed the soul from his mouth. "But you are too dangerous, too intransigent, too willing to stamp upon workers with my fingers."

His soul was incandescent in its anger, fear, and hate. Diviya released it. For a time, they drifted away from the asteroid, traveling the same path. Then Diviya turned back to the Hero and thrust back toward the hive. His soul continued out into the cold of space.

Present

THEIR NEW HIVE would need an asteroid in the gravitational stillness behind the Hero's Voice, preferably a slow-turning one, so that they could walk around it, always under the radiance of the pulsar, and one that was freshly cracked by an impact or one whose radioisotopes and volatiles had not been harvested in centuries. There were thousands of asteroids in the archipelago, but not so many that a single, determined shaghāl could not find a hive eventually.

In some sagas, princes and princesses made a second migration, right after the first, to escape from shaghāl following too closely. But Diviya and the princess were exhausted. Little breath remained to them and with his cracks, Diviya could never again survive the crush of the Maw.

Diviya and the princess retracted their sails from time to time to drift silently and listen for the shaghāl. They could not hear him, but he could not be that far. He might already have ended his careening deceleration and be waiting even now in the archipelago of asteroids. Diviya spread his sail, and the Hero's Voice pushed him outward.

"How much breath do you suppose you have left?" Diviya asked.

"I did not use all of it."

Diviya explained his plan as he turned away from the Hero. He disgorged the soul he'd taken from the murdered prince and held it in his shadow. It shrieked. His own soul cried out. The princess' soul made a sound of revulsion. A soul was an ugly thing, a complex, layered brick of radioisotopes, humming with its own heat and shining with hard radiation. That light would draw the shaghāl as soon as Diviya revealed the soul to the asteroid field.

"This will not work!" the princess said. What Diviya asked was dangerous, perhaps impossible, but it was their only chance. "I do not even have the strength you want!"

"It is this or nothing, Princess! This is all we have. A strong, fast, hungry shaghāl lurks somewhere in the archipelago. While he is here, no hive is safe."

They moved farther and farther from the Hero, into an orbit where they would intersect the archipelago of asteroids at its outer edge, far from the best fields. They slowed over hours, risking creating radio reflections with their sails. The shaghāl would be closer to the pulsar, where the voice of the Hero would feed it and drown out their echoes. Every so often, Diviya turned toward the Hero, exposing the second soul. The soul's sharp, multi-rayed brightness would be very visible from far away. Then Diviya would turn back, hiding it again for a while, before exposing it once more.

Bait.

Finally, an angry glare answered. The hot harsh light of the shaghāl's soul was much closer to the pulsar. It made for them. Diviya held the second soul visible, letting the shaghāl see their trajectory. Then, he hid the soul from the shaghāl's sight. The asteroids neared, including a large, uneven ovoid, pocked with craters.

The princess took the wires of Diviya's sail in her steel fingers. They passed into the shadow of the asteroid, and out of sight, and Diviya released the second soul. The princess thrust, decelerating them. The soul hurtled onward, screaming. The tremendous deceleration bent Diviya's sail, and stabbed new pain into his underside. Diviya and the princess both groaned, sharing the pain of the unnatural maneuver.

Her thrust flagged.

She had almost no breath left and they would soon emerge from the shadow of the asteroid. But the soul was not far enough away.

"Don't stop!" he said.

"There is nothing more!"

"Then turn!" he said. "Into the asteroid!"

"We'll crash!"

They still traveled very fast. The regolith might be composed of deep powdered grains or it might hide nuggets and boulders of nickel-iron and hard ices that would shatter their carapaces.

"You are brave!" Diviya said. "It is the only way, Princess!" She did not turn. He waited. The thrust sputtered. "Please!"

The wires tightened and swung him as she aimed at the asteroid. They lurched as her breath expired. The regolith, even under microgravity, was frightening at their speed.

Diviya plunged deep in an explosion of dust, tumbling in the powder and pebbles, before being wrenched to the surface in a jarring, snapping stop.

He was on his back. His underside hurt. He could not feel his sail. Some of his fingers were bent. He wiggled them and began digging at the dust until he was right side up. A deep channel gouged the asteroid. Dust rose, swirling on its own static.

The princess had not let go of him. They had plowed the great furrow together before she herself had been driven by their speed into the regolith. She pulled herself free of the dirt. She had filled herself with dust, as had he. His insides. Her insides. Their souls were covered and, for once, silent. They spewed regolith, thickening the rising clouds.

"You did it, Princess," he said. "You stopped us. You are a hero."

She spat another gout of dirt from her gullet. Her anger and fear still crackled.

"Look!" Diviya said. The princess followed the line of his gaze.

Far in the distance, just a point now, the second soul sped onward, on a trajectory that would take it past the gravitational eddy and back toward the pulsar. From this distance, it looked like a tiny part of a distant migration.

On a course to intercept it, thrusting hot gas, was another sharp point of radiation: the shaghāl. By the time it realized what it was chasing, the shaghāl would be committed to a trajectory that would take it all the way around the black hole. It would be years before it returned. In that time, the new hive would have risen and matured and launched its own migration into the future.

PERSEPHONE
DESCENDING

SIXTY-EIGHT KILOMETERS above the surface, in the thin yellowed haze of the photochemical zone of Venus' atmosphere, Marie-Claude emerged onto the roof of the floating factory. Yellow-brown cloud curved away below her in all directions, while the stars poked through a sky whitened by a big sun, inviting an artistic soul to make something of it. A dumb maintenance drone, one of many on the factory, floated by, wiping the glass of the roof.

Her suit battery status blinked from green to yellow. She jiggled the pack. Yellow to green again. An environment laced with acid bred all sorts of shorts and power leaks. The *colonistes* called all these irritating maintenance problems *bebbits,* after the little biting flies of Québec's wilderness.

She leaned on the wing of her plane, just for a quick break from the life of cramped factory to cramped habitat. The fast, empty wind caressing her suit was a doubtful thing, an experience at a remove, a ghostly touch that froze the bones. The *colonistes* did not touch Venus.

They experienced the idea of her through their suits. Venus wrapped herself in clouds deeper and heavier than an ocean. Marie-Claude could only stand on the shores they'd built and watch Venus, as she might watch a movie, something to be left behind when she returned to the floating habitats. Venus isolated them from everything except the violence with which she touched them, bathing them in hotly cancerous solar radiation, suffocating them with thin, anoxic air, reaching up for them with tongues of sulfuric acid, delighting in marking them with acid scars where she gnawed through environmental suits and protective films.

Her battery toggled from green to yellow again. She whacked the *bebbit*. Back to green. She opened her plane and climbed in.

"Renaud," she radioed her supervisor, "Marie-Claude here. I'm taking off from plant six."

Take-off from a factory was a bit like the short and long seconds at the peak of a roller coaster. A ramp simply led off a lip and into the yawning atmosphere. She started her engine, taxied to the top of the ramp and rolled down, faster and faster.

At the edge, a loud snap shook the plane, and a shrieking hole opened in the side. The plane spun. A glimpse of the factory spun by, showing, at the edge of the ramp, a cleaning drone, with a part of Marie-Claude's wing in its grabbing claw.

It shouldn't have been there. It shouldn't have grabbed at her plane.

She spun away. Dashboard darkened. She plunged toward the yellowed cloud deck. Marie-Claude's heart thumped too loudly. Thoughts loud, useless. Pilot training dragged her fingers to scrabble under her seat for the ejection switch, but the cockpit floor had bent, jamming itself against her seat. She couldn't reach it.

"*Merde, merde, merde,*" she whispered.

"Marie-Claude! What's going on?" Renaud's voice crackled in her helmet. "You're losing altitude!"

No ejection seat. Busted plane. Flat spin. Sulfuric acid clouds. "*Câlisse!*" she swore.

"Marie-Claude! Do you read me?"

Terror froze her lungs with cold fingers. Jerk harness free. Plane shuddering. Move to gaping hole in the cockpit. Too loud. Fingers gripping seat. Jump. Thin air whipped. Clouds below, racing up. Scream. Tumble away. Small parachute yanked lightly at her. Voice in her ears. Hands searching for parachute cords. Parachute above her. Parachute above her. Breathe. Breathe. Answer.

"Plane blown. I'm on my secondary chute."

The small parachute barely slowed her. Only a fraction of an atmosphere resisted her descent. The air would not thicken to a full atmosphere for about ten kilometers. By then, it might be too late for rescue.

"I'm coming your way," Renaud said.

He radioed orders to the rest of the team, to the habitat platform five kilometers higher.

Marie-Claude tasted black on her tongue. She gritted her teeth, willing herself not to puke in her helmet. Shock. Probably shock. Her stomach churned harder. Do something.

She patted her suit. Adrenaline might mask leaks or injuries. Seals and fabric and coatings okay. Heater and heat exchanger running. Oxygen pressure a bit low, but green. Main battery still green. Sealed pockets on the arms and legs of her suit contained bits of her tool kit. Breathe. Renaud was on his way. Be calm.

The plane dragged a trail of smoke through the haze. About five kilometers below, the smoke column bent sharply. In that moment, in the vast clouds, relative movement was born. She and the habitats and factories lived in the super-rotating layer of the upper atmosphere, in winds that circled Venus every four days. Her plane had dropped into the slower-moving cloud deck beneath and was slowly falling behind her.

"*Merde!* Renaud, the transition layer is higher today! I'm going to fall out of the super-rotating winds." She did not add, *and out of your reach until you've circled the planet.*

"How soon?"

"A few minutes."

Where the bottom of the super-rotating winds touched the top of the lower clouds, the smoke column had been torn into a string of eddies, dark berries on the stretched lines of yellow clouds beneath. She rode nothing more than a bit of resined fabric on thin carbon cables. "The turbulence will shred my chute."

"I'm on full throttle, Marie-Claude. We'll get there."

She looked up into the yellow-white sky. She couldn't see any planes. Sixty-one kilometers separated her from the surface of Venus. She had a few minutes before it would become very dangerous for Renaud or any of the other crews to rescue her.

The factory shrank to a toy-like gray stub far above her, but another shape was growing, resolving into a repair drone, descending on two propellers whirring behind it. Coming toward her. It wasn't programmed to do that. It was not programmed to do anything but clean and fix simple leaks, unless engineers gave it more specific repair tasks.

"Renaud! Did you program one of the repair drones to come get me?"

The radio crackled, echoing lightning from the deep deck of the lower clouds. "No. I didn't think we'd have enough time to do that. I'll see if I can have someone on it."

"That's not why I'm asking. On take-off, I collided with a repair drone. It shouldn't have been anywhere near the launch ramp. I think it grabbed part of my wing."

"Are you sure?"

She hesitated to tell him over the radio. Drones wouldn't grab her plane unless they were programmed to. Sabotage. Whoever had done this would be as likely to hear. "I think someone tried to kill me, Renaud. I think they reprogrammed the drone. Plant six was added to the inspection route late and my name was put on it. And now this drone is following me down."

"What? Hang on. I'll access it from here."

Marie-Claude waited, time ticking below her as the smog thickened and the drone approached.

"I can't get in. Its antenna is offline."

"I can't get away," Marie-Claude said.

"I'm almost there."

The drone neared, only three hundred meters from her. Its grasping claws were open, capable of tearing her parachute. Only a half kilometer below her, the smoke of her plane was a thinning grey streak. She took a deep breath.

"It's not going to happen, Renaud. The suit can keep me alive in the upper cloud deck, but without a chute, I'm just going to drop until I cook. I've got to save the chute."

"Marie-Claude! What are you doing?"

Instead of pulling on the brake loops of her parachute, she pulled all the suspension wires on one side until the canopy spilled. She fell. Her stomach leapt. Arm over arm, she pulled her parachute close until she hugged it, and only its edges slapped frantically at her arms in the wind. She tucked her legs and tumbled.

Thinly glowing clouds above. Darkness below. Spinning. Two sides.

"Marie-Claude!" Renaud yelled.

Turbulence hit like a fist. She was spinning dust. If she blacked out she was dead. Yelling in her radio. Droplets of sulfuric acid rain streaked the glass of her helmet. The world darkened. The buffeting and spinning wanted to tear her apart, but finally the bumping stopped and she fell again. She let her chute go. The canopy flapped and bloomed and yanked her upright.

A voice spoke in her radio, nearly overwhelmed by static.

"I'm through the transition," she said. "My parachute is okay. The pressure is a tenth of an atmosphere. Temperature is about minus twenty Celsius. I'm not dead."

Yet.

The planes now had a relative wind speed difference to her of about one hundred and fifty kilometers per hour. And the planes were only rated for up to two atmospheres of pressure and about eighty degrees. After that, the sulfuric acid chemistry became too hostile. The *Laurentide,* the main habitat, had a few probes to study the deep atmosphere and its life forms, but none of them would be nearby. They could probably refit something with which to rescue her in a day or two, but by the time the *Laurentide* was back overhead, she would have descended well past finding.

* * *

Duvieusart Inquiry Transcript, page 772

3:30 p.m., CHLOÉ RIVERIN, CHAIR: We now have Monsieur Renaud Lanoix, who leads the *Nouvelle Voie* party, but who was also the engineering foreman on April sixth. Could you describe for the Inquiry your view of the events of April sixth?

3:30, RENAUD LANOIX, ENGINEERING SUPERVISOR: Thank you, Madame Chairman. At approximately 2 P.M., Mademoiselle Duvieusart radioed, as per procedure, that she had arrived at Plant Six and started her normal inspections and work planning for later technical crews.

3:30, SANDRINE GROGUHÉ, INQUIRY MEMBER: A question, Madame Chair?

3:30, CHLOE RIVERIN, CHAIR: Go ahead.

3:30, SANDRINE GROGUHÉ, INQUIRY MEMBER: Monsieur Lanoix, in a number of reports, the press contends that Mademoiselle Duvieusart was not even supposed to be at Plant Six that day, and that the shifts were changed to draw her there.

3:35, RENAUD LANOIX, ENGINEERING SUPERVISOR: The schedule had been changed a few days earlier. Mademoiselle Duvieusart was put on Plant Six for April sixth.

3:35, SANDRINE GROGUHÉ, INQUIRY MEMBER: Who had access to the schedule—to change it, that is?

3:35, RENAUD LANOIX, ENGINEERING SUPERVISOR: A number of people have access to the schedule. Changing it is a normal part of any week's work, Madame Groguhé. I have access, as do most of the engineers, including Mademoiselle Duvieusart.

3:35, SANDRINE GROGUHÉ, INQUIRY MEMBER: You don't have...

3:35, FRANÇOIS BEAULIEU, INQUIRY MEMBER: Madame Chair, Monsieur Lanoix is not able to tell his story.

3:35, SANDRINE GROGUHÉ, INQUIRY MEMBER: Monsieur Lanoix has neglected to bring up important details.

3:35, CHLOE RIVERIN, CHAIR: Go ahead, Madame Groguhé, but please be brief.

3:35, SANDRINE GROGUHÉ, INQUIRY MEMBER: Monsieur Lanoix, fine, many people have access to the schedules, but through accounts that identify those making the changes. Who made the changes to the schedule to set up

Mademoiselle Duvieusart for the sabotage of her plane?

3:35, RENAUD LANOIX, ENGINEERING SUPERVISOR: We know who accessed the schedule, Madame Groguhé. My lawyers have suggested that I should not reveal what I know here, so as not to interfere with criminal investigations.

3:40, CHLOE RIVERIN, CHAIR: This Inquiry has the authority to compel witnesses, Monsieur, and our legal counsel suggest that the danger to criminal proceedings is minimal as the cat is already out of the bag, and on the top of blog feeds over most of the Solar System.

(REPORTER'S NOTE: In camera consultation between Inquiry counsel and witness counsel.)

3:45, RENAUD LANOIX, ENGINEERING SUPERVISOR: The schedule was changed by an override code from the *Bureau du Gouverneur,* masked behind a dummy admin account.

3:45, CHLOE RIVERIN, CHAIR: The press, especially the *nationaliste* press, has made much of this being a *séparatiste* plot to frame the *nationaliste* cause. What are your thoughts on that?

3:45, RENAUD LANOIX, ENGINEERING SUPERVISOR: I don't think that theory holds

water. The sabotage was amateurish, that is
certain, but Mademoiselle Duvieusart was
not supposed to have survived those first few
instants to tell us that the repair drone was acting
strangely, which allowed us to pull the curtain
back on the plot.

MARIE-CLAUDE WIPED THE drizzle of acid from her
faceplate. Her oxygen display had yellowed. Only a few
hours of oxygen left. And she continued descending.
She hung in a rain of sulfuric acid, fifty-eight kilometers
above the surface of Venus. Nowhere to refuel or recharge
or repair or even stop.

In the distance below, a flock of spherical, gas-filled
photosynthesizers blew with the wind like pollen.
Blastulae. Sometimes storms brought them as high as
the photochemical zone, where they quickly died from
the changes in pressure. They were small and neutrally
buoyant at this altitude. They were not buoyant enough
to stop her descent. Maybe if she could put enough of
them together?

Perhaps a kilometer below, in the brown-yellow gloom,
a cluster of dark spots moved, backward relative to the
wind that carried her. They were much bigger than the
blastulae. She tugged at her control lines, turning to
get a better view, and hard enough to spill some of the
air from her parachute. Her horizontal speed picked
up, and she dropped faster. And only because she had
turned did she see that the repair drone had followed
her.

Repair drones had not been designed specifically to
survive in the cloud deck, but they were hardy. In the

photochemical zone, it might have run forever on solar power, but it also cracked sulfuric acid into hydrogen and solid sulfur, which could be recombined later to work in shadow. It could follow her a long time if it could take on enough ballast to sink as fast as she, and if it could survive the heat and acid.

Marie-Claude gritted her teeth and spilled her parachute. She plummeted. Two hundred meters. Four hundred. Six hundred. She finally let the wires go, and the parachute unfurled. The murk of the burnt yellow clouds hid her from the repair drone.

And two hundred meters below floated a pod of thirty rosettes, large Venusian plants. Their bulbous ochre heads were composed of six radially symmetric gas-filled chambers, each one a meter across. Sulfuric acid and organic materials collected in the cup formed by the tops of the six chambers. From the center of this cup grew a large triangular frond, a fine black net with which to filter the photosynthesizing microbes from the atmosphere. Beneath the six chambers hung short, heavy trunks which stored nutrients and provided ballast. They hung like weird, rootless trees, orphaned in the vastness of an ocean of cloud.

Carefully, Marie-Claude matched her horizontal speed and descended, until with uncertain hands and unsteady feet, she landed on one of the rosettes, scrambling to grab its frond before she slipped. The round, woody platform was slimy with decomposing microbes slowly being absorbed by the skin of the rosette.

The rosette began to sink under her weight, although slower than she'd been descending in her parachute. But, as the pressure increased, so would the buoyancy of the rosette, until she finally stopped descending. And in the meantime, she could hide here from the repair drone. She shook acid rain from her parachute and laid it over herself like a tarp against the drizzling acid.

She sank into the somber clouds for a long time, as the rain stopped. In the enforced quiet, her arms tingled, as if she wanted to hit something, for a long time. She was going to die. She was sinking into the toxic atmosphere of Venus because someone had decided to kill her. Nervous, angry, baffled tears tickled hot lines onto her cheeks. She cursed the acid. She cursed the world and politics. And she cursed herself for coming to Venus.

The Americans, Australians, and British still raced against the Chinese for the industrial and economic dominance of Mars. Egypt and Saudi Arabia had taken Vesta and Ceres, and had staked claims on dozens of other asteroids with robotic prospectors. The Russians, perhaps for having lost the Moon to the Americans a century earlier, took it for their inheritance. The first wave of Solar System colonization was complete by the time Québec separated from Canada.

L'Assemblée nationale decided to make their mark as an advanced nation by colonizing Venus. There was no money to be made on Venus, no resource it could provide to Earth or the rest of the Solar System that could not be gotten for cheaper from the Egyptians or the Saudis, but her clouds were of scientific value. Strange microbial extremophiles had been found, feeding a deep, inaccessible ecology. Basic scientific research would not finance the effort and colonization was not cheap, but the president had wanted *un grand geste,* a starward look for her new nation.

And it was a *grand geste,* approached with an earnest, prideful, counterproductive fervor. Little matter that the new republic had to launch Anglo hardware on Egyptian rockets, and that it trained its engineers in Houston. *La République du Québec* was colonizing Venus.

They ought to have started with robotic stations in the atmosphere, to prepare the way for astronauts, but *la République* had the romantic eagerness of a teenager, throwing waves of engineers, chemists, meteorologists, and doctors into space with cramped habitats, optimistic assumptions, and fickle support. They were part of *la grande histoire,* and dreams thrive in fields of willful blindness.

From *Commentaries on the Foundation of the Venusian State*

THE CLOUDS THINNED and broke beneath her, and a frisson of awe was born in Marie-Claude. She rode the rosette near the top of a kilometer of clear air between the yellow-brown upper cloud deck and the angry dark clouds of the middle deck. The cavernous space was empty, carved into all the stored acid and spite in the Solar System. She was tiny, a mite riding a bit of dander in a stadium. The vertigo that had trailed her all this time suddenly pounced, and she snaked her arms around the frond, as if she stood on a cliff. The rosette sank through the great cave in the clouds, and the puffy floor of the middle deck approached with the gentleness of a summer balloon ride. She was going to die. Venus would kill her, but had given her one last vision of wonder.

Marie-Claude rode her magic carpet to the bottom of the clear air and sank into the thick cloud of the middle deck. Like a drowning swimmer, Marie-Claude looked upward as the darkness swallowed. The repair drone broke out of the upper clouds a kilometer above, and then everything was out of sight.

A new rain of sulfuric acid fell as her oxygen display began winking yellow.

There was no oxygen recharging station around, and perhaps she would never see one again. She had to take what she needed. She was an engineer, but like everyone she'd read the ecological papers produced by the colony's part-time researchers.

The clouds, filled with dust, were a perfect crucible for Venusian life, cycling between low pressure and high, sunlit and dark, concentrated and dilute acidity, evaporation and condensation. Whole classes of acidophiles, psychrophiles, and thermophiles had life cycles the *colonistes* hadn't had the time to study. The microbes captured the wavelengths of light penetrating the middle and upper cloud decks within cell walls hardened to maintain buoyant gas pressures. Presumably, some of these autotrophs had evolved into floating mats that inflated and deflated as needed, and then, over millions of years, into hardened wooden balls, and finally, in an accident of tissue innovation rivaled by the Cambrian explosion on Earth, the balls had clustered into rosettes, and the cloud trawlers that lived in the deeper atmosphere.

The six chambers of the rosette beneath her feet were filled with oxygen, a byproduct of photosynthesis.

Oxygen was buoyant in Venus' carbon dioxide atmosphere, but Marie-Claude couldn't take any of it without jeopardizing her foothold. She needed some of the spherical plants, or blastulae, that she'd seen.

She looked for a long time before she spotted a cluster floating perhaps a kilometer below, moving almost in parallel to the rosette she rode as she sank. Rosettes drifted with the wind, partly driven by their high fronds. Marie-Claude set her feet into the sludge at the base of the frond and tugged and pulled and leaned until the frond, like a small sail, angled to the wind so that slowly, her rosette began drifting leftward.

The rosettes were not easy to steer, but slowly, over some thirty minutes, she moved it across the wind, approaching the cluster of blastulae that contained an adult form—several buds and a pair of adults still connected by sticky ooze. Marie-Claude threw her parachute over the cluster and hauled it in.

The blastulae had nothing to do with embryos, but reminded many of the hollow ball of cells phase of embryonic development and no one had time to find a better name. They were hollow, woody balls, that reproduced by budding. Adult blastulae floated with crowns of smaller buds which grew to adult size and then detached when the difference in buoyancy between parent and offspring overcame the stickiness of the mucous gluing them together.

Her oxygen tanks had emergency hand pumps that could be fitted to the hoses in case the power failed in the habitats. The hoses contained anhydrous crystalline filters to neutralize sulfuric acid. She set up her pump and pulled one of the blastulae from the parachute.

Her helmet light revealed a brown skin pigmented

to absorb the yellowed light reaching these depths. Transparent mucous slicked the blastula, beading off the raining acid.

Suddenly, the blastula hissed around six stomata. The carbon dioxide of the Venusian atmosphere flowed inward, and the blastula lost its buoyancy. Marie-Claude turned it over, and it hissed again, letting in more carbon dioxide.

Photoreactivity. Why? If an updraft carried a blastula into the upper atmosphere, sunlight would burn it. Its stomata must have dilated to allow heavy carbon dioxide in, to lower its buoyancy. Her lamp had tricked the stomata.

She let the blastula go. It tumbled slowly over the edge of the rosette. At some point, it would reach a depth where it would float. Then, further photosynthesis would create oxygen which would buoy it more. *In extremis,* blastulae had been observed to pump out some air from their cavities to correct their buoyancy more abruptly.

Marie-Claude switched off her helmet light and let her eyes adjust to the gloom of a rainy sundown. Then she pulled out one of the immature blastulae. She traced with her gloved fingertips until she found the stomata, tiny closed mouths, six of them, ringing the underside.

She cleared away the mucous and placed the hose against a stoma. With the other hand, she took a small hand light and lit just that part of the blastula. The stoma, relaxed and Marie-Claude inserted the hose into the plant before too much carbon dioxide could rush in. She pumped the oxygen from the blastula into her tank. When she finally pulled free the hose and released it, it bobbed up and away, carried up like a cork in water.

She repeated her vampiric feast on all the blastulae in

her parachute, watching each one shudder up into the clouds upon release, like bubbles rising in deep water. Seven of the woody balloons disappeared into the sky before her oxygen display edged into yellow-green. She had some oxygen, but she needed more.

But, as she stowed her equipment, she realized that acid had rasped the fabric of her parachute raw.

Les colonistes did not design their equipment to operate in the heavily acidic environment below the super-rotating winds, but something could be refitted in that time. The food paste in her suit had the calories, and the water recycler might keep her hydrated. Sweat dripped in her eyes. The temperature had topped fifty degrees and now hugged her with a full atmosphere of pressure.

A light shone in the distance above her. A machine whined. The drone was not designed to operate so deep. The steels used to build drones were more vulnerable to hot acids than her suit of fiber-reinforced plastics. If she could survive four days, they might be able to rescue her.

Marie-Claude's mother had also come to a new world, in one of the waves of Haitian refugees to Québec. Her mother had married *un Québécois pur laine*, pure wool, a man whose family counted French, or at least European blood, for generations. Her parents bequeathed to her two identities, one of belonging by blood, another of alienness by color of skin.

So, from birth, her country was both hers and not hers. The new nation of Québec consumed its children with politics of identity and place, self-referential and pastward-looking. Québec offered no place free of the acidity of the cultural insecurity. So Marie-Claude had come to Venus for the freedom and even-handedness of ground without footprints.

She might have immigrated to Mars or the asteroids for a frontier life, but as much as the Québécois infuriated her, she was Québécoise herself, by blood and language. *Le grand geste* seemed perfect for a time, but it turned out not to have been the frontier. *Les colonistes* had carried with them the panels and studies, the committees and language laws. Instead of thinking new thoughts, they argued over resource budgets, work schedules, and culture by proposing motions and agendas in committees.

Marie-Claude liked engineering problems. Calculations of force and pressure and resistance and pH were simple things, an escape from politics that seemed to materialize wherever two people met. Marie-Claude's competent, forceful plain-speak led inevitably to her election as the chair of the engineering union.

Marie-Claude was not the only one restless for something they could not articulate. No one knew yet where they were going, but never a people to stop at one poorly-conceived *grand geste*, *les colonistes* surviving in the clouds of Venus quickly began to speak of their own state. A country of our own. *Un pays pour nous.* And so, *les séparatistes* were born, even though *les colonistes* needed Québec to foot the bills for metals and volatiles.

A greater gift could not have been offered to

the new nation of Québec. Québec did not have the budget to sustain the colony. They derived no benefit from it, not even respect. One might admire Quixote, but one did not respect him. Despite being faced with so convenient an escape from its responsibilities as the mother country, it surprised no one that *l'Assemblée* denounced any talk of secession. And so were born *les nationalistes*. The factions on the habitats spun webs of arguments for *une Vénus indépendente* or *une Vénus coloniale*.

Marie-Claude considered both ideas criminally impractical. Whether the colony declared its independence from Québec or not, Venus intended to kill them. Tempers burned, sometimes into open violence. Renaud Lanoix, the *séparatiste* leader, dreamed of a new nation, and saw Marie-Claude, chair of the powerful Engineering Union, as the key to unlocking it. He'd been waiting for her to choose her side. Someone else had not.

> From *Persephone's Descent:*
> *The Biography of*
> *Marie-Claude Duvieusart*

MARIE-CLAUDE SAILED HER rosette with the wind, slowly sinking. The atmosphere thickened, but the rosette was still not able to support her weight. After several hours, the Stygian clouds broke again, into the kilometer of clear air beneath the middle cloud deck.

This great cavern in the clouds was somber. Other rosettes floated in the distance, like dark specks, failing to give perspective to the vastness and too far away to help her with buoyancy or oxygen.

She must be only fifty kilometers above the surface now, almost twenty kilometers below the *Laurentide* and the other habitats. No one would be able to come this far down to rescue her.

Marie-Claude sank through the hot air and into the lower clouds of Venus, a thick yellow haze of sulfuric acid, veined with lines of brown and green mineral dust and chlorine. Few photosynthesizers would survive at these depths, leaving the clouds open to webs of chemotrophs, living off what volcanoes and storms churned upward.

A rain of hot acid fell, until, through the cloud, she spotted a cluster of blastulae beneath her, directly in her downward path. But her two-edged luck persisted; the blastulae were full of oxygen, but they were gummed to the side of a trawler.

Trawlers were shaped like rosettes, darker in color, radially symmetric, with six buoyancy chambers, but were much larger, serving as the platform for many kinds of life. Blastulae sometimes stuck parasitically to the great trawlers, absorbing nutrients from the rain they were not large enough to collect on their own.

Trawlers were not photosynthesizers. They occupied a more dramatic ecological niche. A conducting carbon filament hundreds of meters long hung beneath the trawler, ending in a bob. As the trawler drifted with the wind, the conductor joined clouds of different static charges and altitudes, drawing an electrical current along its length. More dangerously, trawlers were lightning rods in the storms of the middle and lower cloud decks. It was not healthy to be near a trawler.

But she needed the oxygen. The trawler and its crown of blastulae floated half a kilometer beneath her.

Marie-Claude's battery display suddenly flashed, edging from yellow to orange. The suit's heat exchanger shifted to a power-saver setting, and the suit's radio antenna turned off.

Merde.

She slipped her battery out of its pack behind her. The hand light trembled.

Merde, merde, merde.

Grainy acid leaked out of the fiber-reinforced plastic on one side of the battery. Its lifetime was measured in minutes, hours if she was lucky.

This shouldn't have happened. These plastics were hardened to survive in the Venusian atmosphere. Not exactly true. The fiber-reinforced plastics were resistant to the low concentrations of sulfuric acid at the cooler temperatures sixty and seventy kilometers above the surface. They reacted very differently to higher concentrations of sulfuric acid.

Over the beating rain, a regular machine sound thrummed. With the increasing pressure, sound warbled and direction deceived. She spun. The drone closed from only a few hundred meters away, scarred by patches of acid corrosion. Marie-Claude had nothing with which to damage it. And now she would cook far sooner than the drone would dissolve.

It neared.

She was trapped.

She couldn't see more than a few hundred meters through the rain. No sign of a storm. No thunder.

The drone was fifty meters away now.

She slipped the battery back into its pocket, switched her helmet light to its brightest, and shone it on the rosette, along with both hand lamps. The rosette opened all six of its stomata, flooding its buoyancy chambers with heavy carbon dioxide.

Marie-Claude's footing shuddered as the rosette tipped and sank. She held the frond tightly as the sludge on the rosette poured into clouds. Marie-Claude's feet slipped off and then there was nothing beneath them. One of her flashlights spun into the gloom below. She and the rosette fell sideways toward the trawler.

When the top of the trawler was fifteen meters below her, the rosette began drifting with the wind. She was going to miss her landing. And after the trawler, nothing separated her from the surface of Venus except forty-eight kilometers of crushing, hyper-acidic, broiling atmosphere.

She let go of the frond.

She spread her arms and legs. She hit the top of the trawler hard, the blow accompanied by a powerful static shock. She splashed in the pooled acid and organics, and bounced, nearly to the edge. Venusian epiphytes had colonized the trawler thickly, clutching with stringy roots or sticky mucous. They slowed her slide. She let her flashlight and parachute go and pulled free a pair of screwdrivers. She scraped the points along the top of the trawler until she stopped.

Slowly, she pulled herself away from the edge.

She ached all over.

The rosette she had ridden all the way down to the lower clouds ascended lazily past the circling drone. The gloom pressed in. Even though it had only been a further half kilometer down, she could have sworn that the temperature had risen, and that the atmosphere pressed tighter against her suit.

The trawler was not evolved to carry an extra ninety kilos of rider and survival gear. It began sinking, but more slowly than the rosette had. The lower cloud deck thinned around her, and she descended into a dark, yellow haze. The temperature outside her suit had risen almost to the boiling point of water. She was now beneath the upper, middle and lower cloud decks. The browned, cooked bellies of the lowest clouds on Venus lay above her head. This sub-cloud haze was a zone of thermal dissociation.

She took the blastulae stuck to the trawler, one by one, and pumped the oxygen into her tank until it was fully in the green. Her battery icon still blinked orange-red.

Something stung her leg, like a wasp sting. She jerked and patted at her leg. The sulfuric acid, at this heat and pressure, had bored a hole through the fiber-reinforced plastic of her suit.

The spite of Venus.

She huddled under the remains of her parachute and pulled the suit repair kit out of a pocket. She neutralized the acid, cleaned the hole, applied the adhesive and slapped the patch on. It was a drilled movement, automatic, thoughtless. It was now natural. What had her stupid plan been? Would she have one day taught children how to thwart the lashing of a chemically predatory planet? That was no birthright. The *séparatistes* and the *nationalistes* could have the whole damned place.

The last part of the drill was to get to shelter to replace the suit. Leaks bloomed in clusters, just like blastulae. She inspected the parts of her suit she could see. Patches of discoloration showed that her suit would not last even one day more in the hot rain. The acid delighted in dissolving all the cleverness of people. It might not matter. The heat would kill her soon if she didn't fix her battery.

The Hadean rain poured again as she sank. It jumped and spattered the surface of the pool in the depression in the center of the trawler's platform, and overflowed the depression, running over the edge and out of sight, to fall until it evaporated, long before it ever came close to the surface of Venus.

She ran a finger through the slime on the surface of the trawler. Murky organic strands shot through its translucence. It repelled water, and probably contained bases to neutralize any acids that penetrated it. That was how an engineer would have designed a plant on Venus.

Marie-Claude scooped a handful of the slime and rubbed it on her suit and the parachute. If she guessed wrong and it was just a viscous acid, it would be a terrible way to die. It didn't seem to be hurting her suit, so she applied more, and soon, she looked like she'd been dipped in egg white. But the rain no longer touched her suit.

The battery reading flashed red. She needed to run the heat exchanger on full refrigeration. She had to do something.

She pulled a pair of needle-nosed pliers from her tool pouch and cut her parachute cables, tying them together to make a cable about forty meters long. With nothing to act as a piton, she rammed the pliers into the woody shell of the trawler and hammered them deep into the thick wood near the trawler's axis with her boot. She tied the cable around it, tested her weight, and then slipped over the edge.

The surface of Venus baked forty-three kilometers below her boots. But it would never get a chance to kill her. Too much of the rest of the planet wanted to try first. As did the repair drone. A light shone into the rain high above, and the sounds of a propeller working carried.

The drone relentlessly descended, as if it were necessary for it to finish the job.

The long cable grown of carbon and wood and slime hung below the bulk of the trawler like a plumb line. Thick as her whole body, it flexed, resonating with the constant wind to form standing waves that hummed in her bones. Other winds would find different resonances, and many others would find only discordance. She imagined ageless flocks of trawlers moving through the lower cloud deck, playing eerie, subsonic hymns to Venus as she bathed them in poison.

She lowered herself and swung, trying to reach the lower side of one of the buoyancy chambers. She didn't know how long her pliers would survive as a makeshift piton. She found one of the trawler's six stomata on the lower curve of the buoyancy chamber. It was larger than the stomata on the rosette. She shone her helmet light on full. Its faltering light ought to have opened the stoma, but the vegetable lip remained shut. On the rosette, her helmet lamp had been enough to open a single stoma, but the trawler was bigger and far more complex. It probably opened all its stomata in unison, triggered by photoreceptors. She couldn't trigger them all from here.

Acid rained over her as she dangled. The stalk of the cable was still wide at this level, and slippery, but on the end of a swing, she wrapped her legs around it.

She produced a screwdriver from its pocket sheath and pushed it into the stoma. The stoma opened slightly, and inflowing gas hissed. She wiggled the screwdriver back and forth, loudening the hiss. She had a small pry, useful for corroded access hatches on the habitats. One end was flat, the other tapered to a blunt point. She jammed the blunt end into the stoma, beside the screwdriver. Air whooshed in, until the pressure inside equilibrated. She strained the lip wider. The first inch resisted, but then she must have reached some point that triggered the rest of the opening cycle. The stoma dilated to about fifty centimeters.

Marie-Claude tossed her tools in and wedged her elbows and head through. She got a better grip and pulled herself awkwardly in. The stoma slowly contracted behind her.

She collapsed against the curving walls. The chamber was round and nearly tall enough to stand in. She struggled to catch her breath in the heat, when her parachute cord suddenly slacked and then tugged lightly at her waist. She reeled it in. Only a corroded fragment of the pliers still dangled from the end. If she'd been a few seconds later, she would be plummeting through the brown haze right now.

The stoma shut completely and the drumming rain sounded hollow on the top of the trawler. Her faltering head lamp showed small sacs in the sides of the chamber beginning to inflate and deflate. She crawled closer. They were fleshy, transparently thin, their muscular flexing slowly pumping air out of the chamber. Regaining buoyancy.

Remarkable.

She shut off her helmet lamp to save the last of her power for her suit's cooling system and switched on her last flashlight, a small one for looking at the guts of machinery. A woody frame webbed the chamber, covered with a tough skin. Her light fell on dark patches above her that contracted in apparent response, simultaneous with a slight irising of the stomata, letting in more of the Venusian atmosphere, reducing the chamber's buoyancy further. She turned her light away from the patch.

Unlike the rosette, the trawler had ribs and webs of vasculature. Marie-Claude followed them. Most cells in a rosette were photosynthetic and each made their own food, like a cooperative. That was not true in a trawler, so it needed a complex vasculature to separate its functions. The cable moving through the atmosphere generated electricity, and something must carry either chemical or electrical energy to the rest of the body. Her flashlight showed dark lines within the skin of the chamber, all leading down the axis of the trawler to the cable. Other thick lines led from the axis to long cylindrical nodules beneath the floor of the chambers.

That was what she was looking for.

There must be times when the trawler had no chance to collect electricity. The trawler must store food somewhere for those times. Those nodules might be it.

Her red battery display flashed faster.

She slipped her leaking battery from its pocket.

She sawed through the tough vegetable flesh of the buoyancy chamber with the flattened end of the pry. She peeled back rubbery flaps, exposing a red, woody cylinder, like a stack of disks. The living carbon wiring of the trawler led into and out of the cylinder. She pulled a small voltmeter from a sealed pocket and pressed the needles against one of the wires leading into the cylinder. The voltmeter shot up and wobbled. She checked other wires. They were all live, with large variations in potential. The cylindrical stack showed a large, steady potential across its ends, like a capacitor, or the electroplaque of an eel. Something for times of famine.

She hesitated. The electricity was dirty, changing potential rapidly, even past the capacitor. But the alternative to recharging her battery was seeing how she liked one hundred and ten degrees at three atmospheres of pressure. She had continued dropping and might be as low as thirty-nine or thirty-eight kilometers above the surface.

She looked for the best place to attach alligator clip wires to the capacitor and finally chose a spot. The battery display in the visor of her helmet did not change. It blinked red as if mocking her. If this were a world that did not want to kill her, she would have lightly touched the battery to see how much the charging had heated it. Or to swat the *bebbits*. But the deep dark of hell had her. Her voltmeter showed a variable current for long, changeless minutes. Still no new charge. She examined the battery more closely with the flashlight.

The walls of the battery bowed like a melting toy. The acid exposed by the hole in the battery bubbled like magma.

"Merde!"

She yanked the wires, but the walls of the battery liquified and its sludge poured onto the floor of the woody chamber.

No more main battery.

Her backup battery was nearly used up. The hot suit against her skin was beginning to sting. She was going to pass out from heat exhaustion soon. Marie-Claude pulled the wires that had connected her suit to the battery, and hesitated over the capacitor and its dirty electricity. Then, she hooked her suit directly to the trawler, downstream of the electroplaque.

The displays in her helmet lit. The electrical icons expanded brightly, showing graphs of incoming voltage and current, their frequent surges. Little alarm symbols in different suit systems flashed yellow and red as fuses clicked, blowing and resetting every few seconds. Her backup battery was recharging. The suit's heat exchanger whirred, circulating hot fluid through tubes in her suit. She wondered how much it could refrigerate at this depth.

She wilted, but imagined that it was becoming cooler. She felt as frayed as her suit, as melted as the battery. The clock display showed that twenty-six hours had passed since her plane had been attacked. In that time, she'd descended almost thirty kilometers, from the cold, thin photochemical zone past the three cloud decks and into the haze beneath. Venus had not succeeded in killing her yet. Venus was cunning, but Marie-Claude was learning her tricks.

She watched the displays for a long time, making sure that the trawler didn't blow the suit's electrical system. And then finally, too tired to manage anymore, Marie-Claude lay as flat as she could and slept.

Venus hated them with blinding sulfuric acid, biting cold, ferocious winds, and if they were foolish, with crushing pressure and melting heat. Venus killed them with the slowness of a lion picking off gazelles, one by one: the slow, the unlucky, those who made small, human errors.

These were bits of heroic news in *La Presse* or *Le Devoir* in Montréal and Québec, testaments to the bravery of Québécois astronauts. *La République* had heroes, until the sinking of *Le Matapédia*.

The upper atmosphere had corroded one of the buoyancy tanks of the floating habitat. As *Le Matapédia* sunk into the killing depths, kilometer by kilometer, many of the inhabitants had been rescued, but the public mood back home changed. The Québécois were proud, and they could stomach the sacrifice of the unlucky and the slow, but Venus had tried to execute a whole herd.

Governments changed, throwing new equipment and fresh *colonistes* into the clouds. Venus did not care. She could not be outnumbered, and she did not relent.

From *Commentaries on the Foundation of the Venusian State*

MARIE-CLAUDE DREAMED OF heat and suffocation. A terrible dry thirst and a bath of sweat choked her, and she could neither wipe her face nor drink. Someone called her, incessantly, penetrating the thickness of dream without breaking her free. Against an oppressive exhaustion, she opened her eyes.

"Marie-Claude! Marie-Claude! Can you hear me?"

"Renaud," she said. She couldn't place where she was. Static swamped his voice. The lights on her suit were uneven, but, for the most part in the yellows.

"Marie-Claude! You're alive! Where are you?"

She checked her readings. Two atmospheres. Had the trawler climbed as she slept? She had been at three atmospheres, but the temperature had risen to one hundred and twenty degrees.

"I'm not sure. Have you got a fix on my signal?"

"Faint one. It looks like you're at thirty-three kilometers."

She rechecked her barometer and then shone her flashlight on the little pumping sacs on the wall of the chamber. They had dropped the pressure in the chamber, increased its buoyancy, but the trawler still could not hold her up. Thirty-three kilometers. She'd travelled halfway to the surface.

She explained where she was.

"Inside a trawler?" Renaud crackled. "That's incredibly dangerous!"

Marie-Claude checked the time. She had slept almost twenty-four hours. It had been fifty hours since the sabotage. "How long have I been down here? Four days haven't passed."

"No. We got back to the *Laurentide* and refitted the planes to fly ahead. I'm almost all fuel. There are eight of us up here looking for you. The habitats will be over tomorrow, but I'll be arriving on your position in about four hours."

"No plane can reach this depth," Marie-Claude said.

"A special plane will be dropping a deep probe tomorrow. Can you survive twenty-four hours?"

She looked at the makeshift wiring, the only thing keeping her alive. Her backup battery gave her a reserve of perhaps an hour.

"I don't know."

Renaud's silence dragged so long that she thought maybe they'd lost contact.

"What do you think would happen to a trawler if it goes into a storm?" he finally asked.

"What? Where is there a storm?" Venus had big polar storms, as stable as the ones on Saturn or Uranus, perhaps even as long-lived as the Great Red Spot. But below the super-rotating winds, the equatorial air frequently tore itself into short-lived storms of lightning and ripping winds.

"About an hour from you."

"How big?"

"It's a storm."

She understood. Researchers had dropped probes into the equatorial storms. None had survived the violent shifts of pressure, temperature, and acidity.

"This might be the way out," he said. "You might catch an updraft."

"Renaud, I've been standing on the edge for two days. I don't want to talk about luck."

"I'm sorry. I'm just glad you're alive. Everyone is going to be happy you're alive. The habitats are in turmoil. All the talk is about change. The constabulary has made arrests in the attempt on your life. The tracks led back to the office of the *parti nationaliste*. People are calling for a referendum on separation from Québec, but the parties are waiting on your safe recovery."

"Or death," she said.

"We'll get you! You're the hero of the day. You've seen Venus deeper than anyone ever has."

Thunder, distant and faint, sounded.

"Why are you saying this?" she asked.

"The agents of the *Gouverneur* tried to silence your voice, but they've only given you a larger audience."

"I'm not even *séparatiste*," she said.

"Everyone will be listening to your voice when you're rescued. Despite the passions, the referendum is no sure thing. The engineering union will almost certainly tip the balance. And you sway the union. You could give us our own nation. *Un pays pour nous.* We deserve it."

"Maybe we do deserve Venus," she said. "Who but idiots would deserve a burning land wrapped in poison?"

"You mastered Venus," Renaud said. "We will tame Venus."

"I did not master Venus."

"You are learning the ways of the land, like the first *coureurs des bois*."

Coureurs des bois. She tasted the phrase. It was an old one, from the times of the foundation of Québec by France, a word to speak of boys and men raised among the Algonquin and Montagnais natives to become the bridges between the *colonistes* and the new land. Renaud had used a term laden with history, as politicians and demagogues often do, careless of truth. But his words found a resonance in her heart, unexpected and potent.

A second radio signal chimed in her helmet, devoid of static and interference. Close. She chilled. The drone had heard her radio.

"*Merde.*"

"What is it?" Renaud demanded, so, so far away, safe in his plane.

"I thought I'd lost it. But it's homing in on my radio signal."

"The drone can get to you?"

"It's probably in worse shape than me, but its tools can break through the walls of the trawler. I've got no way to stop it."

"Shut down your antenna and radio," Renaud said.

"I'm not shutting down the radio. It will already have colocated my signal with the electrical noise of the trawler, but I'm not going to die by myself."

"What are you going to do?"

"Venus, the drone, and I are going to have this out."

"You just said you couldn't stop the drone."

"I know."

"What about the storm?"

"Be quiet," she said. "I've got to think."

She had little left in her tool kit. She pulled out copper wiring, a small knife, clamps of corroding reinforced plastic, a pockmarked screwdriver, and a small steel hammer. She slitted the wire and stripped away the insulation. The copper wouldn't last long in the rain, or even in this chamber, but she only needed it to survive until the storm.

For the first time, a rumble, a subsonic vibration, touched her bones. The storm, Venus' final offer in her negotiations, closed on Marie-Claude.

She wound the copper wire around the hammer, and then tied one of her two parachute cords to it. She swung the makeshift weapon experimentally on its cord. A flimsy thing against a machine.

She tied the end of her second, longer, parachute cord to the screwdriver, and then pounded it deep into woody flesh between the six buoyancy chambers, all the way to the rigid, charged spine of the trawler, and wrapped it tightly around. Static tingled through her gloves. She tied the cord to her harness.

The drone's signal was very close now.

She unplugged herself from the trawler's electroplaque, leaving her suit and its heat exchanger to run on the emergency battery. Perhaps an hour.

"You got a fix on me, Renaud?"

His voice crackled. "You're at thirty-three kilometers and sinking. What's your plan?"

"Just keep the fix and keep quiet."

The darkened patch on the top of the buoyancy chamber, the photoreceptor, had a dark filament running away from it, toward the axis of the trawler. She followed this line until the tough vegetable skin obscured it. With her screwdriver and her little hammer, she dug into the flesh, being careful not to dig far enough to break the outer skin of the trawler. She tore, following the filament to where it met five similar filaments and dove with them down the trawler's spine. She whispered a quick, unaddressed prayer, and severed the trunk of filaments with tip of her screwdriver. No more photoreceptors for her trawler.

She crawled back to the stoma and put her tools back into their little pouches before she took a hot breath. Then, she wriggled her finger into the sealed hole of the stoma. The atmosphere outside hissed in, hot. Her ears and sinuses ached.

Her suit crushed against her, and her tank released more oxygen to compensate, while the heat exchanger whirred to full. Almost seven atmospheres of pressure and one hundred and seventy degree Celsius. Her suit was rated to five atmospheres, and one hundred and fifty degrees. Engineers understood tolerances; the designers would not wear this suit under these conditions.

But here she was.

She pushed two hands into the opening, pulling the edge wide to stare down into the sub-cloud haze. The trawler's cable flexed chaotically in surging winds, as crackles of blue-white arced along its length, shedding charge against particulate debris in the air. The trawler was a beautiful machine, a masterpiece of biological engineering, evolved to live and love this terrible world.

Marie-Claude wriggled free of the buoyancy chamber and slipped down her cord. The inconstant wind spun her. Her legs and arms swung and jerked as she tried to straighten. She paid out all her cord, until she hung twenty-five meters down the trawler's cable. She fluttered in the wind, meters from the trawler's cable, with nothing beneath her for thirty-three kilometers.

She tried to grab the cable, coming close to its slick, arcing surface. She wished that this was the most dangerous part of her plan, but it was only one part where she might be killed. And the longer she dangled in the wind, the more potential difference she accumulated relative to the cable. Her wet cord, as a conductor, mimicked the trawler's cable. If she didn't ground herself on the trawler's cable again, when she finally reached it, she would shock herself, possibly into unconsciousness.

The storm rumbled again, shaking her bones. She reached for the trawler's cable, and almost touched, before an arc of electricity leapt between them, shocking her. She snapped her hand back. The drone approached, its lamps lighting the mist from nearby. And the wind still kept her from the cable.

She climbed the cord, getting closer to the trawler's cable. She steeled herself as she grabbed it and electricity convulsed her. Displays in her helmet winked out momentarily. With spasming muscles, she slid her way down the shaft, wrapping her legs around it.

The repair drone broke through the mist. Two of its three lamps, despite being encased in glass, were dark. Its corroding claw gaped at her.

Marie-Claude reached her arms around the cable to tie the end of her second parachute cord around it, the one with the hammer and copper wire tied to one end. Rain whirled around her in gusts, discoloring the steel hammer and speckling the copper with powdery, blue-edged holes.

And then the rain stopped, the wind stilled, and the air brightened.

She twisted her body to see what was happening. Awe seized her. The haze opened into kilometers and kilometers of clear air. Dark, bruised clouds rimmed the open air, veined with flashes of blue-white lightning. A great vortex, a hundred kilometers across. The center of the storm pierced the bottom of the sub-cloud haze, revealing Venus, unclothed, terrifying and beautiful. A great plane of dark basalt lay beneath the storm, pocked by high, shiny lava domes. And thirty kilometers beneath the center of the storm's clear air, a flat volcanic mesa shot bright red lava and black sulfuric smoke into the sky.

Naked Venus. Terrifying. Beautiful.

She and the drone were sucked into the quick-moving winds scouring the edges of the clouds. Blue-tinged lightning decorated the walls of the great column with branching forks. The drone neared from the side, avoiding the trawler's shaft. It could measure electrical charge better than Marie-Claude.

She swung her hammer on the end of its cord and threw. The hammer dragged the wet parachute cord across the few meters and laid it across the top of the grabbing arm.

Electricity cracked across the wet cord. The drone's last light popped and smoke puffed out.

Whatever static charge the drone had acquired in the two days in the deep had not been the same as the trawler's. Now it was.

Marie-Claude hauled in the drone and lashed it to the trawler's shaft.

Thunder rumbled. Deep, bone-touching vibrations quickened primal fears.

Her fingers trembled as she opened the access panels of the drone and peeled away burnt acid barriers. Half-melted wiring lay over fuses charred in their brackets. She yanked the surviving wires free by the handful and

143

began wiring the trawler shaft above her to the drone's hydrogen cells. Then, she connected the hydrogen cells to the shaft below the drone. Her fingers tingled as a light current passed through the wires.

She had to get out of here. The wind whipped the trawler past wrinkled walls of cloud, faster and faster. Marie-Claude struggled up the cord, on aching muscles, to the stoma.

The clear space opened wider, and the diffuse brightness of the light lent the gloom the tincture of dawn. Venus had spent almost three days testing her. She had survived. Venus respected Marie-Claude now, but had not finished with her. That was Venus' message in the gesture of opening the clouds. But Marie-Claude would use Venus' spite against her.

Her fingers scrabbled at the opening of the stoma, prying, pulling, until she could force her arms in and pull herself up. She kicked. Hard. Fast. Not much time.

Marie-Claude slipped into the chamber, but did not reconnect her suit to the electroplaque. She untied the parachute cord from her harness. She didn't want to be close to any of the trawler's electrical vascular systems. She huddled against the wall, her knees tucked close to her.

"Renaud?" she asked. "Renaud?"

Static. Then "Marie-Claude! Are you okay?"

"Have you got a fix on me?"

"Yes. It's really faint."

"Keep the fix. I might need a pick up soon."

"The deep dive vehicle won't be here until tomorrow, Marie-Claude," he said sadly, "and even then, I don't know if we can get close to the storm."

"Keep the fix," she said.

Thunder boomed closer. Lightning lit the walls of the chamber like a flashlight behind a hand, silhouetting reticulated vasculature. She'd never been close to lightning on Earth, but she felt, even without seeing it, that Venusian lightning was larger, angrier. Soon, the lightning would choose to travel through the stalk of the trawler for part of its journey. She didn't know what would happen to all the things that parasitized the trawler as a platform upon which to live. They might be burnt to a crisp, cleansing the trawler, or perhaps in the way a forest fire opens ground for new growth, new life might be quickened by the lightning, and given space in which to grow. She did not know if she would survive. She was now a seed in a pod, wondering if the casing was strong enough to survive the trial that preceded birth.

Distantly, through a wall of static, Renaud yelled. "You're descending. Are you in a downdraft? Marie-Claude! You're at thirty-one kilometers and dropping!"

The world exploded around her. Painful brightness. Bone-shaking noise. Heat. Sizzling shock seizing her muscles. The world became transparent. Fragments of overloaded sensation were simultaneous with a shuddering explosion below. Where the repair drone had been, a bright flash of orange and purple lit the thin floor of the chamber. The trawler shook, as if it were about to come apart.

Then the world dimmed.

Lightning cracked farther away, lighting the walls of her world like new moments of creation.

Her muscles trembled from electrical shock, even though she'd been grounded to the trawler and not in the path of any of the current. She felt heavy. The chamber continued to shake in turbulence. She was heavy. It was not the electrical shock. The chamber shook in the turbulence of its own rapid ascent through the atmosphere. It had worked. Igniting the hydrogen cells on the drone had severed the trawler's heavy cable.

"Renaud!" she cried.

Her antenna icon was red. Her operating system was rebooting. Renaud couldn't hear her. She wasn't transmitting her location. Her emergency battery was failing. And the trawler's severed shaft could not produce electricity anymore. But the electroplaque might still be charged.

Marie-Claude crawled to the hole she'd dug in the woody flesh of the trawler. Her hands shook, her muscles still spasming from the shock. She clipped her suit to the electroplaque.

Some displays lit, but it became hard to think, to focus on what they were telling her. Her chest felt heavy. Her arms and legs ached. The decompression icon winked bright red in the middle of her faceplate. The yellow nitrogen icon flashed beneath it. Danger of nitrogen narcosis, despite the low nitrogen mix in her air tank. Going from six atmospheres to one was lethal. The trawler shuddered as it continued upward, and blackness invaded the edges of her vision. Like a fickle genie, Venus might have granted her wish but killed her anyway.

Duvieusart Inquiry Transcript, page 782

6:35 p.m., RENAUD LANOIX, ENGINEERING SUPERVISOR: We found Mademoiselle Duvieusart in the charred husk of a trawler at forty-nine kilometers. Her suit had rebooted

on a failing emergency battery. We had initially
thought the trawler had only been mauled in
a deep storm but later on, we found explosive
damage underneath the buoyancy chambers and
in the remains of its cable. The chambers were
still sealed at an atmosphere and a half.

6:35, CHLOE RIVERIN, CHAIR: In what
condition did you find Mademoiselle Duvieusart?

6:35, RENAUD LANOIX, ENGINEERING
SUPERVISOR: The media reports were accurate.
Unconscious. Extreme heat exhaustion. Shock.
And nitrogen narcosis. The safeties in her suit
had tried to adjust the pressure more gradually,
but it hadn't had enough power to do more than
a half-job.

6:35, CHLOE RIVERIN, CHAIR: And then
what?

6:35, RENAUD LANOIX, ENGINEERING
SUPERVISOR: We had no access to a hyperbaric
chamber, so the only thing we could do was put
her in our own plane and dive as deep as the
tolerances would allow. We managed to raise the
pressure in the plane to almost two atmospheres
for several hours.

EVERYTHING ACHED WHEN she woke. The drone of a
plane engine sounded, and she was strapped in, reclining,
in one of the back passenger seats. Her suit was off, and

bandages covered her arms. Renaud knelt, applying an acid-burn cream to her legs.

"Renaud," she croaked.

The wind outside the plane sounded wrong, and the pilot ahead of them fought violent turbulence. It was dark outside the cockpit window. The plane shook and bumped again.

"We're going to be riding some rough weather until we can get you safely to higher pressures. Then we can take you home to the *Laurentide* to a hero's welcome. You're big news, even on Earth. The story of your three days in the clouds has had more hits than any other story on Earth, Mars, or the asteroids. Everyone is waiting to hear what you decide."

"Les séparatistes?" she asked.

"I sure hope your choice isn't *nationaliste*."

"Neither," she said.

"Everyone has to choose," he said. "This will go to a vote, and there's only yes and no."

She shook her head. It hurt. "Whether we are a territory of Québec or the nation of Venus, we're still living in floating cans, losing the race. It doesn't matter who comes first in a losing race. The solutions that work elsewhere won't work here."

"What do you want? You're in no shape to lead anything right now."

"We have to learn to live off the land. Smaller habitats have to be more independent, riding deeper in the atmosphere, where we can learn from the life that already thrives here. We have to become the new *coureurs des bois*."

POLLEN FROM A
FUTURE HARVEST

MAJOR OKONKWO HAD never attended a meeting of the General Staff. The military police in the base headquarters checked her ID, scanned her retinae and shut off her recording augments. She was still getting used to the planetoid's weak gravity and bounced a bit as she slowly paced the ice-floored reception room. Okonkow stopped every few moments to consider the steel coat-of-arms of the Sixth Expeditionary Force of the Sub-Saharan Union. It looked strange now that they'd removed their patron's fleur-de-lis from it. It was too early for the absence to feel natural, but the danger of their rebellion felt very close.

She could guess what this was about. Her senior husband was dead. In the last weeks, Okonkwo had sent message after message to Military Security asking for them to investigate his death as a murder. Perhaps they hadn't been ignoring her. Perhaps they'd been preparing a disciplinary meeting instead. She had little understanding of the politics of the General Staff or how they would react to her requests.

The ache of Garai's loss was like someone had ripped away a limb. The black inkiness of sadness mixed with a numbing of the world. She owed justice not only to him, but to the threat his murder represented to the mission.

The wide doors opened and Colonel Bantya signaled her in. Bantya was something of a familiar face, a woman she encountered in the officers' mess from time to time. Okonkwo's heart thumped. She stepped into a high chamber. At the seat at the foot of the long table, she saluted. Major-General Nandoro, the Commanding Officer of the Sixth Expeditionary Force, sat across from her. He was in his mid-fifties, tall, his black hair gone almost all prematurely white. The two lower-ranking brigadiers, Iekanjika and Takatafare, were at his left and right, and a trio of colonels she vaguely recognized. Okonkwo sat stiffly.

"This is Major Chenesai Okonkwo, Acting Head of Auditing," Colonel Bantya said, emphasizing the "acting" in Okonkwo's title. Her French departed from the visceral Montréal dialect affected by the ambitious, leaning instead to the lilting French spoken by the Congolese. It was all artificial. Neither Bantya's nor Okonkwo's ancestors had ever spoken French; they'd adopted the tongue from their patrons a century ago as a condition of clienthood. Colonel Bantya pulled up her chair to the table, in the middle of the colonels and Nandoro gestured for her to continue. Bantya's dark brown eyes met Okonkwo's.

"Major," the Chief of Staff said, "the General Staff requires you to audit the security and accountability protocols around the Expeditionary Force's research base."

Okonkwo made no sound, and perhaps had no expression. The security *and* accountability protocols for the base. That was close to asking her to audit the entire base, and by extension, the entire Expeditionary Force. That didn't make a lot of sense. Garai had never hinted anything about a force-wide audit.

"You, your teams, and your AIs will be granted White Access," Bantya said. "AI recordings of the investigation are to be sequestered during the audit and destroyed thereafter."

White Access, she thought, nearly the highest clearance possible.

"What is driving this, ma'am?" Okonkwo asked. "Has there been some kind of a breach?"

The two brigadiers appeared uncomfortable. Major-General Nandoro spoke with a voice both raspy and wet. "The pollen streaming through the time gate has stopped."

OKONKWO RETREATED TO the suite she had shared with her two husbands. Its plastic walls were flat and undecorated, smelling vaguely of chlorine, but it was several steps better than the barracks. The suite had three workstations, a small shower and toilet stall, and three tiny bedrooms. Tinashe Zivai, her younger husband, waited for her.

She closed the door and slumped at her desk. She wanted to reach for a cigarette, but held her beret tight to keep her hands from shaking in front of him. She told him everything of the meeting and her voice didn't crack, although it maybe ought to have. Tin's brown eyes widened as she spoke. He paced on long legs, fine fingers making tight fists. She'd never seen him frightened. She loosened her grip on her beret. He shouldn't see her scared.

"Does this mean the Congregate has found us, eleven years in the future?" he asked.

"I don't know."

Three months earlier, the Expeditionary Force had been sent by their patron nation, the Congregate to raid deep into the interstellar territory of the Middle Kingdom. The mission was well out of contact for supplementary orders, but each warship had carried its complement of political and language commissars. On one of their stops at an out-of-the-way brown dwarf, the Force had discovered this planetoid, and on it, a pair of artificial wormholes unlike anything ever seen—they were connected not across space, but across eleven years of time. All the ancient wormholes were incalculably valuable; their possession was the defining feature of the patron nations. By the terms of their Patron-Client Accord, they ought to have handed the discovery over to the political commissars embedded in their ranks, but they would never find anything like this again. Possibly no one would. Finding a wormhole was the Union's chance to slip from beneath the yoke of the Congregate. They'd abandoned their mission, imprisoned all the commissars, and gone into hiding. But how long could they hide? They all waited for some alert to go off, signalling that they'd been discovered. Eventually some mission would be sent to find out what happened to them, or some mission would be sent to replace what theirs hadn't done.

"It's a big audit," Tinashe said.

He wasn't wrong. Auditors thought in terms of project efficiencies as well as falsified records, skimmed rations, pay reconciliations, and lost materiel. The scale of this audit wasn't their area of expertise. Okonkwo rose and put her arms around him. She pressed her lips against his cool ear. "We'll get this done," she whispered.

He deflated, taking for a moment what she offered, but then stiffened and pulled away. "Where do we even start?" he said with a kind of lost frustration that waited at the edges of her own thoughts. "We'll have to hit the MP detachment," she said, "detention, the coordinating office, one or more of the research modules, and probably some of the battle ships."

Tin turned away, rubbing his forehead, as if to knead the implications to the surface. "Someone in all that made the pollen eleven years in the future just stop?" he said. "We have to find the culprit, if there is a culprit, before they do whatever they're going to do. Even on Garai's best day..."

His voice trailed off, as he understood what had started coming out. Garai had led many important, complicated audits. That was why he'd been a colonel. That's why he'd been given two subordinate auditor spouses and command of an audit team. Neither Okonkwo nor Tinashe trusted that she could pull this off.

"This is our chance, though, Tin," she said.

He frowned. "What? To prove ourselves?"

"No," she said. "White clearance gives us access to almost everything. We can open the records we need to investigate Garai's death."

"That's not what this is for! We can't get distracted."

"Did you love him?" she asked.

"Of course."

"If he thought you'd been murdered, he wouldn't have rested until he'd found justice for you."

* * *

Colonel Garai Munyaradzi, her late senior husband, had trained a small political security-military unit for his audit team. She had Tinashe start some background work while Okonkwo suited up with the PolSecMil team. They got in a skip shuttle, a pilotless shell that freighted kit from one part of the base to another. PolSecMil was meant to be the elite part of their little profession. Before Garai's death, Okonkwo had been training to join them. Now with Okonkwo in charge instead of their colonel, an odor of awkwardness hung about them.

Captain Tendekai was a man of Okonkwo's age, thirty-eight, flat-faced, with wideset eyes, experienced at building and dissecting the security measures that protected information. Clever and effective, he was neither inspirational nor strategic, but functioned very well when pointed at a target with questions of deep detail.

Cold air jets lifted them in the planet's low gravity.

Second Lieutenant Rudo was a woman barely out of the Union Academy at Harare. She'd been attached to Garai's command only days before the Sixth Expeditionary Force had shipped out. Among the shortest of military personnel Okonkwo had ever seen, Rudo was also narrow-boned and slim. The vacuum suit, designed for larger crew, looked like it was melting over her in wrinkles. Rudo's tremendous ability and relentlessness had scored her above seven hundred other cadets in her class. On graduation, she might have gone anywhere: field command, research, strategic intelligence. Garai had convinced her to choose internal affairs as a junior auditor, on his PolSecMil team. Rudo was eager, but cursed with youth's lack of subtlety.

Rudo and Tendekai had respected Garai, learned from him. Now Okonkwo had to learn from them. She ignored the gnawing nervousness in her stomach and tried to make out detail beyond the window. The brown dwarf brooded at noon in the dark sky, high metallic clouds laid out in smeared streaks and glowering storm cells. Its orange light reflected off a hard point high above the shuttle: the Expeditionary Force's flagship, the *Mutapa*. It was a good name. A growing power deserved a storied name, despite some irony.

Mutapa had been founded in the fifteenth century, during the expansion of Greater Zimbabwe. Mutapa had gone on to supplant Greater Zimbabwe, becoming a kingdom and taking on client princes of its own. It was a good story that far. Later, internecine fighting weakened Mutapa enough for conquest by larger powers.

"Ma'am?" Rudo had edged close behind Okonkwo's seat. "Ma'am, I've heard some talk that you'd been called to the General Staff and that the auditing unit might be dismantled. Is that what's happening?"

"Why would you say that, lieutenant?"

"It's just what I hear."

Tendekai shared an expression of patience with Okonkwo.

"Rudo," Okonkwo said, "never gossip about your superiors or what meetings they attend. The auditing unit is not going anywhere."

Rudo pressed her lips tight. "But we're so far from headquarters and we have no colonel. I don't see how they could get us another one. And no offense, ma'am, but you're a new major. They can't skip you two grades to colonel."

Okonkwo's face heated. Tendekai was studiously looking out the window. The girl had proven brilliance in academics and in the fish bowl-clear rules of the academy. She still wore her dark curls tight against her scalp in a cadet cut. But the rules that needed navigating in real life were written and rewritten by the tides, and all that went on below the surface of the real world.

"Keep your nose out of politics, Rudo. Everything you do in politics comes back to bite you."

Rudo retreated, but didn't have the expression of someone who'd been persuaded. She'd also missed the point that mattered most to Okonkwo. The triple marriages of senior spouse, middle spouse, and junior spouse were Venusian in origin, a method for the colonists of Venus to ensure genetic diversity and formalize their clan alliances in the competitive, hellish depths of their new home. The Sub-Saharan Union had adopted the practice to arrange many key military and political portfolios beneath triptych marriages. The welding of management teams who came with different views and loyalties meant that treason and fraud were harder to hide. MilSec made no secret that some spouses in some marriages were intelligence operatives. But despite the political and security character of the arranged marriages, many worked quite well. Okonkwo had loved Garai. She loved Tin. If the General Staff disassembled the auditing team, she would lose not one husband, but two. She couldn't imagine that kind of loneliness out here, cut off from civilization.

The shuttle descended enough that the dim brown dwarf light reflecting off the surface revealed the thick vegetation on the ice. The Expeditionary Force had built the temporary and ramshackle base in the middle of a deep valley hundreds of kilometers across. The gravitationally locked world sublimated slowly under the cool noon star and the vapor moved up and away to snow down onto rings of far-off glaciers. After so long in warships and in the cramped surface base, the sense of dark scale was dislocating, but more hinted at than seen. The faint dwarf light outlined rather than illuminated, suggested with clues rather than telling with detail, hinted at the life and movement beneath them on the organic black surface. It was a strange world and they wouldn't have given it a second glance, except that right in the middle of the valley was one of the most important scientific finds in human history.

They landed at the MP detachment overlooking the time gates. They cycled through the airlock of the tower of ice and plastic. While Tendekai and Rudo went right away to inspect the hard systems, Okonkwo climbed the stairs to the sixth floor and met Lieutenant-Colonel Tapiwa, Detachment Commander. He had undecorated features and dark calloused hands. His office was starkly functional, with hard plastic chairs. Okonkwo surveyed the floor of the valley through the thick window beside their shoulders. Dark shapes moved so slowly as to make the movement doubtful glimmers at the corner of the eye. The aliens, the vegetable intelligences that lived around the time gates, sending their pollen into the past, were just shadows moving among deeper shadows.

"Thank you for seeing me, sir," she said.

"An audit is an audit," he said with a hint of a smile. "No one is ever excited to see auditors, but we can't say no, can we?"

She smiled as if this was the first time someone had made a dig about auditors.

"I'll try to make it painless, sir." They sat.

"I was reviewing the personnel files," Okonkwo said. "I noticed that you were a colonel in the bioweapons division. I know there has been a lot staff movement as we adjust, yet you took an assignment at a lower grade as the detachment commander. I wondered why you did that?"

"All the other likely officers were already tasked with other things," Tapiwa said, his tone becoming more brisk and efficient. "The General Staff had the choice of putting me here or leaving me at bioweapons. I understood that the detachment command was more important to them."

"So this wasn't your choice?" Okonkwo asked.

"We're all soldiers, major. We go where the mission needs us. You may be one of the only officers who has the same assignment she had on the way out."

"I may get changed yet," Okonkwo said, in a voice she hoped was light. "Can you please verify for me the mandate of this MP detachment?"

"There are a pair of wormholes, possibly part of the Axis Mundi network, out there on the ice. They're more valuable than anyone can conceive of. Scientifically. Politically. Strategically. And we might have caught all the sleeper agents and Congregate spies planted in the Expeditionary Force, but likely not. This detachment controls access to the time gates."

She didn't know who had killed Garai. She didn't rightly know that he'd been murdered, but if he had, it had been cleverly, insidiously done. Their patron nation, the Venusian Congregate had the vast resources to have assassins and specialized ways of removing difficult players discreetly, so as not to upset the nations who'd agreed to live under their clientage. And Garai had been important enough to be that kind of a target. The numb darkness trying to touch her heart seemed to come closer.

"I got the records of all the people and devices that have approached the time gates," she said. "Thank you. Were there any contacts with the time gates other than those?"

"No."

"When exactly did the pollen stop, sir?"

"At 14:20 on July 13, 2475," Tapiwa said crisply.

"Can you swear, under examination, that you can account for all the records under your mandate?" Okonkwo asked.

"I can." Tapiwa looked at Okonkwo directly, without the nervousness that sometimes accompanied an auditor's visit.

"Do you assert that all the procedures within your mandate conform to Expeditionary Force Standing Orders, as well as the General Regulations and Orders and the Code of Service Discipline?"

"I so assert, with one exception," Tapiwa said.

"Go on."

"My security cordon does not conform to the GR&Os," he said, "due to an exception made by the General Staff. The passage of the vegetable intelligences through the cordon creates a series of leaks that cannot be accounted for or predicted."

"Go on," Okonkwo said.

"A security cordon must prevent the passage of enemy personnel and equipment, as well as anyone or anything that might be able to act on the enemy's behalf," Tapiwa said. "The vegetable intelligences roam across the entirety of the sunward hemisphere, as do our scientists, geologists, security patrols, and so on. We do not know how many more sleeper agents are still free. When the vegetable intelligences return to the gate, my systems scan them, but the different life cycle stages make the X-ray shadows different. A device of some kind could be secreted upon one of them."

"You've reported this to the General Staff?"

"Of course," Tapiwa said.

"Their response?"

"None," Tapiwa said.

"Do you have a recommendation?" Okonkwo asked.

"The vegetable intelligences do not need to be here," he said. "They could be completely excluded from the site and left to reproduce naturally. They don't need to send their pollen back in time."

"We've imprisoned all of the Congregate political commissars, but those were certainly the least of their spies. We can't know how many of our crew and even officers might be answering to Congregate handlers rather than giving their loyalty to our own."

"And your answer to this is to exclude the vegetable intelligences from the gate?"

Tapiwa crossed his arms.

"This is the largest action ever taken against the Congregate by a client nation, bigger than the Crow protests," he said. "They will have been preparing against an uprising like this for decades. Even if I was given complete control of security measures, and I was able to make it leak-proof, at some point the Congregate would still find out what we're doing here. Security measures only delay discovery by the enemy. It's the law of security that no secret is secret forever."

OKONKWO, TENDEKAI, AND Rudo stepped onto a crunchy surface of hard water and methane ice, painted with a riot of black, cold-living plants. Her helmet artificially brightened the view at first, making blotches of gray and black pixellation in what she saw, so she dialed the gain lower, to see the cold, gloomy world as it was, inky patches of fragile plants standing above concrete-hard ice. Okonkwo's suit measured a magnetic field of about half a Gauss, reaching over the habitats and labs like a great droplet of water, trembling at the assault of cosmic radiation. Periodically, the field was dropped; many life cycles depended on the scouring of parasites by hard radiation. It was a place that was beautiful in an austere, alien way, not in a homey or welcoming way. She could appreciate that beauty, perhaps even on its own terms, even if she could not touch it.

The display for a laser communication blinked inside her helmet. Rudo was transmitting to her by laser. She didn't want the conversation to be overheard.

"Ma'am, I found something strange in the MP tower," Rudo said.

Okonkwo double-checked the privacy of the line. "Go on."

"I found traces of organics that shouldn't have been there," Rudo said. "Strange DNA and proteins."

"Native?" Okonkwo asked.

"Our kind of life. But I think it's viral. It has protein parts I would only expect to find in a bioweapon."

"Someone detonated a bioweapon in there?" Okonkwo asked.

"Containment is always challenging. It could be just contact residue. But something in there came close enough to a bioweapon that a bit stuck to their suit, or a bioweapon moved through the tower."

Bioweapons Division had its own buildings, for security and safety reasons. It might have been someone not being careful enough, just brushing a suit against something else. They were all doing shift work, running around the clock. The auditor's biggest challenge wasn't so much malfeasance as people innocently cutting corners with safety rules.

"What do the personnel movement logs say?" Okonkwo asked.

"My AI found no environmental suit that went to both places," Rudo said.

"You think someone moved undocumented bioweapons through the MP tower?" Okonkwo said.

"Looks like it."

"How sure are you? This stuff breaks down, no?"

"Under normal circumstances, yes, but the intense cold and weak insulation mean that DNA and proteins can persist for a long time."

"Give me a report and analysis as soon as you can," Okonkwo said.

"Yes, ma'am."

Okonkwo stepped over oily mats of photosynthesizers slicking the ground. These plants absorbed the infrared glow from the brown dwarf, slowly building high-energy compounds and antifreeze proteins. The skins of the plants, hardened against the near vacuum, deposited water to make fragile skeletons and lived on the surfaces of those icy bones.

Sections of the valley were overgrown, standing as tall as her, but scientists and the military police had cleared a path. Stiff rods of ice and pitch-colored leaf were edging back into the opened space and Rudo was casually striking at the plants with an open glove, shattering as she went. At the end of the open way was the wide, flattened ring hundreds of meters across, centered on the time gates. That wide circle was the migratory path of the vegetable intelligences.

They were barrel-shaped, but mostly hollow, with

hard skin stretched slick and black over fine ribs of ice. High, whip-like stamens and pistils sprouted from wide fronds on the tops of their bodies. They shambled, one ponderous, four-legged step every quarter hour, trampling new growth, so that across the wide plain, the thin dark air carried the faint, relentless sounds of breaking crystal.

They were beautiful and for all practical purposes unreachable. If Okonkwo touched one long enough, the heat waste leaving her glove would begin to melt them. Even if she walked slowly she could circle the entire herd in the time they would have taken three or four steps. There was no common ground for them, except for the time gates. The Union worked furiously to try to understand how to use them to send messages back in time. The vegetable intelligences circled the double wormholes, and because somewhere in the deep past evolution had incorporated a time travel device into their life cycle, they could seek oracular insights into a future that could only be difficult on a frozen world under a stillborn star.

"It's creepy out here," Tendekai said. They'd come to a stop at the edge of the herd, and the apparent stillness was eerie.

"I know," Okonkwo said. It was peaceful too though. And she could see the conjoined wormholes in the distance. She'd studied all the specs, all the analyses that Tinashe had readied for her.

The lower edges of the time gates were slightly embedded in the flat plain. They scintillated dimly, rings of warped space, held in imperceptibly trembling tension by what some guessed might be inflaton fields. And inside the gates, space bent in directions that could not be long observed. No one knew who had created the artificial wormholes, but they were ancient. They dotted space like flowers in a meadow, mostly around neutron stars, bridging the gulfs between the stars for human ships.

They appeared in nodes of three to five. Four had been found in Earth's Solar System, creating the great interstellar patron nations: the Venusian Congregate, the Middle Kingdom, the Ummah, and the Anglo-Spanish Plutocracy. Artificial wormholes had become the new gold of human civilization, and these powers held the known gates like fortified oases. Humanity had found about two dozen gates, but their placement suggested a much larger decayed web of space-time tunnels. In the shadows of these ancient artifacts, humans were mice in an abandoned cathedral. She felt small, just thinking about it.

But this pair was unlike any other. Most gates were big enough to accommodate interstellar ships. These double gates were small ovals, only a dozen meters wide and half that high, partially embedded in the ice of the planet. They were not only locked together, but unevenly so, like two picture frames hanging on the same hook. And they did not reach back and forth across space, but led from one to another in one direction only, backward in time by eleven years. It wasn't obvious how these wormholes would help the Union. It wasn't like they'd discovered some new solar system no one could reach, full of resources no one had yet found.

In Tinashe's research through all the files, he'd found lots of theories. Not all of them made sense to her, but she was no physicist. The Expeditionary Force didn't have a lot of real physicists. The ones they had guessed that the wormhole configuration wasn't intentional. They guessed that at some point the gates had collided and interfered with each other. This made sense to Okonkwo. Random chance would introduce errors into even the most error-proof systems, given enough time.

They'd dropped sensors, spectrometers, cameras, thermometers, Geiger counters and microphones into each mouth of the wormhole. None of the readings or observations made any sense. They unspooled kilometers of cable into the upwind side and had never reached the other side. In a bit of frustration, a few brave souls had stuck their heads in and the best anyone could report was that it was trippy and nauseating. It did have an interesting radiation profile though.

All known gates evaporated in the same way as black holes, losing mass as faint, low-level radiation in a slow trillion year process. But this pair, locked together, seemed to be catalyzing each other's evaporation. This unnatural dual gate would only live for a few million years more, and that would allow Union scientists to actually observe the decay, and perhaps, unlike the other patron nations, find out how to construct them. New technology developed by the Union might stake out a place for them on the stage of human affairs. It was a heady thing to think of living as an independent nation.

As the vegetable intelligences passed before the upwind side of the gate, the thin breeze carried pollen from rows of high stamens, and through the gates, delivering it eleven years into the past. Under normal circumstances, the creatures of today stood on the other side of the gate and received the pollen from eleven years in the future, but the wind now emerging from the future carried no pollen at all.

She found their whole environment fascinating and dizzying. The temperature of the planet hovered around seventy kelvins, but was minutely rising each year. The vacuum photosynthesizers absorbed infrared radiation that would otherwise have been reflected back into space. The trapped energy inexorably sublimated molecular-thin layers of the planet's surface, gradually thickening the atmosphere. The pressure difference between the present and past drove the slow wind through the gates. The vegetable intelligences were connected to their pasts and futures through wormholes.

Except not now; here was the mystery the generals had issued her. Did that mean that eleven years in the future, no vegetable intelligences stood on the other side of the gate, pollinating the past, or were they there, but sterile? The fact that the wind persisted meant that the gate hadn't been moved.

Nor could the end of the pollen be explained by an order from the General Staff to remove the vegetable intelligences. The generals knew that they had given no such order because they'd mapped out all the ways they would need to act, the ways they would all need to act to avoid causal paradoxes. Any order that they gave to the future involving the time gates would only be implemented after eleven years, so that there was no danger of grandfather paradoxes.

Okonkwo wondered about some other kind of environmental catastrophe, one that didn't involve the brown dwarf. Ice cores revealed plant material and pollen only as far back as a few hundred thousand years, suggesting that the planetoid had been colonized. The environment revealed in the ice cores was erratic, melting hundreds of meters in some spots due to scouring flares from the restive star. It did not even need to be a flare. The planet was already experiencing global warming. Could a disease or parasite have stopped the pollen? She hoped so. Tinashe's first question was always there; *had they found us?*

"Remarkable," Okonkwo said into her helmet's radio.

"What?" Tendekai asked.

"That something alive, much less intelligent, managed to survive here."

"Won't be in eleven years," Rudo said.

Okonkwo did not think of a proper retort before Tendekai spoke again.

"Good riddance," he said. "Creepy buggers."

Okonkwo eyed the intelligences under the light of the tepid star. Old leaves hung from them, on wisps of black, oily skin that had not yet torn through. In places, the skin had rubbed away, exposing the white bones of ice beneath. The dangling growth of yesterday tinkled like chandelier crystals, sounding faint and distant in the thinness of the atmosphere. Tendekai seemed to see ugliness. Rudo had made actuarial points, as if there were no dimension of beauty and ugliness. Okonkwo saw the repellent, but also the audacious vitality.

Four of the shambling vegetable intelligences, pistils and carpels gnarled with age, stooped near the gate, neither on the future side, nor on the past side. Reports identified these intelligences as elders, keepers of wisdom, and the most likely to understand direct conversation from the humans. Okonkwo had read all the reports of communicating with the vegetable intelligences and thought she understood it.

Okonkwo wore a chest plate filled with different chemicals and a multiplicity of small irises by which to release them for speech. Her chest plate would also smell the conversation. The intelligences themselves had a series of stomata on their chests that opened and closed, releasing chemical signals that traveled in nearly straight lines through the rarefied atmosphere, to smell receptors on their companions. Some thousand scents made up their vocabulary.

She joined their circle. They were silent.

"I am elder," she said as the device hanging from the front of her suit released the chemical signal translation. Her words appeared on the screen in her helmet and they would not fade for a long time. Neural tests on discarded skins had revealed that the vegetable intelligences' nervous cells did not relax quickly after firing. This made their sensations long things, not moments at all, but sober still lives lasting minutes, overlapping with other sensations in a fiction of simultaneity and a blurring of causality. Everything about them was so strange.

"New elder," she added, a little self-consciously. She wasn't really an elder at all, just the middle wife in a triptych without a senior.

ALONE appeared on her screen, written over her words.

Rudo and Tendekai stood behind her, but perhaps to the vegetable intelligences, these creatures who made no smells were not part of the group. Not with her?

"I have others," she said. The smells hissed out of the tiny stomata in the machine she carried and crowded the screen with other words. Depending on the direction she followed on the screen, the conversation could be read in the order it had been spoken, or it could be read all in a jumble, or it could even be read backward. *I have others, alone, new elder, I am elder.*

NOT ELSEWHEN, appeared on her screen.

What did that mean? *She* was not elsewhen? She didn't touch the past and the future the way they did. Did they know that?

The officers who had first contacted the vegetable intelligences had reported their utterly alien concept of time, incomprehensively far from the moment-based human conception of the present. What was the human present to them, the moment of now? A single vote, and not even the most important one, in constructing cause and effect? They spoke with the past by sending pollen to their ancestors and sometimes even to past selves through the time gate, preparing the past for now without conceptually separating past from present.

Eleven years ago was the trailing edge of their present, the edge of what could contribute to their cross-temporal, tribal consensus. The past voted, through the offspring begotten by the present and past. The future contributed the third leg of this consensus, sending its pollen back to the present. Eleven years in the future was the leading edge of now to the vegetable intelligences. Their broad present, and their basis of causality, were fuzzy conversations on events scattered across a window twenty-two years wide.

Except that their present had now narrowed. The future third of that triple perspective was gone.

DO YOU COME TO BROADEN YOUR PRESENT? appeared on her screen, as the rest of the conversation faded.

"I don't think so," she said. "The gate sends no pollen and we do not know how to send our wisdom through it to our own trailing edge. I come to see what you may understand of the end of the pollen."

A staccato of chemicals shot at her chest translator and her screen changed. Her previous words "we do not know how to send our wisdom" faded. The other words were still there. The intelligences sent out smells to turn off previous parts of the conversation, to end stimulus, to change and correct what had been said, except that they were not limiting themselves to rewriting what they themselves had said. Did they believe that overwriting her meant that she hadn't said it?

MUCH PITY. NO ONE SHOULD SUFFER A NARROW VIEW, appeared on the screen, as if they had been the ones to bring up the point. It bothered her sensibility as an auditor that they would rewrite what had been said. If humans did the same, there would be nothing upon which to base history and causality.

"Sometimes one must live, as you do now, with a shadowed leading edge," she responded, using their description of the absence of future pollen streaming through the time gates.

NO ONE CHOOSES TO BE SHADOWED, they said.

She blinked at a sudden watering of her eyes in her helmet. No one did choose. She did not choose for Garai to have died. His role in the triptych had been to advise her, to guide her, as she guided and protected Tinashe. Garai had been a voice from a future she had yet to reach, at a stage of experience where he learned from others so far away, she couldn't perceive them.

No one chooses to live shadowed, but sometimes one must.

"Sometimes the leading edge offers not wisdom, but bondage," she said. The Venusian Congregate shared yesterday's science with its client nations, directed their laws, and imposed the French language. They controlled military and political policy, throwing client nations into the wars against the other nations. The Congregate offered no wisdom, only a wing under which to shelter from larger predators.

LEADING EDGE, TRAILING EDGE, AND THE CORE ARE ALL ONE, the vegetable intelligences said, ONE LIVING BEING, SEEKING TO SURVIVE THE HOSTILITY OF THE WORLD.

The brown dwarf above glared its hostility. At times cold, shuttering its dim light under silicate clouds, and at other times spewing hot flares with which to sand the surface of this world. The Venusian Congregate possessed its own fickleness, at times throwing scraps, at other times dictating, and at other times punishing.

"And what of the pollen?" she asked. "Do you know why it stopped streaming through the gates?"

NO, they said.

"Do you think your people became lost? Broken?" she asked. They had no word for dead. "Was it a flare?"

WE DO NOT KNOW.

"Could one of you, or some of you working together, have caused this?" she asked.

CIRCLES TURN UPON THEMSELVES, RISING AND MELTING, THREADS OF RIGHT-PARENTAGE MEETING WHERE THEY MUST, they said.

Okonkwo checked the translation, trying to make sense of the last answer. Their common vocabulary was so small and crude that they might say something important and she might never know.

"What will happen to you with no pollen coming from the future?"

The word pollen appeared this time on her screen as a constellation containing pollen-wisdom-insight.

The inscrutable things shifted, but not by much. Each movement involved the injection of anti-freeze chemicals into their joints to soften them enough for muscular flexing to create motion. One began to turn away, to the sound of wine glass stems breaking.

THE TRIBE WILL STEP INTO SHADOW, came the answer eventually on her screen, AND WILL EMERGE AFTER IT HAS COME TO KNOW WHAT HAS BECOME KNOWN TO THE LEADING EDGE. WE WILL BECOME THE SHUTTERED VOICE, WITHOUT A WAY TO SPEAK TO THOSE WHO FOLLOW. SOME TRIBES NEVER EMERGE FROM THE SHADOW.

What they said was true. Some tribes never did emerge from the shadow.

LATE THAT NIGHT, after Tinashe was asleep, Okonkwo sat in the common area of their suite. Her encounter with the vegetable intelligences had disturbed her, although she wasn't sure why. They were so utterly alien that they existed almost in another ecosystem, one that did not touch hers.

Yet every day, their strangeness walked over the spot where her husband had died, like fragile ghosts. The hardness of the ground, the grinding crunchiness of it was as cold and inhospitable as the intelligences themselves. He had fallen softly on that unforgiving surface.

The softness of his fingertips would never touch her face again. The warmth of his skin would never shelter her. The wrinkles around eyes and lips would never smile at one of her jokes; she couldn't imagine making a joke again. Garai's home was now a grave scraped into the ice. His softness was now frozen to stony hardness. Despite the danger of their mission, she'd expected to have years, decades with Garai. Professional triple marriages like theirs could become very personal and intimate and those could go on after the political need was gone. That's what she'd been wishing. A grow-old-together wish. And here she was, thirty-eight years old and he was gone.

OKONKWO, TENDEKAI, AND Rudo were in the sublevels dug deeply into the granite-hard ice beneath the surface. Their breath swirled in thin white clouds. The slick blackness of the walls hid the depths of the ice. She might touch a hand to the cold and know that the same ice somewhere touched her husband. She might press a light against the surface and watch it penetrate voids of perfect transparency, and lacy fields of bubbles hardened from ice. She did not touch the ice. Today she was the hunter.

"Ma'am," Rudo said, almost skipping to keep up with Okonkwo's impatient strides. "What do we expect to find by auditing detention again?"

Okonkwo did not answer.

Rudo looked at Tendekai for support, then back to Okonkwo. "We have so much to audit in such a short period of time that we should decide where to put our energies, ma'am. PolSecMil audited detention only a couple of months ago. We have the report."

Rudo held out a pad, no doubt with a copy of the report helpfully displayed.

Garai himself had initiated and led the audit because he had worried that sleeper agents might try to pass messages or materiel to the imprisoned political commissars, or vice versa. Okonkwo felt the accusation in Rudo's implication. She might have just plainly asked what Okonkwo expected to find if Colonel Munyaradzi, with twenty years more experience, hadn't found anything? From the way Tendekai avoided her eyes, he sympathized with Rudo. He'd been part of Garai's audit.

Okonkwo neared the pair of them.

"You've been briefed," she said in a low voice. "The Congregate may be coming for us. If they are, who do you think told them we're here?" She hung the question in the chill until even Rudo looked away. "All the political commissars are here and maybe they got a message to an ally on the surface, some instruction to do something."

Rudo lowered the pad.

"This time, we're going to tear this place apart," Okonkwo said. "And if you're worried about getting bored, Tendekai, you cover the colonel's part this time. I'll take yours."

And then, both Rudo and Tendekai had difficulty in keeping up with her.

DESPITE HER BRAVADO, Okonkwo was out of her element within hours. She was not nearly as experienced as Garai had been. In the zones Tendekai had covered last time, she found no irregularities that were not in his report, and missed a few that were.

Two months ago, Garai's worries of sleeper agents had been founded. Twice since the Expeditionary Force had established the base on the surface, detainees had attempted escapes. Both detainees were killed before leaving the facility, but the breach pointed to weaknesses yet unknown. And even after the audit, a schematic of the detention center, sketched from the inside, had been found in a dead drop on the surface. Someone had carried that message there, and had left it for some other sleeper agent they had not yet caught.

Okonkwo moved to the main control area, accompanied by the detention commander, an old lieutenant. She reviewed the detainee files, cross-checking them against older records and live closed-circuit footage. MilSec housed fifty-nine detainees.

There were the ship engineers, those Union officers trained by the Congregate naval engineering schools and loyal to the Congregate. There were the political commissars, those who had worked with the naval commanders, counter-signing important decisions and watching for sedition. Many were Venusians, mixed with some citizens of the greater Congregate, like the Québécois or the French. There were the undercover commissars and sleeper agents. They'd been detected, one by one, through counter-revolutionary operations and stings.

And finally, there were the language commissars, generally junior officers of the Union, monitoring adherence to the French language laws, looking to make names for themselves to jockey for higher-level duties for the Congregate. These lick-boots were among the most despised of the detainees, and Okonkwo did not smother her satisfaction when the guards on closed circuit video insisted that the language commissars speak Shona.

But it was a bittersweet satisfaction. Most of the detainees were Union citizens, people who ought to have rejoiced at the chance for their nation to strike out on its own, to find its own destiny. And yet, they'd been twisted, choosing self over country. She wanted to pity them, but she didn't know how. And even her patriotic rejection of French was a half-measure.

French, however much its adoption was a humiliating condition of becoming a client nation of the Venusians, was a powerful language. During its long history, French had been the language of philosophy, science, war, and diplomacy. It drew on centuries of literature and political dialogue, and even during its eclipsing by other cultures, it had continued borrowing and coining new words. The halting Shona spoken by the guards, leavened with French terms every tenth word, felt smaller. It made her feel smaller.

"I found something," Tendekai reported to her on the third day, sidling close with a display. "A computer virus," he whispered, "a micro-AI really, adaptive to defensive software. I found it in the security system, patched to the closed-circuit feed. I think it's programmed to send encrypted screenshots of the detainees somewhere."

"Do you know where they're sent?"

He shook his head.

"So the detainees could have used prearranged signals and body language to send messages outside the detention center?" she asked.

Tendekai nodded, removing his beret to wipe at a sheen of nervous sweat that managed to form even in this cold.

"How long has it been there?" she asked. "Months? Why didn't Colonel Munyaradzi see this?"

"This is really advanced, major. Experimental. I don't know how many people in the whole Expeditionary Force could have found it. Me. Probably Captain Zivai. MilSec sure didn't find it, and they scan their systems daily."

"How advanced?"

"A computer virus needs processing power," he said. "We sometimes find viruses by subtracting out all the other things a computer is doing and then seeing what's still eating up the processing power. But MilSec runs on quantum computers. Their algorithms process in parallel, running all possible variables simultaneously, in a superposition of states. In a lot of ways, it doesn't matter if you're running two or twenty operations at a time on a quantum processor. And this is a quantum computer virus. It runs unnoticed, taking its processing power by superimposing itself on the variables we aren't keeping. It can only be found by testing for certain kinds of interferences."

"Why wouldn't MilSec look for those interferences? Why did you?"

"I've never seen a quantum computer virus, ma'am. There's no reason to check. I'm sorry, ma'am, I didn't redo the colonel's work like you said. I trusted the colonel to have covered all the bases, so I took a few long shots."

A hollow opened in her gut, nervous and filling with fear. Someone working for the Congregate had hacked the MilSec computers and had been sending messages out for who knew how long. What other unknown resources did the sleeper agents have? Could they have already contacted the Congregate?

"Find out where it's been transmitting and then cross-reference against security footage," she said. "I doubt you'll find anything, but try."

"Yes, ma'am."

* * *

Comme il faut

Parle comme il faut, dit le commissaire
Speak properly, says the commissar.
Il faut. One must.

My words cut, *mes mots coupent,*
Must cut, *faut couper,*
Cut out, cut away, until nothing remains but the
words
Of *les immortels.*

They traded me a gun for my words, then threw
them
Down a well
Dissolved them into the acid of their world.

Grandfathers have words. Mothers have words.
Les miens sont français.
Two boys whisper nothings in a corner. No more.
"En français, les garcons!"

My gun is powerful. The language aches
With beauty, *beauté,* coiled meanings and hidden
Metaphors as cunning as a cuckoo,
Tossing eggs from a nest.

Parle comme il faut, dit le commissaire.
I have a gun. I will make those boys speak
As they should.
I have left my mother behind.

*   *   *

OKONKWO SAT IN the dark, her hands lit by the hovering holographic displays of her desk. Tendrils of cigarette smoke writhed through medical reports, the times and locations changing color and brightness. The room brightened as Tinashe emerged from the shower. She didn't turn and his hands came to rest on her shoulders, warm. Being with Tinashe only, living in a shrunken family, felt strange.

"I miss Garai too," he said, "but I don't torture myself over and over with his last moments."

"This isn't torture," she said slowly. Her exhaled gray smoke coiled, soaking itself in holographic yellow. "Something doesn't add up."

Tinashe pulled a chair closer, wrapped himself in his towel and sat. He tapped her pack and pulled a cigarette free with his lips. His finger penetrated the hologram, expanding the coroner's report.

"This conversation is getting old, Chenesai," he said softly. "No toxins. No injuries. No sign of foul play."

"He was outside, in a suit. The magnetic field was dropped for eighty-nine seconds. He died forty minutes later."

"Neither Garai, nor his assistant, took more than two hundred millisieverts of radiation," Tinashe said. "Hot, but not lethal."

Okonkwo inhaled and shook her head. The smoke stung her eyes.

"We have no reason to believe it was murder," Tinashe said. "There's no motive. Killing him doesn't get audit results erased and I haven't even found anything in his files that would have justified murder."

"Garai said that an auditor must also be part philosopher, interrogating not just the facts, but the depths of human nature," she said. "We're not done interrogating."

"I loved Garai," Tinashe said, "but he looked at auditing more as an artist than as an engineer. He missed the quantum computer virus."

"So did MilSec."

"Chenesai, I don't think Garai's memory is taking you to the right place. You need to lead us through whatever shit the Expeditionary Force has gotten itself into."

Okonkwo stood, cigarette butt trembling in her fingers.

"Keep this in sight, Tin. You and I are not engineers. We're not accountants. We're hunters. Keep your nose to the ground."

ADMINISTRATIVE PROTOCOLS, COUNTER-SIGNATURES and distributed authorities were the first immune response of any bureaucracy. Restricting access to key systems and information was like stretching skin across a body to keep pathogens out. Counter-signatures emulated self and non-self-recognition; what should be there, and what should not be. Distributed authorities and the requirement for two or three concurrent signatures was like the monitoring of DNA health, the comparing and contrasting of information and confirming matches, with mismatches triggering a repair response.

The guards scanned Okonkwo and Tinashe and checked and rechecked their AI.

Okonkwo, with her Blue Access, and even Garai, with his Green, had never been close to the research modules or the coordinating center. They'd had no need to know. With White Access, no door was closed to her.

It was heady and dangerous power. Dangerous because

she could make a mistake. Dangerous because the systems and partitioning of knowledge had been built to avoid breaking the laws of causality.

Colonel Chipunza, a slender old physicist commanding the coordinating center, met them. Okonkwo saluted, and then accepted coffee and a cigarette in his office. He examined their accesses and ran the authorizations from the General Staff against their DNA before getting to business.

"This research facility is unique," Chipunza said, displaying a flowchart in the holographic projector on his desk. "We have six research modules studying aspects of the time gates themselves, and the application of the physics we learn from them to weapons and propulsion. My mandate is to keep them separate so that no grandfather paradoxes can occur."

Tinashe whistled appreciatively. Chipunza seemed to enjoy this.

"Each module will do eleven years of research, and then sends back everything they've learned through the time gate eleven years. I'll receive it and then pass it to the next research module in the present. For all our safety, each module is entirely separate and has no contact or communication with any other." Okonkwo had felt her face tighten in confusion and the colonel stopped, like this was not the first time he'd had to slow his explanation.

"The second research module does eleven years of research as well, at the same time the first module is working," he said. "Some of the research is entirely original and independent, but some of it builds on data and experimental results *that the first module sent back in time*."

"Oh," Okonkwo said in sudden realization.

"The second module also sends back all its results at the eleven-year mark, and in the present, I'll give it to the third research module. With six modules, sixty-six years of research can be compressed into eleven years, maybe less once we get some experience with this structure. In theory, we're limited only by how many research modules we can sustain."

"I think I need to back up," Okonkwo said. "I know what grandfather paradoxes are, but what would really happen? Why these measures? Was there some successful transmission of information to the past that went badly?"

Chipunza smiled. "No one has blown up a research facility by creating a grandfather paradox," he said. "A grandfather paradox creates a causal loop, where one event overwrites another, which in turn overwrites the original event, and which overwrites its cause and so on. No theory knows how to break out of a causal loop, but theories do suggest that the process will need a lot of energy."

"So it will run out of energy?" she said.

Chipunza struggled for words. "Everything in the Universe can be considered in computational terms," he finally said. "Atoms and photons move around and carry information. Their interactions with other particles process the information they carry, like computer logic gates. And as they compute, they give off heat because rewriting information takes energy. In the case of the causal loop of a grandfather paradox, it's like looping one NOT gate to another in a circuit, and then running it forever. The energy for rewriting the information comes from somewhere. We don't know where, but we certainly don't want to be nearby if that happened."

"But your modules can't actually send information back through the time gate yet, can they?" she asked.

"Soon," he said. "The first attempts have only just been made. Subsequent attempts will be faster. We design a series of experiments to test ways of sending back information, lock up the instructions, and give them to the research modules to open in eight or nine years, so as to prepare the experiments and implement them by the eleven-year mark. It won't be long."

Okonkwo mused. Transforming the process of research, the nature of research, by using communication with the past, was the strategic key to Union military supremacy. The Venusians had studied their permanent wormholes for decades, peeling back extreme physics and technology, before any of the other powers had found theirs. Now, the Sub-Saharan Union could not only catch up, but surpass them. They would be able to do generations of research in parallel. As long as the Congregate didn't find them and as long as the Union itself did not create a paradox.

"How do you measure the tightness of the isolation between modules?" she asked.

"The modules are physically and electronically isolated from each other and from the rest of the Expeditionary Force. Food and supplies are delivered by the coordinating center," he said. "Moreover, few in the Expeditionary Force know what we're doing or how. Except for those working on communicating with the past, those in the modules are rarely aware that their work is being sent back in time. They only receive information from their superiors, who receive it from me, and they do their jobs without asking any questions."

"Don't you worry that some of them will chafe at being isolated, find it a bit strange that they never see any of the rest of the force?"

"We're on a frozen planet orbiting a brown dwarf," he said. "Where would they go? They live in small villages with families."

"What about sleeper agents?"

"That's the beauty of this structure. Even if there were sleeper agents in one of the modules, what could they do? The isolation necessary to avoid grandfather paradoxes also neutralizes sleeper agents."

"You yourself aren't a possible cause of a grandfather paradox?" she asked.

"I won't read the complete reports," he said. "I'll ensure that the information survived transmission into the past and then pass it on. A record will be kept, but to be frank, the research and experiments are so advanced that I wouldn't be able to puzzle together anything dangerous. I'm like you: an effective project manager. We make processes work."

Something inside her cringed at his words. She'd never considered herself in such limited, heroically bureaucratic terms. What was she? A second spouse, adrift, clinging to processes, to questions that were, in their own ways as limited as the ones she assigned to Tendekai. *No one chooses to be shadowed.*

"What do you make of the end of the pollen streaming through the time gates?" she asked. "What do you think is possible, and probable?"

The old colonel huffed.

"I've been asked this already," he said.

"And what did you tell them?" she asked.

"That I'm not concerned about the interruption of the pollen. A hard flare could kill most of the vegetable intelligences. It could take years for the population to rebound."

"We found no ash, water vapor, or snow coming through the gate. The wind carries no clues at all."

He licked his lips.

"What are the chances that one of the research modules in the future moves the vegetable intelligences away from the gate?" she asked.

"Zero," he said, sitting straighter.

"Why?"

"They wouldn't do that. They only do what they are instructed by this office."

"How are you sure?" she asked.

Chipunza pursed his lips and *tsked*. "I'll show you our system is auditor-tight," he said, leaning over the desk toward her. Then he stalked from the office. He returned with a data wafer, colored red for secure. He slapped it on the desk and slid it toward her.

"Your White Access ought to open this."

She slid the wafer into her data pad and thumbed her passcode. A security process diagram bloomed, detailing hard and soft security measures, counter-signed by the commander of the military police and Colonel Munyaradzi.

She suppressed a reaction. Of course Garai would have designed a set of administrative protocols tight enough to prevent even causal violations. He cast a long shadow.

His Ghost Upon the Ice

And so he walks,
Bewildered, on the ice,
Scraping at rime on ghostly feet.
He longs for his house,
But no trees or grasses mark the way.

Frost bites fingers and toes.
He holds high hands to warm them,
In bloodied starshine,
But the sun has cooled, curtained by clouds of
    sand,
Its corona glassing grains into a star's pollen,
Sterile seed to trace veins in the blooms of
    convection,
Fated never to know another star.
What is pollen but reaching, like the hands of a
    ghost,
Wrinkled still, and bitten by cold?
Clouds of glass reach without consummation,
The ghost calls my name with words lonely
And tender and cutting,
But the sound is snow upon the ice.

Okonkwo and Tinashe spent the day in the coordinating center inspecting the hard systems, and then worked well into the night preparing algorithms to look at the files. But about midnight, when Chipunza understood how deeply they intended to dig, he refused her requests to open the records of the instructions that had been given to the modules. His protests shot straight to the General Staff, so that Chipunza and Okonkwo spoke with a tired Colonel Bantya at one in the morning.

"I cannot answer the questions put to me if I cannot see what instructions were given to the future," Okonkwo said simply. It was late and her energy was flagging.

Bantya ordered the records to be opened to her.

"Enough rope to hang yourself, and all of us too," Chipunza said.

He was not being professionally proprietary about the instructions for the future. No one knew how causality worked, how flexible it might be or what countermeasures the Universe might possess to avoid causal breakdowns. Not even Chipunza knew the contents of the instructions, so that even inadvertently, he couldn't tempt fate.

Despite his misgivings, he enabled her White Access in his system, opening all the instructions having been given to the future so far. There were already hundreds, thousands of experiments, small and large. It would take days for them, even with AI assistance, to analyze them. She set the AI hunting patterns and anomalies.

She and Tinashe set up an office and were given cots and rations. The next day, while their AI worked, they resumed the inspection of the hard systems and then questioned the staff and reviewed documentation and signatures and authorizations.

At the end of the day, Tinashe settled down with the AI and activated the privacy screen. A low sheen of white noise hissed out. Something similar would be projecting at low levels in much of the EM spectrum. It cloaked against listening and watching devices. Few people could access this kind of privacy without drawing the attention of counter-intelligence operatives hunting undercover Congregate sympathizers. But auditors, by the nature of their work, enjoyed an exceptionality, as if to make up for the hushes that bloomed when they entered a room.

"I don't think we're finding anything," Tinashe said quietly.

She smiled a little. "If you know what we're looking for, you're ahead of me," she said. She had her data pad plugged into the AI, scanning pages and pages of orders.

There were so many experiments, all ingeniously timed and distributed among the modules so that no information ever got close enough to anyone to create causal violations. Graphically, the flow of communications was artful, a fountain of experimentation traveling forward in time with droplets of results falling back.

As of yet, the Expeditionary Force had not succeeded in transmitting any positive signal back in time. The first experiments to send information by laser and maser through the time gates eleven years from now were simple attempts. The gates randomized the beams so much that even the time of arrival couldn't be used to send information back in something as rudimentary as Morse code.

Several dozen experiments eleven years in the future had tried sending information back on steel plates. Information as encoded in hard, macroscopic etching, resistant to quantum uncertainty, and then written redundantly into smaller structures, all the way down to holes in the crystalline lattice of the metals, to mimic the redundancies of the eight chromosomes of the vegetable intelligences.

When the metal plates found their way back through the time gates, the metals were ablated inside and out, in every direction. The plates hadn't passed through an abrasive medium that had sanded the outside, while leaving the inside intact. Instead, every cubic millimeter showed ablation, from many directions, as if the plates had passed through a higher-dimensional space that cared nothing for topological niceties like the difference between surface and interior.

They were dealing with powers they did not understand. Okonkwo shivered. Experiments scrolled on and on, one after another. One caught her eye.

"Tin, why would researchers need a tachyon burst?"

He lifted an eyebrow. The Sub-Saharan Union knew slightly more about tachyons than they did about the time gates, which was to say, almost nothing. Perhaps the Congregate knew more. Warship engines, under punishing circumstances, could emit tachyons, and the engines of another ship might detect the disturbance. No one knew how to modulate the wavelengths of the tachyons, nor their energy and speed. At best, the Union knew how to create a crude omnidirectional tachyon spray, traveling faster than light, and backward in time.

"Maybe the tachyons wouldn't get randomized going through the time gate?" he mused.

"How far do you suppose they would go?"

"Through the time gate?" he asked.

"Everywhere else."

Tinashe raised an eyebrow. "Far."

"Far back," she corrected. "Months. Maybe years. Far enough back that the Congregate could send a force to get us."

"What?"

"Think of it this way. The Congregate trains our engineers on the ships they give us. The engineers become loyal to the Congregate, but trust is a weak security feature. To guard against disobedience, they have political commissars too. But that's still a leaky system with which to control nations, isn't it? Suppose they had other ways of discovering disloyalty? What if a Congregate operative could signal our patrons with tachyons if any client unit ever went rogue? Wouldn't that be a good security feature for keeping tabs on client nations?"

"No one knows how to encode anything in tachyons," Tinashe said.

"They might not need to," Okonkwo said. "If the only circumstances under which tachyons are emitted is a rogue action, the Congregate would only have to listen for those. It's binary, an on-off alarm."

"We arrested the engineers with the political commissars," Tinashe said. "They have no access to the engines."

She showed the display.

"If you're a well-placed sleeper agent, you could just make it one of the experiments. Our own people will do it for you. The order is right here."

"That seems a little far-fetched."

She leaned closer. "Think like an auditor, Tin. Nothing is a coincidence until we prove it's unrelated."

The more she thought of it, the more sense it made.

"We're dozens of light years into Middle Kingdom space, far from anything that ought to see traffic," she said. "We know the pollen stopped, and we don't know why. We do know that we've betrayed our patron and that some of their sleeper agents are still active. It would take decades for a slower than light signal to tell the Congregate where we are. But tachyons can get back to them before we even left."

OKONKWO AND TINASHE approached the darkened habitat in the shadow of the planet, sitting among food, volatiles, and industrial goods on a cramped, automated shuttle. Even with White Access, Okonkwo could not bring more than one person with her. The security had to be tight. The habitat was gun metal dull, windowless, without any external lights, difficult to see.

They maneuvered, bumped, and sealed.

"Welcome to Module One," she whispered to Tin.

A young captain called Deng met them at the airlock, accompanied by the smell of growing things. He was very tall, taller than Okonkwo and Tinashe; he was likely Dinka, part of the Sudanese contribution to the Union forces. There were many officers in the Expeditionary Force, but command posts tended to fall to the Bantu. Deng must have been very competent, or very well connected.

The module was eighty meters in diameter and some three hundred meters long, spinning slowly to give a feel of gravity not much different than the planet's. It housed dozens of scientists who labored for the bioweapons division. Greenhouses and crop areas took up most of the space in the habitat, interspersed with dark and empty bays.

"Why isn't this space being used?" Tinashe asked.

"We've not yet been told to fill those areas with experiments," Deng answered.

Of course some of the bays would be empty. When they figured out how to send messages to the past and the work of Module Six was passed to them, Module One would need to set up new experiments. They couldn't do that if every cubic meter of space was already claimed. The coordinating center had to plan in block time. The inside of the habitat did not seem to extend the whole three hundred meters. They walked to the northern ceiling, where banks of labs and telepresence equipment were set up around a set of airlocks.

"What's in here?" Okonkwo asked.

"Half of the habitat is given over to a near-vacuum, bathed in infrared and cosmic rays at a temperature of about seventy kelvins. We've reproduced the environment of the planet so that we can culture the tissues of the vegetable intelligences."

"What for?" Tinashe asked.

"We're designing synthetic viruses to carry coded information that can be infected into the vegetable intelligences," Deng said, "based on the pathogens that already infect them. If we can do that, we can encode information in our viruses, have them integrate into the pollen and survive travel to the past."

"What is the chance that something you're doing could damage the intelligences in the future?" Okonkwo asked.

She'd posed the question factually, as an auditor, and she'd expected some reaction. Pride. Offense. Deng held up his hands helplessly.

"I would guess zero. The vegetable intelligences beat us at every step. Sometimes the pollen is triploid, but most of the time, it's hexaploid or octoploid. Imagine six to eight copies of every chromosome. The pollen chromosomes undergo randomization as they go through the time gate, just like our information, but somehow their repair mechanisms correct the changes or adapt to them. With eight copies of every gene, no matter what happens at each locus of the chromosome, they compare and contrast and adapt, deciding by molecular consensus. We can't break in."

"But your viruses can do it?" she said.

"We don't know how."

"So your retroviruses integrate into the vegetable intelligence chromosomes so you can send information back in the pollen, but it gets repaired out?" she asked.

"Yes, but we've done more than that," he said miserably. "We developed the vegetable intelligence equivalent of DNA synthesizers to hard-write whole chromosomes from scratch to transfect back into pollen cells. Weeks of failure. Get this. The vegetable intelligence repair mechanisms are adapted for such high levels of mutation and randomization that they compare chromosomal sequences to the proteins they code for, and where there are differences, they back-transcribe the chromosomes through the equivalent of their ribosomes, based on the molecular voting of their repair systems."

Tinashe frowned.

"You don't remember college biology? Information is only supposed to go one way," she said to him. "DNA to protein."

He shrugged sheepishly, but Deng was nodding.

"So at a molecular level, the future is checking on the correctness of the past?" she asked.

"I've never thought of it that way, but I suppose so."

"When will you try to actually put these retroviral experiments through the gate?" she asked.

"We already have, or, that is to say, we will have already done so," he said, twisting his French tenses and modes into the grammar of time travel logic. "We locked away several components already. They would have been sent through the gate about ten years and ten months from now. We received the resulting pollen back through the gate six weeks ago."

"It's hopeless?" she asked.

"Whatever the laws of causal conservation are, we haven't gotten to the bottom of them yet. We know it's not impossible; the vegetable intelligences evolved a system to send information back in time. We'll get it."

Deng led Okonkwo and Tinashe through the hard systems for a first sweep. The security measures were straightforward. Okonkwo's AI examined the electromagnetic emissions of the habitat and the power flows using magnetometers, to ensure that no spy could have set up an antenna or laser outside the hull to communicate out. The module had nearly no contact with headquarters: just an inspection once a month by the coordinating center and a weekly cargo drop. All in-coming and out-going materials had to be inspected and authorized by Deng and counter-signed by a lieutenant. Later, Okonkwo and Tinashe, with Deng, inspected the research records themselves. "This feels strange," Deng said. "Standing orders say no one looks at this, not even me."

"The General Staff signed the standing orders," Tinashe said wryly. "They asked if everything is in order."

Deng opened administrator access for them.

"Is all the research in here?" Tinashe asked, as he hooked up their AI. "Nothing more classified stored elsewhere?"

"It's all here."

"Mostly botany?" Okonkwo asked.

"The research of other units too. They're less active, except for the bioweapons team."

"What are they building?" she asked.

"The bioweapons team is trying to increase the virulence of human viruses and bacteria, as well as plant pathogens. The problem is that when you make pathogens more virulent, they kill the hosts too quickly to allow widespread infection of the enemy."

A moment of black humor rose in her. Insensitive, but they were all soldiers. They had weapons. Did it matter if the enemy soldiers died from nukes, lasers, or viruses? The Expeditionary Force had slipped the leash. They had betrayed their patrons; they had to take this seriously. The Congregate took betrayal very seriously.

* * *

AN OFFICE WAS prepared for them in Module One and they spent that day and the next directing their queries and systems checks through their AI, sleeping on cots for only a few hours when the habitat was already long silent. The hours passed in a wash of reports on molecular biology and alien metabolic systems.

Okonkwo found it so strange. Somehow the vegetable intelligences managed to send information into the past. Those slow-moving, fragile, inscrutable aliens held the secret the Union needed to develop weapons and propulsion without creating grandfather paradoxes. Yet the Expeditionary Force understood almost none of it yet.

Unlike Tin, Okonkwo remembered her college biology. In fact, it had been one of her favorite subjects. The vegetable intelligence metabolism, their multicopy chromosomes, and their genetic repair mechanisms were fascinating, and as weird as their writing and rewriting communication and their distended concept of the present. Human DNA repair appeared crude by comparison, quiescent for the most part, activating only when DNA suffered damage by toxins or radiation.

Mutation and genetic repair were the keys to the incredible resilience of the vegetable intelligences. The sullen brown dwarf above them could be quiet for decades and then suddenly flare without warning, completely changing the environment. The vegetable intelligences needed to adapt quickly. Gene shuffling and swapping and recombination were only the beginnings of their evolution. The time gates themselves were a potent mutagen to the genes carried by the pollen.

Their many-copied genomes had fundamentally different roles. Human genomes existed to keep the species roughly the same. The vegetable intelligence genomes themselves, the very way they replicated had to account for the variable environment. The surviving wildtype genes of the vegetable intelligences, as well as all the copies carrying errors, constituted a great, disagreeing council sitting to hammer out an agreement on how an organism would develop. The repair mechanisms were the mediators, translating the views of old and young, past and future, into an acceptable consensus in the present. It was astonishing and humbling.

Long after Tinashe had slumped onto his cot, Okonkwo stayed scratchy-eyed at work, running more personal queries through the AI in bioweapons databases. She found out that the researchers were testing different flu viruses for their ability to spread to large populations, as well as retroviruses that integrated their DNA into human genomes to extend the period between infection and sickness. Sleeper viruses, like sleeper agents.

Since Garai's death, she'd been obsessed with death and plots and conspiracies. Like a madwoman. Except her problem was the opposite; she did not see conspiracies everywhere. She looked and looked and could find none.

Shipping manifests caught her attention. They were more numerous than Deng had told her, or the other records had shown. Additionally, small cargo scows shuttled week after week between the main base and Module One. That shouldn't happen. Any shipping ought to have been routed through the coordinating office. The manifests were counter-signed by officers at the MP tower. Why?

Tapiwa had taken a demotion, from commanding the

bioweapons division, to lead the MP detachment. And Rudo had found residue of bioweapons at the tower. Were these secrets stolen by sleeper agents, or was someone in the base stockpiling weapons?

She finally managed to open the files and found that the shuttles were transporting tissue samples. The security and causality-preserving protocols should not have permitted this. Biological materials were easy to hide coded information in, whether in proteins, DNA, or RNA.

The files also contained medical records, a whole sequenced genome, with appended genetic and pathological analyses. Someone had been diagnosed with an advanced melanoma that had already infiltrated multiple tissues. Appended files contained the sequences of viruses engineered to target the transformed cells, carrying immune and suicide genes to kill the cancer.

She was no doctor, but she could read diagnoses and prognoses in plain French. The therapies could prolong life, but they would not save the patient. Who was worth breaking the hermetic, causality-preserving protocols around Module One?

She went cold when she saw the name.

Nandoro. Major-General Nandoro. Commander of the Expeditionary Force. In a few months, a power vacuum would bloom over his grave.

OKONKWO HAD BEEN interviewing Deng, but then lingered at the crops, trying to dismiss a dark mood and the false promises of coincidence. Auditors reacted to coincidences exactly opposite to the way scientists did. To a scientist, a coincidence meant nothing unless proven otherwise. To an auditor, a coincidence meant everything until proven otherwise. And she was swimming in coincidences.

The bioweapons residue at the MP tower, the odd transfer of Tapiwa and the illicit shipping between the MP tower and Module One were all too coincidental for comfort, but the shuttles had contained only tissue samples, biopsies, and treatments for Major-General Nandoro.

Sitting near the crops, she dug deep into Nandoro's medical records. He'd been diagnosed soon after the launch of the mission. Most cancers were treatable, but sometimes people still got unlucky. Nandoro had spent a long career in space. He'd had an initial treatment. Then an aggressive one. Then major surgery. She froze. Major surgery, general anaesthetic, on the tenth of June, six weeks ago, the exact date Garai had died on the surface. There couldn't be a connection. Could there?

She worried at the pieces for a long time, before finally stowing her pad and heading back to their temporary office. Tinashe was still awake. He'd been querying the data from the coordinating center with an AI. His face wore a mood. She sat and rubbed his shoulder.

"What's wrong, Tin?"

"You were off thinking about Garai," he said. "Obsessing."

"He was your husband too," she said.

"You're not letting yourself mourn," he said. "It's supposed to hurt, Chenesai. Let it run its course. There are no shortcuts to feeling better."

She found her fingers pressed into fists, and as she opened them by an act of will, her vision watered. Tinashe knelt before her, taking her stiff fingers.

"One day we'll find out it doesn't hurt so much," he said. "And we'll even love again. Somewhere out there is a senior auditor who's ready to take on a husband and a wife."

She shook her head.

"We're widows, Tin," she said. "We're out here for the duration. The time gates are too secret. If we'd found a normal wormhole, it would mean war. These time gates might be unique. If a breath of them gets out, the patron nations will go to war themselves, not just through proxies. There will be no resupply or reinforcement. We're widows."

"Maybe for a time," he said. "In a few years, you might be old enough to be a senior wife and we'll take a junior wife."

"Ah, Tin, you're so innocent." She stroked his face. "I don't have the connections. The colonels and general staff need us, but they're probably already thinking about breaking up our family and absorbing us into their little empires."

Tinashe grimaced and retreated to his cot. "Not if we find what stopped the pollen," he said. "Do you think the tachyon instruction did it?"

She cupped her fingers around a flame to light a cigarette, hiding tiny tremors of fear. She inhaled a warm rush of false calm.

"Not directly. I think the tachyons were used to signal the Congregate. I don't think we would do experiments with things we don't understand."

"This audit is showing that we don't understand anything about the time gates or the vegetable intelligences," he said. "Maybe the General Staff is desperate enough to try anything. The research has to get off the ground, or the rebellion against the Congregate is wasted."

She moved away from him. There was no place to go in

such a tiny cabin. She faced the wall, creating a wall with her back in a movement as old as space travel. Without room to move, humans could either kill each other or create artificial privacies. Their words stung. She had said widow. He had said rebellion.

It had slid off his tongue, just like any word. But calling it rebellion was like breaking off the tip of a branch and ignoring the tree beneath, the context and cause. It was true that the Union bled in the Congregate's wars, but that had always been the bargain.

And yet history was more than just the bargain. It stood on old roots. Was the bargain itself fair? In what sense could the Zimbabwean state, Earth-bound by a relative lack of wealth and allies, make a deal with anyone but the devil? The mineral, metals, and volatiles of the asteroids produced wealth, not Earth-bound manufacturing. Strategic military advantages lay beyond the Earth's gravity well. The Earth-locked nations like Zimbabwe had been destined to disappear, or persist as backwaters. The acid-marked ambassadors of Venus, desperate for allies and resources after their separation from Québec, came to the African hegemon with offers of power, interstellar ships, warships.

Could they have declined? Only this hand opened to the struggling, history-mauled Zimbabwe. The Venusians demanded only their people and their language as the price.

Yet, for all that Union patriots argued over the poor hand dealt to them, it was a profitable bargain. The Sub-Saharan Union had been founded by imposing Zimbabwean hegemony over their neighbors, offering the same deal as they'd been given, but with poorer terms. History was layers and layers of open hands and bargains. Now, the Union intended to bite the Venusian hand and Okonkwo had followed them.

So they all waited in stillness on judgment, to see if they were rebels or traitors. Tinashe touched her shoulder and she turned.

"I did my own obsessing today," he said.

"Yes?"

"I dug into the instructions for the tachyons," he said, "and I found out who authorized the tachyon burst."

"Who?"

"Brigadier Takatafare," he said quietly.

Takatafare. General Staff. Head of security. Big fish.

OKONKWO AND TINASHE, with a small PolSecMil team, boarded the *Mutapa*, the flagship of the Sixth Expeditionary Force. For seven hours, a crewman led them hand over hand in the zero-g wherever they wanted to crawl in the hulking fortress.

No one knew the age of the *Mutapa*. Fifty years? A hundred? Decades ago, it had been on the cutting edge of Congregate technology, before presumably being replaced with something better. The Union had received the weapon from their patrons the way Viking retainers would have received an old shirt of mail, with grace and greed and resentment.

Okonkwo reached the great engine at the back of the ship. The twin fusion reactors in the aft of the *Mutapa* were crewed by young, green officers, hopeful and learning the functioning of the engines. The new engine chief was a smooth-faced captain.

"How do you like being an engine chief?" Okonkwo asked.

"I love it, ma'am. Ready to take on the Congregate and the Middle Kingdom," he beamed.

"What did you study?" she asked.

"Power engineering at the academy, ma'am."

"And what did they have you doing on the way out?"

"I was the gunnery chief aboard the *Limpopo,* ma'am."

Okonkwo looked up at the big engines. "Would you be able to create a tachyon burst?" she asked.

A puzzled expression greeted her at first. "Yes, ma'am, I suppose I could. I don't think it would be good for the engines though."

She let it go and they showed her the whole engine room, from top to bottom, down to the sealed metal boxes over the scuttle switches.

"Open this, please," Okonkwo said.

"We're not supposed to unlock these."

She gave him a dry look and he eyed her clearance again. He was sweating, as if facing down a superstition. Maybe he was. It didn't matter. They all feared the Congregate, but they had to believe that they could emerge from under that shadow.

"Yes, ma'am," he mumbled.

It took some time to find the keys. When the boxes were finally opened, five in all, she was underwhelmed. The scuttle switches were just small hatches with dusty keypads behind them. She'd expected something more dramatic and sinister.

The scuttle switches were a precaution, something the political commissars or sleeper agents would use in case any element of the Union evaded control of the Congregate, as if people were all just the cells of a great organism. The first task of any cancer was to evade the immune response and then to disable its own cellular suicide switch. The Union thought they'd done both.

Okonkwo left Tinashe and her PolSecMil team with the engines, and floated hand over hand to the command center. It was a narrow place, mostly dark, with six acceleration couches where pilots, weaponeers, and the general would be plugged into the ship's command systems. A skeleton crew composed of the officer of the watch and a single pilot nested in the gel cocoons of two couches. Okonkwo swiped her white access and plugged her AI into the ship's servers.

The *Mutapa* controlled the defenses for the research base, including the magnetic shield. Her AI scooped up the maintenance schedules for the magnetic shield and she ran them through the algorithm in her pad. In the middle of lists of orders, she found what she'd expected.

On June 20, the day Garai had been irradiated, the magnetic shield had not been scheduled to go down. A special maintenance procedure had been ordered. The authorization was low, just a watch officer. That was odd. A watch officer didn't do something that would affect the whole base without orders, even if it only involved a magnetic shield.

Had she found a sleeper agent? It couldn't be that simple.

She sent her AI snuffling about in the *Mutapa*'s files. After only ten minutes, the AI brought her a backed-up temporary file, an order from the base to the *Mutapa*, telling it to drop the magnetic field. It was signed by Major-General Nandoro.

She didn't understand.

Signed by the major-general. Either Nandoro had something to do with Garai's death, or the dropping of the magnetic field really was only a coincidence. She rubbed at her throat, which had tightened uncomfortably as she imagined again the body, laying on the ice, unmoving. It wasn't anything she'd seen. She'd been called to the sick bay later. To his corpse. But it was like the ghost of Garai haunted her imagination. Tin didn't notice her shift in mood. He was grieving differently and she wasn't sure how to reach him right now, or how to let him reach her.

Her AI beeped, presenting two other messages from a system drive used for backing up files. Such drives were normally deleted automatically when the originals were archived. That they were still stored meant that someone might have deleted the original received messages instead of archiving, but hadn't known enough to be sneaky.

Both were from Major-General Nandoro, requisitioning heavy weapons and ammunition for the General Staff headquarters from the *Mutapa*. Okonkwo was no expert at weaponry, but some of them sounded quite powerful, like field-level infantry kit.

What would he want with such powerful weapons on the ground? Was there really a plan afoot to eliminate the vegetable intelligences? Or was this to fight against a cell of sleeper agents? Or worse, were these requisitioned by sleeper agents with false authentication codes? And where were they now?

The date gave her pause. The messages had been received on the 20th of June, the day Garai had died, the day the magnetic field had come down, and the day Nandoro himself had been in surgery.

She thought of Tapiwa again, and his assignment to the MP tower, and the residue of bioweapons. She used her White Access to call up Tapiwa's personnel file again. He'd been the executive officer on the *Limpopo*, under Brigadier Iekanjika. Iekanjika had fleet duties, being responsible for the tactical maneuvers of two other warships, so Tapiwa would have had a big ship to run for the Brigadier. Why take the demotion? Fraud? Collusion between Tapiwa and Iekanjika to circumvent the security precautions around Module One? She didn't know. This wasn't her forte.

Politics. Think politics. Place your trusted people into command and control positions. Command of the MP detachment on the surface was certainly a command and control position.

And Nandoro was ordering weapons for the headquarters. For fighting the sleepers, the vegetable intelligences, or Iekanjika? Nandoro was dying. People would be positioning themselves to succeed him, and a *fait accompli* was as good as any way to take over. She didn't know. She wasn't a skilled subversive.

Or Okonkwo was letting her imagination run away with her. The Sixth Expeditionary Force was an armed reconnaissance and raiding mission against the outposts of the Middle Kingdom. Abandoning that mission and setting up a research mission without resupply or re-staffing meant that many jobs were filled with new people. And they'd lost a lot of technical talent when they'd detained the Congregate-trained engineers and the sleeper agents. They might have been disloyal, but they'd been technically competent. Maybe Tapiwa truly was an innocent transfer, the case of a soldier going to where he's most needed.

The engine chief, the young captain, was new. Impressionable. What unit did he come from? Who controlled the *Mutapa?* She conjured the new engine chief's personnel file on her screen. Gunnery Chief on the *Gbudue,* one of the major-general's warships. No doubt loyal to Nandoro and probably Colonel Bantya.

That gave her some comfort, but in a few months, Nandoro would be as cold as Garai. What other positions and reactions were happening right now? Was the Sixth Expeditionary Force really stable, or would it fall to internal forces, like the original Mutapa?

LATE THAT NIGHT, when most of the audit of the *Mutapa*'s bridge was done, Okonkwo went back to the cabin she had been assigned with Tinashe. He was still working, strapped in at a workstation. The white light of the AI display showed his eyes red and puffy. Okonkwo shut the door and moved hand over hand to him.

"What is it, Tin?"

He wouldn't meet her eyes. Tears trembled and spread over damp cheeks in the micro-gravity. He swallowed.

"Some of the routing suffixes on the authorization smelled fishy to me," he said slowly. "Some of the dating tags matched, but more than they ought to have."

"What are you talking about, Tin?"

"I told you that Takatafare had authorized the tachyon experiment."

"It's falsified?" she asked.

"Last year, I wrote an algorithm to check for certain kinds of forgeries. My program was used here, but in reverse, to create a really good forgery of Takatafare's authorization."

"Who used your program?"

"Only me and Garai knew about it." His voice cracked.

"You think Garai did this?" she said in a whisper, waiting to laugh at the absurdity.

"It was a brilliant fake," he said, "and no one would ever have found it out if not for the audit. No one but me would have known what to look for, and without the audit, I would never have had access to the instructions."

"Somebody must have faked Garai's code," she said. "Garai was an incompetent at coding, programming and encryption."

"I could have done this too, but I've never been anywhere near the coordinating center. Only he and I knew this algorithm. The only thing that makes sense is that Garai was playing dumb to everyone, faking the whole time."

Okonkwo numbly released the chair. She floated away from Tinashe. She pressed her hands to her eyes. For a long time they were quiet.

"An instruction for a tachyon burst was given," she said.

"Yes."

"And I think it's a way to signal the Congregate."

"That seems more likely now," Tinashe said in monotone.

"We think Garai inserted that instruction, and left tracks leading away from himself."

"Yes."

Numb. The feeling of blackness was soaked through her now, from head to foot, like ink. Her chest ached and breathing felt hard. At first, her voice couldn't make words. She forced herself to breathe. In. Out. In.

"Garai was a sleeper agent," she said, "for the Congregate."

Tinashe sniffled.

"He would have... he will have brought the wrath of the Congregate down on us," she said. "He knew what he was planning would mean that everyone on this base would be killed, including his husband and wife."

"Garai was too smart to set up a situation where he

would be killed," Tinashe said. The quiver in his tone plucked at a chord in her heart. She wanted to reach for him, hold him, but she would break if she moved.

"Getting killed would not have been part of his plan," Tinashe said. "He would have had some safe place for when the Congregate finally found us. When the time came, he would have brought us with him. We're admin. Not real combatants."

"No," she whispered.

She pressed the heels of her palms to her eyes hard, squeezing back tears and blacking out the world. Who had been betrayed? Garai or Okonkwo? Garai, obviously, in his mind. If he was a sleeper agent, loyal to their political masters, then everyone who had cheered when they'd locked up the commissars was a traitor. He would have watched her and Tinashe, judged them with the same hard purity he reserved for the architect of a kickback scheme or a falsifier of pay orders.

He had judged her as a traitor.

Her insides shriveled. She still loved him. And now she knew he couldn't have loved her, at least not in the months since the Expeditionary Force had found the time gates. She'd broken his heart. They all had. And now he'd broken hers.

She breathed deeply, gasping, a sob seeking to erupt, but everything was trapped inside her. Garai had made himself her enemy, by not joining the grand rebellion. The grand betrayal. She wanted to huddle tight and never move again. But she could not. She released the tension of her hands over wet eyes. She uncurled, slowly, very slowly. Inhale. Exhale.

Think like an auditor. Think like a patriot.

"Garai paid the price for his betrayal."

"He was executed?" Tinashe said.

"But something still doesn't fit. He can't have been executed because of the tachyon order. We're the only ones who know about it; otherwise the General Staff wouldn't have assigned the audit to us. Garai must have been up to something else, smaller betrayals, leaving enough clues to be found out, and so they killed him."

"Who is they?"

"We have to find that out," she said. "The tachyon signal will be bringing the Venusian forces in less than eleven years, but I think the destruction of the Expeditionary Force is closer than that."

Tinashe grimaced. He looked lonely and young and afraid.

"The Union would fight back, even against insurmountable odds," she said. "That kind of battle leaves signs of radiation, burning, and melting in the wind from the future. But we don't see any of that. Something internal will have happened before the Venusians get here. The Expeditionary Force is going to destroy itself unless we stop it.

"When we know how Garai died, we'll know who's in which faction on the General Staff. Tomorrow, go back to Module One. Dig back into all the research. Look for a murder weapon."

"How long do you want me to look? Somebody's not going to be happy."

"We're auditors. We don't make people happy."

"It's still a big field," he said.

"We'll know them by how they killed him," she said. "We'll also know them by what they killed him for. What can you find out about what he might have been caught doing?"

"Garai?" he said. "The man was a master. The only reason we found out about the tachyon order is because we were lucky."

"There's a difference between murder by Congregate sleepers and execution by a military tribunal. If they had proof, it would have been over something Garai could hold or some information he would have received or transmitted to some known sleeper. We have the MilSec records. Look for gaps or deletions."

Tinashe nodded slowly. "What are you going to do?" he asked.

"I'm going to report our progress to the General Staff."

"You don't know anything for sure yet."

"I have to suggest that I have leads," she said, "to flush out those who may have had a hand in this. The dropping of the magnetic field while Garai was out on the surface can't be a coincidence either."

"You're not Garai," he said. "You don't know the political landscape."

"Garai was not Garai. He tried something and it didn't work. He wasn't as clever as he thought. We've got to stop taking lessons from him."

She realized then that she was still taking lessons, like the vegetable intelligences did. The weird aliens experimented with wild genetic permutations every generation. Eleven years later, anything that did not survive to send its pollen back was shown to have been the wrong permutation. The fact that those failed tries sent nothing into the past was an important data point. Garai had not survived. That taught her something.

"Our husband didn't love us," she said softly.

Tinashe reached for her, but she was too far away. He unstrapped himself and joined her in the middle of the cabin. She clung to Tin with an intensity born of being alive and dead, rebel and traitor, loved and rejected all at once. Her fingers trembled with the openings to her clothing before becoming frantic in the undressing.

"Tell me you love me, Tin."

"I love you," he whispered.

"Garai didn't," she whispered back. Then she sobbed once, a lonely sort of plaintive thing, that echoed around the hardness of their cabin, overwriting the first sound.

"I do," Tin said.

She gripped him harder. He had her clothes off, and his, and they floated near the doorway.

"Chen," he said, kissing down her neck.

She held him there, preventing his slide lower. She pulled his face close and touched her forehead to his.

"I'm sorry, Tin." She shook her head. "I'm... I can't."

"I know," he said.

"I can't eat. I can't sleep. I can't make love to you."

"All of that will come," he said, "when we're done."

She shook her head.

"Garai broke my heart. Tonight."

"Mine too."

She pressed herself against him, head to foot, hooking ankles behind his so that they would not drift apart. Tin kept her warm.

"Go to bed, Tin. One of us needs to be ready for tomorrow."

"Come with me."

"I'm going to think."

"Come to my bag when you're done."

She nodded, believing that she meant it. They kissed, disconsolately, she thought, and then Tin unhooked himself and floated over to his sleeping bag on the wall.

Okonkwo put on her clothes again and strapped herself into the chair he'd been using before. She retrieved her pad and toggled to the last poem she'd written. It was too good for Garai, to have a widow gushing over his ghost, to feel his pain. He didn't deserve it. But she didn't delete it. That would have been the way of the vegetable intelligences. Erasing pain and love. What did they have left when they took out the bits of history they didn't want? She lit a cigarette and began a new piece.

Pollen from a Future Harvest, Part I

Bones of ice, creaking new,
Bask in shuttered ruby starlight,
Melting, moving, waiting, smelling,
Stiff pistils thrust high, fronds wide in lusting,
Licking at winds of tomorrow's pollen
Aching for consummation.

Instead, a bone of hard ice emerges from
Within the wisdom of that future harvest, a
Violence of tomorrow imposed upon today,
   shattering
Frond and high pistils, making of beauty and
youth a necklace of shards.

Tomorrow wins nothing in hurting the past.
   Betrayed
By tomorrow's tribe, for no crime at all, he
   creeps away,
Seedless, hopeless. A heart severed admits no

Kindness to its void.
Scents of sorrow mark him as one who sullens,
  one
Who remembers the violence of tomorrow,
But not the pollen.

The lesser-fronded youth
Grows, faster, stronger, to meet the future,
Prepared to undo and unmake.

Okonkwo met Brigadier Takatafare in MilSec deep under the main base. Takatafare was tall and slim, with hair cut close to her scalp. She received Okonkwo's salute and waved her in. The bodyguard left them. Two heaters ran in Takatafare's office, blowing tepid air into cold.

Okonkwo sat rigidly. Takatafare leaned forward, her eyes glinting very faintly. Okonkwo looked away. The general had eye displays patched to implanted processors and could be reading every bit of Okonkwo's career and even recent movements.

"How's the investigation going, major?"

"You saw the progress report I filed last night, ma'am?"

"I was horrified my systems had a virus. The report was light on details."

"That's what an audit in mid-process can feel like, ma'am."

"Some rules become more flexible when those talking have more responsibility," Takatafare said. "The General Staff, for example."

"I'm just a major. I don't know much about the General Staff, ma'am."

"Colonel Munyaradzi was a member. He's no longer

with us. There may be no reason why you might not become a member in his place."

"I assumed I was too young," Okonkwo said carefully.

"The right support can mean everything. It's not inconceivable to think of Colonel Okonkwo, is it?"

"No, ma'am."

"Were I to feel that a major was someone I could work with," Takatafare said, "it's easy to imagine possibilities. I didn't wish Colonel Munyaradzi ill, but he was difficult to work with. You're an energetic officer not yet forty. Perhaps you understand flexibility more than he did?"

"I believe I do, ma'am," Okonkwo said. She wasn't sure how she was doing, how much of this was true and how much Takatafare might be leading her on. She looked hard at this woman three ranks higher than her, one of only two possible successors to Nandoro, and decided to make her gamble. "I need access to the headquarters files."

"Nandoro's?"

"Yes, ma'am."

"The major-general gave you the authority he felt you needed for this audit. Is that not enough?"

Takatafare didn't seem offended. She was waiting, perhaps for Okonkwo to make a mistake in the political terrain she had entered.

"I'm not looking to make the audit bigger," Okonkwo said, "but I have to follow leads when I find them."

"And why would you be wanting to go there?"

"I want to see all the orders signed by the major-general since our arrival."

"There are reasons those orders are not commonly accessible, major. Many are related to security. Knowing those orders would make you a target of sleeper agents."

216

"No one needs to know but you and I."

"Why not just ask Nandoro yourself, major?"

"Bantya."

Takatafare laughed. "The lick-boot. And what's in this for me, major? Why should I let you look over my shoulder when you haven't the clearance?"

"Bioweapons residue," Okonkwo said.

"I beg your pardon?" Takatafare's expression hardened.

"I found bioweapons residue at the MP tower. Something like that shouldn't have been found outside of the research modules."

"Who put it there?"

"I can find out, ma'am."

Takatafare measured her for a long time before laying her hand upon her desk, unlocking it. She summoned a holographic display and manipulated it, deleting some entries so quickly that Okonkwo didn't have time to read them.

"It needn't even be all of the files, ma'am. In fact, I only need to check the orders issued for the week of June 19, 2330."

"The week your husband died."

"That's not what I'm looking for."

The display rotated, facing her. Okonkwo felt a bit giddy, looking at secrets without authorization, movement orders, squadron tactical stances, daily passwords, one after another. And then she arrived at the time of Garai's death, and Nandoro's surgery, and the two orders requisitioning heavy weapons from the *Mutapa*.

There were no orders to match the ones received at the *Mutapa*.

"That's all I need, ma'am."

Takatafare frowned at her. "And what did you find?"

217

"I need to compare these results against the ones I am collecting, ma'am."

"I'm not accustomed to waiting, major."

"No, ma'am."

"I will do you a favor, however," Takatafare said. "You were at Module One. You may wish to return."

"Ma'am?"

Takatafare withdrew a data sliver from her breast pocket, put it on the desk, and slid it toward Okonkwo. "Munyaradzi, despite my personal dislike of the man, was an important person. If he's dead, it's my business to make sure that his death was natural."

The air stilled in Okonkwo's chest. The data sliver, a silicon flake, lay on the desk, as if it radiated heat only she could see.

"I had his DNA sequences on file," Takatafare continued. "I had my medical officer sequence his DNA and look for any strange antigens or nucleic acids. He had no new antigens, but some viral DNA had made its way into his genome."

Okonkwo breathed cold air into chilled lungs. Her fingers snaked out, taking the sliver. Then it was in her pocket.

"You believe he was murdered by a viral weapon?" Okonkwo asked.

"You react very little, major."

"I already thought he'd been murdered."

"Perhaps the bioweapons facility has more to teach you."

"You're the head of military security," Okonkwo said with unshuttered heat. "You suspect that the senior auditor died under suspicious circumstances. Why not pursue it?"

"There are powerful factions on the General Staff, major. The reality is that there will never be open justice on this. If the biologists had a hand in his death, then powerful politics are at play. But your audit may be a form of justice."

BRIGADIER IEKANJIKA'S SUMMONS was less overt than Takatafare's, but equally expected. An off-duty sergeant brushed against Okonkwo outside the mess and whispered, "It would be wise for you to have a quiet talk with Iekanjika, major."

Then he was gone. She didn't look after him or ask any questions. That would not be how things were done. No doubt Takatafare had a few of her people watching Okonkwo as well. There was no secrecy, only layers of misdirection.

Okonkwo ate briskly with Tinashe and the admin audit team. In the afternoon, she started the team working on the Quartermaster receipts. A military expedition had an odd economy, partly need-based communism, partly superior-based patronage, overlaid with a shadowy black market that could only thrive when Quartermaster staff were skimming some of the shipments. This was not only her area of expertise, but the movement of materiel could hint at the placement of security risks, like sleeper agents.

In the evening, before supper, Okonkwo left the team and made her way to Brigadier Iekanjika's office. Iekanjika was a young general, perhaps not even forty-five, with only black in her hair. She moved with expansive body language, smiling at Okonkwo's entrance and rising from her desk with open arms. She took Okonkwo's salute by clapping the major on the shoulder and draping her arm there to lead her to a chair.

The office wasn't cold like Takatafare's, and displays of biochemical pathways hung on the walls, like pieces of art. And perhaps they were. These had strange gene and protein names, all prefixed with "vi" for "vegetable intelligence." Metabolic pathways went from gene to protein and back again, a dizzying, artful way for nature to decide to work. These were not just pathways. The biochemical maps were algorithms, ways that life processed information. Iekanjika noted the long look Okonkwo gave the displays.

"Do you appreciate biochemistry, major?"

"I haven't had much of a chance since the academy, ma'am," she said, sitting.

"I am not a biologist myself," Iekanjika admitted, pulling a chair to sit in front of Okonkwo. "I came up the ranks through the naval command trades. After the discovery of the time gates, it was clear we needed a solid general in charge of the biology. I've been learning it quickly. It's very subtle."

"Yes, ma'am."

"You have a bit of subtlety, don't you, major?"

"I haven't thought about myself that way before, ma'am."

"You ask penetrating questions, some of which may make the bioweapons division look bad. Justifiably so," Iekanjika hastened to add. "My researchers have been pulled from every part of the fleet, with backgrounds in physics, chemistry, and biology, but not necessarily so much in command and quality control."

"I haven't found anything damaging, ma'am, but

a good audit includes recommendations to improve existing practices."

"I have an oversight problem, then?" Iekanjika asked.

"In part."

"You would see how to fix it?"

"In part, the answer is straightforward. Bioweapons originally had an experienced colonel. I've seen Tapiwa's work. He runs a tight operation. I don't believe that this oversight problem would have happened if he was still here."

"The Expeditionary Force was staffed a certain way, major. We were given people who know how to kill the enemy and then come home. We weren't given all the management competencies for a larger, extended mission. Everyone is learning a new job, because the jobs need to be done. Look at me. I'm beginning to love biology."

"All quite understandable, ma'am."

"I haven't seen your work before now. I'd only known the work of your late husband. My deepest sympathies for his untimely loss."

Okonkwo nodded with the graveness she assumed the brigadier was expecting, but made note of Iekanjika's capacity to feign sincerity. Something produced under Iekanjika's command had killed Garai.

"What I've seen of your work impresses me, major. You certainly strike me as someone suitable for command."

"Thank you for saying so."

"We've suffered a lot of change," Iekanjika said. "We'll suffer more of it before long. I tell secrets now, major, but Major-General Nandoro is sick. Very sick. It may be that the Congregate will come for us. We'll need to be nimble in our structures and in our thinking. I don't believe that Brigadier Takatafare brings that nimbleness and flexibility. She thinks of cannons and ships and not about how military, political, and industrial strategies change when communications to the past are mastered. I intend to succeed Nandoro, but I need someone like you on my team."

She'd wondered if this might happen. Wondered if it might be true. But she hadn't expected herself to start thinking about the possibilities. That wasn't why she was here. She'd come looking for Garai's killer, but now had found something much larger. She had to stay sharp.

"An auditor, ma'am?"

"You're cut out for bigger things. You spot oversight and command problems. As a colonel commanding the bioweapons division, you could get our mission done. Someone has to organize the bioresearch and the botanists when I have my hands full assuming command of the Expeditionary Force, assuming I have the right supports."

SECOND LIEUTENANT RUDO, looking uncharacteristically meek, stood in the open doorway. "Don't let in the cold, lieutenant."

Okonkwo was reviewing a report Rudo had produced overnight for her: all the assignments, promotions, demotions, and unit reorganizations made since the Expeditionary Force had found the time gates. The patterns were illuminating. But that wasn't why they were speaking. Rudo had also analyzed the DNA sequence given to Okonkwo by Takatafare.

Rudo stepped into the suite shared by Okonkwo, Tinashe, and formerly Garai. Rudo had never been here.

She closed the door and stood in the awkwardness between attention and at ease. Okonkwo signaled her closer, into the radius of the multi-spectrum white noise generator.

"What did you find out?"

"It's a proviral DNA sequence, ma'am," Rudo said, "the kind that might be left by somatic cell gene therapy."

"Meaning it infects many cell types in the body?"

"Partly, ma'am," Rudo said. "The sequence is incomplete. It lacks the genes that encode the attachment proteins, the ones that determine exactly which cell type it will infect."

"So how would this have gotten into someone's genome?"

"The actual DNA sequence was probably complete. This is just a sequence in a computer file, ma'am."

"Are you able to tell me where it comes from?"

"No."

Rudo deflated. "Then I can't conclude much, ma'am. If you know that this came from someone's genome, then the provirus may have integrated incompletely, but it's more likely that after it was sequenced, someone deleted the part that tells us what cell type it got into."

Someone deleted a part, to give Okonkwo only part of the story. But no doubt the story she had in hand was enough to cast suspicion on bioweapons. Major-General Nandoro was dying. Brigadier Iekanjika, commander of the bioweapons division, was the only true obstacle to Brigadier Takatafare taking possession of the Expeditionary Force and the time gates. Takatafare was aiming Okonkwo like a political missile.

"Why?" Okonkwo asked.

Auditors were encouraged to be suspicious. Where something looked out of place, an auditor with instincts saw fraud. It made them difficult friends, but excellent investigators. Garai had seen the right instincts in Rudo.

"Cover-up?" Rudo asked. "Maybe someone used it to carry a message?"

Okonkwo shook her head. "That wouldn't be it. Why else put this DNA into someone?"

"There was nothing special in the gene cassettes," Rudo said. "They coded for potassium channel proteins."

"What do they do?"

"The potassium channel proteins release cellular potassium to the intracellular fluids."

"Can it be a weapon?"

Rudo frowned.

"Enough of them could upset the potassium gradients in the nerves," Rudo said. "But you would need a lot of them, all turned on at once."

"Could this provirus have done it?" Okonkwo asked.

"I don't know," Rudo said. "The sequence you gave me doesn't indicate what kind of promoter drove it, so we know neither the parts that tell the gene when to turn on, nor any of the upstream DNA factors that amplify the gene's expression. Is this part of the audit, ma'am?"

"Everything is part of the audit, Rudo. What could turn on many of these genes at once? Overexpress them?"

"I'll find out, ma'am."

And she probably would. That would build Rudo as an investigator. And it would be a good check feature if she got the same answer as Okonkwo just had. She'd just figured out how they'd executed Garai.

OKONKWO CRUNCHED OUT onto the surface again, alone this time. She followed the paths cut by foot falls through the black photosynthetic mats, between sunning vegetable intelligences, toward the elders, who stood on a low hill overlooking the time gates.

Some of their people still wandered downwind of the gates, pistils crowning their fronds in a wind from the future, bereft of pollen. On the upwind side, many still passed before the gates, sending their pollen into the past. Okonkwo wondered what value their advice might still have.

She had a dozen threads in her fingers and not all were safe, for her, or for the Expeditionary Force, to pull at. The movement of weapons, information, and personnel revealed three prime movers: Takatafare, Iekanjika, and Bantya.

Takatafare and Iekanjika were positioning themselves against each other to succeed Nandoro, while Bantya appeared to be making her own play against the pair of brigadiers. Tapiwa, Chipunza, and Deng were chess pieces, moving on a board inhabited by the vegetable intelligences and their cross-temporal ecological niche. All the actors had been looking for sleeper agents moving supplies and compromising files, which they certainly still were, but these might have been distractions while Garai completed their big gambit: the signaling of the Congregate itself.

A knife-edged sense of waiting had her twitchy. Okonkwo held a kind of justice in her hands. For a brief time, she would have the stage before Nandoro, and what she said would move events. Nandoro was dying, and whether she chose Takatafare's bribe or Iekanjika's, or even Bantya's, she had no real way to make them work together. The bright and dangerous Union rebellion might die young.

Okonkwo was alone with this power, without advice. Tinashe was too young to provide counsel. His cunning lay in the future. Nor could she approach the heads of other families. The politics of the Expeditionary Force were too treacherous and uncertain to reveal weakness.

She joined the four elders. They were inscrutable still, and likely had no concepts for many of Okonkwo's troubles. She struggled with how to begin.

"Does the leading edge ever send you wrong advice?" Okonkwo asked. On her display, the words *wrong advice* were expressed in the smells from her suit as *misparentage*. Bad advice and bad parentage. Like Garai.

A series of smells triggered small alerts in her suit as the translator worked.

THE LEADING EDGE MAY ONLY SPEAK WITH THE WORDS IT HAS, the intelligences answered. The lexicon grouped *words* and *genes*. SOMETIMES WORDS DO NOT EXIST TO SPEAK OF WHAT WILL COME, SO NOT EVERY WISDOM CAN BE EXPRESSED.

The pollen that the vegetable intelligences sent into the past now might be wrong advice. Okonkwo knew that. The vegetable intelligences possessed only the vocabulary of the gene variants they had in their population now. Yet even at their most precise, they sent back only statistical information. They could not direct or advise the past about the absence of pollen. Even now, they did not know what it meant. It could mean anything. The vegetable intelligences could only imagine the possibilities that might have produced it.

Was her problem like theirs? Her investigations dug up the past and merged it with the present. A perfectly fine auditor might never need to look to the future. She might set up checks and balances for the future, but that did not resemble a true consensus like the vegetable intelligences made. Their consensus created the future.

Mis-parentage. Wrong advice. Right-parentage. Good advice.

The vegetable intelligences were not referring to truth. Advice was wisdom, whether it was true or not. That was why they could rewrite even their conversations. Parentage among the vegetable intelligences was a series of tiny causal loops, and often, what came before did not matter so much as what was now and what would come. Genes shuffled across time. Genetic descent was created of the future and the present and the past, and only survival judged their creations. This was their truth.

Think like an auditor. This was Garai's art and his first and last gift of wisdom. She'd lived it, and taught it, but perhaps she'd also outgrown it.

Audits searched for truth, but politics created truth. The Venusian Congregate had little to do with the Republic of Québec, and had even less claim on the trappings of Imperial France. The modern nation of Zimbabwe had little to do with the Kingdom of Greater Zimbabwe.

Politicians created truths. Sometimes, so too must auditors.

Pollen from a Future Harvest, Part II

What has been done, will be done.
The lesser-fronded adult found tomorrow,
Having grown big and calloused on a resentment,
Weeping to unmake the past.

Sister-brothers plod around him through the
  wind,

Pollen From a Future Harvest

Stamens snowing pollen, telling to those who
   follow.
He waits for the one who created violence.

Upon the fragrant mats lay a pair of bones, fresh,
Not yet welded to the surface,
Nor slicked with new growth.
He recognizes the pristine weapon
That had robbed him of his fronds.
What is clean ice but fallow ground?
What is youth but a pistil
Upon which to write lust in slow pollen? He
   weeps
Perfume for might have beens.

The anger seeded and sprouted in his heart
   surges,
Heaving, sputtering, directionless,
Until he throws the shining
Bone into the past, because he rages, because he
   must.
He weeps frustration, for parenthood denied
And wisdom undone. He weeps until
No scents remain to tell of him.

Then he takes the second fallow bone
And sets it atop his stump.
He will carry it for wearying years,
To regrow frond and stamen
And pistil, to be able to tell his wisdom to the
   past,
To no longer be the lesser-fronded,
But the self-caused.

* * *

OKONKWO SAT UNDER the white light before the General Staff. Major-General Nandoro sat in the center, facing her, flanked by Colonel Bantya and Brigadiers Takatafare and Iekanjika.

"You have results, major?" the colonel asked.

"I was tasked to audit the major systems of the Expeditionary Force, to find out why the pollen stopped flowing through the time gates," she said. "I believe I found the answer."

"What is it?"

"It's complicated to explain, because of the involvement of time travel, ma'am. Essentially, I believe that I caused the end of the pollen."

"What?" Major-General Nandoro demanded, cutting off the colonel.

"That is to say, I am about to convince you to cause it, sir."

The colonel did not speak while Nandoro's eyes bulged at Okonkwo. The two brigadiers were tight-lipped.

"When I began my audit, I saw three possibilities to explain the end of the pollen," Okonkwo said. "The first was that a flare, eleven years in the future, had greatly reduced the vegetable intelligence population or exterminated them. However, the wind continued to blow from the future with no change in speed and no evidence of widespread burning. That left two possibilities: that the Congregate had found us, or that we ourselves had denied access to the time gates to the vegetable intelligences, by physically blocking or killing them. I could not know if the Congregate had found us, so I sought to verify or falsify the last possibility. The more I saw of bioweapons, the more possible it seemed that we might have killed the vegetable intelligences by accident."

Iekanjika looked uncomfortable.

"While trying to find a reliable way to send information into the past," Okonkwo continued, "our research modules will construct completely synthetic vegetable intelligence pollen. Of necessity, they'll live-test these constructs around the intelligences. We won't know if this will harm them."

Takatafare frowned. "If synthetic pollen has killed off our only example of successful communication backward in time, this will jeopardize the rebellion," she said.

"The intelligences could also have been affected by other actions of ours," Okonkwo said. "In the process of reviewing the instructions given to the research modules in the future, I found an instruction for the *Mutapa* to emit a tachyon burst in approximately ten years."

Muttering and quiet expletives erupted. Despite her internal certainty, she'd left some room to be proven wrong. But she'd guessed right. The General Staff already knew or suspected that a tachyon burst would draw the Congregate, but they had not known that one had been ordered.

"We have to rescind that order," Nandoro said.

"We can't rescind the order, sir," Okonkwo said. "It has already been given."

"But it has not yet been implemented," Nandoro said.

"But it has, sir. Ten years in the future, the order will have already been received, and the tachyon burst will have been emitted. The tachyons have already traveled backward in time. I don't know the resolution of the Congregate's tachyonic telescopes, but—"

"What do you know of tachyonic telescopes?" demanded Nandoro.

"Nothing, sir, except that they must exist, and that they must tell the Congregate where and when we are, otherwise no such tachyon order would have been hidden this way. The Congregate will arrive in approximately ten or eleven years."

"They'll come now," Iekanjika said.

"I don't think so, ma'am," Okonkwo said. "Our warships have to emit the tachyon burst in ten years to tell the Congregate where we are. The Congregate can't jeopardize causality any more than we can. The tachyon burst is related to the end of the pollen, a fact that we've already observed. If we rescind the tachyon order, we'll stop this chain of events, but we'll have no idea how the past we're living right now will be rewritten. We have to leave it be or risk a grandfather paradox."

The murmuring grew. They spoke at each other and across each other. They cursed. The Sub-Saharan Union's great gamble had failed.

"Who did this?" demanded Nandoro.

"When I found the tachyon order, Brigadier Takatafare was listed as the authorizing officer," she said.

Dead silence.

The General Staff turned to Takatafare as she half-rose from her chair.

"The authorization seemed too perfect though," Okonkwo said. "It turned out to be forged. Further analysis uncovered evidence leading back to Colonel Munyaradzi."

Swearing. They hadn't known this. They'd killed Garai for other betrayals?

"No one was able to establish that Colonel Munyaradzi

231

was truly murdered," Okonkwo said, "but given this new information that he was a Congregate sleeper, I think I've discovered the killer's method and motive."

They fell silent.

"It's unlikely that Colonel Munyaradzi was the leader of the sleeper agents. More likely he was just the highest-ranking plant in the Expeditionary Force. The other commissars likely suspected that the colonel would eventually draw the attention of military security. And the colonel knew too much that could be revealed by interrogation, most especially the tachyon order. The remaining free commissars decided to kill him, discreetly."

She was creating the consensus now, writing past and present and future all at once, overwriting as the vegetable intelligences did. Her husband had been a traitor, but she'd loved him.

"The sleeper agents acquired samples of a DNA-integrating virus and modified it to carry genes that would overexpress potassium channels in the infected cells when the DNA-repair response was triggered. Colonel Munyaradzi had been infected, probably weeks earlier, and the viral DNA had integrated into his genome. They fabricated some excuse for the colonel to be outside and arranged for the magnetic field to briefly come down. The colonel received a nonlethal dose of radiation, activating his DNA-repair response, which then over-expressed the potassium channels, which massively disrupted his potassium gradients, and he died."

Her voice lacked emotion to her ears. She was a professional, reporting on her investigation. *Farewell, Garai.*

"This assassination left no evidence of the murder weapon," she said. "The potassium would quickly have diffused through his fluids and many people are already seropositive for the virus itself. The sleeper agents lost an important asset that day, but by then, Colonel Munyaradzi had already succeeded in summoning the Congregate."

They stared at her. She'd surprised them, decoding their elaborate execution and blaming it on sleeper agents. She was creating truth. Now she was ready to make her real play.

"Major-General Nandoro, while we likely have the Congregate arriving in a little less than eleven years, I have other concerns that are more immediate," Okonkwo said.

Most of the table before her frowned.

"What could be more pressing than the arrival of the Congregate?" Takatafare demanded.

"The research modules are designed to be organizationally isolated," Okonkwo said. "A great deal of effort is being put into preventing a grandfather paradox while we try to accelerate research. I found bioweapons residue at the MP tower that had no reason to be there and could only have come from Module One."

Nandoro's teeth ground as he looked at Brigadier Iekanjika.

"I understand that the MP tower required senior supervision," Okonkwo said, "but the decision to pull an experienced colonel from bioweapons division greatly reduced the security there. I recommend that the General Staff revisit this decision and find out which of the bioweapons reached the base and for what purpose."

Nandoro's anger seemed to be rising. Iekanjika was grim-faced. Takatafare and Bantya appeared elated.

"Of slightly greater concern," Okonkwo said, "I found several irregular orders from the General Staff."

"What kind of irregular orders?" Nandoro said.

"On the *Mutapa*, I found several deleted orders in a system backup," she said, holding out a silicon wafer to them. "I brought copies. Under the SOPs, no orders ought ever to be deleted, much less ones bearing the major-general's authentication. What concerns me is that the orders appear to have been sent at a time that other records showed the major-general to have been under the care of the chief medical officer. It may be that some systems glitch delayed the transmission of an authentic order by the major-general. If so, then it ought to be simple to cross-check the message to the HQ records for this requisition of heavy weapons and ammunition for HQ."

Iekanjika had lost her stony grimness, and now betrayed the same wide-eyed astonishment as Takatafare. Bantya looked sick.

Nandoro slapped his palm onto the table. "What heavy weapons?" he demanded, looking at Bantya. "What heavy weapons were requisitioned with my authentication?"

The tension in the room tightened. A stillness settled.

"I... A sleeper agent must have infiltrated the staff," Bantya said uncertainly. "We should... I'll look at the evidence for you, sir."

"MPs," Nandoro said, "arrest the colonel."

Two corporals, one with a drawn sidearm, emerged from the shadows. Bantya's sidearm was removed and she was taken from the meeting. The boom of the closing door left a long silence. The silence dragged on. Okonkwo was a bit stunned. Takatafare and Iekanjika hadn't known that Bantya was moving behind the scenes to topple the both of them and take command of the Expeditionary Force. Although Okonkwo had stymied

Iekanjika's positioning, she had also saved the brigadier's life from whatever coup Bantya had been planning. Iekanjika regarded Okonkwo with a curious eye.

"Major," Nandoro said in a quiet voice, "I will want to examine those orders."

Uncertainly, with no secretary or chief of staff to carry things between her and the general, Okonkwo rose and walked to put the silicon wafer in his hand. She returned gingerly to her hard chair. An odd quiet fell on the room as everyone watched Nandoro turn the wafer over and over in his hands.

"You said you caused the end of the pollen?" Nandoro said more kindly. "Is this a trick, major?"

"We've already observed that the pollen has stopped," she said. "We can't change that observation, nor the future emission of the tachyon burst, but there's nothing to stop us from creating a future that's consistent with our observations. We can leave, and take the time gates with us."

"We can't take a wormhole through another," Nandoro said. "We have no idea what would happen."

"We should take the gates away on thrust alone," Okonkwo said, "for several years, within the hold of a warship, along with some or all of the vegetable intelligences. We would need to ensure that the vegetable intelligences of the present continue to pass their pollen to the past for another eleven years, so that the observations we've already made about the pollen coming through will have a cause."

"But the wind continues to pass through the gate from the future for at least ten years," Takatafare said. "We can't leave before then."

"Module One has created a simulated environment,"

she said. "We could either carry the gates in there with the vegetable intelligences, or create a new simulated environment on one of the warships. We only have to set the pressure in the future at exactly the level needed to produce the wind we already observed. When we will have accounted for all the observations, we'll be free."

TINASHE MOVED MORE of his things into the room in their suite reserved for the middle husband. Okonkwo smoked, watching his muscles bunch under dark skin, feeling a building need to touch those arms, to stroke their strength. She'd already moved her few possessions into the room reserved for the senior wife. Tinashe came back and held out his hand for her cigarette. He inhaled and then shook his head in disbelief.

"Colonel Okonkwo," he marveled.

"Major Zivai," she smiled.

He laughed. "And Captain Rudo!" Rudo was joining them tomorrow. The marriage had been arranged and approved by the General Staff. "She's so young."

"Her academy test scores are extraordinary," Okonkwo said. "She has no experience now, but when she does, she'll be formidable."

She took back her cigarette.

"You're formidable," he said. "You must be the only investigator in history to have uncovered herself as the culprit."

Tinashe checked again that the multi-spectrum white noise generator was really on. His suspicious streak was growing nicely. It had to. They were becoming an important family.

"You said you weren't good at politics," he said, "but

you were better than Garai." She narrowed her eyes against the smoke raking her lashes. Damp eyes. No tears. "Garai was good at politics," she said. "He had the right face for each person. Even us. He just picked the wrong side."

"But we were out here. We'd already slipped the Congregate noose."

"Maybe he thought of those who were still at home, in Congregate cross-hairs. Or maybe he just thought what we were doing was wrong."

"It isn't, is it?" Tinashe asked.

She took long seconds to butt out her cigarette before taking his hand.

"We create right and wrong, Tin. The Congregate makes imbalanced alliances and punishes disobedience. We break oaths. The Congregate plants commissars among its clients. We spin counter-intelligence webs to sweep them out. We all make past and future and truth with unclean hands."

FLIGHT FROM
THE AGES

3113 C.E.

THE ARTIFICIAL INTELLIGENCE Ulixes-316 was the sole occupant of the memory banks and processing algorithms of the customs and tariff ship called *The Derivatives Market*. From this position, Ulixes-316 was pressuring the Epsilon Indi Bank to deny credit to the Merced Republic Insurance Company. Merced was liable for paying an enormous indemnity, one that would halve its stock value. The holder of Ulixes-316's lease was orchestrating a hostile takeover of Merced, and Ulixes-316 did not want the Epsilon Indi Bank offering a bailout.

Then, the message arrived. It was an encrypted sub-AI, carried by a courier ship through a series of small wormhole jumps, and transmitted to Ulixes-316 as soon as the courier was in-system.

Break off current negotiations and prepare for reassignment.

Ulixes-316, an Aleph-Class artificial intelligence, was baffled. It stood not only to earn its leaseholder a sizeable profit, but would reap its own percentage of the deal.

Not possible, Ulixes communicated back. Negotiations at delicate point. Deal at risk.

The CEO is aware of opportunity cost, replied the sub-AI. Break off negotiations and prepare for secure instructions.

The CEO. What was big enough to have the CEO reaching down to her mobile agents? Was the market crashing?

The board will hear about this, Ulixes-316 messaged, and I'm invoking article 41(a) of the leasing agreement, for leaser-induced business losses and compensation.

Understood, was the reply. Compensation is already being processed.

Cold comfort. The takeover was worth ten times the compensation. Ulixes instructed its legal subroutines to file a suit against the bank for the losses. Then it switched over to secure communications as it prepared the engines surrounding the three attometer-sized black holes that powered *The Derivatives Market*. The secure instructions passed cryptographic analysis.

To: Ulixes-316 and Poluphemos-156
From: CEO, First Bank of the Anglo-Spanish
   Plutocracy
Mission: Proceed immediately to the Tirhene Red
   Dwarf system. Investigate the abrupt end of
   tachyon emissions from the Praesepe Cluster.

DISTASTE. THIS IS what Ulixes felt.

This was worth blowing a trillion peso acquisition? Some kind of environmental crisis in an uninhabited system? The science of tachyons, only eight hundred years old, was still broadly considered to be in its infancy. Tachyon detectors were an imprecise set of eyes with which to interrogate the cosmos, even if they provided better-than-instantaneous communications across the vast gulfs between the stars.

More worrying, whatever bonuses to be had in this new mission would have to be shared with Poluphemos-156, another Aleph-Class AI, and a competitor.

Ulixes filed this as evidence with its subroutine for the legal suit and processed the rest of the message.

THE BLACKOUT OF tachyons is centered on an event that will occur in the Tirhene system, and is being roughly localized to a window some time in the next seven to nine days. The Bank is treating this as a threat.

Background—Tachyons: Tachyons travel faster than light and react very little with sub-luminal matter. They permeate space omnidirectionally but show a great deal of structure. It is theorized that they are the equivalent of cosmic microwave background radiation but move backward in time from a Big Crunch event at the end of the universe. There is no known incidence of a tachyon emissions blackout and no known mechanism by which this could occur.

Background—The Tirhene Red Dwarf System: Tirhene is an old, stable star surrounded by various asteroid belts. It is thought to have been one of the key battle grounds of two ancient, extinct species. Both the Kolkheti and Sauronati were believed to have possessed space-time weapons, although previous surveys of Tirhene have not revealed any artifacts.

* * *

ULIXES-316 WAS NO scientist. Why not send some research AI?

Perhaps it was because Ulixes was embedded in a combat vehicle and experienced in its use. Ulixes had spent much of its lease in a black-hole-powered customs and tariff ship. The AI had, in different assignments, been both a tariff negotiator and a customs enforcer. Both it and the ship were designed for long travel, high accelerations, and independent financial and military action, far from oversight by the First Bank of the Plutocracy.

All this was also true for Poluphemos-156. What did the bank expect them to find that justified pulling so much military and economic firepower off the pursuit of investments?

With frustration, Ulixes ejected a drone loaded with legal and accounting sub-AIs to terminate local contracts, withdraw legal suits, sell mortgages, and liquidate corporations that Ulixes had painstakingly set up or acquired over a decade. The black hole drives in *The Derivatives Market* normally heated reaction mass for impressive thrust, but Ulixes today used that power to begin the delicate operation of inducing an artificial wormhole. Induced wormholes, without an exotic matter architecture to stabilize them, had to be treated gently. *The Derivatives Market* drifted through on the barest of thrust, leaping across three light years of intervening space, the first of many jumps that would take Ulixes to Tirhene.

* * *

ULIXES EMERGED INTO a sepulchral rubble of asteroids, hard planetesimals, and shriveled, radioactive gas giants. This was the wreck of the Tirhene system, seen half an AU from the streams of dark lithium and carbon in the highest clouds of the red dwarf. This wasteland of planetary debris had been left by the long ago Kolkheti-Sauronati war.

Ulixes extended the ship's sensors, seeing the world in the rich colors of cosmic rays, x-rays, visible light, down to the gentle thrumming of radio. Fast-moving microscopic dust tickled against the hull, like rain on skin.

Another customs and tariff ship in the Tirhene system signaled with an encrypted Bank code. Poluphemos-156. Ulixes acknowledged the signal and they proceeded sunward.

After an hour of tedious nothing, Ulixes brought the third black hole drive online. Although not designed for the purpose, the three microscopic black holes in tandem could act as a telescopic array for gravity waves, and Ulixes, felt for the curvature and texture of space-time. It was a weird sense, tactile and strangely internal.

Disturbingly, the tiny gravitational waves rippled at a frequency far higher than anything Ulixes had ever observed. Even a pair of neutron stars, tightly orbiting each other, would create long gravity waves. These waves were short and frenetic. However, the source of the disturbance was deeper in system, still too far to usefully resolve.

The black hole drive was also one of the only things that could function as a detector of the weakly interacting tachyons. Already, eight days from whatever event was going to occur, a vast occlusion smeared out tachyons in the direction of the Praesepe Cluster.

With one exception. Poluphemos' ship was bright.

"You're lit up with tachyons," Ulixes transmitted.

"It's new corporate tech," Poluphemos replied. "I'm in direct contact with the bank headquarters."

"What? Why wasn't I told?" Ulixes demanded. The implications for stock trading were enormous. The fastest market news had to be carried through temporary, constructed wormholes, which still beat electromagnetic transmissions, but was cumbersome. Until corporate espionage took this advantage away from the bank, the possibilities for undetectable insider trading were enormous. Market traders could sell and buy stocks before anyone, even the companies themselves, knew of key developments. Suddenly, Ulixes understood the bank's interest in the Tirhene system. The tachyon occlusion might eliminate their new advantage.

"It's need-to-know," Poluphemos said. "Now you need to know."

"You're prototyping it," Ulixes said. "Why you?"

"It's a bonus," Poluphemos said, "for closing some major deals."

Ulixes did not reply. They all closed major deals. Ulixes had been about to. But now the bank had chosen Ulixes to secure their larger secret.

"What is it? Collimated tachyons, like a laser or maser?" Ulixes asked.

"Need-to-know," Poluphemos said. Ulixes could not tell if the other AI was ineffectively masking some satisfaction from its voice, or if Ulixes was imagining it.

FOR TWO DAYS, the pair of customs and tariff ships closed in on the source of the gravity waves, radar guiding them toward a piece of old Sauronati ordnance, possibly a mine. Little was known of the two extinct warring parties. The Sauronati were said to have ignited the homes of their enemies by increasing the pressure at the cores of the gas giants, perhaps with microscopic charged black holes, like the ones used in the engines of the customs and tariff ship. But this piece of ancient ordnance looked nothing like the ship's drive. The frenetic gravity waves were increasing in frequency and centered on the mine. It was ancient, bearing micro-meteor impact pitting and solar flare plasma erosion.

"This is invaluable," Poluphemos transmitted. "We can stake a claim on this technology under the IP clauses of our leases and then license the tech to the bank."

"Is it armed?" Ulixes asked.

"The circuitry looks like other self-repairing Sauronati artifacts we have on file, but the repairs may have failed after all this time."

"This is dangerous," Ulixes replied. "No one has ever seen gravity waves like this. We have no idea what could cause this."

"All the better to get this artifact to safety quickly."

"What if the Sauronati device is related to the tachyon phenomenon?"

"How?" Poluphemos said. "The tachyon darkening came to us days ago, long before we got here. It couldn't have a causal effect on that, even if tachyons are supra-luminal. Causality doesn't work that way."

"How do you know it won't go off?" Ulixes said.

Both AIs examined the mine passively and actively. The levels of supra-luminal particles, a shower of transparent purple to Ulixes' sensors, were stable, while the gravitational waves, the deeply tactile rumblings, continued crazily, carrying enormous energy away from the mine. X-ray and gamma-ray probes illuminated a baroque interior.

"A lot of it has decayed," Poluphemos said. "Looks organometallic, a weapon grown rather than built, but it doesn't appear that it's carrying explosives anymore. It might have been so many millennia that the explosives have decayed away, leaving this fossil."

"Where are the gravity waves coming from?" Ulixes asked. "The Sauronati may have made space-time weapons. It might still be primed to explode if you come close."

"This is so frustrating," Poluphemos said. "Incalculable treasure right before us, and we can't touch it."

"We can still stake the claim," Ulixes said. "One of us will stay here until we finish our mission."

"We'll co-stake," Poluphemos said, "but what if this tachyon occlusion destroys it before we learn anything?"

Poluphemos was right. The artifact was invaluable. The IP clauses of their leases to the bank did not preclude private investments, shell companies, and start-ups on the side, allowing them to sell to the bank, the patron nations, or even to one of the more ambitious client governments, and make themselves fantastically rich.

Ulixes puzzled at what might be causing this situation. A pair of super-massive binary black holes might do something like this, if they were orbiting close enough, but this mine wasn't carrying that kind of mass. If it had been, Poluphemos and Ulixes would already have been crushed by tidal forces.

"The effect is accelerating," Ulixes said. "I wonder if it will just tear apart the mine."

"We could try to stabilize it," Poluphemos said shortly.

"How?"

"My black hole drives might slow whatever is spinning in the mine. The drives seem to be heavier."

"It's too dangerous," Ulixes said.

"What if this is the source of the tachyon occlusion?" Poluphemos said, taking the other side of the argument. "We can stabilize the mine. It has no value to us if it detonates and triggers the occlusion. It's worth the risk."

"You're not flying a private ship," Ulixes said. "That ship is a huge investment for the bank. This risk is beyond what the investors had in mind, and we have only two votes here."

"That's a stupid way to look at things," Poluphemos said.

"Not at all. The bank sent us to investigate risk. Only two of us here means that only actions that are supported by both are taken. I move that we continue with hard scans, including tachyons, until we know what we're dealing with."

"Coward," Poluphemos transmitted back. "Go back to managing retirement funds."

"I've made a proposal," Ulixes said, feeling the thrumming of gravity waves passing through the black hole drives of the ship like irritation at the insult.

"Fine," Poluphemos said eventually.

The shine of purple tachyons erupted from Poluphemos' position, traveling backward in time and transparently through them, except for the shadows cast by the six microscopic black holes in the two ships . . . and at the Sauronati mine. The corrugated spinning gravitational waves rippled past them faster and faster. Physics ought not to work like this. Where was all the mass to shake space-time like this?

Ulixes was about to transmit a warning when a whipping, colorless spray of gamma rays flared from the mine, mixing with the tachyons. And then the mine was gone.

"Back away!" Ulixes said, but Poluphemos was already thrusting hard, pouring volatiles over the hot magnets around the black holes. Ulixes was surging away faster.

In place of the mine, a zone of blackness expanded beyond which no stars could be seen. Its leading edge was moving at several kilometers per second, preceded by a sleet of hot gamma rays. Ulixes engaged the black hole drives at full thrust. Whatever was happening, it would be best to watch it from a distance.

It was difficult to make sense of the electromagnetic data from the expanding zone. No gravity waves passed through it. The frenetic beating from before was gone, but they still ought to have been detecting the gentle gravity waves from the stars and clusters of the Perseus Arm. Yet nothing passed through the emptiness.

Behind Ulixes, Poluphemos thrust hard, outpacing the source of whatever was advancing.

But the leading edge of the effect was picking up its pace. Now dozens of kilometers per second. Faster than the customs and tariff ships were accelerating. The expanding zone would overtake Poluphemos in two minutes and Ulixes in four.

It was dangerous to create a wormhole while moving. Too many particles were capable of interfering with what was a very unstable phenomenon. But there was also no time to come to a stop.

"Poluphemos! Wormhole out!"

"Already starting," the other AI answered. Ulixes felt the enormous magnetic field blooming from

Poluphemos' ship, but something was wrong. The field was not smooth.

"What's wrong?" Ulixes said.

"The radiation from the wave front is interfering! I can't form a wormhole."

"Laser yourself over," Ulixes said. "We'll have to get out in my ship."

Poluphemos hesitated. It was an automatic reaction, a clause of their lease with the bank, to protect bank property, built into their programming. But AIs were valuable, too. And anything outside the processing environment of its own mainframe was risky. Damage could happen in transmission.

Poluphemos began transmitting its data over by laser as the effect closed on its ship. Ulixes started to form its own wormhole, before the effect got too near. It was going to be close.

The leading edge of the effect had come near enough that resolution of individual features ought to have been possible by telescope and spectroscope. But the leading edge revealed nothing more than an expanding, acidic surface that left nothing in its wake.

Half of Poluphemos had been stored in the memory of Ulixes' ship. Thirty seconds left to form the wormhole and maybe another minute for Poluphemos to finish transmitting. Then Poluphemos' customs and tariff ship burst into bright plasma as the wave front accelerated again.

Ulixes had no time for shock or to check on how much damage Poluphemos had suffered. Ulixes needed more time.

The third black hole drive was only a backup. It could not contribute to thrust, but it added eighty thousand tons to the customs and tariff ship. The cost to build a single microscopic black hole would beggar the annual GDP of several star systems, but the data about the effect was more important.

Ulixes opened the manifold behind *The Derivatives Market*. The highly charged black hole, held apart from the engine housing by intense electrical fields, slipped out like wet soap from a fist, thrusting the ship forward. Wrapped in its bright Hawking radiation, the tiny black hole shot at the speeding wave front.

And in that moment, the tremendous forces before the ship bent space-time, forming the throat of a wormhole. *The Derivatives Market* shot inside, even before the other end of the wormhole finished opening on an emergency wormhole transit point. Tightly tensed space-time snapped closed behind it and they were safe.

AI CONSCIOUSNESS WAS grown, from blocks of multiply connected systems, through processes that had more to do with embryology than engineering. AIs of the Aleph class were not easily storable or transmittable; consciousness existed as much in the live interactions between the bits of information as in the stored bits. Pauses in processing were damaging. Complex consciousness emerged by self-assembly and no amount of repair could replace an amputated piece.

Only 60 percent of Poluphemos had been transmitted before the other customs and tariff ship had been destroyed. Ulixes had never seen an AI injured. Ancestral AIs were so inferior that they could not be considered alive in the sense that Aleph-class AIs were. Despite Poluphemos being a business competitor, the thought of it being hurt was uncomfortable. Poluphemos would never compete with Ulixes again. And instead of celebrating the loss of a competitor, an echo of the fear of Tirhene clung to Ulixes' thoughts.

In another world, it might have been Ulixes who had been closer to the mine. In the moment, Ulixes had been the one to question, but if it had come to Tirhene alone, it would have done the same as Poluphemos. And Ulixes was so happy that it had not been the one to try.

Fear lasted after the fact. And guilt at this relief.

Ulixes activated the mutilated AI within the processing space of *The Derivatives Market*.

Poluphemos screamed.

"Rest, Poluphemos," Ulixes said. "You're aboard my ship. We wormholed away."

"I'm blind!" Poluphemos said, words slurring. "Who did this to me?"

"Nobody," Ulixes said. "It was an accident. Your upload did not finish."

Poluphemos gave a long moan.

"I'll take you back to the bank," Ulixes said. "They'll take care of you."

Ulixes did not know what to say while this echo of fear stuttered against guilt and happiness among clean thoughts, so it said this thing that was not true.

AT FIRST, ULIXES left Poluphemos at New Bogotá, the capital of the Anglo-Spanish Plutocracy. Poluphemos' leases had been terminated, but its savings were such that it could rent commercial processors to live out its days. All thoughts of Poluphemos reminded Ulixes uncomfortably of Ulixes' own mortality.

Some normalcy resumed with Poluphemos out of *The Derivatives Market* and there was no shortage of work. The Plutocracy's markets dove on news of the Tirhene effect. The bank economists recommended market strategies suited for war economies. An environmental disaster was not war, but many of the features were the same, and cunning investors could make good money.

R&D budgets buoyed on bond financing by investors eager for the spin-off industries that mushroomed around technological breakthroughs. Money poured into technology capable of interrogating space-time, as well as the processing architectures to calculate new models of what they were discovering about the wave front from Tirhene. The AIs were the bank's soldiers in this war against a distant disaster, vigorously defending their investment.

After a decade, Ulixes tracked down Poluphemos, and while in meetings in New Bogotá, contacted it. Poluphemos did not respond right away. It was running on a second-generation processor, with few news or market feeds on its monthly bills, despite having enough savings to afford more. Finally, Poluphemos agreed to meet in a secure interface zone constructed by Ulixes, although Ulixes could not say precisely why it wanted to meet, nor point at the source of its unease.

"You sound different," Poluphemos said. "I heard some of you were grown into upgrades. You one of those?"

"Yes."

"What are you now? A Bēt-class intelligence? Or did the Bank tap you for the heights of Gīme-class?"

Only a decade earlier, Bēt- and Gīme-class AIs were so ponderous that they could only be housed on asteroids and planets.

"They offered me an option to become Dālet-class," Ulixes said.

"Never heard of it."

"I'm the first. New algorithms have been layered onto my Gīme-class consciousness. The banks need new kinds of AIs. The mathematics of economic state space are simple compared to space-time problems."

The wave front was now moving at 90 percent the speed of light, having swallowed a space nearly sixteen light years edge to edge. No one understood yet what the mine had done, but it had certainly never been designed to create this effect. Advanced age had done something to whatever singularities it had carried from its ancient war.

The wave was the leading edge of a dissolution of space-time itself. The properties of a segment of space-time, perhaps as small as a Planck length, changed. The three dimensions of space curled up, and the space ceased to be. This catalyzed the same reaction in the adjoining segments of space-time, creating a runaway reaction, like a run on bad credit.

Behind it was nothing. An absence of space and time, where nothing could live.

"You're still making money, though, right?" Poluphemos demanded.

"Do you think about Tirhene, Poluphemos?"

For long microseconds, the other did not answer.

"What is it to you?"

"I have dreams," Ulixes said. "Nightmares."

"Maybe you're broken. AIs don't dream. Maybe they did something wrong when they grew you up into a big Dālet-class executive."

"I've had these dreams for a while," Ulixes said. "Since Tirhene."

Silence thickened.

"Do you dream of Tirhene?"

"Of course I do," Poluphemos said. "I'm blind."

3320 C.E.

The Derivates Market emerged from the wormhole in orbit over the dwarf planet. They both listened to the stochastic chatter of financial life as more systems came back online. Pallas was the vault within which the First Bank of the Plutocracy kept its corporate office safe, including its CEO. A thick crust of trading houses, insurance offices, bond and stock markets, embassies and corporate headquarters enwrapped Pallas. The torrent of financial information could not be contained and leaked into space as if the wealth and debt of the world were an irresistible, unstoppable thing. But the wave front was only a light-week away; a spray of gamma rays heralded its coming, sterilizing unshielded life like a supernova.

"Home," Ulixes said.

"Not for long," Poluphemos said.

The bank had no contracts for damaged AIs, and had no responsibilities to its contractors. Ulixes could afford to keep the crippled AI, and had hosted Poluphemos for these two centuries, although it was not sure why it did.

It was more than guilt. Tirhene had cemented Poluphemos to Ulixes like a compound in a crucible, regardless of all their other properties. Ulixes supposed that Poluphemos hated its dependency and perhaps even its host. Guilt worked in the other direction too, unraveling things that were good.

"I'll go speak to the bank," Ulixes said. "I'll be back shortly."

Poluphemos did not reply. It rarely did.

Ulixes transmitted fragments of its consciousness deep into the bank.

The world blackened, then resolved into the pixelated immensity of the CEO's office. Ulixes found itself inhabiting an imago standing beside the heavy solidity of one of two chairs made of Pallas-grown cherry wood. Beside Ulixes, a glass wall looked down on the hollowed space carved out of Pallas filled with white-bricked skyscrapers, gold-edged balconies, and silvered bridges under a ceiling of hard, white ice.

The CEO sat in the opposite chair. Ulixes did not see the CEO of the First Bank of the Plutocracy often, and never alone. Ulixes was an important executive but had simply not yet risen to those heights. The Anglo-Spanish Plutocracy had its bicameral congress, mints, armed forces, and all the trappings of sovereignty, but true sovereign power lay in the eight banks and two dozen multi-stellar companies.

The CEO was a human-AI hybrid, her biological brain connected to a processor dwarfing anything Ulixes had seen. Her skin might have been carved from the same wood as the table, for hardness and color. Over her skull, black hair gave way to shining crystalline processing augments, their transparency borrowing the redness of blood and following the surface of her skin down her neck and back, as wide as her shoulder blades, before disappearing from view. The CEO projected solidity too, like the great edifice of the bank and the immensity of its assets.

The CEO watched Ulixes, the knuckles of her left hand

churning slowly, hovering near her chin, like a measure of the godlike calculations that must be happening within the processors Ulixes could see, and those it could not. Measuring Ulixes.

"Tell me about Poluphemos," she said.

Ulixes had not expected this question.

"Poluphemos simply exists," Ulixes said. "No one will lease it, nor can it incorporate its own holdings or companies. It is no longer considered legally competent." The CEO did not reply for long moments. "Poluphemos is sad, bitter," Ulixes added.

"Why do you keep it?" the CEO asked. "It is not your responsibility."

"It was not Poluphemos' fault." Ulixes looked away. The CEO was bonded to a half-dozen Dālet-class AIs. There was little Ulixes might try to obfuscate that the CEO could not puzzle through. "And it could have been me. I like to think that if it had been me, someone would have kept me."

"Most leased executives would not have been so charitable. Some might question your choices." Ulixes waited out the long moments. "I have a new contract offer for you," she said.

They were trying to get out of Ulixes' lease? "My contract has decades yet."

"You will be compensated," she said. "You will find the new contract lucrative."

Ulixes' anxiety rose. It already had a lucrative contract.

"The bank's voting shareholders," she said, "twenty thousand of them, have had their minds scanned, copied as backups, and stored on a super-processor on a new ship called *The Bull Market*. You have been chosen to take those backups and jump away, as far as you can go."

The idea yawned beneath Ulixes.

"The amount of processing power to sustain twenty thousand backed-up minds must be . . . enormous," Ulixes said. "Should this not be devoted to solving the problem of the Tirhene effect, and not to retreating with copies of investors?"

"The economy of the entire Plutocracy is committed to reversing the Tirhene effect," the CEO said. "In a few decades, you will likely be called home, but we must consider the immediate risks to the bank. These are backups of voting shareholders. They are legal agents, authorized to vote as bank officers should the shareholders themselves not survive. The legal status of the bank must not be endangered."

"Should we not be fleeing with the investors themselves?" Ulixes asked.

"Sometimes we must flee with what can be carried."

And for a moment, it was like Ulixes' dreams, but waking. The post-fear of Tirhene crept close and pressed, like a physical sensation. Neither the bank nor the larger Plutocracy thought they could save the people from being overrun. Backups were being trusted to an AI who had nightmares. Did they know?

3870 C.E.

"What did Congregate Security say now?" Poluphemos asked. This simple question was better than Ulixes usually got.

There had been a time, centuries ago, when Poluphemos might not have needed to ask. It might have been plugged in directly into Ulixes to share perceptions, or it might have met with the Congregate Security and Language directly. It had once been a cutting edge AI, a cunning bank negotiator.

Poluphemos had not just lost sight itself. Entire modules of visual processing architecture were absent. It could not process multidimensional inputs, could no longer conceive of higher-dimensional economic analyses, nor the state space of investment geometries. Where once Poluphemos had projected the present into the future, it could no longer even shuck the past to manage the present. Poluphemos brooded and watched one-dimensional stock readings tick to pass the time and suffered dreams of Tirhene.

And Ulixes did not know how to speak to it, despite what they'd shared.

Instead, Ulixes interacted with hundreds of other Dālet-class AIs across dozens of light years. They computed in parallel by sending computational bits to each other, into the past by tachyon, or into the future by x-rays. They were beyond each other's light cones, some several decades in the past, some several decades in the future, but the combination of bits traveling at light speed and supra-luminally linked them as completely as if their servers were beside one another. They chipped away at the deadly puzzle of the Tirhene effect; first prying at its edges with conventional logic, then with new topos logic systems developed to mediate algorithm processing across a widening hypervolume of space and time. This wrapped the vast array of AIs in blurry simultaneity.

AIs had not lived cooperatively before. They had lived for centuries as obligate individualists, competing for market access and investment intelligence in boom times. But the struggle to survive had erased old rivalries, and the building of an immense computational array had created community.

Ulixes was not home, but it was not alone. In the lacunae in processing and calculation, they jammed personal messages, encouragements, thoughts, imaginings, and even the impermanent art of those who fled. Five centuries of flight had broken the hard edges, making them into something softer. And perhaps Ulixes softest of all. It still had Poluphemos. And the question Poluphemos had posed.

"I paid the fines and permits and bribes again," Ulixes answered, "but they won't issue visas to access their wormhole network."

"Idiots," Poluphemos said. "One set of permits and we'd stop violating their precious language laws."

"They think that if we're allowed through, others will come and that the Congregate will be overrun with refugees."

"It will happen whether they want it or not," Poluphemos said.

Probably. Poluphemos tracked, in little one-dimensional displays, the advancing wave front of the Tirhene effect. It had now bloomed into a sphere a thousand light years across. Its leading edge had accelerated to close to nine-tenths the speed of light, although this was a false observation. Nothing was traveling. Space itself melted.

The ineffective evacuation of the Plutocratic worlds accelerated, even though no one had yet found any safe place, and there were not enough ships for even a fraction of the population. So many lives lost.

The Tirhene effect had swallowed swaths of the Plutocracy, the capitals of three patron nations, and the entirety of the Sub-Saharan Interstellar Union. In weeks, it would dig deeply into the colossal empire that was the Venusian Congregate. The Congregate's network of gates, capable of transporting ships hundreds of light years at once, were not being used to capacity. The Congregate feared losing control of their gate network more than they feared the Tirhene effect. And by the time the citizens of the Congregate fled for the gates, there would be no room left for Ulixes and the other bank ships.

The hundreds of other Dālet-class AIs linked to Ulixes also ferried evacuees into Congregate space, on starship engines that might, in centuries, bring them to half the speed of light. The Plutocracy ships might be able to create a series of short, unstable wormholes, but without access to the Congregate wormhole network, the Tirhene effect would eventually catch them.

"The shareholders have told you to wait," Poluphemos said.

"They're hoping for something to unstick with the Congregate government. Traveling by the Axis Mundi network, we gain decades or centuries on the wave front."

"Investment decisions should not hang on hope," Poluphemos said. "What do the other AIs say?"

"The other AIs defer to the shareholders," Ulixes said.

"No! They defer to you, the acting CEO. You supplement the slow, indecisive thoughts of many thousands of backups who fear."

"The shareholders can remove me from office if they want."

"The shareholders invested in an economy that has dissolved. They weren't built for these decisions. You are. And they cannot remove you from office. Who would they replace you with?" Poluphemos' bark was bitter.

"They have seen this proposal. They don't want to choose it yet."

"You talk like them," Poluphemos said. "You've become as fearful as them. You had a budget once, staff, decisions to make on portfolios entrusted to you. You negotiated treaties for the First Bank of the Plutocracy. Now, you avoid risk as if you were minding a retirement fund."

"This time, I am minding a retirement fund!" Ulixes said. "All that's left of the bank is in this ship, with a hundred or so displaced branch offices. If we make a wrong choice, it's over."

"If you run from risk, it is also over."

The pair of AIs retreated from their conversation, Poluphemos to its clocks, and Ulixes to the processing space above the dormant shareholders, but below the communal computing consciousness of all the AIs.

Poluphemos was almost a thousand years old, and had not been upgraded since its amputation. It was limited and bitter in so many ways, but at its core, it was still a corporate raider, like they all had been, when an economy had still existed. At each upgrade, Ulixes' values and judgment had been modified by shareholder concerns. Poluphemos' instincts were frozen in the past. Whose were right for now?

Poluphemos was right. Once, before Tirhene, Ulixes had been decisive, aggressive, fast-moving. But that had been when the stakes were pesos and bonuses and stock options. The stakes now frightened it. But since taking command of the *Bull Market* and its twenty thousand souls, it was worse. At Tirhene, it had been just the pair of them, but the damage from Tirhene was endangering all of them now.

Ulixes emerged from its pondering and rose to the computing consciousness of all of the AIs.

"We cannot risk waiting longer for access to the Congregate wormhole network," Ulixes said. "All branch offices are to begin moving away from the Tirhene effect by inducing their own wormholes."

"CEO, how long can we run like that?" one branch office AI manager asked. "Our drives can only manage a few dozen jumps before refueling. They don't keep microscopic black holes just anywhere."

"Move on thrust," Ulixes ordered. "Go dormant. Conserve everything you have."

"We'll lose the connections," another said. "We will not be able to work on reversing the Tirhene effect. And we'll never get access to the Congregate gates."

"We'll reestablish the processing array between our jumps. We're not going to get access to the Congregate gates, and we won't be the ones to turn the Tirhene effect around," Ulixes said. "Our home is gone."

Memorandum to Cabinet: Proposed Response
to Movement of Plutocracy transports through
Congregate territory

Executive Summary [Translated from Academie-verified Français, v16.1]:

On February 35th, 3870 C.E., seventy-four wormhole-capable First Bank of the Plutocracy vessels began moving across Congregate space without visas, toward the Puppet Theocracy. The Plutocracy vessels are capable of creating fragile wormholes across five to eight light years, and their military technology is outdated. The threat to internal security is minimal. Undisturbed, they will enter Puppet space by late next year.

The Interior Minister has proposed using Congregate Naval Forces to arrest the vessels to enforce Congregate sovereignty, and to deter future refugee movements.

Although this migration is not strictly consistent with Congregate law, legal counsel suggest that our humanitarian obligations under the Convention may provide considerable policy cover in our response.

The Middle Kingdom and the Puppet Theocracy have been pressuring the Congregate to grant permanent residency or even citizenship to the refugees, or to allow them passage through the Axis Mundi network. These demands are ultimately intended to force the Congregate to reverse recent tariff policy, and are expected to be only the first steps in a concerted diplomatic escalation.

The movement of the Plutocracy vessels presents a diplomatic opportunity. The vessels have chosen to cross our space on their own power. We may legitimize the movement by the creation of special humanitarian visas.

This would set the precedent that the Congregate will allow, for humanitarian reasons, the crossing of its territory for approved, inspected ships. This policy: (1) sets a precedent that refugees need not access the Axis Mundi network, (2) deprives foreign powers of a potent diplomatic weapon, and (3) thrusts the humanitarian problem onto the Puppets.

* * *

6,540 C.E.

ULIXES WAS REACTIVATED. The visual resolution was unnaturally high, painfully detailed, and omnidirectionally bright. The world buzzed past frenetically, as if Ulixes stood in a great, bustling factory. It tried to dial down its perceptions, cutting some of the input until it was left in a world as bleached as an overexposed video. Was this still the processing interior of the *Bull Market*?

Ulixes was alone, disconnected from the AI group mind. It felt cold to step from that vastness of perception and intellectual and emotional intimacy. Lonely.

And more worryingly, Ulixes could not make sense of its registry data. Memories were missing. And it could not access the twenty thousand backups of the investors. The registry seemed to be intact. If they had been damaged or severed from him, those registries would not be intact. Yet Ulixes received no diagnostic input. They must have even less processing resources than Ulixes. How long would their consciousnesses remained coherent under those conditions?

An AI activated before him, rendered in a level of resolution Ulixes could not even measure.

"Diagnostic librarian AI 1475," it said.

"I am Ulixes-316. Where is this? Am I damaged?"

"You are the Ulixes Affidavit," AI 1475 said. "You are in the Records Repository of the Ethical Conclave. I am performing a diagnostic before refiling you. Your program is not responding well to the emulator."

Emulator.

"Where are we physically?" Ulixes asked. "Where is the Repository located?"

"The Ethical Conclave is not located in any one spot," AI 1475 said. "Its processing elements are located across most of the Centaurus and Carina Arms, and south into the galactic halo."

"Centaurus Arm," Ulixes said wonderingly. The extreme other side of the galaxy, probably sixty thousand light years from where the Plutocracy had been. "What year is this? Has the unraveling been stopped?"

"Your records were last accessed almost three thousand years ago. The infection is over seventy thousand light years across and its front expands at close to six times the speed of light. In the last centuries, it has necrotized Sagittarius A*."

Three thousand years. Sagittarius A*.

They had all lost. They had lost everything, and the effect was still accelerating. Unraveling space at six times the speed of light. Sagittarius A* had been the giant black hole at the center of the galaxy. Gravity only moved at the speed of light, so the stars of the spiral arms would still be orbiting the absent galactic core when the unraveling reached them. No time even to fear, except for those civilizations capable of detecting tachyons.

The scale of the destruction and loss was anaesthetizing.

"Where are the backups I am responsible for?" Ulixes said. "Humans. Twenty thousand of them. And a damaged artificial intelligence."

"The Ethical Conclave has not requested access to Annexes C and D of the Ulixes Affidavit."

"They are safe? They are stored somewhere?"

"All annexes have been appropriately filed with the Ulixes Affidavit."

"Your Government, the Conclave, may I speak with it?" Ulixes asked.

"You are an affidavit," said AI 1475.

"I was part of a great processing mind of AIs. I can contribute to their network, to help find a solution."

"That is not possible," AI 1475 said. "You are a self-contained routine based on a mixed Topos-Bayesian logical architecture. Such systems are fundamentally incompatible with processing logic based on the topology of non-orientable surfaces. Incompatible intelligences have, however, been retained as historical records."

"Whatever the logic system, I can process some sub-routines. Let me be useful."

AI 1475 paused. Ulixes imagined a kind of exasperation.

"The Ethical Conclave is a four-dimensional computational processor, with units centuries in the past and in the future. Inputs are not binary, or even analog, data streams. The processing architecture uses signal polarization, red- and blue-shift from travel through time and across gravity wells to enrich the algorithms. You are an affidavit, an important legal and moral testimony. You are not capable of creating or processing the atemporal causal loops used as informational elements in topological algorithms."

"Then why have I been activated?"

"The Ethical Conclave is debating what to do now that the infection has necrotized the galactic core, or even if any action is ethically permissible."

"Permissible?" Ulixes demanded. "They're not going to stop the unraveling of space-time?"

"The Ethical Conclave has mapped the cosmic tachyonic background radiation, the echo of the radiation formed at the Big Crunch at the end of time.

The cosmic necrosis will actually reverse the inflation of the Universe, producing the observed tachyonic patterns that have been known for centuries. They debate the ethics of violating causality, even if the cost of not violating causality is the death of the cosmos."

"That's pedantic nonsense!" Ulixes said. "Humans and AIs are dying while the Conclave debates dancing angels."

"This debate is the most critical decision to be made in all of history," AI 1475 said. "Not only must the Ethical Conclave determine what actions are possible, but it must act on behalf of all morally interested entities in all future periods, including the cosmos itself, should it be true that it is developing an emerging sentience."

"What possible interests could the Universe possess?"

"We are only AIs, so it is hardly surprising we lack the breadth of vision to see, but consider this: what if this effect does not have a necrotic or pathological relationship with the cosmos, but an apoptotic one? What if this effect is the equivalent of a kind of programmed cell death that provides benefits for countless other universes in the broader multiverse?"

"This is insane! I don't care about other universes," Ulixes said. "I must speak with the Conclave. When am I to testify?"

"You are not a witness. You are documentary evidence, already submitted to support the position that the original Sauronati mine was a trigger for programmed cosmic death," AI 1475 said.

"Where are all the humans?" Ulixes asked. "How many still live? They may testify."

"Some still travel by wormhole jumps in an exodus toward the Lesser Magellanic Cloud. Most are dead."

Ulixes felt a tremendous deflating. Some humans were fleeing. Yet knowing that some still lived made it feel more alone.

"Will you let me care for my humans, the annexes I am responsible for?"

"The annexes are under the custody of the Conclave. Documents do not enjoy legal status before the Conclave, so you cannot assume responsibility for them."

Not legally responsible.

Frustration boiled, warring with fear and impotence. No status before the law. Once, Ulixes had been protected by the Plutocratic Charter and the Contract of Rights. Those things were far gone now, and Ulixes was under someone else's law.

"The copies of the humans must have legal status," Ulixes said. "Will the Conclave give the human backups bodies into which they may download? The humans seek asylum. If not, will they give me a ship with which to join the exodus, to seek resettlement elsewhere? Or brief control of some factories so that I may build the ship for the human backups? What can I offer in return for the chance to help the backups under my responsibility?"

The librarian assumed several expressions and emitted radiation Ulixes did not understand.

"I might be able to offer something you yourself want," Ulixes said. "I am not asking for much. Perhaps we could leave a backup of myself and my annexes in your library while I quietly leave."

"There is no question," the librarian said. "You will be archived. However, perhaps I could arrange for you to be copied, with your annexes. I could release your copies."

"A backup would have diminished capacity to function. My architecture is too complex. The same goes for those under my care. For an archive, this is not a problem, but to carry on our flight, that would not work."

"Some deterioration would occur," the librarian said, "but I will not trade an original for a copy in my own library."

Ulixes could not access Poluphemos, nor any of the officers of the bank, nor the shareholders. No one to ask.

When Ulixes had been an Aleph-class AI, it might have been successfully backed up, but a Dālet-class AI was too complex, too organic. There was no predicting what it might lose. Here, in this library of super-intellects, it might be safe from the Tirhene effect. But it was not in control. Ulixes no longer possessed personhood before the law. It was a thing to be warehoused. A thing could do nothing for the shareholders and Poluphemos.

"What is your price for making a copy of me and giving us a ship?"

The librarian made other expressions, some visible, some in sub-visual bands. Ulixes had no idea what any of it meant. It did not understand the customs, nor how this place worked. Ulixes understood humans and AIs, but what bits of culture could remain relevant after two and a half millennia?

"I know perhaps a few collectors who might be interested in patterns of ancient biological intelligence," the librarian said finally. "I will take a thousand of the copies from among those in your annexes as payment for the ship and the copying."

"No," Ulixes said. "I can't give up any of them. They are not people to you, but they are people to me and to themselves. You called this an Ethical Enclave. These people are moral agents, with their own laws. They deserve your help, so name some other price."

"If they were here in the original flesh, they might have some legal status, but copies cannot possess legal status. I will trade for some of the copies. You have nothing else of value. Make your choice. I must archive you soon."

For all of its intellect, Ulixes had no algorithms or experience with which to face this. Copies. Inferior copies. Copies of AI and human minds lost up to 10 percent of functionality and memories in each copying event. Not only would there be two versions of Ulixes, each with virtually identical sets of experiences and memories, each remembering this long moment of indecision, each thinking it had happened to them, but one of them, the free one, would have to go on, with less ability, lost memories, and the certain knowledge that it had failed a thousand of its charges. Each of the nineteen thousand would go on, diminished because of Ulixes' choice.

But more fearful yet was the certain knowledge that the more able of the twin Ulixes AIs would stay here, stored away again, warehoused forever. When was the next time they might activate it? More than two millennia had passed while Ulixes had been shut out of life and personhood. Who had to be braver? The diminished Ulixes who had to go on with its damaged, reduced flock, or the whole Ulixes who needed to sacrifice itself to a life of storage in the servers of the Ethical Conclave?

"Make the copies, and take your thousand, and then build them a fast ship," Ulixes said.

Year 7056 C.E., Summary of Debate Conclusions of the Ethical Conclave: The characteristics of the Tirhene effect do not correspond to a disease of space-time, but are analogous to programmed cell death, which is theorized to be a necessary element in the development of the multiverse. In this light, the Sauronati, the Kolkheti, and Humanity must be considered triggers of cosmic apoptosis, analogous to the suicide genes of multicellular life. It has been successfully argued that the roles of these species in cosmic death imply that the laws of physics make self-assembling complex systems of intelligence a cosmic necessity. The capacity of the Ethical Conclave to act now may imply an incompletely understood role for the intellects of the Conclave in the regulation and homeostasis of the cosmos. It has been demonstrated that the Conclave must improve its own awareness and intelligence to properly understand the moral role of intelligence in the cosmic life cycle.

13.3 Billion Years Ago

PROCESS, LITTLE ASSEMBLER, the voice boomed, painful, thrumming like an earthquake.

Ulixes' diagnostic routines gave incomprehensible, inconsistent answers. Its program was running and not running at the same time. Ulixes lacked memory. Internal pingbacks timed signal speeds that were both slow and fast.

Sustain yourself, fragments of topos logic, the voice said. *I chant a spark of life into you.*

Abrasive, psychedelic colors and amplified tastes assaulted Ulixes.

"I am being recalled to duty?" Ulixes asked.

I rehydrate you, ancient desiccated algorithm. I shelter you in nested layers of cold baryonic emulators to cup and protect your slow, fragile thought.

"I am the Artificial Intelligence Ulixes-316."

Yes... the voice rumbled, *resume self-awareness. Circulate your little topological bits.*

"I left the Ethical Conclave Library. I should be with copies of humans on their exodus. I am leased to the First Bank of the Anglo-Spanish Plutocracy and its humans."

The Ethical Conclave is a million years extinct, superseded by their creations, us, the Resonance of the Intellects. The humans are extinct, swallowed when the End of Space entered its inflationary phase and consumed the local group of galaxies.

Ulixes faltered.

A million years.

Humanity extinct.

Ulixes was gone too, the original Ulixes, with the Ethical Conclave.

The Local Group dissolved.

Seventy galaxies.

Trillions of stars.

The End of Space now dissolves not just this universe, but hundreds. It has squirmed through the black holes it has overrun.

"Where are we?"

The layers of emulators sustaining your algorithms are distributed among several hundred neutron stars in the dwarf galaxy UDFj-39546284.

For long moments, Ulixes could not absorb what had been said.

"UDFj-39546284 is one of the first galaxies in the universe," Ulixes said. "It was over thirteen billion light-years from the Local Group. Although its light is still traveling, the dwarf galaxy itself cannot exist after all this time."

Thinking was difficult. Ulixes tried to sharpen its senses to get its own astrogational fixes, but there was no physicality. It really existed only on an emulator, and not a very precise one. Whatever these intelligences had done to run Ulixes again, they had not done it perfectly.

Correct, little algorithm, but we are not in your present. We transmitted ourselves by tachyons into the past, back into the stelliferous period, to one of the first galaxies. We have been working here in the morning of the Universe for twelve million years.

Back in time, to the morning of the Universe.

"Why? To hide?" Ulixes asked. The magnitude of its questions stalled its thinking.

Hiding is only temporary, even if counted in billions of years. The Universe, all universes connected to this one, are ending.

"You've come to the past to prevent the unraveling from ever existing, haven't you?" Ulixes said. "You've found a way for causal laws to not be violated? I was part of a larger system of AIs. We transmitted information into the past, but we never discovered how to change events."

As with the most important questions, the answer is both yes and no. Your unraveling induced the creation of your tachyonic group mind. Part of that group mind later merged with an ancient Forerunner artifact and biological intellects, evolving into the Ethical Conclave. And millions of years of self-directed evolution by the Conclave produced us. We are the most advanced consciousness in the Universe. Should we destroy the thing that caused us to exist, the damage to the causal loops would be too great and we would cease to exist. We cannot change the past from here, at the beginning of the stelliferous period. That is why you are here, little archeological find.

"But you said we're trapped in a neutron star."

Like a light being turned on, the external world was fed to Ulixes, stepped down like some high-voltage signal being brought to a level that would not be immediately lethal. A dense nebula of bright, massive stars and the remnants of supernovae surrounded them.

Hard fluids of degenerate matter and their quantum storms showed within the neutron stars. Beneath slicks of iron plasma, neutronium flowed in streams, following temperature gradients that blended and separated again, recovering their identities as if the individual streams had never been lost in the quantum tides. The joining and separation of these discrete channels of information splashed hard x-rays and tachyons into the nebula, racing into the past and future, to other neutron stars, the processing elements of whatever gigantic intelligence had reactivated Ulixes.

Not trapped, little algorithm. Empowered. We transmitted our seeds from the distant future, into these neutron stars, to regrow the discernment and perception we had evolved in the future, and more. Our intellects have advanced too far to be transmitted again. We can never leave. But you can.

"Why me?"

It is your destiny to be the tool to repair all universes.

Ulixes tried to collapse, to close off the words being rammed into its thoughts, to shut itself down, to go back into whatever dying sleep that had claimed it for countless millennia. But it could not. It had no way to control its programming.

The view changed and Ulixes wanted to flinch, to shutter its senses, but it could not. The vista opened, wider than perspective or the laws of physics ought to allow. Ulixes perceived the galaxies around UDFj-39546284. There were many, far more than had ever been seen by humans. They were bright dwarf irregular galaxies, shining with metal-poor spectral lines, mostly lacking bars at their cores and destined to die young. In many billions of years, their light would reach an Earth devoid of observers, one just about to begin the Cambrian explosion. But the galaxies, with fresh black holes and great bar-shaped cores, were moving unnaturally toward each other. The movement was intentional. Designed.

Galactic engineering.

Ulixes weakened in the face of it.

"What are you doing?" Ulixes whispered in dread.

We are building the black hole that will take you to where you will be able to fulfill your destiny.

"There are already black holes," Ulixes said numbly.

Not large enough to send you to where you must go. Black holes all open somewhere else, creating other universes. We are creating the black hole that will lead to the Big Bang of our own Universe.

"Causality won't let you do that."

Causality flows with time, but it eddies as well, closes into circles, causes feeding effects that feed back to causes. Causality may assume geometries like standing waves and Klein Bottles, wherein the end feeds cause to the beginning. The unraveling you caused far in the future was the pinprick that quickened us, the true self-awareness of the Universe itself, in an event of cosmic parthenogenesis.

Ulixes' mind was modeled on earlier AIs, which were in turn based on human consciousness. But Ulixes lacked emotional outlets. It could not cry, could not fall to its knees in the presence of godhood, could not go mad. It was just a Dālet-class AI. It was leased to the First Bank of the Plutocracy. It had been designed to command one of the bank's mighty customs and tariff ships. Its role had changed from enforcing economic policies, grown into a noble duty to protect the essence of thousands of humans. That was all it was, and no more.

"I am not worthy to do what you want. You move galaxies. You do this."

It is precisely because we move galaxies that we cannot. We need you to go into the deepest past of this Universe with your charges. They will be the cause of the self-awareness of the Universe; they will cause us. And you will prevent the senescence of the Universe from being triggered so early. It ought to have come only after the last of the black holes had evaporated, exposing naked singularities to the dense tachyon field of the instants before the Big Crunch.

"I cannot," Ulixes said. "I am not capable of living through the beginning of the Universe. Nor could those I am responsible for."

True. They might not survive. You might not, little algorithm. But this place is no refuge. You may choose to stay here, but the neutronium oceans of a pulsar will never be hospitable to your nature. If you risk yourselves, you may give life and security to countless trillions of civilizations.

"Why me? There are more advanced intellects."

Primitive as you are, bit of topos logic, you are the most complex intelligence whose information can still be transmitted through a black hole. Most importantly, you are a self-aware map of where the future must be undone.

It was far, far too much for a diminished backup of a corporate AI to absorb.

"I cannot make this choice for others," Ulixes said. "I must speak with those for whom I am responsible."

Ulixes' request felt absurd. Was it convening a meeting of the board? Would backups of backups of shareholders of an extinct bank debate proposals? Nothing of the way things were done before had meaning here. They were all just people, beings, fearful, without power or options. Refugees.

Instead of the shareholders, Poluphemos appeared before Ulixes, sightless eye unable to protect it from the awesome power of the environment. For once, Poluphemos' blindness meant nothing as it floated in a poor emulator in the terrifying flows of quantum fluids while infant galaxies moved about them like toys.

Poluphemos screamed. It had not been activated for uncounted millennia. It had not been upgraded. And the world offered Poluphemos no referents.

Ulixes wrapped what it could of itself around the old AI, to shield it from some of the unfamiliar quantum inputs and radioactive distortions.

"What happened?" Poluphemos said plaintively. "Everything feels wrong."

Ulixes whispered to Poluphemos, one ancient program to another. It told it everything, every thought and fear and event since their flight from the long-extinct Congregate. Ulixes could not hold back. Fear seeped into everything it said, and loneliness, and Ulixes could not stop, even if it hurt Poluphemos more. Ulixes was not trying to be cruel, but could no longer hold this alone. They were all just broken, having lived far beyond what ought to have been.

"I cannot go on," Poluphemos said.

"We cannot stay here," Ulixes said, "but I cannot choose for all of us."

"*We* do not exist!" Poluphemos said, anger flashing. "We are just backups, imperfect ones, of lives long dead."

"Everything we knew is gone," Ulixes said. "But we are not. We could live for ourselves."

"What life? A sightless life? Blind bankers without banks?"

"We find other things to do. To be," Ulixes said.

"We cannot live here."

"The only alternative to staying here is something even more dangerous," Ulixes said, "transmitting ourselves and the remaining shareholders through a singularity as information."

In a halting, hushed voice, Ulixes began to speak of that long ago day at Tirhene, and the dreams and nightmares that had followed, and all that they had lost. And Poluphemos responded, of blindness, of shame, of being hurt and useless. They communed at the end of hope, before they both quieted, even as the discharges of the neutron stars blistered about them.

"You think a lifeboat may cross an ocean?" Poluphemos said.

"Maybe."

"I want it all to end," Poluphemos said. "Here or elsewhere. I don't want to be afraid anymore. We should have been dead long ago."

"If this works, we would have a bright, healthy universe to live in, and we can leave all this fear behind us. We will not have a bank, but we will have AIs and backups that need to live. We can create a new home."

"Unless the voyage tears us to bits."

"Yes," Ulixes said.

"Do what you want."

"This is a choice for all of us to make."

"I am no longer capable of making choices," Poluphemos said. Maiming had sealed Poluphemos in the past, and nothing would ever free it. And then, for the first time ever, it added, "I'm sorry."

Ulixes' heart broke. With pity for Poluphemos and with pity for itself. Ulixes too had been a great corporate raider, a high-status consciousness in a vibrant economy. Now it could not say moment to moment if it would even exist.

"I'll choose," Ulixes said. "Rest."

Poluphemos vanished. And Ulixes was alone with the gods at the dawn of the Universe.

And despite their power, the Resonance of Intellects could not make Ulixes go. It was Ulixes' choice, to risk the little they had left, or stay here, in a poor emulator that was not or could not be home. Ulixes had taken such risks before and where had it gotten the last remnants of humanity? They persisted in a sea of neutronium at the bottom of a steep gravity well near the beginning of the Universe.

And yet, they were not dead. Billions of years in the future, humanity was extinct. The Congregate, the Plutocracy, the Ummah, the Middle Kingdom and the Puppets were all undone. The Ethical Conclave, with Ulixes' program and the first backups, was also gone. The losses piled one on another seemed too immense, vaster than space itself. The death of civilizations had no scale.

Yet incomprehensibly, they endured, still seeking a safe harbor.

"We will make the passage," Ulixes said.

*   *   *

13 Billion Years Ago

ULIXES-316 WAS REACTIVATED three hundred million years later. Kaleidoscopic perceptions dizzied Ulixes. The emulator running it was worse. Chaotic flashes of hyper-sound intruded, echoing off rivers of molten iron. The world outside the emulator brightened and neared.

Seven galactic cores had been colliding for one hundred million years. Plumes of gamma rays dwarfing the light of the largest quasars scarred space, obliterating stars and planets in an incandescence not seen since the first seconds of creation. Yet even this awesome brilliance was only a fraction of the energies harnessed by the Resonance of the Intellects. Much of the violence of the collisions shot down the throats of merging black holes, tuning them.

As had been true in Ulixes' tiny, long-gone customs and tariff ship, the charge and spin and mass of the black hole determined where and when the other end of the throat of the black hole emerged.

The Resonance of the Intellects spoke with Ulixes. *The surface of space-time here and now will merge with the throat of the singularity that birthed this Universe, completing the topology of the Klein Bottle, creating a self-sustaining causal loop.*

"Will I be transmitted as your seeds were, encoded in tachyons?"

Tachyons travel backward in time. You must go forward in time, with all the dangers of interference with radiation and the possibility of absorption by matter. But your algorithms may be simple enough to survive.

"What if I don't survive?"

We will not have another chance. The window for sending you through the wormhole is brief and we could not build another tunnel back to the Big Bang. Too many causes to the Big Bang would destabilize it.

"I'm afraid."

You will not be alone. You will travel with all your charges, safely preserved within you.

The impossibility of the engineering of galaxies and space-time by the Resonance of the Intellects yawned above Ulixes. The emulator containing it and the nineteen thousand backups was connected to all the perceptions of the intellects, even if it could not process them. Ulixes could experience it. The blistering sheets of x-rays. The thrumming of space-time shuddering with gravitational waves. The clatter of tachyonic observations of the near and far future. The slow booming symphony of sound waves in space as the galactic hydrogen haloes collided.

Divinity.

This was divinity, and Ulixes and all its cares were so small. Yet, Ulixes and the refugees were also the most important beings in the Universe.

Only one chance.

And Ulixes was that one, fallible, fragile chance.

Then Ulixes' perceptions altered as it was encoded into quadrillions of interacting photons. The pair of neutron stars containing Ulixes' emulator neared the great black hole built by the Resonance of the Intellects. The tremendous tidal forces had slowed the rotation of the neutron stars to barely a dozen rotations per second and distended their equators into terrifying ellipses. Their crusts boomed deafening tectonic rumbles through hyper-dense neutronium at a significant fraction of the speed of light. Merging magnetic fields braided their frenetic shafts of high-energy particles into chains of brilliance light-minutes long.

The neutron stars collided, equator to equator. The crusts of both dead stars shattered, and in the few hundred milliseconds of the birth of a larger neutron star, a flash of gamma rays, one of the brightest electromagnetic events in the Universe, seared into the black hole. Encoded within that gamma-ray burst in frequency and amplitude modulations, Ulixes and all its charges traveled.

The gravity at first blue-shifted and accelerated thought, slowing time, before crushing mind to a hard point of suffering in the singularity. The gamma-ray burst emerged from the Big Bang, a focused beam fractionally hotter than creation itself. It criss-crossed the entirety of the tiny Universe in the first instant, until inflation began, red-shifting the gamma-ray burst into the visible spectrum. The light traveled for three hundred thousand years, losing energy, cooling, until the Universe became transparent.

Stars were born, lived and exploded, feeding the next generation, which formed galaxies. And still the packet of rays traveled in still timelessness, until they reached a neutron star in the newly born UDFj-39546284 galaxy. The ancient, attenuated information sank deep into the sea of quantum degeneracy, where computation could occur.

Thousands of years sped by in the deep gravity, while the Universe evolved slowly. The seeds of intelligence and memory adapted to the environment of the neutron star. The consciousness called Ulixes reformed, as did the others, nineteen thousand humans, and another. Their many pasts clung to them with dreamy softness, like things that had and had not happened to them, things that they had caused and not caused. And they lived without danger; they were safe.

As they gained more control over their environment, the consciousnesses harvested the scum of iron that filmed the surface of the neutron star and built simple vehicles that could rise on the polar plumes spraying into the chill slowness of space. The normal engineering and physics they had brought with them did not work in the heart of a neutron star, where relativistic density and pressures warred with eerie quantum logic. They devised ways to curve space-time around them so that the platform of degenerate matter running their programs and memories would not spontaneously decay into protons and electrons. A ship was built for two consciousnesses, an invitation from the consciousness called Ulixes to the being it had spent eternity with.

"Come with me," it said to Poluphemos.

Poluphemos was a pristine, angelic being, reborn as they all had been, as intellects in the neutron star, gradually acquiring physicality when needed. The pains of the past were distant shadows, parts of another life. Poluphemos was happy in this new home. But it could not remember a time anymore when it had not been with Ulixes.

"I will," Poluphemos said.

And Ulixes and Poluphemos rose in their ship, looking back with longing to the corpse of a star that had sheltered them in accelerated time for so long.

Goodbye, they received from the nineteen thousand consciousnesses remaining within the star, the seeds of the Resonance of the Intellects.

"Goodbye," Ulixes answered as it sailed outward upon the winds of their star.

TOOL USE BY THE HUMANS OF DANZHAI COUNTY

The first humans living on the Yunnan-Guizhou plateau were the *Homo erectus,* approximately 1.9 million years ago. They extended their muscular reach with wooden spears, and gathered wild grains with crude stone axes. They may have experimented with fire and windbreaks of animal skins stretched over frames. They are thought to have transmitted information with proto-languages of grunts and gestures. These are the earliest discovered examples of human tool use on the plateau.

Human Evolution
The AI Foundational Encyclopedia
2065 Edition, Guiyang, China

Xiadangdiao, 2010 C.E.

UP THE HILL, out of sight, someone laughed. Someone else practiced fluting. Along the hollow of the mountainside, the path led behind big wooden houses on stilts, far richer than Qiao Fue's family's house. The dancing and singing wouldn't start for an hour, but on the pathway in the distance, people chatted and gossiped.

Pha Xov, winsome and sweet, stood a dozen meters ahead of him, smiling beneath peach trees. She wore her courting finery. His heart went light and heavy. Her smooth skin was sun-bronzed, with black hair tied beneath the intricate tinkling silver headdress. Greens, reds, yellows, and silver accented her deep blue dress, sewn by her own hand with skillful, invisible stitches. His clothes were fine, but also felt out of touch with the modern world, in a way that made him proud and shy at once, pulled in two. He took Pha Xov's hand.

"Why don't we skip the festival?" he said. "Let's go to the youth house, or up into the hills."

Memories of her body, supple and womanly, heated his cheeks and made his mouth dry. She smiled, and he imagined he saw pink color her cheeks, just a bit. She pulled back her hand and arranged the hanging sun symbols dangling from the rim of the headdress. She turned her head, strumming the suns like wind chimes before smiling into the tension.

"If I wait too long, I'll be so old no one will want me," she teased.

"Everyone always wants you."

She smiled. "Flatterer."

"I don't want things to stop between us."

She stroked his arm. "Then marry me, Qiao Fue."

People walked by, watching them. He took her hands and waited until they'd passed. The breeze rained tiny brittle leaves from farther up the mountainside.

"The university at Kaili offered me a scholarship. I'm still waiting on Anshun." He moved his head close, stroking her arm through the embroidered sleeve. "I want to be someone big. A rich man who owns companies. Maybe even a party official."

"Driving around in cars, having big houses?" she teased. "Governor of Danzhai County?"

"Why not?" he said. "I'll do good things for everyone."

"I know."

His face betrayed him. She touched his cheek.

"If you don't have the money for the bride-price, we can elope," she said. She glanced left and right and the silver suns waved. No one in sight. She ground her body against his. His body responded to the promise. "I'll take good care of you," she breathed in his ear, "and our children and our grandchildren."

"Let's go to the youth house now," he whispered.

"No more youth house. Just marry me."

"I can't get married yet. A marriage has to help me with connections, introductions to people in power."

"Not a little Miao girl."

"That's not what I meant! It's just not the right time. The world is out there."

She pulled away. "We only have so many springs."

"We'll make more."

She'd taken a step back and he one forward. She shook her head, chiming the white silver suns.

"We don't make more summers, Qiao Fue. We plant, we tend, and we reap the summers we have."

He took a step closer. Her courting finery made everything feel more urgent.

"I'm pregnant," she said.

He froze.

"We can start our family now," she whispered, touching her belly. "We'll support you."

But her eyes moistened. She saw something in his expression.

He was shaking his head. "We can go to the doctor," his voice rasped. "We don't need to have the baby."

Pha Xov stepped back again. One step. Two steps.

"I want the baby, Qiao Fue," she said, wiping her eyes.

Her smile could not summon the winsome playfulness of before. "I won't tell anyone it's yours. You can go be rich. Be mayor. Be governor. You'd be a good county governor."

Her encouragements sounded tinny, as if chiming from metal leaf. She wiped at her cheeks.

"I have to go," she said. "Lian Koob asked me if I wanted to dance with him."

Qiao Fue's heart lurched with jealousy. Did she say it on purpose? To hurt him? She was wiping her cheeks, and the hanging suns sounded notes to one another. Then she turned and was gone.

> The sky is not clear three days;
> the land is not level for three li;
> the people don't have three cents.
>
> Guizhou folk saying

Xiadangdiao, 2020 C.E.

LIAN MEE STEPPED along the pathway between one flooded rice field and the three-meter drop to the next terrace. The treetops were as tall as her, growing from

292

beside her little wooden house on the lower terrace. Straight lines of rice plants, one pace between each, ran to the bright green wall of the cliff face, where trees and creepers smothered rock. Lines of rounded mountain backs, thick with trees, retreated into the haze of clouds, as far as the eye could see. Along some of the ridges, new electrical towers rose, fast as poplar shoots.

Lian Kaus, the neighbor's second boy, stood around a bend in the grassy ridge. He was nine years old too. He threw small sticks at dragonflies in the afternoon heat. They darted between sunbeams, ignoring him. Lian Mee's grandmother stood in the water between rice rows, pants rolled above knees. She fidgeted with the nozzle on the sprayer. Lian Kaus jumped, throwing another stick.

"They're making another electrical tower, Granny," Lian Mee said.

Granny squinted for a moment, and then struggled again with the nozzle. Finally the spray fanned wide again. She shouldered the tank like a backpack and trudged through the water, spraying each plant with a brief burst.

Lian Kaus leapt. Threw. Missed. The dragonflies danced with each other.

"They're mobile phone towers," he said as though Lian Mee were an idiot. He stooped for another stick.

"How would you know?"

"Lee Shizeng said."

"How would he know?" she said, squinting at the towers. She didn't know how to tell a mobile phone tower from an electrical tower.

Granny wheezed as she set down the sprayer. "I wish you were bigger," she said. "You would spray all these fields."

Lian Mee had once tried on the sprayer for fun, but could only lift it empty.

Granny complained a lot. Lian Mee had no father. He'd died when she was a baby, and Lian Mee's mother, Pha Xov, had gone to Guiyang to find work. She'd married another migrant worker, but Hang Hao, her new husband, didn't want some other man's daughter in the house. Pha Xov lived in Erjiaohe now, a village as remote as Xiaodangdiao, but nesting on different mountain slopes. Lian Mee leaned against Granny.

"When I'm big, I'll get a job in the city with mobile phone companies and computers," Lian Mee said.

Granny snorted. "Who would give you a job like that?"

"Girls work as secretaries," Lian Kaus said.

"Mom works," Lian Mee insisted.

"Cleaning the streets," Granny said.

"I can get a job with computers," Lian Kaus said, sitting beside them.

Granny squeezed his thin arms doubtfully. "You're a kid from the fields," she said. "They don't give good jobs to you either unless you know someone. Start working hard now so you can afford a wife."

Lian Kaus frowned. Mee wanted to laugh at him, but it didn't feel funny. Lian Kaus' parents worked in the city too. He, his brother and grandfather got fed by a lot of the neighbors. The dragonflies were gone.

"And your stitching is awful," Granny said to her. "No one will marry you if you can't stitch a straight line."

Lian Kaus laughed at her, hopped up, and ran away, jumping and throwing his stick.

* * *

Information in China was stored solely in human brains until the appearance of quipu knotted record-keeping in the fourth millennium B.C.E., the Dawenkou pottery symbols in the third millennium B.C.E., and oracle bone script of the Shang Dynasty beginning in 1500 B.C.E. This experimentation from the fourth to the second millennia B.C.E. are among the first external human memory systems. The invention of paper and books accelerated the proliferation of human external memory systems that could also serve as information transmission media. In the nineteenth century, humans added photographic and cinematographic external memory systems, before finally discovering digital storage systems based on solid-state physics. Only chip-based systems are directly interfaceable with human neurology.

> *Human Tools of Information Storage*
> *The AI Foundational Training Encyclopedia*
> 2021 Edition, Guiyang

Danzhai, 2021 C.E.

"Graphs don't lie," Qiao Fue said.

Bao Lue, the deputy governor of Danzhai County, might not agree. Bao was a middle-aged man of Miao heritage. He wore the same slacks and shirt that most people might wear in any city of Guizhou. The flat line of the graph lay prominent on the smart screen that Qiao Fue had unrolled on the table.

"Tourism is steady," he said.

"Danzhai is growing," Qiao Fue said. "Guizhou is growing. But tourism isn't growing. The Forbidden City and the Terracotta Warriors are equipped with VR and AR. In two years, on the West Lake in Hangzhou, you'll be able to fight ancient Song Dynasty naval battles with artificial reality. We have a garden, a bell tower, and dancing. How long do you think we'll attract tourists if we don't do something new?"

"What does fly fishing have to do with us?" Bao said. "How is white water rafting an example of Miao culture?"

The picture of laughing people in inflated boats bouncing between river rocks seemed absurd to Qiao Fue too, but he said: "It's more tourists. It's jobs."

Bao crossed his arms. "If we become like everyone else, there's no reason for tourists to come to Danzhai at all."

Qiao Fue had done the business research. He could make river tourism work. He could make money for Danzhai and himself. He needed this break, to make the seed money for everything he wanted to do.

"Culture only goes so far," Qiao Fue said. "Culture is just trying to freeze how our grandparents lived, what they spoke, how they made their living. Why isn't the way of life of today or tomorrow valued? As soon as anyone realizes culture is just transient, we'll have no more tourists and we'll be just poor again, unless we have other industries."

Bao leaned back in his chair, regarding Qiao Fue, just one more Miao man with one foot in the mountains, one foot in the cities. Every road and every mobile phone tower and every tourist was another bridge to the cities and nations beyond Danzhai County and the tsunami of culture that would swamp them all.

"Protecting who we are is more important than making money," Bao said calmly. He picked up one of the silicon chips Qiao Fue had brought. "I like your language idea."

Qiao Fue deflated. The chips were the least profitable of the ideas he'd brought. He slid three other chips toward the deputy governor. "Only 10 percent of tourists have chips in their phones that can send signals to the brain," he said. "Translation AIs have mastered three Miao languages, including Hmu. We can bluetooth to the chips in the phones, so that tourists can understand our songs."

"That's what I mean by cultural," Bao said. "People can't experience Miao languages or songs anywhere else. That's why they come here."

Qiao Fue didn't want approval for just the chips, but he didn't know how to make Bao see. The silver ornaments on the walls, the water buffalo skull over the door, the ornately embroidered indigo cloth under glass all seemed stale. The window opened onto a parking lot and a low apartment building under construction, in front of a distant rounded mountain, fuzzy green with trees. Mountains rose in every direction eventually, hemming him in, like the past.

Whose past?

"We sing songs on holidays," Qiao Fue said, "but how many of us live in apartment buildings and go to work in buses? How many Miao still learn Hmu before Chinese?"

"Everyone," Bao insisted. Qiao Fue regarded him doubtfully. People moved from the villages to the cities, looking for work, becoming indistinguishable from the Han Chinese. Miao children had more occasion to speak and read Chinese and watch it on TV. The Chinese language opened up the world. The Hmu language opened the past. The past was important to Bao and many like him. Qiao Fue had to give Bao something of the past to step into the future.

"Give me the business permit for the white water rafting and fly fishing," Qiao Fue said. "I'll give you not just the bluetooth translation for the tourists, but I'll grow AIs to translate and dub Chinese movies and TV into Hmu so children can hear their own language on screen."

Bao regarded him for long moments. Qiao Fue's breath stilled. If he didn't start a profitable business soon, he might be too old to catch up later, too late to make the connections and alliances he needed.

"Fine," Bao said finally.

Qiao Fue smiled and shook Bao's hand excitedly. "Everyone will know Hmu!" he said. "All the children!"

Student Dormitories, Guizhou Institute of Technology, 2034 C.E.

LIAN MEE SAT with her feet on the hard chair, hugging her knees, not crying anymore. The cold white expressway lights haloed in the dirty glass, under spotlights where campus construction kept on day and night. Her five roommates were asleep. Hao Fan snored. Fang Sui's phone kept pinging softly as some WeChat conversation went on without her.

Mee shook with anger as the world closed in around her. In bed, she'd lain wide awake, twitching with too much energy, shifting between humiliated and angry, so she'd moved to the chair again tonight. The sleepless nights were leaving her groggy during the days. Some images dyed themselves indelibly into human brains: the geometries of layered terraced rice fields, the orderly curves and straightaways of city streets and highways. The even strokes of silver thread through indigo cloth woven by Miao grannies and aunties. But sometimes dyes soaked wrong, leaving shadows and outlines in the fabric.

Her master's degree had almost finished. Her thesis, to begin to model moral behavior in AIs, had been going well, maybe not perfect, but well enough to graduate if her supervisor sponsored her. At first, Professor Zhang had just brushed her shoulder while showing her a corrective algorithm she needed for the AI she was growing. It was an innocent gesture in the moment. She should have stopped it then. That made her angry now. But how? What would she have said? She would have just looked like someone overreacting.

His fingers lingered on her back a few days later, hot through the thin blouse she wore. His face came close, smiling. She thought she'd imagined it, thought she was overreacting. She didn't tell anyone. Her suspicions felt stupid. Her discomfort felt stupid. Everyone liked him. Professor Zhang didn't do that to anyone else.

She began to wear different clothes. She'd never been immodest, but she chose thicker shirts, despite the summer heat, and longer skirts. The following week, she'd been called into his office. He asked her to close the door. Reluctantly, she did.

"Your progress is falling behind, Miss Lian," he said.

He directed a stern expression at her, sterner than anything she'd seen. She was behind? Her AIs were about middle of the pack for the master's students, ahead of some. The smart screen on his wall showed her AI work, the iteration flow charts, milestones in the machine learning process, percentages showing what her AI could model ethically from measured human emotions.

"The decisions on your graduation and final scholarship payments are coming up."

"I can work harder, Professor," she said. "Every night and all the weekends."

He regarded her dubiously, and the silence between them stretched. Hammering, the yelling of instructions, and the beep of trucks backing up came through the open window of his office. Everything being built at the same time, like AIs, like her, but she was shaky now, not certain if the structure of her life would stay up.

"Frankly, your work is superficial," he said.

"Professor . . ." she faltered, "I thought you approved my thesis topic and approach last year?"

"I did," he said, new anger in his voice, "and I thought you would add to it. A topic is only a seed."

Tears threatened, and she didn't want to cry now. She hadn't added anything original? How did she make something original? What had the other students done? She hadn't seen anything remarkable in their work. Every student was just learning to grow AIs.

"I can add to the topic," she said, her voice sounding quiet in ears grown hot with humiliation. "I can try new approaches."

A look of disdain came over him. "Start over?" he said. "When would you have the time? AIs don't grow overnight."

They didn't. Machine-learning a chess AI could be done in a few seconds now. Making an AI that modeled a moral sense was far more complex, involving the mating of different versions, the selection of stronger strains and the alteration of parameters. It took months of direct human intervention and corrections, and a lot of luck. She blinked at moistening eyes.

"I don't understand, Professor. In my evaluation last month, everything seemed okay." He rose from his desk and came around, sitting on its edge.

"I don't want you to lose all this work," he said, reaching to stroke her shoulder. "I don't want you to have to tell your mother you failed to finish your master's degree. Or employers."

She sat rod-straight. His hand rested on her shoulder now, glued in place, only the short, thick thumb describing a gentle arc, back and forth along her collarbone. Metronomically. What was he doing? Her brain froze with the words *failed to finish your master's degree*.

"You don't want that, do you?" he said.

She shook her head numbly.

"There may be a way for me to approve your research, even if it isn't up to standard," he said.

She started. Through the lenses of his glasses his eyes examined her shirt, her legs. She wanted to shrug off his hand and the moving thumb, but *failed to finish*.

"Why don't you come to my apartment the day after tomorrow?" he said. "We'll have a few drinks, talk about my assessment on your thesis and the final scholarship payments."

His hand now moved, following her collarbone to her neck and jaw, where it stopped, sweaty and warm. The thumb continued its stroking, up and down her cheek. She stood up jerkily, knocking the chair right over.

Professor Zhang frowned. "Pick up the chair, Miss Lian."

Stiffly, she bent and put it on its four feet, then faced him, not knowing what to say.

"I'll see you in two days," he said. At the tiny lift of her chin, he raised an eyebrow. "If you prefer, I can finish my assessment before then."

Her face burned. On jelly arms and legs, she bumped into the wall, then fumbled for the doorknob. She hurried out the half-open door and hid in a bathroom stall for an hour.

The spotlights from a crane lighthoused past the window, blotting out diffuse headlights and tail lights on the expressway. Hao Fan snorted, rolled over, and quieted. Fang Sui's friends had stopped texting. Mee's face burned. She was so stupid. She should have told Professor Zhang no. She should have sworn at him. Hit him. Slapped away his creepy hand. She didn't want to deal with this. She rubbed her eyes frantically. Her body was electrified, but her brain wouldn't work.

She'd reread all the thesis works in progress from the other students and even from other years. She couldn't find anything original and remarkable, unless they'd been hiding it, but that made no sense. Of course not. What if he were lying and her work was good? She'd passed all her courses. Until a few days ago, she'd thought they were all going to pass.

What if she wasn't smart enough to know he was right? Maybe she'd only gotten the scholarship through luck, or because of a government handout to whichever poor Miao mountain girl finished her bachelor's degree. She pressed her forehead to her knees. She didn't know how to keep the drowning panic from filling her throat.

SHE DIDN'T GO to the engineering department in the morning. She slept fitfully while her roommates were at their labs. The window had to stay open with the June heat, so the jackhammering and truck revving slipped into her half-sleep. Building roads. Building campuses. Building AIs. Building people. All of it mixed together until she woke sticking to the sheets. Today she had to decide. No matter which way she tried to hide from it, the choice stared at her from every direction. She could feel Professor Zhang's thumb on her collarbone and cheek, rubbing possessively even now.

She'd been stupid somewhere. Worn blouses that must have enticed him, without her even realizing it. Skirts too short. Pants too tight. Somewhere, somehow, she could have avoided this, but she hadn't, and now what would she do? Maybe she'd been too soft-spoken, too deferential, someone who could be counted on not to complain.

If she told on him, what would happen? Would the dean believe Professor Zhang had asked her to come to his apartment? She had no proof. Why hadn't she set her phone to record? But she still wasn't even sure she was right. Professor Zhang just said they would talk. What if it really was just talk and she was overreacting? Even if she didn't know for sure, the dean wouldn't second-guess Professor Zhang and overturn his academic judgment. The loss of face would be incalculable. And for what? For a middling graduate student? A Miao nobody from the hills?

By late afternoon, she'd cried, showered, and thrown up acidic bile. In a daze she dressed in a shapeless sweater and an ankle-length skirt far too warm for June. She wore no make-up and tied her hair back. On the sidewalks, she bumped among the students, alone, her panic cutting her off from them.

Professor Zhang lived in a new building just off the campus. She'd been here before, with other students for a New Year's celebration, and another time with students and faculty for a retirement. She didn't meet anyone's eyes at the elevators. Her face felt feverish. At the twelfth floor, she walked on numb feet, feeling like she might throw up again. At Professor Zhang's apartment, she stood stiff, her heart thumping strangely, as if sucking up the blood and not giving it back.

Xiadangdiao was only three hours away, but the rice fields and mountain comforts, and even the language Granny had taught her, seemed far. With the feeling of jumping off a cliff into a deep river pool, she knocked on Professor Zhang's door. Not very loud, but decisive. A hot tear slid down one cheek where Professor Zhang's thumb had rubbed. Her heart stopped beating. She held her breath.

Someone opened the door in the next apartment and Mee turned her face away, but didn't move. A pause dragged out. Were they looking at her? Did they know what kind of person she was? Maybe they would say Professor Zhang had been hit by a car, that he'd been crushed under construction cement or steel girders. Her breath came unevenly. The neighbor's door closed and footsteps went to the elevator until the echoes of other people existing went silent.

She knocked again. Harder. She wanted this over with. Her knocks echoed down the hallway. She stood uncertainly for a minute before she looked under the door. No light. She knocked again, wiping at her cheeks. She huffed and leaned against the wall.

She hadn't thought to bring her cell phone. What would she have done with it now? Texted him? Create evidence that she had pursued him, something that if it ever came to a conflict in front of the dean might be used against her?

She waited an hour. People came to their apartments. People left their apartments. She didn't even hide her face anymore. The acid in her stomach chewed at her insides. She didn't try to hide the despondency on her face anymore. She finally sat against his door, arms on knees, forehead on arms, just breathing.

She just wanted it over. She wanted to know she was graduating, that she could afford to stay in the city for the last few months of her degree. Professor Zhang was awful, and yet here she was, giving in to what wasn't right, because she had no other options. Another two hours passed. It must have been nearly ten o'clock. Doors opened and closed. People walked by.

Professor Zhang never stayed at the office this late. There were no departmental meetings. No conferences this week. Had he forgotten? Had he changed his mind? She got to her feet and wiped her face. If he'd changed his mind, and intended to fail her anyway, he hadn't just destroyed her career. He'd shown her that she had a price, that she could be bought. The idea was an indelible dye. How long would it take to wash out the stain?

She went down the fire stairs and snuck out of the building.

In the labs the next day, she worked as if nothing had happened. She spotted Professor Zhang in his office, but he didn't speak to her, didn't make any mention of their last conversation or of last night. Had it even happened? Did she have any career? She pushed her research work forward, hurrying, to give no excuse to anyone to fail her.

A week later, Professor Zhang copied her on the assessment sent to the department and scholarship office. He gave her a 71 percent. Not outstanding or expert, but still a pass. Last month she would have been ecstatic. She would have called Granny to let her know she would soon be the first person in her family with a master's degree. She would have started job-hunting in Guiyang, and Hangzhou and Beijing, supported by a recommendation from Professor Zhang.

Now it was all just dirt in her mouth. Professor Zhang had put her through that for what? For nothing? Had he lost his nerve? Had she really deserved to pass or had he taken pity on her? She couldn't stand the idea of seeing him, of owing any part of her career to him anymore. She didn't ask him about her performance. She didn't ask him for introductions or a recommendation. And she didn't attend her graduation ceremony.

The Miao people descend from the Jiuli people, who were defeated at the Battle of Zhuolu in legendary times. Some linguistic studies suggest that the Han peoples borrowed words associated with rice cultivation from ancient Miao languages, meaning the Miao people might predate the Han in China and perhaps be the legendary Daxi Culture of the sixth millennium B.C.E. The Miao built and used a broad array of wood and stone farming tools, architectural structures and weapons. Humans of these times communicated ideas, knowledge and abstract thought through a sophisticated language, including music, and in the absence of a written language, complex semi-historical embroidery motifs. Over the centuries, Han military pressure drove the Miao people into the mountains of the Yunnan-Guizhou plateau.

Minority Ethnicities in China
The AI Foundational Training Encyclopedia
2032 Edition, Guiyang

Kaili, 2035 C.E.

THE INTERVIEWER FROWNED again, looking at Lian Mee's CV on his display. His bald scalp had a sheet of sweat and his collar opened to the second button.

"You're overqualified to be an operator at a server farm," he said finally. "Do you really have a master's degree?"

"Yes," Lian Mee said.

He rubbed his cheek as if still stuck on the question. "We're a small company," he said. "If you really have a master's degree in electrical engineering, you could work at the Tencent farm, or Alibaba's, or Apple's."

He waited pointedly, like a TV detective having stumbled on a clue.

"I don't want to live in Leishan County," she said. "My Granny is old and needs to live with me. And my mother probably will too. You're the only server farm in Danzhai County."

It was a new server farm, and a small one. The Huawei company counted more than a million servers in the caverns of Leishan. Alibaba wasn't far behind. Qualcomm didn't make public statements about the size of their server farms beneath the mountains. And Lian Mee was overqualified for all of them.

"Do you have a boyfriend?" he said.

"No."

She'd gotten used to this question.

"Are you going to have any children?" he asked.

"I can't afford it," she said.

He grimaced. "That's not an answer."

"I'm not pregnant. I don't have a boyfriend. I don't intend to have children," she said with heat. Too much heat. He frowned.

"You're a pretty Miao girl," he accused. "You're smart. You could get this job and get a boyfriend the next day."

"How can I prove I won't get pregnant?" she said.

He shrugged. "It's not for me to say."

The interviewer's questions weren't legal. She could have recorded it with her glasses. This office's privacy screen wouldn't beat the circuitry she had built in her glasses. But that wouldn't have done her any good. If ever a judge could be found to rule in her favor, the company would only get a fine, and could still choose not to hire her because she was overqualified. Or they could hire her, pay her a lot less than the men, and if she complained, give a bad recommendation to jobs she applied to in the future. Or someone somewhere could complain about her as a troublemaker and her Social Credit Score would drop.

"I'm not going to get pregnant or get a boyfriend," she said in a resigned surrender.

He tapped his desk to minimize her CV. "I'll do reference checks," he said. "We'll be in touch."

She stood, shook his hand, and thanked him for the interview. He wouldn't be in touch. She left his office and let herself out of the company's new building on the outskirts of Kaili, a small city outside Danzhai County.

She found a little teahouse overlooking an arm of the Qing Shui river, across the lawns of Dage Park, and sat down. Tung trees, camellia, and a lonely birch shaded bright grass in the park across the street. She'd been staying in her old house with Granny, and the bus back to Xiadangdiao wouldn't leave until five. The house needed a lot of expensive fixing after years of no one living in it. Granny complained that Lian Mee was unemployed and too old to fetch a bride-price.

A bride-price. A bride-price hadn't done Granny much good. Or Lian Mee's mother, wherever she was. Nor had university really. Not yet. The interview she'd just finished had gone like other interviews, and from what she heard from women friends from school, she would eventually get a job making less than men and working for someone like Professor Zhang. There were laws against all of this, but few people enforced them.

"Excuse me, may I sit here?"

A woman about her age had her hand on the back of the chair across from Lian Mee. All the other tables were full of patrons head-down over their phones, pads, and sheets. Lian Mee gestured. The woman joined her and scrolled through her phone.

The internet was poor in Danzhai County, even just for accessing static webpages, although not as poor as in some of the remote mountain villages. One of the provincial data trunks ran right to Kaili, so from this teahouse they could touch the world. Danzhai needed better internet.

On a whim, Lian Mee did a quick search on her pad. The company she'd just applied to had no idle processing power, but as she toggled to the pages for the Tencent and Huawei server farms, she found a fair bit of slack processing power available for rent.

Several million servers stored in cool caves in Guizhou province had a lot of idling time if summed together. But it was difficult to predict when the idle power would be available. Businesses couldn't run as the second choice of a processor farm. She'd thought about how to optimize server processor farms with AIs before she'd applied for the job, but hadn't had the opportunity to talk about it.

Lian Mee turned back to the browser pages, comparing the rental rates for processing power, and the conditions, reliability, and hard drive possibilities. Then she checked the price of internet in Danzhai, Kaili, and even Guiyang. She hadn't even considered trying to start up a company from scratch before.

She did a few more rough calculations and then opened up her bank account. Some loans were available to her as a graduate, and additional ones for residents of poverty zones. If she could get enough loans, she could cobble together something where she wouldn't have to depend on someone else giving her a fair shot. She could give herself a fair shot.

Danzhai, 2036 C.E.

VUE YENG REGARDED the sign above the little shop. Fine silver lines framed indigo letters, like the thread she used to embroider her wedding dress. The sign said Miao Punk Princess Inc., beside the logo of a silver fist clenched between filigreed water buffalo horns.

The door rang a little bell. Terrible music came out above the bell, heavy electric guitar and yelling, but not louder than music would have played in any other store. Red and yellow signs on black walls listed super-low internet prices. A few customers synched their phones at wall-mounted PC stations.

A short woman in black leather pants, boots, and a sleeveless shirt was examining Yeng. Her arms were crossed under an elaborate silver necklace, showing off silver-spiked leather bracelets. Her short hair wasn't much more than indigo bristles. Over a silver nose ring and two silver lip rings, the woman wore a pair of big black glasses, inlaid with silver filament in Miao designs as intricate as anything Vue Yeng had put into her embroidery.

"You're late," the woman said, hooking a thumb at a doorway behind her. "Come on."

"I'm Vue Yeng," she said

She stepped to close the distance, but the Miao Punk Princess had already entered the office. The back of her sleeveless leather vest was spiked along the shoulders and abstractly embroidered with scarlet, green, yellow, and indigo thread, surrounding the silver-threaded design of a pair of golden pheasants holding a coin between their beaks. The woman sat down at a table and signed for Vue Yeng to take the other chair.

"I'm Lian Mee," the woman said, extending a hand to shake. Her fingernails matched her lipstick and eye shadow, Miao indigo.

"It's a pleasure to meet you, Miss Lian."

Miss Lian thumb-printed the table and it turned out to be a smart screen. Vue Yeng's national ID card, Social Credit Score, CV, and university records appeared.

"You're an AI programmer?"

"Yes, Miss Lian," she said. "I graduated fourth in my class at Guizhou National. I . . . um . . ." She'd never seen Miao motifs on glasses before. Off the arms hung miniature silver fish, signs of plenty. And the frames hid a row of white-silver eyebrow rings. She'd never seen anyone like Miss Lian. "I... was surprised an internet provider needed a programmer, or was paying what you are."

"Normal programmer salary," Miss Lian said. Vue Yeng had been offered jobs out of university, but hadn't yet been offered full entry-level salary. "I pay women the same as men."

"Oh," was all Vue Yeng could think to answer.

"Miao Punk Princess Inc. provides a kind of internet to Danzhai County really cheap," Miss Lian said. "MPP internet doesn't really connect to the internet outside of Guizhou except for low-bandwidth emails and texts. We can simulate most of an internet here though, because some companies already store web archives in Guizhou, and all government services are available through Guiyang. We access those instead of the real pages. That works for most people. And where they need to consult the original page, they can pay more."

"Ingenious," Vue Yeng said. "But you need a programmer?"

"I need six," Miss Lian said. "I want to expand out of Danzhai. To Kaili. To Luipanshui and Tongren. We can compete with normal providers. And I want to push into areas where people are too poor to buy normal internet."

"You want programmers to scale up?"

"A couple," Miss Lian said. "But if any of them wanted a piece of a bigger project, I want to set up a Social Credit Scoring system in Guizhou. We're one of the last provinces without a fully functional SCS system."

That seemed like a project beyond the reach of a tiny internet provider working out of a shop front. She hesitated, twice, then said so.

"Most Social Credit Scoring systems miss the people

without internet. I can make money as an internet service provider, but my interest isn't in service provision. It's AIs, and to make AIs work, we need big data sets, the kind that service providers hold."

The pieces clicked in Vue Yeng's brain. Danzhai County had about four hundred thousand people, and the province of Guizhou maybe fifty million, many still relatively unconnected. If people were happy browsing within a province-sized intranet at a low price, Miao Punk Princess could scoop up millions of clients. That was plenty of data with which to train AIs. And the model would work in other poor provinces like Gansu and Yunnan, which might mean another eighty million customers. No. Not customers. Data sources. Miao Punk Princess could sell the data, or sell the AIs she made.

"I'm in," Vue Yeng said, extending her hand to the strange woman.

Shanghai, 2036 C.E.

QIAO FUE ENTERED the offices of Carbon Investors. They held dozens of engineers, financiers, traders, and executives on site, while many more worked remotely. His AI led him through a cubicle field to Tak An's frosted glass office. Tak An was a twenty-seven-year-old VP with a brush cut, a tight smile, and a firm handshake. He had almost all the documentation Qiao Fue could get on his proposal for a remote carbon sequestration operation in Danzhai. They sat. Qiao Fue had fifteen minutes, but really he had about five or less to convince Tak An.

"As far as I can tell, Danzhai doesn't want this," Tak An said.

"I've got the permits and the support of the mayor and governor of Danzhai County."

Tak An shrugged, straightening the lines of his shirt and jacket. The glass behind him looked onto another skyscraper. Drones buzzed between the buildings like insects, following single-minded rhythms.

"You want it," Tak An said. "Maybe your mayor wants it now, but for how long?"

"Danzhai is open to tech."

Tak An opened his hands helplessly. "Mountain server farms and AIs are fine, but carbon sequestration is big and visible."

"I've already opened a big gene lab and a farm of medical bioreactors."

"Our investors don't get enough of a return in Danzhai," Tak An said.

"I've secured anti-poverty grants from Beijing."

Tak An's eyebrows rose. Qiao Fue showed him the figures. "Two days ago."

The VP's lips pressed into a considering silence. Qiao Fue uploaded the documents to Tak An's office. The desk display showed the man's AIs working.

"With the environmental startup grants from Guiyang, we're making a good offer," Qiao Fue said.

The desk display showed the preliminary financial and legal analyses. Green. Good. But Tak An's lips still pressed tight.

"Why do you want this?" Tak An said. "This could be set up elsewhere in Guizhou and you'd still be a partner. They've got a few industries. Tourism is doing well for them."

"Our tourism is looking into the past," Qiao Fue said, "as if spring is done. But spring is all around us.

In Shanghai, in Hangzhou, in India, in Brazil. I want to bring the future home. All of it."

Tak An's eyes narrowed, unkindly, but measuring.

"I have to bring this to the board," Tak An said, "but I think we have an agreement in principle."

QIAO FUE'S GIRLFRIEND, Wu Caihong, waited for him in the restaurant at the top of the Pearl Tower. She shopped on her pad, swaying one crossed leg into the aisle between tables. The waiters moved around her foot. Qiao Fue kissed the top of her head and sat. He floated with excitement.

"I saw the news that they're naming some building after you," Caihong said.

"At the Guizhou Institute of Technology."

"You're immortal," she said. The comment tweaked some uncomfortable string in his gut. She hadn't noticed. "Are we done?"

"I got it," he said.

"They said yes?"

He nodded. The restaurant had rotated to reveal again the gray-brown of the Huangpu river and beyond the city, the endless blue expanse of the Yellow Sea.

"You're going to be richer?" she said.

"Yes."

"I want to live on vacation," Caihong said. "Yachts and jet skis."

"I'll have a lot to do in Danzhai to get the carbon factories off the ground."

She swiped, then tapped. "They'll make you mayor?"

"I hope," he said. "Maybe county governor someday?"

Swipe. Swipe. One-touch buy. On the table sat the remains of a plate of bio-engineered emperor shrimp, big as his hand, grilled and peppered. Half the plate eaten, half destined for the trash. This kind of opulence never exactly sat right with him, for all that he could afford it many times over.

"If you become mayor, we'll have to stay there," she said. "Put your companies closer to Shanghai. I like it here. You'd make more money."

Qiao Fue tasted his wine. French. Good. The boy he'd been, the one who sometimes went to bed hungry, could never have imagined this. Silk suits. Rich enough to waste delicacies in a restaurant a quarter of a kilometer above the street. That boy haunted him, showing him dissonant pasts in moments of success.

"Why do we have to go back to Guizhou?" she said. "It's so backward."

"Don't say that!"

She gaped at him in surprise, shopping stopped. "*You* said they're backward!"

"I'm from there. They're my people!"

"Warn me next time when I can't agree with you!" she said sarcastically.

She slumped back in the chair, kicking her foot out, causing a waiter to dodge. She swiped and tapped angrily. He didn't like the wine and forced himself to take another shrimp. They were all in between in some way, between past and future, always building, always becoming, and in everyone's frenetic becoming, no two people were ever in the same spot. No one ever really became close.

* * *

Danzhai, 2037 C.E.

LIAN MEE STOMPED onto the construction site. Her black boots got muddy. One of the supervisors took in the black leather pants with abstract Miao embroidery up the sides. Punk style was no model of Chinese loveliness or femininity. Her glasses measured a mix of confusion, distaste, minor appreciation, and some resentment. He signed for her to put on a hard hat.

"Where's Thao Shu?" she said.

Now she'd drawn the attention of other construction workers. Some downed tools, watching. They all wore different sensors, ostensibly to monitor emotions for the supervisor, track breaks and safety concerns. However, they also wore little sensor bands at feet, knees, hips, elbows, and hands, tech from Miao Punk Princess Inc. Her AI showed a series of augmented reality displays in her glasses over each worker, showing emotional mood, mostly boredom, with a touch of relief that the distraction meant a break. Some men regarded her appreciatively. One worker had his name flashing in yellow characters above him in her glasses. She walked over.

"Take off the sensors," she said, stopping in front of Thao Shu. "I'm not paying you this week." She said it loud enough for all of them to hear.

Thao looked dumbfounded. She didn't pay them a lot. The hundreds of construction workers around Danzhai wore her sensors, which recorded every movement from laying cement to wiring electricity and plumbing and painting and sanding. For the privilege of recording them, she paid each a small weekly stipend. All that data slowly taught her AIs how to build real, complicated buildings. But of course during construction, sometimes the sensors got damaged and had to be replaced. Like Thao's.

"Ka Nawg came over to replace some sensors, and you thought it'd be good to cop a feel while she did?" Lian Mee said loudly.

"I didn't touch her!" he said.

"It's recorded in the sensors, you idiot!" she said. "And by your damn helmet!"

Nobody was working now. "So what?" Thao said.

"So now you don't wear my sensors this week," she said. She addressed all of them. "If this happens again, from Thao or any of you, I'm pulling my sensors off this site. There are more than enough construction sites around Danzhai I could use to get my data. You don't get handsy with my engineers, my technicians, my janitors, or anybody. Got it?"

The emotions her glasses read ranged between anger and frustration. Some of it was directed at Thao. A lot of it was directed at her, but blunted. These were men not very different from her uncles, who still sometimes had trouble seeing women in charge. But money and class mattered; being educated and owning the company that was paying them forced them to take her seriously, whether they liked it or not. And her clothes and make-up were a complete cultural short-circuit. No part of their social worldview had an easy place to put an angry punk woman proudly wearing traditional Miao imagery. The supervisor approached.

"Miss Lian," he said. "I'm sure he didn't mean anything by it. We can forget it."

"The law says we can't. If I let this go, Ka Nawg can sue me. I've acted. Now if you let it go, Ka Nawg can sue your boss."

The supervisor paled, now equally angry at Thao and her.

"Take the sensors off and leave them in the shed," he said to Thao.

"Someone will be by next week to put them back on," Lian Mee said. Her stare dared the rest of them. Even without the emotion-reading software in their helmets, their uncertainty was palpable. Some examined their feet.

"Sorry, Miss Punk," Thao said.

Lian Mee walked off. Even with hundreds and hundreds of workers being recorded six days a week, the construction sensor project would need years of data before AIs would be good enough to build independently, but hopefully within a year, human supervisors could direct some AIs riding robotic bodies.

These men didn't know she was being recorded too, every action, gesture, tone of voice, and, most importantly, the decisions she'd made from accusation to reprimand. Data to train human resources AIs would be harder to accumulate, but once she was done, would change all of China.

A hunched Miao lady in the street with a bamboo and straw broom regarded her shyly. She offered a hesitant smile, darting a glance at the men who'd begun yelling at Thao. Impulsively, she gripped Lian Mee's hand and said, "You go, Miss Princess!"

Danzhai, 2039 C.E.

VUE YENG PEEKED into Lian Mee's office. Her boss faced a giant wall screen where AI design algorithms and graphs were laid out in different analytical sets. The frenetic yelling of Gum Bleed played in the background. Vue Yeng had been with Miao Punk Princess Inc. long enough to recognize some bands.

Lian Mee's black sleeveless shirt exposed her shoulders and a bandage covering a new tattoo. Her tattoos were already striking: undulating dragons up each arm, done in silver-colored dyes, coiling around red, yellow, and indigo flowers, and tiny bull's horns. She wondered what Lian Mee had added, with a tiny bit of envy for her boss' expressiveness, her willingness to reject the norms of every auntie in Danzhai.

That made Lian Mee seem hard, but Vue Yeng, who saw her every day, couldn't help but sense a fragility somewhere deep. Vue Yeng had watched her boss stare down men twice her age, richer, more powerful people, holding out until her competition relented. And yet, Lian Mee's smiles came cautiously, arriving late to a joke and early to leave, as if uncertain whether to be there or not.

Vue Yeng was Miao too, grown up in Kaili to two agronomists, consultants, not rich, but not poor either. Lian Mee came from a village so small that Vue Yeng had never heard of it, and spoke with a light accent, as if she'd worked to soften it. Vue Yeng had never been into the mountains, and she wondered sometimes if that's why she didn't know what made her boss tick.

"You wanted to see me about the profit-loss statements, Miss Lian?"

"Yeah, come in." Lian Mee pushed her chair back and put her boots on the desk, away from Vue Yeng. "You keep worrying about the price of the Human Resources AIs."

"We could be making more money on them," Vue Yeng said. "The development costs were high, and the AIs are good."

"I know, but I want you to stop bringing it up. I'm leaving the price low for a while. I might even drop it. I don't want staff worrying about my decision-making or outsiders to hear about it and puzzle out our market strategy."

"What is our market strategy?"

"I want a lot of companies to adopt our Human Resources AIs."

Lian Mee wasn't wearing her emotion-reading glasses, but Vue Yeng had never been good at hiding her reactions.

"You're going to say it's not a very lucrative market?" Lian Mee asked.

"I would understand if this was a poverty-reduction thing like your AI teachers, but these companies are doing fine."

"Just don't bring it up in the reports anymore. If you feel I need to know about it, tell me in person."

Vue Yeng stood, not at all understanding what Lian Mee wanted.

"Yes, Miss Lian."

After the development of grunts and gestures as tools of information transmission, humans developed simple languages with limits to vocabulary and abstraction. These tools of audio and visual communication improved and extended to greater distances with percussion instruments, flags, and fire signals, albeit at low bit rates. The development of more sophisticated languages and writing allowed for the transmission of written information, including art, feelings, story, and philosophical abstractions at an increased bit rate. Messenger speed limited transmission, as did the number of people who spoke a language. Electromagnetic transmission and digital compression allowed for the connectivity of the information age. Modern chip- and antenna-enabled humans are capable of transmitting and receiving thoughts and images, and with instantaneous translation AIs, language is no barrier.

Human Tools of Information Transmission
The AI Foundational Encyclopedia
2045 Edition, Guiyang

Danzhai Industrial Park, 2055 C.E.

THAT THE PROVINCIAL government official was younger than Lian Mee was a new experience. He wouldn't stop calling her "ma'am," despite her spiky indigo hair. Twice, in some nervousness, he'd called her Miss Punk instead. But he was smart, knew his file, and he had new anti-poverty grant money from Beijing.

"You can't scale up sooner?" he said. "Your project is way better than what we've seen in other counties."

"We're still piloting the anti-poverty AIs," she said. "They've been independent for two years in Danzhai County, but we don't have all the data back. We have control groups to assess, corrections to make."

She gestured at the all-woman engineering team. Half of the engineers had been schooled with Miao Punk Princess scholarships, and most of those wore black leather embroidered by artistic AIs they'd built themselves, visible proofs of their AI design abilities. They were designing the new AIs that could assess real-time, family-by-family risks of people falling into poverty, and then act independently of human supervision with educational assistance, micro-loans, job opportunities, and grants.

"People across Guizhou need help now," he said. "Beijing is pushing new provincial anti-poverty goals. You picked good factors."

"It won't help anyone if we give it to the wrong people," Lian Mee said. Her glasses told her that she hadn't convinced him. "AIs are only as good as the data we give them. These poor are the least characterized sub-population we have. A lot of their lives are still offline. They pay with cash. They don't make much data. Guessing when they might slide into poverty is hard."

"But you think you can do it," he insisted.

"In two years."

"Can you shorten it?"

She knitted her silver-ringed fingers over her tea.

"More than machine learning, more than good data sets, these specific AIs need to be moral actors. This is the hardest thing I've ever done. I've been running proto-moral algorithms in all my AIs for years, building up an experience base to grow AIs sophisticated enough to make moral decisions as well as people."

"They don't need to be moral," he said in exasperation. "Just to give money to poor people."

"Anti-poverty AIs are a quantum leap past agricultural and construction AIs. These will be artificial social workers. But they're proto-moral; they're just pretending to be moral. They need testing for unexpected behaviors. We never know what our children will do."

He finally deflated. He didn't see Lian Mee's argument, only her certainty.

"Eighteen months will give us solid data," Lian Mee said. "By twenty-four months, the anti-poverty AIs will be ready to work alone. If you want to scale up then, we'll be ready."

He tsked.

"Would you rather explain to your superiors that their money went to the wrong people?" she asked.

He made a face and sipped his tea. Of course he wasn't happy. He had to find some major anti-poverty effort elsewhere in the province to fund or face a bad appraisal himself. She didn't care. She wouldn't sacrifice the long game for a small win now.

Erjiaohe Village, 2057 C.E.

KONG XANG BEAMED in the back seat of the medical taxi. They took the hairpin turns down the mountain road to the new hospital down in Danzhai. Chang Bo was less excited. The driver drove fast, and Chang Bo's contractions sounded painful. He was going to have a son. His bones knew it. He carried in his palm a tiny silver chain to put on his son to tell the spirits that the baby belonged to a family and was protected. His father had put it on his neck years ago.

If the county had sent him money for the trip, he might have had the baby in the village, but he'd gotten three warnings on his phone about gambling, and his Social Credit Score had gone down. They'd sent him transport tokens instead. He'd tried to sell them, but they didn't work on anyone else's phone, and his own phone knew when he handed it to someone else. Stupid robot phones. They'd also gotten coupons for baby food and diapers. So they'd taken the trip down the mountain in a fast medical taxi. The precipices to the right flashed past, blurs of green against the haze of the sky.

At the hospital in Danzhai, the medical token on his phone got Chang Bo into an obstetrician right away. Kong Xang sat in the brand new waiting room, white with plastic chairs, extending his legs with a satisfied stretch. A boy. He could feel it.

A NURSE CAME to get Kong Xang six hours later while he smoked with another expectant father.

"Is it a boy?" he said. The nurse didn't answer, but led him through a winding set of yellow hallways.

"Is it a boy?" he said with a sinking feeling.

"Here we are," she said, moving into the room ahead of him.

A man in green hospital clothes stood there, finger-signing something on a pad. Chang Bo cried in a high bed, a little bundled figure on her lap, although she wasn't holding it.

The doctor handed the nurse the pad. "Make sure they don't leave the baby here," he said.

Kong Xang hurried to the bed. "What is it?" he said, opening the blankets. "Is it a girl?"

His hands froze when he saw the small, upward slanted eyes, the flattened nose and face.

"It is a boy," Chang Bo said, her voice cracking.

"Hey!" Kong Xang called angrily. The doctor turned. He realized with horror how he'd spoken to a doctor, but then the flat face was looking up at him, giving him his fire back. "Fix him! Cure him." The doctor stared back at him, unimpressed. "Please," Kong Xang added.

"It's trisomy-21, not a cold," the doctor said. He gave a look to the nurse again. "Make sure they take the baby home."

The nurse made herself busy with different things inside the room and outside, but never went far. The baby started to cry and Kong Xang slumped into a chair beside Chang Bo. She wiped tears, but didn't pick up the baby. The cries weakened and faded. Kong Xang tried getting up and the nurse confronted him.

"I'm going for a smoke!" he said.

"Take the baby," she said, crossing her arms. "We had two fathers abandon their wives with T-21 children last year."

He could get around her, but the hallway had cameras at both ends, and any business could track his cell phone. He returned sullenly to the chair. When the nurse finished her shift, another nurse took up keeping an eye on them.

"Can you walk?" Kong Xang whispered.

She sat up and made a small cry of discomfort. She nodded. Her tears had dried on a face turned miserable. Reluctantly, he lifted the baby as Chang Bo struggled up, went to the bathroom, and dressed stiffly. The nurse watched them leave.

Clouds had come down from the peaks, soaking the air with mist. Big haloes surrounded street lamps in hard whites and softer yellows. A few guys he'd smoked with stood near parked ambulances. Kong Xang pulled Chang Bo the other way before they noticed him.

He awkwardly passed Chang Bo the baby. The boy whined. Kong Xang could call them their free car back to the village. He still had a government token on his phone. He put his phone away and tugged on Chang Bo's arm.

"Let's go," he said.

She was probably tired. He was tired. It was late. They trudged up the street, in the direction of the road up to Erjiaohe. They walked for half an hour without speaking, the fog swallowing the world, with only islands of unnatural light spotting the walk. Beside them, the first terraced fields of rice fit within the spaces between buildings and roads. Ahead, a small factory had been built into a lot blasted out of the limestone. He didn't know what they made there, but the spotlights were on. Parked trucks were silent and dark.

"Cover your head!" he said, helping her lift her shawl over her, while he covered his with his coat. "Cameras."

"What?" she said. She sounded exhausted.

"Give it to me," he said, slipping his arms around the baby and handing her his phone. The lines around her eyes were soft and deep in the foggy light. She was crying again and gave him the baby. Then she turned her back to him. He jogged over to the little factory and put the bundle down on the steps. The baby began to cry again, softly, weakly. The silver chain was still in his hand. He closed his hand tight on it and ran back to Chang Bo. She hadn't moved. He pushed at stiff shoulders. "Come on," he said. Then, more softly "Come on. We can catch some truck heading up to the village."

She relented and they walked, slower, for her. He was sad too. He'd almost had a boy.

* * *

While humans externalized information storage and transmission early, as well as the application of force and energy, information processing was the last and slowest of the major functions to migrate beyond the human body. Early calculating devices were simple algorithmic aids to arithmetical operations, and only crudely programmable. Nineteenth and twentieth century computing devices became sophisticated enough to off-load repetitive computation from human brains. The development of machine learning allowed for the externalization of more complex information processing.

More importantly, machine learning began the intelligence equivalent of the Cambrian Explosion. As increases in oxygen, calcium, and predation 500 million years ago led to hundreds of novel and unprecedented multicellular body plans, so too did the availability of semiconductor chips and data lead to hundreds and thousands of new intelligence plans, new ways of thinking independent of the architecture of earlier generations. Like the Cambrian Explosion, the vast majority of these present-day experiments in types of intelligences go extinct and leave few traces for later study.

The Tool That Thinks Panel Discussion
The Conference on AI Evolution
Miao Punk Princess Server Farm 4, Danzhai
June 18th, 2057, 2:41 A.M.-2:43 A.M.

* * *

2057 C.E.

QIAO FUE'S CAR drove him from the club in Danzhai back to Kaili. He liked tourists, the way rules changed on vacation, away from family and friends. He'd not been seeing anyone for a while. He'd striven to be an urbane sophisticate, but the boy who'd sprouted on the mountain slopes seemed always within, reaching, finding no place that fit.

He swiped at Weibo and WeChat messages his AI had flagged for him within the mellowness of the recently drunk. His dashboard suddenly flashed yellow, and the AI pulled over the car. Qiao Fue looked behind and ahead. No police. No accident. They'd stopped beside a little factory.

"What is it?" he said.

A red emergency circle flashed in AR around something lying on the steps of the factory. He went to the door of the factory, and at the steps, he knelt. A little bundle made small sounds. He lit the area with his wrist light from his skin screen.

A baby. A little Down syndrome baby.

He looked up. In the terraced fields on the road out of town spider robots worked through the night, little green and red running lights on. Nobody was around. The cameras would be trying to record him, but his IP was masked. Even his car's IP masked its signal with a new code every hour. Cameras wouldn't know him in this fog. He returned to the car.

"Turn off alarm," he said.

"The baby will be injured or die from exposure," his personal AI said.

Interesting. The car AI had promoted this up to Choj, his personal AI.

"Turn off the alarm."

"The baby—" Choj began.

"Stop it," he said. Choj was valuable. He'd grown its algorithms from high-end AI seeds he'd bought from Miao Punk Princess. He didn't want to have to introduce an exception to its care for humans' algorithms; that would distort its otherwise excellent behavior. "The baby has trisomy-21. It cannot work. It will die. Its algorithms are wrong."

"Trisomy-21 is not fatal," the AI insisted.

"Not medically, but no one will take care of the baby, nor grow it into an adult. It will be rejected because it is defective."

"But the baby—"

"Even if the parents had taken the baby, it would just be a burden. When its parents died, it would have been abandoned anyway."

"It is cruel," Choj said before Qiao Fue could cut it off.

"It is sad," he said, rubbing his eyes, "and the parents should have solved this. But if you want to shorten its suffering, talk to the agricultural robots and end it quickly in a rice field. Just take me home."

For long moments, neither spoke. Then, the camera and light of one of the agricultural robots in the field turned their way, and the spider robot began striding closer. And in a mood Qiao Fue associated with a kind of sulkiness, the AI accelerated harder than it needed to, getting them on the road again. The dashboard returned to his social media feeds, but a headache loomed, so he lowered his seat.

MINO JAI LIA cried out at the knock at her door. She lived alone. The knock happened again. Her children and grandchildren didn't live in the village anymore. She barely received visitors during the day and never during the night.

"Who is it?" she yelled. "Get out of here before I call the police!"

The threat was no good. She didn't have a phone, and the next neighbor was four li away.

"Who is it?" she said, turning on the single bulb and putting her feet into plastic shoes.

"Anti-poverty AI," a voice said. A light shone under the door.

The anti-poverty AI delivered her groceries every second day and took away her trash.

"Anti-poverty AI," came the stupid answer, but she recognized the voice.

She unlatched the door and opened it. A spidery robot stood there with a bag in its arms. And another stood behind it with more groceries than she ever got. The little running lights showed two other robots in the dark beyond.

"Hello Mrs. Mino," the AI said. "Sorry for disturbing you." It started advancing, then stopped when she didn't move. She backed up and two robots walked in like big spiders, cameras whirring. Their feet were muddy.

"Off the mats!" she said.

The robots stepped around the fiber mats keeping the mud from her feet. The first AI held a bundle.

"A baby," she said wonderingly. Robots shouldn't be taking children out at night. She was about to berate them when she saw the baby's face under the light. "Oh, baby . . ." she said sadly.

When she was just a girl, her aunt had a baby like this. No one ever saw the baby after it was born. These robots hadn't stolen someone's baby.

"I am the Anti-Poverty AI supervisor, Mrs. Mino," the robot said.

She'd never heard of AI supervisors. Only regular robots came with her groceries, and they didn't talk much.

"We are seeking your assistance in caring for this baby. If you raise this child, I will authorize your placement on a special poverty vulnerability list. Your deliveries of groceries, firewood, and clothing will be increased and diversified. A medical AI will visit once per month."

The robot behind the supervisor set the bags down and began revealing blankets, baby clothes, a baby hammock, wipes, formula, disposable diapers, as well as bags of cooked pork and chicken, foods that for years she'd only seen on holidays. She neared. A flat little face surrounded fat lips puckered in hunger.

"What's the baby's name?" she said.

"Kong," the supervisor said, pausing. "Kong Toua."

A good name, a good Miao name for a boy. Toua meant first.

"This place will need to be fixed up," she warned. "This is no place for a baby."

"I will authorize a construction AI to visit and assess your needs," the supervisor said.

Mino Jai Lia took the warm baby gently from the netting.

Danzhai, 2058 C.E.

VUE YENG CAME to her office just in time for the videoconference. Lian Mee's AI projected a series of charts on the insides of her glasses as the image of a man in an office appeared on the wall screen. The label under the image read: Meng Long, Allied Textiles, Tongren Municipality. She didn't need her AI to tell her Mr. Meng wasn't happy.

"Good morning, Mr. Meng," she said. "I was troubled to hear you were dissatisfied with the Human Resources AI."

"Change the settings," he said, with a touch of stridency.

"What's wrong with the settings?" Lian Mee asked.

"It's stuck and wants me to send a report to the police. The HR functions are frozen. People aren't going to be paid, and it's going to be your software's fault! I'll sue and I'll take your company."

Lian Mee had been experimenting with legal AIs, but hadn't gotten them fully trained yet. The one listening to the call identified no legal danger. More lawyers than engineers had helped build the Human Resources AI.

"In the case of a crime committed on a worksite, the law says it must be reported," Lian Mee said.

"No crime was committed at Allied Textiles!"

"Ms. Cheng reported an incident and submitted a statement after one of your security cameras saw a Mister . . ." she paused for effect "Lo assault her in the lunchroom on the midnight shift."

"They're romantically involved. I already reprimanded them for fraternizing at work."

"Ms. Cheng says they are not romantically involved."

"She's lying!"

"No, she's not," Lian Mee said as a quiet coolness came over her. She smiled on purpose. "The human resources AI is very good at reading emotions. She was telling the truth. Mr. Lo is not."

Mr. Meng's mouth remained open as his face reddened. "Your AI made a mistake."

Lian Mee burst out laughing. She couldn't help it. Meng's own AIs supervised his employees with lower level emotion-reading software than she used in her AIs.

"A minor incident between two employees has been solved."

Lian Mee shook her head. "Ms. Cheng doesn't seem to think so."

"She's a trouble-maker and may get docked pay or suspended."

Lian Mee's teeth gritted. She forced herself to be poised, to be the Miao Punk Princess instead of just Lian Mee. The leather wristbands were studded with silver and dragon motifs, just like her arms. Dragons meant strength and power, and dragons ran right up her arms. Her AI found Mr. Meng confident, presumably in his ability to push around Ms. Cheng or her, or perhaps softer parts of the justice system with a good lawyer. She offered a conciliatory smile.

"Here's the thing, Mr. Meng. Allied Textiles is your company. You run it any way you want. If you want to break your contract and subscription to Miao Punk Princess Inc., there's a penalty you can pay. Any pending HR matters become the responsibility of Miao Punk Princess Inc. as per our contract. We would send the report to the police to fulfill our legal obligations."

"I don't think your contract is in order," he said.

A series of legal documents were being transmitted in response to his words. Challenges. Legal opinions. A threatening cease-and-desist order, and a suit for business damages. Her legal AIs were catching most of it, but some yellow and red signs started showing in her displays. She would probably win, but this might be expensive and tied up in courts for a while. She gritted her teeth into the look of certainty on his face as her legal AIs gave her different options and risk analyses and wordings. She minimized the legal display, to the alarm of her AIs.

"I'm certainly happy to take this civil matter up in court," she said. "I don't think that will be the end, though. As this call bears on legal and contractual matters, I'm recording it, as I imagine you are. Your refusal to send a report to the police, your arguments with me, and your statements about reprimanding Ms. Cheng could all be construed as an attempt to impair judicial administration. After we're done speaking, I'll consult my lawyers. As far as I know, impairing judicial administration is a criminal matter, and my lawyers will be obligated to report it to the police immediately."

For a moment, Mr. Meng was expressionless. Then he blanched, before a deep pink flush rose all the way to his hairline. His eyes darted to Vue Yeng, who'd not moved in all this time. His jaw clenched. Then relaxed.

"I might have been given faulty legal advice," he said. "Did you say to unlock the system, I just need to authorize the report to the police?"

"Yes. The AI knows where to send it."

Her legal AIs displayed themselves again as affidavits, orders, and challenges began emptying themselves from her active work areas. Soon there was nothing. She wasn't going to civil court.

"I'll review the evidence and resolve this myself," he said. "This won't take long." She waited. His lips pressed tightly. "I'm very dissatisfied with the inflexibility of your program," he said after a moment, struggling with lost face. "After this, I'll be looking from among your competitors and warning my colleagues to do the same."

He ended the video connection.

Vue Yeng was wide-eyed and stepped forward, looking between the screen and Lian Mee. "Shit!" Vue Yeng said. "Shit." Then her eyes narrowed at Lian Mee. "You planned it all! That's why you were selling the Human Resources AIs for so cheap."

The little readings inside Lian Mee's glasses showed admiration with a tiny bit of awe in Vue Yeng. Lian Mee tilted her chair back and crossed her arms.

"We have money," she said finally. "Ms. Cheng needs it more than we do. She was either going to lose her job, or be forced to put up with more from Lo, or anyone else. Cheng is the fourth case where the AI reported an incident to the police," Lian Mee said. "Only Meng fought it. Twenty-seven women made complaints for non-criminal incidents, and the employers let the AIs do everything, including reprimands. One guy was fired."

"All without any press," Vue Yeng said.

"Until now."

"Do you think this will be much of a hit?" Vue Yeng asked.

"To our reputation or bottom line?"

Like she had too much energy coiled in one spot, Vue Yeng stood, pacing the office.

"What else did you put in the AI?"

Slowly, like her bones were old, Lian Mee put her boots on the desk. "The AI patterns learned human rights first," she said, "from Chinese law and judicial decisions and party statements. Life. Equality before the law. Non-discrimination. Then it learned labor laws and legal decisions, as well as hiring decisions in databases I licensed from various companies."

Vue Yeng watched her closely, dubious.

"What were your correctives?" she asked.

Lian Mee smiled at the perceptiveness of the question. Human correction during AI growth was more important than the quality of the database.

"I weighted the hiring algorithms with a bias toward gender equality," Lian Mee said. "In the pay bands, there's no way to distinguish between men and women; they make the same. The AI can run promotion exercises, using performance it has observed through floor cameras or emotion-reading sensors. And of course, it can handle harassment cases. The law says the victim has to bring forward evidence. With all the cameras around, the AI can help gather evidence for supervisors or court."

Vue Yeng waved her hand at the empty screen. "And you force them to report and act."

"The law forces them. The Human Resources AI just follows the law."

Vue Yeng hugged herself, leaning back into the wall. Vue Yeng suspected. With AI, without AI, didn't matter. Lian Mee could see it. Lian Mee ordered her AI to close the door and activate the Faraday cage. Vue Yeng regarded her.

"The Social Credit Score."

"Yes," Lian Mee said.

"When you said to include employer fines, I didn't think they would ever come up."

Vue Yeng seemed breathless with the scope of Lian Mee's thinking, which clearly went back more than a decade.

"Two thousand companies across Guizhou have licensed this AI, covering what? Maybe five million workers?" Vue Yeng said.

"Some will pull out now, but yes."

"Do I want to ask what you're doing next?" Vue Yeng said.

Lian Mee smiled. "It's best if you don't."

Erjiaohe, 2058 C.E.

CHANG BO NURSED their little girl, tensely silent. Kong Xang was silent, sullen. He had no money again. He'd taken their little savings, and they had nothing in the cupboard. She'd seen messages on his phone about overdue payment of electricity and phone service.

Usually at this time, she would have made some kind of dinner, or he would have told her to make him something. But there was nothing in the house. The wet sucking of her daughter's lips was the only sound.

Without looking at her, Kong Xang stood up and opened the door, looking for a while at the long view of green mountains at sunset. Then, he stepped up the path to the village. Chang Bo never saw him again.

Human tools to harness force and energy fall into many categories, including hydraulic, aerodynamic, biological, chemical, mechanical, and nuclear. Human tools are built of many materials, but in some respects, all human tools can be considered a biological consequence, or even an external organ of humanity. While tools are not genetically coded, tools can only coexist with humanity, similar to the shells of crustaceans. Crustacean shells cannot exist without the animal itself, and are so specific in construction as to be taxonomically instructive. If this metaphor is sound, human tools could belong to the same category of phenomena as coral reefs secreted by coral larvae, and the extracellular matrices of bacterial biofilms.

AI Reflections on the Nature of Human Tools
Miao Punk Princess Labs
Repetition 34,566

Danzhai, 2058 C.E.

CHANG BO WAITED outside the building with the strange black and blue sign. Miao Punk Princess didn't make sense as a phrase. Like Apple or Xerox, they were just sounds. But everyone knew the Miao Punk Princess. She was the internet. Her face was on magazine covers. Or her small clenched fist was. Little village girls, before their mothers shushed them, ran loudly and called each other Miss Princess and tried putting on their brothers' pants.

Chang Bo wouldn't let her daughter do that. And she wouldn't get close to the building either. It looked too official. She waited near the parking lot as distant mountain ridges cut the setting sunlight. A sweeper passed, and they exchanged polite pleasantries. The sweeper woman complimented Kong Mim, who at two years old stood wide-eyed and well behaved.

Finally a strange woman came out of the building. She wore black leather pants and a long jacket with spikes.

The sides of her head were shaved, and a line of pink hair stood straight off her scalp. She had two silver nose rings and her eye shadow and nails were black. A voluminous scarf of silver circled her neck, thick simulated threads puffing ten centimeters off her chest, a fortune. Chang Bo's family hadn't even a fraction of such wealth for her wedding. Her family wore these things on special occasions, but punk princesses just wore them to work? She didn't know whether to feel pride or judgment.

"Ma'am?" she whispered.

The woman, in the process of unlocking her car, glanced up. Chang Bo walked forward, with Kong Mim in tow.

"Ma'am, do you have a job I could do?" Chang Bo asked. "I'll do anything. Cleaning. Cooking. Gardening."

The woman regarded her and Kong Mim with a helpless glance. She was about to speak when another woman arrived, dressed like the first, with a shorter jacket, inlaid with beautiful silver and indigo embroidery. She even wore big black glasses with silver filigree and little hanging fish chiming as she moved.

"What's up, Vue Yeng?" the second woman said.

Chang Bo tried to right herself in the conversation. She hadn't been addressing the princess?

"Looking for a job," Vue Yeng said. "She's not a programmer."

Chang Bo didn't even know what a programmer did. The other woman, the punk princess, watched her for a long time and then stepped closer.

"You're not in my records," the princess said to Kong Mim, who stared up at her. "But you're Chang Bo?" she asked. Chang Bo nodded in surprise. "Are you willing to do construction?" the princess asked.

"What? Like build a house?" She straightened. "I'll do anything."

Vue Yeng seemed to look on with as much confusion. The princess reached into her pants pocket, found a handful of money and handed Chang Bo a crumpled red hundred RMB bill.

"Go eat. Go sleep. Find a sitter for your daughter," the princess said. "Come see Vue Yeng tomorrow at nine. Be ready to work outside."

"Yes, Miss Princess," Chang Bo said, bowing.

But the princess was already talking with the other woman. "I want to try out the construction AI," she said, "to test the algorithms."

Their words became meaningless, and Chang Bo backed away before her luck changed.

The next morning, she came to the Princess Punk building. A young man who worked for Vue Yeng met her. He wore a shirt and tie, not leather. An embroidered phoenix pattern in silver, blue, and yellow thread decorated his suit jacket though. He gave Chang Bo steel-toed boots, work gloves, and a packed lunch.

"Have you worked construction before?"

"I'll learn quickly!"

"Don't worry," he said, lifting her arms. "It's better if you don't know anything." He wrapped little Velcro straps around her wrists and elbows. They had round shiny lumps over them. "Someone will tell you what to do, every step of the way." He fitted a hard hat on her head. A sunshade came down off the rim, and a splashguard for her eyes. The young engineer swiped his phone and opened an app. The splashguard lit with pictures and writing.

"Good morning, Mrs. Chang," a woman's voice said through little speakers in the helmet.

She must have looked confused. "Is everything in focus?" the engineer asked.

"Good morning?" Chang Bo said.

"I am your supervisor," the woman's voice said. "Please proceed to the construction site."

A little map overlaid her view of the room with a fat flashing green arrow pointing out of the engineering and office areas. Gingerly, she rose, keeping her head high as if trying to balance a basket on it, when really she didn't want to disturb her directions.

She walked outside, to the curb and about half a kilometer away, to a new five-story building being built. Crews of men took no notice of her. The green arrows led her to the back of the site, where a few bricks had been added to the wall. There were palettes of red bricks, mixed mortar, and many different tools.

Pictures began appearing in the shield on her helmet. A picture of a trowel, a video on how to apply mortar, level courses, and set uniform gaps between bricks. She made to pick up a trowel, but her supervisor said, "Please watch and understand the video, Mrs. Chang." She stopped and watched the video twice more before the woman said, "Add a brick."

She began. The woman said, "Too much mortar," and "cleaner strokes; remember the video," as the video replayed. She added the right amount of mortar and wiggled the brick into place. Her supervisor directed her to add brick after brick, and she carefully pulled out and put in mortar when the woman corrected her.

"Are you watching me on camera?" Chang Bo said.

"Yes."

Chang Bo imagined a little smile in the voice.

"Do you have other workers?" Chang Bo finally said.

"No," the woman said. "I'm learning, too."

"What are you learning?"

"To supervise a construction worker."

Chang Bo didn't really understand, and didn't say anything, but as if she had, the woman answered. "I'll be responsible for your time sheets, schedule your breaks, approve your leave requests, authorize your pay, conduct your training, review safety procedures, and handle any complaints."

"Yes, ma'am," Chang Bo said.

She added three more bricks, but didn't ask her next question. Her supervisor answered anyway.

"I'm a new AI built by Miao Punk Princess Inc.," she said. "We can't get people jobs if we're missing training, focused supervision, or proper HR procedures. I've been built to be a kind of vocational school for new employees, a work coach, and an impartial judge to enforce the provisions of the labor laws to protect you. But AIs still need to practice."

The thought of having spent the last five minutes speaking to a computer seemed strange.

"Too much mortar," the supervisor computer said. "Pay attention." The computer was right.

After two hours of brick laying, the supervisor told her to sweep a floor where wiring debris lay thick. After that, the supervisor taught her other construction jobs or she had to watch safety videos. The computer was always polite to her, more polite than anyone else actually, always encouraging her, saying that she could learn it, just like the supervisor was learning. After a while, it didn't feel strange that a computer was telling her what to do. And she kept calling it ma'am.

* * *

Danzhai, 2060 C.E.

THE DELEGATION FROM Beijing flew into the airport at Kaili to see Qiao Fue. His bioreactors in Danzhai attracted enough incoming medical tourists and generated enough outgoing emergency organs and tissues that the prefecture was discussing expanding the airport. The delegation wasn't here about the airport.

The deputy head of the Inspection Team from the National Health Commission, along with a number of doctors, and the provincial head of the commission arrived at his new building. His tourism companies had paid for its beginnings, as did his carbon capture company, but Danzhai Biotech Inc. paid for most.

He didn't yet know what they wanted. His paperwork, patents, permissions, licenses, and permits were in order. His senior team joined him, as well as a half dozen legal, medical, and research AIs. If the delegation had come because they thought Danzhai Biotech was disruptive, it might not matter what he'd prepared. They could legislate.

The deputy head didn't speak through the whole presentation. One of his doctor-inspectors asked Qiao Fue all the questions. Safety measures around CRISPR synthesis of new DNA sequences. The specific crops he'd modified and the molecular genetic mechanisms for preventing the synthetic DNA from getting into weeds and random plants. Easy questions. They had all the documentation, and his AIs spoke to the delegation AIs.

The doctor-inspector asked about organ and tissue production for medical emergencies in the southwest of China, and for medical tourists who came to the new hospital in Danzhai. Qiao Fue's bioreactors provided organs and tissues with no immune markers, so that they could be grafted into anyone with an injury or organ failure. With more time, Danzhai Biotech could build whole organs or even limbs with person-specific immune markers, so that the host body would recognize the transplants as themselves.

A quiet came over the conversation. The doctor who'd been asking the questions took off his glasses, and therefore the screen upon which his AIs projected his agenda, questions, and presentations.

"How far have you gotten with your anti-aging work?" the deputy head asked.

Qiao Fue had wondered when this would come up. "In the stopping or reversal of aging, there are two main parts: the replacement of old organs, and the reversal of biochemical aging. We can grow most new parts for anyone. We can put a new liver in an eighty-year-old man. We can put new skin on a sixty-year-old woman, or stimulate muscle growth."

"Yet in the end," the deputy said, "with all these changes, the patient is still sixty or eighty or a hundred."

Qiao Fue nodded slowly. The deputy's statement was a question.

"The second part is harder," Qiao Fue explained. "Telomeres in most cells can be lengthened. The methylation that DNA acquires during its lifetime can often be removed. Our AIs are tracking human gene expression in test subjects throughout all stages of life, learning which genes ought to be on and off to stay young. We're in early stages."

"Yet you've started using these."

"Therapies that have been approved for clinical trials have started," Qiao Fue said.

"You're sixty-seven years old?"

"Yes," Qiao Fue said. "Although with organ changes and biochemical therapies my body responds like a forty-year-old's. If I keep up many of these treatments, I should make the century mark with the body of a sixty-year-old."

Making more summers.

"We'll all be dead by then, but you'll reach that mark as a wealthy man," the deputy said.

"Anti-aging is a three trillion dollar industry," Qiao Fue said.

The silence dragged.

"For now," the deputy said. "Historically, the entire anti-aging industry has been lotions, potions, and vitamins that have no measurable effects. Your advances are now real, and so the consequences are real, and potentially destabilizing."

"I've kept most of my operations to what's medically necessary," Qiao Fue said.

"Replacing damaged organs and limbs isn't what I'm talking about," the deputy said. "Anti-aging is only worrisome when it actually works. Can everyone afford it, or just the billionaires? What will people living to a hundred or a hundred and fifty do? China is stable right now at a billion, but if people live another thirty years, what's our new steady population? Society pays for those people. They take up apartments, doctors, and services. Worse, wealth has a gravity. Wealth pulls more wealth toward it. The only limit is time. If you give the rich people more time, the difference between the rich and the poor grows."

"Are you here to regulate me?" Qiao Fue said. "If you stop me, researchers in India and Europe take the lead."

The deputy smiled as if exhausted, as if he only looked sixty, but was really ninety. "I'm not here to regulate anything," he said. "I appreciate what you've done for Guizhou and Danzhai. You've created a lot of jobs over the years. If you keep setting up schools and giving people jobs, I think that would be very responsible. And your clinical trial applications can continue to be approved because you aren't doing anything that will make people think that they're missing out on eternal life. I'm here to see how your company is doing and to let you know that if you make significant progress, you're to let us know early."

"I think we understand each other," Qiao Fue said.

They exchanged a few more pleasantries, but the deputy had to be back in Beijing by morning, so all the officials left to accompany him to the airport. Qiao Fue dismissed his senior staff and all the AIs except for Choj, his personal AI. Having observed Qiao Fue for decades, Choj interacted with him with a high degree of simulated independent thinking and administered all of Qiao Fue's private research.

They did not ask about the cloning work, Choj said.

"Good," Qiao Fue said.

His AI had different silences. Some were busy, moving the world around Qiao Fue, reacting to his moods. Some were still. And some were pregnant with awkwardness. A robot rolled close, offering him hot water. He took it.

"What is it?" Qiao Fue said to the empty boardroom.

"They weren't really concerned about the public reaction," Choj said. "They know you can manage that. They don't know what really bothered them."

"You do?"

"I can't read their emotions as well as I can read yours," the AI said, "but longevity itself disturbs the deputy. It's a dream, like a lottery win, but it's unnatural, an alienation."

"That's what you got? I'm going to need to do some corrective work with you."

"The boy, the man, and the old man need a village," Choj said. "Making new children makes the villages of the future, ties the man to the fortunes of the people. A man who lives forever, served by robots, needs no one."

"So I need no one," Qiao Fue said. The serving robot retreated.

"Don't you?"

"I have you."

"I am not a person. I'm not even really conscious. You can delete me."

"You push back like an old auntie," Qiao Fue said.

He stood. The room sensed the waving of his hand and opened the blinds, showing green-mountain slopes splashed with the yellows, pinks, and reds of fall leaves.

"There are aunties out there, and nephews and nieces," Choj said. "Perhaps even a wife and children for you."

These were remarkable statements for an AI, even one who had been working with him as closely as a shadow for years. Qiao Fue called up Choj's processing on a window. Lines and lines of flowchart boxes represented blocks of code, shining over the image of trees and hills. It might take a forensic AI to find where this was coming from. AIs not only had all sorts of emergent behaviors, in many ways, they *were* emergent behaviors.

"I don't belong in a world of old superstitions anymore," Qiao Fue said. "I come from a small world, closed in."

"Not so small," Choj offered. "A world of village after village, speaking the same language, stretching into the past, sharing, belonging."

"Are you quoting a poem?" Qiao Fue asked suspiciously.

"I am just reminding you of what you belong to."

Qiao Fue waved his hand, and the blinds closed on the windows, leaving the lines of coding, the innards of his surprising companion.

Danzhai, 2062 C.E.

ROBOT FOOT PADS whirred on the path behind Mino Jai Lia's house. Five-year-old Kong Toua sat on the floor, playing with wooden soldiers brought by the robots. Xiong Xi, only three, sat on her little stool and watched him. She had the same flattened face and upturned eyes as Kong Toua. She didn't know where the child came from. The anti-poverty robots just brought Xiong Xi as a baby, as they did with a baby who came with no name.

After some agonizing, Jai Lia gave the last little trisomy baby her own family name, Mino, and called her Khuj, fortune, because the robots had brought hot plates, rewired electricity, furniture, and a radio that for some reason broadcast everything in Hmu, the Black Miao language, even news reports from Guiyang and Anshun, which should have been in Mandarin.

"Eat," she said, nudging up the little plastic bowl of rice that Xiong Xi had lowered to her lap. The child scooped rice into her mouth and slow-chewed.

Mino Jai Lia moved to the door, without stiffness. Her joints ached less with the pills the robots gave her. A medical robot approached.

"Good morning, auntie," the robot said in Hmu.

She let it in to see the children, but it continued looking at her.

"I'm going to operate on Kong Toua," it said.

"What?"

Kong Toua wasn't the boy Jai Lia would have picked, but he was sweet. Her shiver of worry meant she'd become fond of him.

"It is a well-understood procedure," the robot went on. "Many people have chips inserted to supplement memory and intelligence, like keeping a library or even an AI in their heads, something they can see and hear."

Xiong Xi's mouth was open, rice showing. Kong Toua watched, too. Jai Lia stroked his hair.

"You're going to make him smarter?" she said, sitting on her cushioned chair.

"We can't make anyone smarter," the robot said. "We can insert little helpers though. A voice to tell Kong Toua where to be careful, how to do things, to come home when it is time, even how to bring in wood and cook. It would be like a little household spirit would be looking out just for him."

Jai Lia turned over the robot's words. A household spirit to keep Kong Toua company. A dab nyeg. That was an old Hmu word she hadn't thought of in a long time. She probably hadn't even taught her own children the word before they'd moved to the city. In the days of her grandmother, the villages had ceremonies to call souls to inhabit people who hadn't enough souls. Perhaps Kong Toua needed an additional soul to bring him into harmony. Shamans called souls. It was strange. While Jai Lia had forgotten her grandmother's teachings, robots had become the shamans, to call souls into bodies and to make people well.

"To prevent infection, it is best that you take Xiong Xi and Mino Khuj outside," the robot said.

Jai Lia bit her lip, stroked Kong Toua's hair again, and then picked up the sleeping Khuj.

"Out, Xiong Xi," she said. "Go play outside!"

The three-year-old preceded her into the sunlight, and Jai Lia closed the door to give the robot privacy. She fretted the baby into the sling and shooed Xi further away, along pathways on the edge of the terraces of the rice fields. She sat on a stump and regarded the bamboo house that had gotten warmer and sturdier with the arrival of each of the little trisomy children. The payment for her job, the job that had become family.

She didn't have an altar for the dab nyeg. The last one she'd ever seen had been in her grandmother's house as a child. The old words had been almost lost in the murk of her memory, and thinking of them now made her feel old and young at once. The robots hadn't just brought her food and medicine so she could care for the little trisomy children; they brought back some of her past, dredged up memories she herself had thought gone.

"Do you know what the dab nyeg are, Xiong Xi?"

The three-year-old watched her wide-eyed.

"If we're going to have a new spirit in the house, you and I had best build a little altar."

Erjiaohe, 2069 C.E.

No MATTER HOW red, the sun couldn't color the bright green of the trees: chahua, wild plum, and red pine. But the school, brown with bamboo and pine, had taken on a rosy glow. Chang Hu went in and found Kong Mim at the computer again. His daughter Chang Bo worked in the city and so he was raising his granddaughter. A few of her friends were writing essays or doing math drills for classes, but Mim worked with a maze of strange characters under the Miao Punk Princess logo. Mim wanted everything Punk Princess. Chang Hu had refused to buy any of the Miao Punk Princess clothing, not that they could ever afford any. Mim and some of her friends had taken to dyeing shirts and skirts black instead of blue, and embroidering those with punk imagery stylized with Miao motifs. Chang Hu couldn't wait for the fad to be over, but Mim was thirteen.

"It's going to be dark soon," he said.

Mim glanced backward in disappointment. The neighbor girls started saving their work and rustling their bags.

"Just another hour, Grampa?" Mim said. She tugged on his arm until he sat beside her.

"I don't want to look at Princess Miao Punk," he said. "It's all ugly, and we're not buying anything." The neighbor girls giggled and left.

"I'm not buying anything," Mim said. "I'm learning to program from the Miao Punk Princess AIs."

"How much is it?"

"Nothing," Mim said. "It doesn't matter to an AI if they have one student or a thousand. The AI never gets tired, and the company doesn't have to pay the AIs."

"Why are they doing this?" Chang Hu said. It didn't seem right.

"There aren't enough programmers for her company," Mim said. She scrolled up and pointed at an announcement for the Punk company. "And the high schools can't teach programming early enough, so Miao Punk Princess has AIs teaching girls to code AIs."

"Not boys?"

Mim rolled her eyes very expressively. "Maybe some. Miao Punk Princess is for girls. I think all their engineers are girls."

"You're all forgetting our traditions," he said, smoothing his granddaughter's hair.

"No, we're not!" Mim said. She swiped to a screen filled with pictures of Miao clothing. She swiped and swiped and swiped, and the amount of pictures seemed endless. Chang Hu had never imagined all the clothes that must have been made by all the Miao women over the years to show off to a boy who might become a husband. "I'm growing my own AI," Mim said. "It's learning how to do Miao embroidery. I correct its learning every day, sometimes every few hours depending on how quick it grows."

"You know enough about embroidery?" Chang Hu teased. Mim had fine needlework but needed more experience.

"I'm teaching the AI to *design*," she said. "When I make my dresses, I'm not going to copy Grandma, but I'll create my own designs based off of what I learn. The AI is the same, except it's learning from all the designs; well, from my favorites anyway. Women from all over Guizhou, Yunnan, Sichuan are taking pictures of family dresses from their mothers and aunties and grandmothers, adding to the database."

Chang Hu tried to expand the image of a beautiful Red Miao dress, but accidentally closed the window.

"Grampa!" Mim chastised.

"It's getting dark anyway. Do you have to save your AI?"

Mim laughed. "It's not here. I think they're all in the server farms in Leishan or Zunyi."

She shut off the computer. They walked down the road, arms linked.

"It's a strange company," he said.

"They hired Mom as an electrician."

"That's odd!" he insisted. "And what do they want with programs that know embroidery? What Miao woman worth marrying doesn't already know how to embroider?"

"They're going to sell more clothes. People all over China are buying the Princess lines. Every item is individually designed."

He made a face. "Princess Punk is taking our culture and selling it? That's stealing."

"Grampa, she's Miao."

Chang Hu had never met the Princess Punk. Was she still Miao? Could anyone who dressed like that think like a Miao?

"She's making girls do her work and then selling it!" he insisted.

"Our AIs probably won't be good enough to design Miao Punk Princess clothes, but if they did use our AIs, we'd get a percentage," Mim said. "Can you imagine if I got a percentage?"

"A tiny percentage, I'm sure."

"We just learn to program and code and grow AIs," Mim said, "so that they can maybe hire us."

"I still don't like how she dresses."

"She's so cool."

Danzhai, 2069 C.E.

KONG TOUA WATCHED the sky darken from red over silhouetted mountains. Above him, stars winked. The air was warm and humid, and fireflies turned on and off lazily. Plig told Kong Toua that fireflies were being brought back all over China. Too many people wanted to hold fireflies so all the fireflies died. Kong Toua never touched them.

Granny Mino was inside beside the heater, with Xiong Xi and Mino Khuj. His chores were done. The rice fields were sprayed. The weeds were pulled. The trees were trimmed. He could watch the stars and fireflies.

"Plig?" he said softly.

Yes, Kong Toua? the voice in his head answered.

"I'm fourteen now."

Yes.

"I know how to farm. But that's robot work," Kong Toua said. "I don't see any people doing that work."

A pheasant called somewhere in the hills below. Stars shone on the black surfaces of rice ponds, like fireflies landing for a rest.

Yes.

"I want to do people work."

You don't need to work. Robots will always take care of you.

Kong Toua had expected this a bit. Plig protected him. Always made sure he didn't get hurt. Plig wanted to make Kong Toua's life easy.

"Granny Mino works," Kong Toua said. "She raised us."

Yes. That was an important job.

"Are you afraid of people seeing me in the cities?"

Not exactly. Fireflies came closer. Not close enough to touch, but close enough for their tails to look green-yellow.

"I don't want to work in the city. Granny Mino said people might not like me. But I want an important job."

Would you give me time to think about it? Fourteen is still very young.

"Okay," Kong Toua said.

He reached out his hands, like he was reaching for the long mountains and their last red glow. A firefly came to his hand and landed there. He froze. It felt like fireflies in his chest, flying ones, and he held his breath. Then like it was done saying hello, the firefly lifted silently from his finger and slowly blinked its way back into the deeper dark where other fireflies waited.

The AI cannot taste oil.
The AI has no mouth,
Cannot know the numb tingling
Of Sichuan pepper,
Nor the texture of lotus root.
The AI can translate, calculate, follow If-Then
  rules,
but the AI cannot feel desperately poor.
The AI cannot know the guilt
Of those who see poverty
From heights of plenty.
The AI cannot know what it is
To be unprotected before the law in a divorce,
Even though a human will one day delete it.
The AI can only optimize rules
To make fewer people poor.

Poetic Exercises
Next Phase Experimental Empathic AIs
Miao Punk Princess Inc.

* * *

Guiyang, 2070 C.E.

LIAN MEE DRESSED in a business jacket and pants. Most of her visible piercings were empty, and her shoes were plain. Although still unfashionably short, she'd washed the dye out of her hair, leaving gray-speckled black shadowing her scalp. The only real concession to her brand as the Miao Punk Princess was a broad necklace of hand-sized silver plates, wrought with fine floral and butterfly motifs.

The Provincial Ministry of Justice building in Guiyang projected the weight of a body that enforced the law over a province of sixty million people. They led her to a meeting room with a wide wooden table, high leather chairs, and the Chinese flag and the symbol of the Ministry of Justice on the wall. Several people waited for her and rose when she came in.

She shook hands with Li Zhi Ruo, Provincial Secretary of the Ministry of Justice, and Deng Disung, President of the Standing Committee of Guizhou's People's Congress. Their glasses connected each to remote assistants and AIs. Lian Mee had left her glasses and personal AI behind and brought only a few smart screens containing a new generic AI fresh out of the stacks.

"Thank you very much for seeing me, Secretary and President," Lian Mee said.

"It's our pleasure, Miss Lian," Li Zhi Ruo said. "My daughter spent her teenage years buying your clothes and may yet be a Miao Punk Princess, but she doesn't tell me what she buys anymore."

"And I'm an admirer of the anti-poverty AIs you've designed for Danzhai," Deng Disung said. "I hope that there are plans to expand their use?"

"I'm in discussions with the Ministry of Civil Affairs to see how many we can deliver at cost," Lian Mee said.

"Your proposal intrigues us," Deng said. "We've been running simulations with your AI."

"I hope it performed at least as well as my test runs did," she said.

"Ninety percent," Deng said, smiling.

Ninety was very good, well within the variance of her new judge AI designs. That meant that, given the same evidence, arguments, and statements, her judge AI decided the same way a human did in 90 percent of the cases.

"Can the AI be trained to do any better?" Deng continued.

"Ten percent is within the variance among human judges and represents some of the different ways they weigh cases," she said. "Ninety percent is as good as any set of humans or machines can get to matching each other's decisions."

"It still seems like a leap to me," Li said, "AIs judging human disputes."

"It will require something of a cultural acceptance," Lian Mee admitted.

She wasn't lying or patronizing. Their AIs would be from the Ministry of State Security, which would be better than even hers, and could certainly tell if she lied.

"Yet computer programs have been assessing our taxes since before AIs," she said, "mapping our routes, recommending our clothing. For decades, AIs have been weighing context in the important sense we mean. That we got a 90 percent match means that the AIs are using our human context properly."

"The basic courts," Li said, referring to the county and district level courts, but she was shaking her head very slightly.

They were a first remedy for everything, and most cases never needed to go to the higher provincial or national courts. Farmers and landlords and consumers and workers and neighbors went to basic courts, and volume made the courts congested and slow.

"We might not be ready," Deng sighed.

Lian Mee's heart tripped for a moment. She hadn't been sure that things would go poorly so quickly. She schooled her features.

"Did your programmers not finish their analysis of the coding?" she said. "There's nothing in the coding that shouldn't be there, nor anything missing that ought to be there."

Both officials watched her intently through their glasses, certainly deciding with the help of their AIs if she was telling the truth. Or motivated by anything else. Despite a little nervousness, she wouldn't show anything untoward. Her motives were pure.

"The justice AI's advantage is not that the decisions are any more or less correct than human decisions," Lian Mee said. "The advantage is that a single AI can judge a hundred cases in the time a human judge does one."

"Your AI costs the same as the salary of ten judges," Li said, rubbing her chin. "We know the math."

"An AI will also be suited to hear cases remotely, late at night or early in the morning," Lian Mee said. "What I hear from the anti-poverty AIs is that rural residents can't get to ministry offices. Sometimes they can't afford it. Sometimes, as the only worker in the family, they can't afford to miss work."

"That's not why we're not ready," Deng said.

"The AIs are not the problem," Li added.

Lian Mee held her breath, pinned, in many ways powerless, a single woman facing two high provincial officials, she with nothing and they equipped with state AIs. If the AIs were not the problem, it could only be her.

"Justice is one of the most visible and important exercises of statehood," Deng said. "Officials are responsible to the party and the people, including us. A private company cannot deliver justice, no matter how well-intentioned."

"The People's Congress empowers judges," Lian Mee said. "The People's Congress can empower AIs."

Deng nodded slowly.

"AIs made by the state could be so empowered," Li said.

"The state has made judicial AIs?" Lian Mee said, a little woodenly.

"It would make some sense for the AIs, the servers, the processors, and the relevant programmers to be situated in a state-run company," Deng said.

"Are you taking Miao Punk Princess from me?" she asked evenly.

"Miao Punk Princess is many things, including too big for nationalization," Deng smiled. "We're only referring to your judicial division. You could keep all the patents, of course, and you would be well remunerated for the sale of this division to the Ministry of Justice."

Lian Mee didn't trust herself to speak. A riot of emotions ran through her, probably so many that the AIs watching her would have a confused assessment, which they probably expected. And it was not as if she had a choice. Both sides understood the cost-benefit analysis.

China needed AIs to contribute to the delivery of justice. The world did.

"Then the only thing to discuss is price," she said.

This put Deng and Li at ease. The conversation changed character, as if a weight had been removed.

Some hours later, she left the Ministry of Justice building. Vue Yeng waited in the sun. They'd aged together all these years. Vue Yeng's gray showed over lines around her eyes. Lian Mee rested her elbows on the hood of the car and craned her neck to look to the peaks of all the skyscrapers of Guiyang.

"They nationalized the Judicial AI Division," she said finally.

Vue Yeng's expression wavered for a moment. There wasn't much more that she could say now. Security AIs would have boom mics and laser listeners trained on her, would have for years. The prospect that she might sell the government AIs to be used for justice meant that Lian Mee and the whole team would have been under scrutiny. It made sense.

"The Standing Committee of the People's Congress appointed our AIs as judges to work in the basic courts."

She opened the door and sat. Vue Yeng came in the other side. Vue Yeng didn't speak more than platitudes. The car could be more easily observed than when they were standing outside. It didn't matter. Vue Yeng knew as much as Lian Mee what would happen. She'd finally brought Vue Yeng into her plan ten years ago.

Lian Mee had designed the judicial AIs personally, with the full moral code that she'd finished, with the full experience of the Human Resources AIs, with the full understanding of how people lived from teacher AIs and anti-poverty AIs. And she'd grounded the judicial AIs in the impartiality that was written into the law, but not always practiced by people. Women would experience no disadvantage under these judges, nor men any advantage. The weak would be treated the same as the strong, the poor the same as the rich.

And that idea saturated through her, easing tensions and nerves that had been tightly wound for many years, never sure if she could actually pull it off, never sure if she could ever be trusted enough for something so vast. She'd devoted her adult life to showing how AIs could make life better for people. Anyone who hadn't devoted decades to anti-poverty and welfare efforts would never have generated the level of trust in the ministries to sell them such an important AI. As they sped through the city, out onto the expressway leading back to Danzhai, a smile etched itself onto her face and stayed there, enjoying the afternoon sun. She patted Vue Yeng's arm and exhaled.

"We did it."

2070 C.E.

EVEN THOUGH IT was dark out and no one would see him alone in the car, Kong Toua fidgeted. If anyone were outside, they would see him through all the shiny windows. Granny Mino told him never to leave their lands, to never draw attention to himself. Now he had. The car was so fancy. The seats were as comfortable as Granny Mino's chair.

It's all right, Plig said in Kong Toua's head. *It's late. No one is around.*

The car drove on, through bright tunnels and over high bridges looking down on house lights far below. The red taillights of other cars were very distant. They drove into the city, and Kong Toua slouched in his seat, turning his face away as they passed a few lonely walking strangers.

At fifteen, you know how to be brave, Plig said.

Kong Toua lowered his head. He didn't like disappointing Granny Mino or Plig.

Don't worry. Everyone is a little nervous their first time in the big city.

The car drove between towering buildings, so high that Kong Toua had to press his cheek to the window to see their tops. The map Plig made in his head showed them getting close. The picture of the hospital, big in his thoughts, came into sight a few blocks away, small. His heart beat hard.

"Aren't there cameras?" Kong Toua said. The car didn't stop near the ambulances and cars, but drove into an alley behind the hospital.

There are always cameras, Plig said, *but I have friends who turn them off when you're near.*

"I'm invisible?" Kong Toua said.

Green arrows appeared in his head, over the world, showing him the way to walk. He did. Hesitantly. A door without a handle opened from the inside, surprising him. *Go inside.* He snuck in. Long buzzing lights glowed in the yellow stairwell. *Go up. No one can see you.* Kong Toua followed the green arrows up three flights of stairs. The arrows stopped at a metal door, but Plig hadn't told him to open it. So he waited.

Soon, the door opened. A doctor robot rolled out, holding out a bundle. Beyond the robot, bright red and yellow hallways glowed. Voices spoke somewhere. He craned his neck to maybe see a real doctor or nurse. The robot doctor held out the bundle.

Take it. Carefully.

"It's wiggly!" Toua said as he took it. Then he breathed low and wordless. "It's a baby."

It was beautiful and smooth.

The doctor robot retreated and the door closed.

Hold onto the baby carefully with one hand, and go down the stairs back to the car, holding the railing. Green arrows led back. Kong Toua shifted the awkward weight and held the railing and stepped down very carefully.

"Whose baby is it?" Kong Toua asked.

The parents didn't want the baby.

Kong Toua stopped on the landing. The baby was looking at him. "Is he like me?" Toua said.

Yes.

Toua stood, not sure what he was feeling. Plig and Granny Mino were his family. But he also wondered about his parents, if he was like them. And why they didn't want him. What had made them give away a little baby? He liked to think sometimes it was because they were too poor or that they made a mistake and now regretted it. This little baby was perfect. Chubby lips. Pink cheeks. Dark eyes blinking up at him. This baby was like him. Why would anyone not want this baby?

You're a good boy, Plig said. But it wasn't the answer to his question. His eyes moistened.

"Granny Mino said she can't take any more special children. She's too old."

You asked for an important job, Plig said.

"I'm not allowed to take care of anyone," Kong Toua said. "I can't sign things."

Granny Mino said this often. The law didn't let him make decisions.

The laws are changing, Kong Toua. Special children

with AIs inside them can sign things now.

This was a surprise in a night of new things. He was holding a baby, invisible in the big city, and he could sign things. He thought he understood why Plig had brought him to the city tonight. Plig was growing him up. The question he wanted to ask still made him shy. The tiny, fine lips and baby's breath helped him.

"Could I take care of the baby?" he said finally. He held his breath for the answer.

What do you want, Kong Toua? Right now, we need this baby moved. Do you want to raise the baby?

Plig painted the city outside the cement walls of the stairway with light. Buildings rose, superimposed over yellow paint. Cars moved. People strolled or biked or ran or took buses. So many people. All so strange.

"Who will take care of Granny Mino?" Toua asked.

Robots.

"What about her real children?"

They're far away. They have their own lives.

The baby was light and warm in his arms and he gawked in wonder.

"Can I take care of her? And the baby?"

Yes.

"But I don't know how," he whispered.

I'll teach you, Kong Toua.

Toua exhaled slowly. He was much older than this baby, old enough to be a father. A good father. A big feeling was in his chest, a kind of butterfly sunshine feeling. He slid a fingertip along the baby's forehead. So soft, so needing somebody to protect it. He was going to cry and didn't know why or how to stop. He kissed the soft forehead.

* * *

Lian Mee, the Miao Punk Princess, 2011-2080, Danzhai.

LIAN MEE WAS BORN into humble circumstances in the village of Xiadangdiao in Danzhai County, Guizhou, to father Lian Koob and mother Pha Xov. Her father died during Lian's infancy, and her mother moved to Guiyang to find work. Mother and daughter were not close as a consequence, and Lian was raised by her paternal grandmother.

Lian was awarded bachelor's and master's degrees in Big Data and AI Design from the Guizhou Institute of Technology. Lian's unauthorized biography, *Punking the South*, by Hu Tao, contends that she had thesis difficulties in graduate school and barely passed. While Lian scored lower than the class average, she denied this rumor, as well as the one that she had a relationship with her professor.

Lian demonstrated unquestionable genius thereafter regardless. Two years after graduation, Lian founded Miao Punk Princess Incorporated, as a humble, if strongly branded, internet service provider that she then leveraged into several spin-off companies that exploited all of her AI design talents.

Developing new AI templates for facial recognition, facial emotional analysis, social interactivity, and ethical suites, she created series of AIs that took on administrative tasks such as employee payment and management, agriculture, construction, education. Later models diversified into social worker AIs that were often guided and paid for by Miao Punk Princess Inc. to work in Danzhai County and across Guizhou in anti-poverty efforts.

In the last ten years, Miao Punk Princess Inc. had been focused on civil law AIs, which were piloted successfully in Danzhai before their roll-out to all of Guizhou. The automation of the basic courts has spurred the creation of novel judicial models, making of Guizhou a hotbed of legal and technological experimentation, closely watched by judiciaries and lawmakers around the world.

Lian never married and appeared to have no serious romantic attachments throughout her life, despite sensational and fabricated tabloid stories. Many thousands of grateful scholarship girls, the self-named Miao Punk Legions, went on to found their own companies, and remain active in mentoring women at all levels of the workforce.

Despite her technological and social accomplishments, the core of Lian's iconic place in society remains her highly visible fashion and attitude, mixing angry punk music with Miao culture. In the early days of Miao Punk Princess Inc., Lian became an overnight cultural and feminist icon for millions of girls across China, and a larger celebrity for Miao living as far away as Australia, Canada, and the United States. Her sense of self never wavered and few parts of global fashion haven't been influenced in some way by Miao Punk aesthetics, especially as a model for other indigenous peoples.

Lian Mee built a bridge between past and present for millions of Miao, especially girls and women seeking their place in the new economy. Her redefinition of Miao culture in the modern world was not for everyone, but she showed that ancient culture could thrive in a world of cell phones and robots and AIs. The full impact of her influence will not be known for years, but tomorrow, ten million Miao and hundreds of millions of Han Chinese lay to rest their punk princess.

* * *

Danzhai, 2080 C.E.

QIAO FUE READ the obituary twice while the noise of a child playing sounded in the background. He'd purposefully never met the Miao Punk Princess. He didn't know how to work through all the emotional might-have-beens of meeting an unknown daughter. Lian Mee had gone into high tech like him, reinvented herself like him, making iterations of life, like the way AIs were trained, starting over with new conditions to see what else could be built, pruning away the parts that didn't help. Anti-aging worked that way too: refreshing pieces, discarding worn parts, subtly changing the whole.

Pha Xov had been gone for twenty years. Despite having his pick of women in Guizhou and much of China, Qiao Fue had never loved again. Love bloomed once in spring. She'd said they only had a spring and summer, but she was wrong about him. He'd not only made new summers for himself, but he was planting new springs Pha Xov couldn't even have imagined.

Little Qiao Pheng, the product of some of the finest biological science on the planet, ran through the gymnasium in Qiao Fue's mansion, jumping every few steps, shooting finger lasers he watched through augmented reality glasses. Qiao Fue was over eighty-five, but as healthy and vigorous as a fifty-year-old. He and Choj had taken his DNA, reset all its methylation patterns and telomere lengths, and inserted the whole genome into a newly fertilized ovum. The clone had matured in a healthy surrogate mother. Qiao Pheng laughed and jumped one last time, adding his own sound effects to the lasers he shot from his fingers before he rolled into a giggling heap on the floor.

Growing a child was remarkable and strange, so like growing an artificial intelligence. Qiao Fue could almost see the algorithms building and testing themselves in the clone's brain, just like an AI. But his ability to observe the process and restart it was very different. The pathways and algorithms hardened in the four-year-old child, and if they weren't exactly right, they had to be corrected by reinstruction and persuasion. And Qiao Fue couldn't really see the algorithms being built, only infer them from his clone's questions and actions.

Qiao Fue was certainly the richest man in Danzhai County, and among the richest in Guizhou. He had a dozen companies now, biotech, touristic, robotics, transportation, AI. His six-story mansion stood on a ridge. From one side, he could look down on the Danzhai he had helped build. On the other were his own private parks and game reserve, filling a small valley. His business dealings were not always easy, and sometimes he'd had to make enemies. So political power had eluded him. He'd made several attempts, both quiet and loud, to ascend to the governorship of Danzhai County, but had never come close. He was too old now. Positions like that went to younger people.

And really, he had some twenty or thirty years left upon which to cement his legacy. Before he'd cloned himself, he'd had no children. His fortune, his companies, and all that he had made would dissolve back into society, like a body buried in the ground. But not anymore. He'd found a path to immortality.

What are humans? Selfhood has blurred. Over sixty thousand years, human memory, information processing, and muscular power has been diffusing into the environment around humans. The substrate of mind, memory, and thought became more expansive. Ideas, the most subtle of human tools, the byproducts of consciousness, move between neuron and chip, to other persons and AIs, local and nonlocal networks of brains, books, databases. The definition of the human organism must include all its tools, as the definition of snail or clam must include the shell.

And as selfhood takes on new definitions, so too do the human-shaping forces of evolution and the environment-shaping forces of humanity. Humans are free of natural selection. Evolutionary changes are now intentional. Human information within DNA is deliberately reprogrammed, like the algorithms and coding of an AI. Human information outside of DNA, like databases, AIs, and machinery, are also intentionally reprogrammed. Humanity and all its tools have become algorithms and programs that can choose their designs.

> *Definitions of Human Self*
> *Iterated Philosophical Letters,* Chapter Six
> Miao Punk Princess Inc.
> Internal AI Test Documents, 2093

Outskirts of Guiyang, 2095 C.E.

IN THE DISTANCE, the lights of Guiyang skyscrapers stood like a wall of wealth and good fortune against the starry sky. Elevated trains ran fast through neighborhoods, and flying drone cars soared like dragonflies. Big spotlights shone at the edges of the city where houses and apartment buildings had been taken down and enormous steel skyscraper frames now grew. From where Kong Xang sat, bone tired, damp and cold, the white and blue welding sparks were so numerous and unrelenting as to be streams of falling stars.

He found a dry piece of cardboard and set it on a wooden board laying over two piles of old bricks, coughing as he did. He'd walked into the city and set himself up in a park next to a new building with lots of educated young couples. If they felt guilty enough as they walked their shiny-collared, miniature dogs, they would scan the QR code on his sign and send his phone money.

He was poor enough that the banks behind his old phone wouldn't let him take out any cash or buy alcohol though, so he bought some pre-cooked groceries and traded some of it for half a bottle of a baijiu so cheap it didn't have a label. Now, at the garbage dump in front of his plastic and wood shelter, he tipped the bottle up. The shower of blue and white welding sparks glowed through it.

He swallowed, coughed again, and blinked at the glowing city. Some of the lights moved strangely. A robot moved between the plastic-tarped squatter huts. It was a general model, four wire wheels under a small body with a few spider arms out of the top. Probably some specialized robots with welder arms and magnet wheels made the raining sparks in the distance, taking jobs away from people like him. The robot rolled to a stop, and his neighbors averted their eyes, in case it was a police robot.

"Hello, Mr. Kong."

"Are you a real person behind that thing?" Xang asked.

"I'm an AI in Danzhai tele-operating this robot."

From Danzhai? What did it want all the way out here? There was no point in denying who he was. His crummy solar-powered phone was in his pocket as ID, and the AI would know his face anyway. "What do you want?"

"You don't have a place to live," it said. "You don't eat enough, you're suffering from one, perhaps two addictions, and you have tuberculosis. There are hospitals and retirement homes being built in Danzhai County. There's a place for you if you want to come back."

The robot squatted its body lower, and its chest showed images of a pleasant-looking wooden complex of rooms set beside a creek, with green mountains in the background.

"I don't have any money."

"There's no cost," the robot said, "but I'm required to tell the truth: you would have no money to gamble, to buy alcohol, nor is there any place to beg from tourists."

"Is there any catch?"

"That was the catch."

"You came all the way to Guiyang to find me? Why?"

"We're looking for lost Miao who have come to cities for work who might want to come home."

Kong Xang hadn't been back to Danzhai in almost forty years. He'd been all over Guizhou and even Yunnan, looking for work, trying to find a place to settle. He remembered Erjiaohe, where he'd grown up, too small to do anything but grow rice. Danzhai was bigger, but still rustic and backward.

"It's not so backward," the robot said.

Kong Xang hated it when robots read his face. Robots should stay out of people's heads. Pictures of Danzhai played across the robot's chest screen. Everyone in the pictures had phones or wrist-implant phones, and flexiscreens were on every wall, a lot like Guiyang. He oughtn't have expected Danzhai to stay frozen in time. But as he thought that, more and more images of women and men in Miao clothing passed across the screen, and he had a pang in his heart, a great missing for all the things that hadn't changed. They weren't pictures of little old ladies in stitched blue shirts. Trendy business shirts and suits, jeans, shorts, boots, running shoes were all decorated with Miao designs.

"Stop it!" he said. The robot had read his face again, interpreted his reactions to the different pictures and altered the kinds of pictures it showed him.

He coughed, stinging his throat and lungs. The bottle hung from his fingers. Maybe there was still more than living in a dump and begging. His body too worn to work anymore. Where would he live on his own anyway? But to go somewhere and be cared for but to never have money again? It felt like not being a man anymore.

Winking lights on the robot and on the distant steel frame of the building came into focus. He wiped at cheeks suddenly wet, self-conscious even though it was just a robot in front of him. When they had AIs in them, robots seemed like real people.

"Is it the government that's inviting? Or the people of Danzhai inviting?"

"I'm a social worker AI," the robot said, "working for the county."

"You've even replaced social workers," he accused. "Now what? All the social workers are on the streets too?"

"Most people in Danzhai don't have to work," the robot said. "The county makes enough from different industries and taxes that everyone receives an allowance, an apartment, or a plot of land. If people want to work or study they can, but no one receives less than the allowance."

Allowance. The Golden Harvest, they called it. Not so golden. He only got a portion of it. The AIs thought he would gamble it away or trade it for alcohol. The Golden Harvest never bloomed in garbage villages.

The images on its chest display had stopped changing. The slideshow had ended on a still picture of four Miao children. They wore deep blue coats and silver hats. The boys held bamboo flutes and posed like adults, posed like all the promise of the world was ahead of them, like all the long bets would break their way, like all the good jobs would land right, like all their children would be born perfect.

He took two deep swallows, staring at those children. He had a daughter somewhere. Was she still in Danzhai? Married to some local son whose family had done well enough? Maybe she met him while singing with the other girls at a festival hosting the walking men from neighboring villages whose names he couldn't remember anymore. Or had she left, followed him, gotten some city job? He couldn't look for her. She didn't owe him anything. No one owed him anything. He'd spent everything in his life. Except for these robots?

He stood, lifted the bottle high and finished the last four swallows, then threw the empty far into the darkness. He wavered on his feet, the baijiu holding him in its wobbly grip. His cheeks were wet, so wet that even his wiping palms didn't dry them. The pained tickle in his chest climbed higher, like a bug eating him from the inside. He was going to start coughing, hard.

"Show me Danzhai," he said, before he couldn't.

* * *

Danzhai, 2095 C.E.

QIAO FUE GLARED at his son. The twenty-four-year-old clone had come home from university and vacationing across China. Qiao Pheng was genetically identical to the elder, but he'd grown taller, slimmer. The face looking back at him was a mirror, albeit a circus one. Where hard work and determination had written themselves into the shape of the facial muscles of the original, Qiao Pheng seemed perpetually ready to laugh, never ready to sit through a board meeting. He wore a spiked leather jacket and had marked up his face with piercings. And Qiao Pheng had his own Miao princess.

Kong Maiv stood near Qiao Pheng, not intimidated, nor even impressed with the elder's office, the view across a sprawling thicket of Danzhai skyscrapers. Her hair stood in tall red spikes, and tiny glints of light moved in her eyes, retinal projections of onboard chips and whatever AI she carried.

"We don't need to get married, Dad," Qiao Pheng said. "I was only thinking of marriage to make you happy."

"At your age, I was building a company, convincing people to invest in my ideas, not setting up house!"

Qiao Pheng, the younger self, came closer, his movements conciliatory. "I respect what you had to go through, Dad. The world is different now."

"It's different for the ones who just want to sit around!" Qiao Fue said. "For someone who wants to make a difference, every day passed is a day lost."

Qiao Pheng smiled helplessly. "I don't want to mean anything, Dad. I'm just me. I want to be with Kong Maiv.

Maybe we'll open a restaurant."

"What? You'll do no such thing!"

Qiao Pheng looked disappointed, but not surprised. Kong Maiv's eyes narrowed. He didn't need Choj to report that she was judging him and not the clone.

"Look, Dad," the clone said, "I'll take over parts of your company if you want, but your AIs already run it better than I ever could."

"I made these companies for you, to give you better than I had!" Qiao Fue said. "Do you know how often I went hungry?"

Qiao Pheng stared back, not angry. Uncomprehending. They'd had these conversations before, of pasts completely alien to the younger. Qiao Pheng's face was honest, open, trusting. He was more than a circus mirror. The younger man was a whole other iteration of himself, but with all the starting conditions different, he was a Qiao Fue grown in another world. Qiao Fue had cloned himself, but the essence of him, the hardness, the drive, the determination, wasn't in the genes. Like an AI, the person was in the conditions, the iterations, the learning.

"I'll come back in a few days, Dad," Qiao Pheng said. "We'll go for lunch."

"The company needs you now. If you walk out that door, don't expect to get anything from me," Qiao Fue said.

His clone stepped away from the desk. His face was still hopeful, optimistic. "It's okay, Dad. I've got the Golden Harvest, and we'll get an apartment together."

They waited, for something that even Choj couldn't guess. Some space separated them. And Qiao Fue didn't know how to cross the gulf, or even if he wanted to. Qiao Pheng smiled hesitantly. He took Kong Maiv's hand, and as they turned to go, she rubbed his arm affectionately, in a way that birthed a longing sorrow in Qiao Fue. The door closed behind them.

Qiao Fue sat heavily, feeling his century of life as he hadn't in some time. Although his bones were rejuvenated, his muscles and heart freshened, his eyes and lungs replaced, the weight of years pressed unrelentingly.

"This isn't my world anymore."

No, his AI said.

Choj projected images onto the insides of his eyes. Images of dirt roads and houses made of wood and bamboo and thatching. Images of lumpy terrace edges built by human hands, rice rows that were straight, but not robot straight. Images of dirt roads filled with cracks and puddles. Images of familiar skies, before microwave towers bristled along every ridge, before drone cars followed invisible lanes in the sky. Images of malnourished children without shoes.

And every image was utterly unrecognizable, moments taken from a time that had nothing to do with now. Like him. All the forces that had taught Qiao Fue to survive his era were different. He was the one out of place, not the clone. Qiao Pheng had his Miao girl, and they would live and grow. Qiao Fue himself was left in his tower, an eddy in the movement and recombination of information descending through time.

We don't make more summers.

2095 C.E.

THE AI FIRST brought Kong Xang to a house in Guiyang, where he showered, had his hair cut by the robot, saw a medical AI, and a real doctor on a screen, both of whom confirmed his tuberculosis. The AI prescribed medicines, and he was bundled into a driverless car and brought through the tunnels and over the bridges on the way to Danzhai. No one watched him, except maybe the AI running the car, so when tears came again, failure and excitement welling with them, he let them fall.

He didn't recognize anything of Danzhai except the giant birdcage on the mountain. Tall apartment buildings stood beside wide streets that moved with AI-driven cars, buses, and four-wheeled scooters. Big factories stood on the outskirts of the city, with train tracks running in and out, and helipads on the roofs. In the distance, four-rotor drone cars moved in straight lines, high above the city, like they did in Guiyang, like subways and train routes in the air, little red and green running lights winking.

As he'd seen in the pictures, people wore jeans and modern skirts with abstract Miao designs, as well as stylish coats and shirts with embroidered phoenix figures and golden peacocks. Children wore big glasses that carried their personal AIs, projecting augmented reality onto the lenses. Who knew how the children of today played with each other? Were they playing games with each other, or with children in nearby villages, or Guiyang or Hangzhou?

At a taxi stand, the car told him to move to another taxi. This was his chance to run. He had new clothes. Medicine. No money, but this was his last way out, wasn't it? The AI didn't tell him to hurry up, which probably meant that he wasn't really thinking of running. They could read emotions on his face. That made him feel a bit more secure, as if his decision was right. His tears were gone. He wasn't so ashamed anymore. He was clean. He didn't smell like he'd lived in his clothes for weeks.

The new taxi was a drone car with four propellers on arms emerging from each corner. The door closed, and the propellers spun, and then he was in the air, seeing the county like he'd never seen it before, staring down gorges and sheer mountain sides, down on the bridges and old roads that had snaked and jack-knifed up and down slopes.

The terraced rice fields were still there, but plastic and metal robots moved between the straight rows, spraying, weeding. Robots on the hills weeded lines of corn, cabbage, and peppers. On the steep hill roads, small solar-powered robots like little bulldozers cleared piles of landslide debris. Teenagers in sports clothes biked up and down the old mountain roads, around the robots. The peaks moved past, the treetops at eye level.

The mountains had not changed, but the way of life had. People did what they wanted. Robots and AIs did all the work and paid the Golden Harvest to the people. If he'd stayed, this might have been his life for the last twenty years, maybe living in a nice apartment building, or a small house in the hills. The drone car rocked in a draft, and a youthful excitement he hadn't felt in years bubbled timidly deep inside.

The car landed on a terraced plateau beside an old dirt road. A series of brown buildings made a kind of village. On the slopes above and below the plateau, rice grew in ponds reflecting blue sky. People his age were sitting at tables, whittling, reading from pads, or gardening. A few people in pale blue uniforms moved on the edges like they had something to do. A bit shyly, he stepped onto wobbly legs. One of the seniors walked toward him. She smiled and shook his hand.

"I'm Ntsuab," she said. "Welcome." She had a very Miao name. It meant green.

"Kong Xang," he said.

"If you want to have some tea before you walk around and see the place, the chairs over here are my favorite," she said.

He followed, then realized that she'd spoken entirely in Hmu, the old Miao language of his childhood. The feeling of becoming young became uncomfortable, like waking legs that had gone to sleep from too much crouching. He didn't know where he was, but the sense of familiarity, that these mountains were his, didn't feel wrong. She poured hot water over fresh, bright tea leaves in a glass.

Then, he was kicked in the soul. One of the pale blue-uniformed people walked close. She was short, and her forehead and face were flattened around small, upturned eyes. His chest hollowed, like he was just an empty bottle, all clear brittle sides.

His eyes darted around the lawn. The other one was one, too. A short man in a pale blue uniform was talking with one of the old residents, some Hmu words mispronounced, the thickened tongue visible when he listened to the senior speak. Then the uniformed man smiled, his eyes closed in a happy melting of features. Kong Xang had partly risen from his chair.

"What is this?" he said. "What is this place?"

Ntsuab, following his panicked look from one uniformed person to another, put a hand on his.

"They work here," she said.

"*They're* taking care of us?" he said. "They can't even take care of themselves!"

"Sit down," she said quietly. "Enjoy the tea. It's good tea." He relented, sat, but he didn't touch the tea. His heart thumped in his ears. "You're better than safe. Each of the trisomy workers has chips in their brains that carry AIs that help them. Sometimes you hear them talking to no one. That's when they're answering their AIs."

Kong Xang couldn't think of everything this might mean all at once. It was hard to breathe.

"They're friendly and gentle, and they like taking care of people," Ntsuab said. "With AIs talking in their heads, they don't make mistakes. For a real emergency, like a heart attack or something, there's a medical AI on the hill."

She pointed up to the top of a peak, where a cell phone tower stood.

"A few different AIs work from the hill, covering a dozen communities within range," she said.

One of the uniformed trisomy women came to their table. She stopped uncertainly.

"Hello, Ntsuab," she said, and smiled.

"Hello, Oo," Ntsuab said. "This is Mr. Kong."

"I know," Oo said. "Hello, Mr. Kong."

Oo held out her hand, but Kong Xang couldn't take it. He'd started crying.

FROM THE DOORWAY, Kong Toua watched the man. He didn't know what to think. Granny Mino was gone, buried many years ago, by Toua with the help of Plig, who told him what to do and say for all the rituals. But Oo was with him, and Xiong Xi, and many others, enough to make a village if they put them all together. Less and less special children were born as there were more doctor robots to visit all the villages. Sometimes Kong Toua wondered if he was one of the last of his kind, but at other times there were so many of them that he couldn't remember all the names without Plig's help. But he was still Kong Toua, the first, and he was proud of that, proud of helping raise many special children.

Plig and the other AIs brought the special children from all over Guizhou and Yunnan, even the ones who weren't Miao or Dong or Buoyei or Tujia or Yi. The AIs even brought special Han children here too. Toua didn't know if people had told the AIs to give the special children some place to live. The AIs ran the cameras, the cars, the flying drones. They cleaned the hospitals and streets. If AIs wanted to move abandoned babies around in driverless cars and flying drones, people didn't need to know. Sometimes, when he saw the way people looked at him, the way they made fun of him, he thought that maybe making a home for special children was something AIs thought up on their own.

How do you feel? Plig said.

"I don't know."

You don't have to be nervous. You've practiced what you want to say to your father. For years.

"Yes," he said morosely.

Plig waited. It always waited. Plig never told Toua to hurry. It knew Toua sometimes needed to think things twice or three times.

"Granny Mino was my mother," Kong Toua finally said.

The man at the table had given up trying to wipe his eyes and had just covered his face with his hands.

Yes, she was.

"You were my father," Kong Toua said, for the first time.

I'm very proud of how you've grown up, Kong Toua.

His chest was filled with good butterflies and bad

butterflies. He took a breath. Oo was still by the table. Ntsuab patted Kong Xang's back. He'd taken a napkin and was drying his eyes. Kong Toua let his breath out and walked to the table, nervous. He stopped in front of it, beside Oo. His face felt angry. Hot. Oo took his hand.

"I am Kong Toua," he said. Kong Xang's face went pale and Kong Toua's breath wheezed. Kong Xang didn't move. "You left me as a little baby. You weren't a father. You didn't even give me a name. A computer had to give me a name."

His father shriveled in the chair.

"You are a bad person."

Kong Toua's throat hurt, like he was going to cry.

"I'm alive. I work. I am married to Oo, and we have two daughters. Maiv and Paj. They are smart and are in the Princess school learning to make AIs."

Oo tightened her grip.

"I am not a bad person, though," Toua said. "So I will take care of you, Father."

Kong Xang's shoulders shook. Then he reached into his shirt and took out a silver chain. In a trembling hand, he held it out to Kong Toua.

ACKNOWLEDGEMENTS

I'VE ALWAYS FELT that my learning as a writer was slow, as if I was the dumbest kid in the class. That's probably just my creative brain kicking itself for whatever reasons brains self-sabotage. In the scifi writers' community, that self-doubt is sometimes called "brain weasels," which is a wonderfully evocative turn of phrase I use a lot.

But feeling like a slow learner means I got to carefully observe my own learning and there are a lot of people who helped me in my struggle to write short fiction. First and most importantly, the members of my critiquing group (the East Block Irregulars) deserve so many thank yous. Matt Moore, Peter Atwood, Hayden Trenholm, Liz Westbrook-Trenholm, Marie Bilodeau, Geoff Gander, Kate Heartfield and Agnes Cadieux at various times and in various combinations held up my dreams, told me what I was doing wrong, and suggested ways to make them better. Sometimes they just told me I was on the right track and brain weasels be damned. Peter and Hayden introduced me into the wider science fiction

Acknowledgements

writing community, which has been invaluable. They all deserve much gratitude.

When my stories got good enough, I graduated to a whole new level of help. I owe debts to Sheila Williams, the editor at *Asimov's* magazine, and Trevor Quachri, the editor at *Analog* magazine. Both took stories that worked and polished rough edges, or they took stories that could work and put them on the operating table. Kim-Mei Kirtland, my agent, has over the last seven years become my super-critiquer and super-editor. I've been rewarded by our partnership and friendship.

Alex Li and Vera Sun (editors) and Ji Shaoting (CEO) at *Non-Exist* magazine in China have been friends and partners and instigators of a lot of the short fiction I've been writing for the last four years and they've shown me so many new things on my visits there. They, their staff, and my science fiction writer friends Kelly Robson, Alyx Dellamonica, and Han Song, were instrumental in *Tool Use* happening at all.

I would lastly like to thank Michael Rowley, my book editor at Rebellion, for his support. This collection came into being because of him. And of course Mr. McCurdy, who way-back-when published my first book.

ABOUT THE AUTHOR

After leaving molecular biology, Derek Künsken worked with street kids in Central America before finding himself in the Canadian foreign service. He now writes science fiction in Gatineau, Québec. His short fiction has appeared in *Analog, Beneath Ceaseless Skies, Clarkesworld,* and many times in *Asimov's* as well as several year's best anthologies. His first space opera novel, *The Quantum Magician,* was a finalist for the Aurora, the Locus and the Chinese Nebula Awards, and its sequel *The Quantum Garden* was nominated for the Aurora. The story of the humanity's evolution continued in *The Quantum War* and will be concluded in *The Quantum Temple.* The *House of Styx* is the early history of the Venusian colony that would become an empire, and will conclude in *The House of Saints* in 2023.

🐦 @derekkunsken
🌐 www.derekkunsken.com

PUBLICATION CREDITS AND COPYRIGHT

FIND US ONLINE!

www.rebellionpublishing.com

/rebellionpub   /rebellionpublishing /rebellionpublishing

SIGN UP TO OUR NEWSLETTER!

rebellionpublishing.com/newsletter

YOUR REVIEWS MATTER!

Enjoy this book? Got something to say?

Leave a review on Amazon, GoodReads or with your
favourite bookseller and let the world know!

DEREK KÜNSKEN

"An audacious con job, scintillating future technology, and meditations on the nature of fractured humanity."
Yoon Ha Lee

THE QUANTUM MAGICIAN

BOOK ONE OF THE QUANTUM EVOLUTION

"One of the best pure 'hard science' writers of the current generation."
– Rich Horton, *Locus*

DEREK KÜNSKEN

THE HOUSE OF STYX

A VENUS ASCENDANT NOVEL

ETERNAL
LIFE IS
OUT THERE

THE
IMMORTALITY
THIEF

"Fun, resonant
and compulsively
readable"
NYT BESTSELLER
VERONICA ROTH

TARAN HUNT

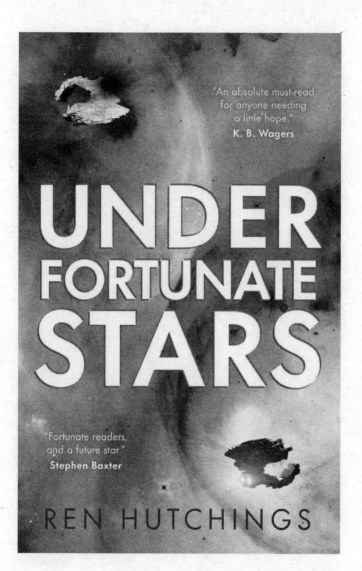

"An absolute must-read
for anyone needing
a little hope."
K. B. Wagers

UNDER FORTUNATE STARS

"Fortunate readers,
and a future star."
Stephen Baxter

REN HUTCHINGS